Alec H

SECOND

To Sarah & Family,

With thanks for being there at the start of
the journey - David Bryant's; and Alec's...

SIGHT

Hope you
enjoy the
read...

Very best
wishes,

Alec Hyde

www.alechyde.com

BrightSpark

www.selfpublishforfree.co.uk

This Book was published in 2013 by Alec Hyde
under the guidance of BrightSpark Publishing
under their SelfPublishFor Free.co.uk service.

First Edition.
© Copyright Alec Hyde 2013.

ISBN 978-1-908295-12-5

The Author, namely Alec Hyde, asserts the moral rights
to be identified as the author of this book.

Disclaimer: All characters in this publication are fictional and any
resemblance to real persons, living or dead, is purely coincidental.

Designed, edited, typeset, printed, and bound completely
in-house by BrightSpark Publishing.

www.brightsparkpublishing.co.uk

ALEC HYDE

Alec Hyde grew up in rural Worcestershire. After studying Ancient History & Latin at Edinburgh University, he went on to work in London for the Civil Service – with much of his career spent in the intelligence and security fields.

In 2007 he relocated to the Scottish Highlands to enjoy a better work-life balance.

When he isn't writing, Alec enjoys playing guitar and drums, trying – with varying degrees of success – to emulate his favourite rock bands.

Second Sight is the first book of *The False Light Conspiracy* trilogy.

For more information about Alec, please visit www.alechyde.com

DEDICATION

A long time in the making, this book is dedicated to my family, friends, and all members of the Sutherland Writers' Group.

Special thanks must also go to my wife, Nicola. Her unwavering support, belief and encouragement ensured that David Bryant made it this far...

He had a cloak of gold
And eyes of fire;
And as he spoke, I felt a deep desire
To free the world of its fear and pain
And help the people to feel free again.

Uriah Heep, 'The Wizard'

PROLOGUE

FOR A MAN with less than forty minutes to live, Peter Meddings seemed decidedly unconcerned – but then ignorance did that; it armoured the soul.

Thirty-nine minutes till impact.

A warm glow of self-satisfaction suffused Meddings, complementing the twelve-year-old malt he was finishing. In truth, the man did have every reason to be feeling pleased with himself – his best ever sales' pitch; the memory of the girl from the bar the night before; and securing a ticket on the heavily over-booked flight. In Peter Meddings' self-centred world, life didn't get much better.

No armour was that impenetrable though, and death could always find an opening. The tiniest chink all that was needed to admit a well-aimed shaft of chill breath, fletched with the promise of eternal sleep. At 14:27 death would loose an arrow of finality and Meddings would breathe no more. As it was, Meddings had been on borrowed time. Years before, with the kids gone and two divorces under his belt, he'd run headlong into his midlife crisis. He'd bought a Harley Davidson in the misguided belief he could recapture his youth. On a dark September's evening, he'd glimpsed a pair of dazzling headlights racing up behind him. An experienced biker would have given it full throttle and torn quickly away from the approaching danger. Not so Meddings. He'd hesitated – only as long as it had taken to adjust the mirrors, to redirect the glare – but in that time the joyrider had covered the intervening distance. The car had nudged the Harley's rear wheel as the driver had gone to overtake too late before a bend. Bike and rider had been catapulted to the side of the road as the stolen vehicle had sped away. Peter Meddings had been impaled on a fence-post. The emergency services had attributed his survival to passing out from the pain. They'd later told him that, had he tried to pull himself free, they were in no doubt he would have bled to death. Meddings' local paper had picked up the story, describing his survival as miraculous. He'd even got a passing mention on regional TV.

Thirty-five minutes till impact.

But there'd be no miracle this time. Meddings would die. And a tragedy on this scale was guaranteed to generate extensive media coverage. All the nationals would carry the story for at least a week; their news-hungry reporting packs gnawing away daily at whatever remaining courage grieving relatives had left to display. And with yet greater immediacy television reporters would interview aviation experts real-time – even while the clear-up operation was ongoing – inviting informed opinions for the cause of the crash. But two to three weeks down the line, the terrible loss of life would be old news; flagged only for the briefest of mentions when the accident report came out. Column inches and air-time would instead be given over again to the more important things in life – like exposing the adulterous lifestyles of premiership footballers, snapping the latest batch of reality-TV stars leaving nightclubs the worse for wear, and covering the vain attempts of jaded politicians to raise their profiles by engaging in cheap publicity stunts.

Thirty-two minutes till impact.

Even at the height of the media interest, however, one fact would go unnoticed; something that not even the most accomplished reporter would uncover – for every person taking that flight had already cheated death at one time or another in their lives. Had that link but been made, a whole new dynamic might yet have ensued; with spin-off articles on conspiracy theories – as well as calculations of the statistical improbabilities involved – being just the tip of the journalistic iceberg. But it was not to be. And so there would be no reports about the pilot, Brian Webster's, heart stopping shortly after birth and the frantic efforts of the delivery-room team to save him. Nor would mention be made of how Webster's co-pilot, Steve Harkness, a former RAF Flight Lieutenant, had escaped a car-bomb during his last tour of Northern Ireland. Likewise, nothing would be said about Marianne Sévigny, the occupant of seat 75B, whose brother had grabbed the wheel when she'd suffered an epileptic fit while driving. Nor would any attention be paid to Ike Greene, 12D, who'd cut through a buzz saw's power cord when helping his father build the new family home in Arizona. And so the list would have gone on for every man, woman, child, and member of the flight-crew who'd been on board that plane.

But death was patient. Eternally so. And no matter how lucky the lethean escapees had so far been, death had always known there'd come a time when they'd finally have to walk down the one-way street of life. And that moment was nearly upon them; a mere thirty-one minutes away. Death began sharpening its scythe in anticipation of a bumper harvest.

269 souls there for the taking.

269.

But that still left *one* unaccounted for. One lone soul whose survival, whose very existence, had always answered to a different set of laws.

And who was now being allowed to walk safely away.

Again...

CHAPTER ONE

ONLY THE UPPER half of the man's body was visible – everything from the base of the spine down seemed to have been corkscrewed deep into the ground.

The head had suffered significant trauma. Sheared away at the crown, it sported a row of neat undulations – similar to those made by a pastry cutter – that ringed the now-exposed cranium; puréed, bloodied grey-matter replaced the once sentient brain. The agony of the man's last moment alive had been preserved on what remained of his face – muscles frozen into a contorted mask of pain; teeth locked around words he'd never finished.

Not far away there were other bodies – an adult female, judging by the clothes; and, more recognisably, a child. The latter was tightly curled into the foetal position; a throwback to the safety of the womb. Not that it had offered any protection when the end had finally come.

'Move back, please. Nothing to see.'

Nothing to see. To the policeman saying the words, the stock phrase came easily. But years of experience had long since taught Detective Superintendent Ray Tomlinson the futility of the instruction. People were naturally curious and those three words served only to whet the inquisitive appetite still further. A crowd of onlookers had already begun to gather.

Tomlinson had been first on the scene. He knew he needn't have got involved at all – he was on leave – but then for him, like so many in his profession, the job wasn't just a job; it was *the* job; one that took over his whole life. Crime didn't take a breather just because he'd packed his suitcase for a fortnight away.

He'd managed to set up a primitive cordon, to help preserve any evidence – a procedural necessity, as he expected the site would be designated a crime scene before the day was out.

'Move back, please,' he repeated, wondering how much longer it would take before the local boys arrived…

A siren's piercing tones cut through the air and blue lights strobed in the superintendent's peripheral vision. Idly, Tomlinson looked up from his newspaper. He realised at once that he couldn't consciously have been reading it for several minutes; that he'd allowed his mind to wander; to create a distraction from the crowded railway station; from the chaos that was London Waterloo that evening. Instead he'd been immersed in the memory of a summer holiday that had not quite gone to plan; the two weeks when he was meant to have been touring the Scottish west coast with his wife, Brenda. The first week had passed uneventfully, but the second had been interrupted. Suddenly.

Unexpectedly. When the bodies had been found. He'd put it down to nothing more than chance – his being there; right man, wrong time; on duty, even off duty. So he'd taken charge; at least, to begin with.

Tomlinson made to close the paper and then, there in the bottom right-hand corner, he saw it; understood what had triggered his mental reverie. It was an article about a Highlands distillery being bought out by a Japanese conglomerate. He recalled their having visited it; remembered too the pleasant half hour he'd spent in the tasting room at the end of the guided tour – and how Brenda had had to drive them back to the guest-house that night. She'd been annoyed with him and had given him the silent treatment for most of the next day. Still, he was determined to make amends for the inconvenience he'd caused her. Not just on that holiday, but for the disruption to their personal life throughout his whole career – the late nights, the telephone calls at unsocial hours; the occasional disappearing act he'd necessarily had to pull. Just another two years to go, then he'd be free to retire at fifty-five. The plan was to sell up and see out their retirement in Portugal. He'd chosen Portugal over Spain deliberately – too many expatriate criminals on the *Costa del Crime* for his liking. Tomlinson allowed himself a brief smile, thinking of the good times that lay ahead.

The siren gave a quick *whoop* and he turned towards the blue lights, watching as an ambulance slowly inched its way across the concourse. In almost biblical fashion, a red sea of commuters parted just long enough to let it through, before the black waves of suits and coats collapsed in on themselves again. The ambulance came to a halt beside a miniature island of yellow, where station officials in fluorescent jackets crowded protectively around a woman who'd fainted. The hours she'd had to endure, standing jam-packed amid the horde of delayed commuters, had finally taken their toll; both physically and emotionally. The doors opened and the paramedics stepped down. Tomlinson was surprised there hadn't been more incidents. Outside the October evening was cold, but the body-heat from the thousands of people packed into the station had seen the temperature steadily rise. To the superintendent, the whole atmosphere seemed to have become decidedly oppressive. He'd arrived just after six-thirty and, as soon as he'd realised he was going to be in for a long wait, had gone to the toilets to freshen up, before purchasing a bottle of water and a baguette from one of the kiosks. He'd called Brenda to let her know he wouldn't be home any time soon.

Tomlinson had heard the same apology being played over the Tannoys every quarter of an hour since his arrival. He couldn't see the point any longer. The station was full to capacity, so no-one else would be getting in. He expected that the entrances at street level, as well as in

10

the tunnels coming up from the underground, had already been closed. So, like himself, those already crowded onto the concourse must have known the announcement off by heart. But the recorded message played on, explaining how vandals had damaged a transformer, and how that had led to all train services being severely disrupted since mid-afternoon. It continued, reassuring passengers that engineers were working as quickly as possible to restore power across the central network. A seasoned commuter, Tomlinson knew what that euphemism meant – no trains in or out until further notice. He, for one, didn't want to hear another vacuous apology; he just wanted information. Even a well-intentioned estimate of when the first trains were likely to run again would have helped. At least then he, and the thousands like him, could have weighed up the situation and decided on the next move – whether to wait it out; try to find alternative transport; or go get a meal; maybe down a few pints in a nearby pub to kill a few hours; or admit defeat and book into a hotel for the night.

The crowd had been patient up till then, but Tomlinson felt there was a tension building – a collective irritability, exacerbated by tiredness, hunger and thirst; ordinary people just wanting to get home; to see loved ones; to put the kids to bed. Even those who'd waited quietly – having laid claim early on to their own bit of space – were now feeling the strain; were becoming less tolerant as time passed and late-comers intruded, eroding their personal area. As he looked around – scanning faces, the way people held themselves, how they were dressed – the superintendent was drawing on investigative experience to read the non-verbal language, the subtle behavioural tells that everyone displayed. His subconscious was on autopilot, rapidly categorising those he scrutinised into one of three groups.

First, the submissive. Those who retreated into themselves at the first sign of danger. Many of whom would be destined for a nervous breakdown; or, worse, a bottle of pills and no morning after. Next, the aggressors. People whose overbearing nature appeared to be rooted in a bedrock of total confidence. But years spent harassing others came at a price – high blood pressure, clogged arteries, and a body seldom fit for long-term purpose. He knew each group, though poles apart, was headed on a collision course with reduced life expectancy. Finally, there was the silent majority. Mr and Mrs Average who, like himself, just got on with it; accepting that, if it was a bad day today, it would probably end up a better one tomorrow.

Against this backdrop, Tomlinson predicted it could only be a matter of time before someone finally snapped; did something stupid.

He wasn't wrong.

It was like white noise.

Only black.

And silent.

But he felt it was having the same effect – a deafening of his senses that was leading to complete disorientation. He knew he had to refocus, and quickly. To do otherwise meant he risked losing himself – *within* his very self – once and for all. Something deep inside was telling him that, if only he could hear himself say the word, the mirror of silence would shatter; its illusory shards would fall away to reveal the reality being denied him. Concentrating hard, he tried one last time to ensnare it...

And then – he had it.

Claustrophobic.

He'd done it. He'd found it. He repeated the word at once, before it had a chance to escape. He repeated it again, taking time over each syllable; carefully traced every letter on the roof of his mouth with his tongue; hoping that in this way he was giving the word permanency, a solidity of form. He had to guard against it being snatched away into the void. For a final time he repeated it – *claustrophobic.*

Albeit a small victory, it had been hard-won; and it bore witness to his determination. The significance of his achievement was not lost on the dark-white, silent-noise. Sensing the need for greater stealth, it ceased its mental assault; allowed its place to be taken by another. It only took a moment for him to recognise the new adversary for what it was – a familiar old foe which, while different, was equally as dangerous. He knew – remembered – it would be harder to resist. Unlike its forerunner, it wouldn't try to crush him. Instead it would seek to wrap him in comforting psychological oblivion, as it had so nearly succeeded in doing the last time they'd met. He became aware of the surrounding darkness softening, losing its oppressive density, as wispy clouds of apathy drifted in to settle over the mountain ranges of his comprehension; as layers of forgetfulness began to settle on the peaks of his rationality.

He had to escape – now, or the moment would be gone. In his mind's eye, from there high on his rocky plateau, he began scanning the landscape around him; below him. His action didn't go unnoticed and, in response, the darkness grew suddenly more intense; limiting his vision, his sense of direction. He needed to concentrate more. He took a moment to steady himself; to firm his resolve; to plan how to get away. But even as he tried to think of options, a single overriding thought kept pushing to the fore. Refusing to be ignored...

Cave.

He heard his own voice speak the word – or, at least, what he took to be his own voice; only it seemed somehow different. It left him confused, for he couldn't be certain he'd actually said the word out loud. The word was there again – *cave* – echoing all around him; passing through him. His confusion began to give way to foreboding. An intuition that the time was fast approaching – when he'd have to face his greatest fear; when he'd have to enter the narrow opening that was even now appearing in the jet-black rock-face behind him. Involuntarily he felt his body tense up. He didn't want to go in there. He couldn't. Not yet. And maybe he'd never find the courage needed to do so. For he sensed there were *things* in the cave. Hidden things. That watched his every move from deep within the gloom. Things that were waiting for *him* to see *them…*

He stopped himself just in time –

A sudden realisation of what was going on. The confusion. The fear. The cave. All of it was a distraction; a deliberate one. To keep him occupied. To buy the clouds of apathy the final few moments they needed to finish their work – to bury everything away; to suppress his emotions; to squeeze his remaining memories into some long-forgotten cranial corner. The very building blocks of his self were being dismantled; systematically; row by careful row; one at a time. He thought he could almost hear words being carried on a breeze – like the gentle echoes in a sea-shell clasped by a child to its ear – inviting him to lie back and let go; to cease to exist; telling him it really could be that easy. And he was feeling tempted. So very tempted. He wondered why he should keep fighting. Whether it could ever be worth it…

But in that same instant, his self-survival instincts rounded on him. They weren't prepared to let him surrender himself. Not without good reason. And certainly not before he'd had his questions answered. In quick succession they released them – the *hows*, the *whys*, the *whens* – like neural distress flares sent skyward from a mountain side; signalling his position; inviting the answers to come and rescue him.

It worked.

He wanted to know how long he'd been there. How he'd got there. Where *there* even was…

A flash of memory made a sudden break for it, as pure cerebral energy arced its way clear of the surrounding confusion to earth itself in what yet remained of his consciousness. He saw a school bag; his school bag. He remembered now, he'd been looking for it. Blue canvas, with double shoulder-straps. But he only ever used the one, because that's what everyone else did. He'd bought it from the local army surplus store. He'd gone back there ten, maybe fifteen, years later. The shop had long since closed down and, in place of all things militaria – uniforms, commando knives, German helmets, replica Iron Crosses –

he'd found an end-of-the-line discount bookshop. Ironic proof if ever it was needed that the pen was mightier than the sword.

Another spark of remembrance...

The daily pilgrimage he'd make every lunch-time to the market stalls, ever hopeful of finding a bargain. And just enough time afterwards for a game of *Space Invaders* at the riverside café. It had been a favourite haunt of the truckers and bus drivers – where else could they get a full fry-up for under a pound? Paper had still been the legal tender back then; no such thing as a pound coin. The temptation to stay on for just one more game – one final chance to save Earth from the aliens – had often proved too great to resist; and then he'd be up against it, racing back to get in through the school gates before the afternoon bell sounded. It seemed he'd never left himself enough time to get there and, yet, somehow he always managed to do so.

He wanted to reason that one out. But even as the mental cogs started turning, the darkness was already encroaching on his faculties. He persevered, determined to see this one through. The black clouds lifted; retreated – but he knew they were there, waiting to rush in again if his concentration wavered. Two words – *children's time* – came into his mind. He wondered if that's how he'd done it, how he'd always beaten the clock. For children's time, he figured, must be flexible; able to be pulled into strands like chewing gum. Expandable, it had given him those last few minutes; the extra seconds he'd needed. All of which gave rise to another question; to a temporal conundrum. For at some stage there had to have been a change – a point at which he'd grown up, had left his childhood behind – and adult time had taken over. Adult time. Inflexible. Forever in short supply. When deadlines and work pressures became the norm. When there was no longer time for play; for enjoying weekends with the family. When there was almost too little time even for time. But when had it all changed, and how could he have missed something so important? The more he thought about it, the more complex it became. Somehow both times needed to co-exist; the world of the adult merging with that of the child...

Perception.

The word appeared of its own accord. That was it. Surely that had to be the key? He promised himself he'd be sure to act like a child again the next time he saw his son. When *Papi* came home to offer a kiss and a cuddle at bedtime... But it was as if the darkness had suddenly stabbed at him, punching home the realisation he'd never have that chance again. Luisa's parents had seen to that –

Red-faced now and out of breath, he was at the school gates – just as the bell rang. He could still get to his classroom on time, but first he had to find his bag. He ran across the playground and stopped.

Something wasn't right. He looked round for the madcap scrum of kids, all trying to get into the main building at the same time. His eyes darted left, then right, searching for the handful of prefects who were always on hand to round up the stragglers. But the place was deserted. He began to panic. He wondered if he was too late. He checked his watch. His first thought was that it must have stopped, but he could see the second hand was still moving. He felt sure they'd all laugh at him when he walked in; that he'd get a detention for being late. He resigned himself to the humiliation.

The darkness was there again, closing in on him. He tried to focus on the playground, picturing its familiarity; remembering where he'd left his... But he couldn't even think of the word now. He knew it was something he needed. Something that he... If only he could...

All of a sudden, a final distress flare was loosed. It raced quickly up towards the leaden clouds of oblivion that hung overhead; that threatened at any moment to rain down a shower of forgetfulness on him. Only this time the flare didn't carry a question but, rather, a single instruction.

Find yourself –

Without warning, a train was suddenly advertised on the electronic departure boards. Platform sixteen. The sea of black surged instantly forwards. Few people had actually had enough time to register the destination; it was just an instinctive reaction – everyone else was moving, so they felt they had to as well. Tomlinson allowed himself a wry smile at the stupidity of it all; at the prime example he was witnessing of Stone-age mentality overriding the twenty-first century brain.

'Coming through.'

'Sorry. Can I get past?'

Polite British reserve was still there, but only just. Soon, though, tempers began to fray as people didn't – or couldn't – move out of the way.

'Come on! We've got a train to catch...'

The mask of courtesy was slipping.

'Yeah? Haven't we all?'

It was then that a thick-set man with a clean-shaven head, wearing combat trousers and hooded top, elbowed one of the suits out of the way. The touch paper had been lit. The suit seemed unsteady on his feet, slurred words accompanying uncoordinated movements. He'd been in one of the station bars for the past hour, drinking away the wasted time; getting himself wasted in the process.

'Watch it!' he shouted; the threat empty – he couldn't even

focus properly. But his friends weren't as half-cut.

'Get back and wait your turn, you tosser!' barked one of them – the pinstripe, loud tie and braces all hinting at a job in the City.

'You what!' roared the thick-set man, having none of it. He'd been on a building site since dawn. He ached all over. His muscles were tired from an honest day's graft. But he knew his own strength and was confident he had enough left in reserve to deal with the three of them. 'Come on, then! You want some?'

The Transport Police were quick to act.

Seemingly from out of nowhere, a wedge of officers piled in; CCTV operators skilfully guiding them to the seat of the would-be disturbance. Arm-locks were applied with well-practised ease. There was no need for cuffs. Quick. Quiet. No fuss. There'd be no charges. Just time enough for the men to cool off in the cells.

Tomlinson nodded his approval as he watched events from his little oasis of calm – a recess at the entrance to platform thirteen; just up from the flower girl's stall. He'd chosen the spot deliberately, after noticing there was no natural through-flow of passengers. Consequently he'd have no-one barging past, treading on his toes. There was one major drawback though. Being out of the way meant he wasn't able to see the central departure screens so, instead, he was entirely reliant on the smaller, localised TV-monitors, with their truncated information and all but illegible script. If the train he wanted didn't happen to arrive on either of the two platforms immediately behind him, by the time he'd heard the announcement and made his way over to the designated one, he'd likely be unable to board – with the seats and standing room already having been taken. It was a question of balance, Tomlinson knew that, and for the sake of a little more comfort now it was a compromise he was happy to accept.

The Tannoy suddenly burst into life, crackling loudly with static. A distinctly nervous-sounding voice began to speak, 'Platform six... *teen* for the delayed 17:00 Basingstoke service. Calling at...'

For those crowded into the station, it was as if a lighthouse of lucidity had appeared on the horizon, its beam shining brightly; finally allowing a course to be plotted home. But for the fact that a squall of confusion was about to blow in; that would catch the good ship, *Commuter*, unawares. For to reach port safely, to navigate a clear channel through the underwater hazards, concerted effort would be needed – all hands on deck and the whole crew necessarily pulling together in the same direction.

But it wasn't to be.

Single-mindedness – the seductress siren of the sea – called softly to those onboard, inviting them to abandon ship; luring them to a

16

premature, watery end. Waves of commuters swirled; surged forward; stirred up eddies of uncertainty around platform entrances, as people were buffeted; their bodies forced one against the other; arms and bags flailing.

Then, more disconcertingly still, the referential lighthouse beam proved suddenly illusory; unreliable in its capacity as a guide –

'*Correction*,' the announcer's voice broke, as he had to own up to his mistake. 'This is a platform alteration. Platform *six* for the delayed 17:00 Basingstoke service.' The man hurriedly cleared his throat. 'I do apologise for any inconvenience caused by my earlier announcement...'

His words were drowned out by an angry tsunami of sound – a roar of expletives; whistles of derision; sighs of disbelief and laughter all rolled into one.

Holed now below the waterline – keel splintered on unseen rocks – *Commuter* began to take in water; began to sink.

'Looks like a long night.' A woman, blonde, attractive, in her mid-forties had taken refuge next to Tomlinson.

'Seems so.' He smiled.

'You don't want Basingstoke?'

'No, Guildford. You?'

'Earlsfield.' She produced a packet of cigarettes. 'Don't suppose you've got a light?'

'Sorry, no. Besides...' But he didn't have to finish the sentence; the sounds of disapproval from several of those near the woman did the talking for him.

'Ah... The smoke police and all that...' The blonde put the packet away. 'Are you happy now?' she asked, directly challenging a man who, until then, had been looking down his nose at her. He reddened and turned away. 'Been trying to give up for ages, anyway,' she said, switching her attention back to Tomlinson. She smiled and flicked her hair back.

Harmless banter; potentially flirtatious had it continued, that could have helped pass the time and made the two of them feel all the better for it. But it was over before it had even begun. Tomlinson let out a knowing sigh as he made a discrete, habitual movement – one cupped hand coming to rest against his waist.

'Sorry,' he shrugged apologetically, 'I've got to go.'

The blonde looked disappointed – he noticed the down-turned creases either side of her mouth; years of putting on a brave face having left their mark – but she nodded as he left.

It took him five minutes to navigate his way through the crowd, to cover the thirty yards to the taxi rank at the front of the station. Even there, commuters spilled out onto the pavement. He kept on walking, bearing left as he made his way down the hill and on past the steps at the entrance to Waterloo. He crossed the road by the corner of the Shell Building, adjacent to the London Eye. The giant wheel loomed up in front of him, flashbulbs exploding inside the pods every so often as tourists eagerly snapped the Capital's famous skyline.

It was then that Tomlinson's pager went off for the second time. Without even thinking about it, his hand was once again there; drawn to his belt; years of Pavlovian-style conditioning leaving as much of a mark on him as the woman's creases had on her.

He'd expected as much, knowing they'd be wondering why he hadn't already called in. He took out his mobile and tapped in the number.

Two rings later, 'Commander Peters' Office...'

'Sally, it's Ray. You paged me?'

'Oh, Ray. Sorry. I know you were on your way home. But something's come up. The Commander would like you back here straightaway.'

'Not a problem. Waterloo's complete chaos tonight anyway. It's been like that for hours. The first trains are only just running again.'

'Do you want me to send a car?'

'No, I could do with the walk, thanks. It'll wake me up a bit.'

'See you in... ten minutes?'

'Yes, that's fine.' He rang off.

It was noticeably chillier now, not helped by a breeze coming in off the Thames. Tomlinson retreated into his overcoat, pulling up the collar as high as it would go, and set off along the Embankment for Westminster Bridge. Once over the other side, the Yard was only a short walk away.

Find yourself –

He tried harder to focus; desperately sought to recall where he was. But it was no use. Eyes blinded by the gloom, his mind stayed equally in the dark. What he did know was that he couldn't afford to give up. He caught his breath and forced himself to slow down; made himself concentrate.

He didn't feel afraid, so he reasoned he wasn't in any immediate danger.

Got to get a grip, he said to himself. *It's clearly just a dream. One of those where you think you can't wake up. Go on, test it... try reaching out and touching something. You won't be able to...* He moved his right hand to one side, probing in the dark. He didn't want any surprises. But he got one. He managed to topple a glass – his hand too slow to react before it fell to the floor. *Fool. What are you playing at? You could've cut yourself. Stupid.* But there was no crash. He

18

traced the same hand down his legs, giving it a chance to redeem itself. He couldn't remember if he was barefoot but, if he was, he'd need to take care in case the glass had smashed. His fingers told him his feet were bare. More, he was bare. Naked, but not cold. He was aware of a ruffled, silky sheet beneath him. And the gentle hint of a fragrance that hung in the air; something floral – jasmine, perhaps. *But if I can feel this, I can't be dreaming.*

'Hello?' he said out loud. 'Hello?' he repeated, addressing the unknown when there was no reply.

His eyes were adjusting to the gloom now and he thought he could make out a faint shimmer of orange; over to his right – a hazy, luminous tear in a curtain of black. He tried to figure out what it was; to judge the distance; but everything was so deceptive in the dark. He felt around where the glass had been for a bedside lamp. Table, yes; but lamp, no. He'd have to make his way over there if he wanted to know more. He edged lengthways down the bed, reasoning he'd be clear if there was any broken glass. But he still needed to take care; there might be other obstacles in the room. He dropped his legs gingerly down onto what felt like a deep pile carpet –

That explains the silent glass...

He stood, then moved slowly forward, checking the way ahead with little side-to-side swings of one foot; mimicking a blind man with a cane. As he crossed the room, the orange light grew steadily brighter; became more distinct – an ingot of pure amber floating in a strong-room of darkness. It was mesmerising; began to draw him in.

Now or never...

He reached towards the light, expecting to feel warmth. But there wasn't any. In fact, there was little sensation at all. Instead, his hand just passed straight through the etheric amber substance. Blackness billowed all around him and the ingot changed shape, becoming momentarily amorphous. Another shape-change followed and then reddish-orange flooded into the room. It lit his surroundings just long enough for him to turn briefly, to register the bed and side table. And then the light was gone – the curtain he'd disturbed falling back into place – cutting off the orange glow from the street lamp outside.

He laughed; half in relief, half at his own stupidity; banishing the childhood demons and fears he'd been imagining. Brave now after the event, he pulled the curtain aside with a flourish and looked out of the window. He was greeted by an unexceptional suburban view – cars parked in white-lined bays, pavements wet from rain and a solitary pedestrian crossing the road below. He tugged a little more at the fabric, letting in more of the artificial light. He scanned the room. Door. Bed. Matching bedside tables – a lamp on the far side, adjacent to the wall.

So that's why I didn't find one –
An easy chair in one corner. Folding luggage cradle. Another door. Dressing table. TV. Mini-bar. Standard hotel fare. An environment that was only too familiar to him, given the amount of time he'd spent holed up in them of late – living out of a suitcase four nights in every seven. And on the floor by the chair he saw his discarded clothes. His, as well as a *second* set –
He did a double-take.
But even as the sentence *Whose are those?* was forming, he heard a latch being snapped open...

CHAPTER TWO

THE SUPERINTENDENT WAS standing in the commander's office. Dual aspect, it had enviable views across London and was perched on the corner of New Scotland Yard; one floor down from the SB – Special Branch – nerve centre.

Tomlinson knew the SB offices like the back of his hand. He'd spent many a year working out of there, in what now seemed a previous life – or, rather, lives; plural. And all because of the multiple aliases he'd assumed; the non-existent addresses with which he'd been provided; and the cover stories upon which he'd had to rely. Of necessity every element of his lives – each of his operational *alter egos* – had had to be carefully crafted to safeguard his, as well as his family's, personal safety. And not just at the time, but also to withstand any future scrutiny.

The superintendent gazed out of the window, staring through his own reflection at the panorama of buildings arrayed before him – the floodlit Houses of Parliament; MI5's Headquarters at Thames House; and the beige and green edifice that was MI6. *Eggs in one basket* he thought to himself. A co-ordinated terrorist *spectacular* against that vista would see the UK's security and intelligence machinery hit hard; as well as central Government, if Whitehall itself was included in any plan. Tomlinson knew it could only be a matter of time before some organisation tried its luck…

The commander strode purposefully into the room from his secretary's outer office, a folder tucked underneath one arm. At 5' 10" Graeme Peters was around Tomlinson's height, but his build was slight, not stocky like the superintendent. He had a full head of grey hair, silvering in places, which complemented perfectly his charcoal Savile Row suit. Both men had joined the Metropolitan Police force at about the same time but Peters, already having graduated from Cambridge, had been slightly older.

Even from his earliest days, Peters had been a smart thinker, second-guessing how the force would change; how there'd be a clear need for its future leaders to operate as if they were chief executives running multi-national corporations; how the Met itself would come to evolve into a crime-fighting business – the totality of its output represented annually by a single line on a spreadsheet. And so Graeme Peters had deliberately sought out those posts where he knew he would gain experience of finance, planning and personnel – the very areas that so many of his contemporaries avoided; that were considered backroom functions; as far removed from front-line policing as it was possible to get. But Peters had been careful, taking steps to ensure he didn't get stranded in a No Man's Land of policy documents; to avoid being seen as a number-cruncher. He'd made sure he returned to operational duties as often as was needed to keep his hand in. And so, thanks to his tactical manoeuvring, time and again he'd found himself in pole position when the next promotion opportunity had come along.

A shrewd operator, calculating in everything he did, Peters was also one of the select few – a senior officer who'd successfully managed to tread that most delicate of paths; retaining the trust of the rank and file while also gaining the ear of the Met's political masters: the changeable Ministers and their semi-permanent officials at the Home Office.

Like every large organisation Scotland Yard's corridors were forever alive with Chinese whispers, and the latest talk was all about Peters; about how, if he was prepared to stay on for another three to five years, he might yet become Britain's top cop – Commissioner for the Metropolitan Police. Already many felt he was being lined up for a Deputy Assistant Commissioner's post; and it was believed his name had also been put forward for suitable recognition in the New Year Honours' List.

There was no denying that Graeme Peters moved in influential circles – but it was a far cry from the superintendent's world.

The young Tomlinson had been an above-average student, and his teachers had earmarked him for university. He'd wanted to read chemistry, but his father's premature death had forced a change of plan. He'd known straightaway that he needed to find work so he could support his mother and younger sister. He'd known, too, he needed a job that offered good pay and long-term prospects. After exploring options with his careers adviser, he'd decided police work wasn't so far removed from chemistry – uncovering the reasons why things happened; seeing if outcomes could be changed – and he'd attended for interview soon after. Thanks to his eventual grades, his common sense and his overall level of fitness, the Met had welcomed Tomlinson with open arms. The new recruit had taken to policing from day one. The more he learned, the more he'd wanted to learn. He found he enjoyed pitting his wits against the criminal mind, treating it much like a game of chess. And although he would be the first to admit he'd lost many games during his career, still he was able to take pride in the fact that his dogged policing style had seen him win far more tournaments than his law-breaking adversaries. He knew too his many successes had contributed to his own rise through the ranks. He would have been happy to retire as a chief inspector, so his elevation to superintendent had been an unexpected boon. He doubted he'd go any further, but he didn't mind. What counted most was that his mother had lived long enough to witness his achievements – for though she never spoke of it, he'd long suspected she'd blamed herself for his missing out on university.

Just occasionally, though, Tomlinson did wonder *what if...*

What if he had gone on to study? Maybe he'd have ended up pushing the boundaries of forensic science – DNA profiling, or driving forward some other investigative technology? Something told him he would have ended up working with the police no matter what path he'd chosen. Unlike Peters though Tomlinson didn't have the knack, or rather the desire, to appease the politicians. He told it like it was. Always had. Always would. A trait his mother often said he'd inherited from his father. Tomlinson never set out to offend, but he did feel that the truth, the reality of situations, needed to be told. As a result, some considered him rude; gruff even. He just considered himself a straight talker.

But he got on well enough with Peters, each man recognising the other's strengths.

'Ray, sorry to have kept you waiting. Thanks for getting back so quickly.' The commander made a beeline for his conference table. He pulled out one of the chairs and sat down, beckoning Tomlinson to join him while he opened the folder. 'I understand you hadn't got far. Problems at Waterloo?'

'That's right,' Tomlinson sighed. He removed his overcoat, folded it loosely and placed it on the floor beside one of the table legs. 'I'd been thinking of coming back anyway – catching up on some paperwork, then heading back to Waterloo in a couple of hours' time. Maybe by then the –'

'Right, well, we'd better get on...' Peters' interruption signalled that the small talk was over. Taking a deep breath, he began, 'We've got a double murder, Ray. The details are still a bit sketchy,' he pulled a two-page briefing note from the folder, scanning the contents to refresh his earlier understanding, 'so I'd like you to get over there as soon as we're done here.' A flash of Tomlinson's eyebrows questioned the location. 'South London; outskirts of Croydon,' the commander added. 'Committed some time this afternoon.'

'The victims?'

'Two pensioners. A Mr and Mrs Wilson. Beaten to death.'

'Burglary gone wrong?'

'No, doesn't seem so...'

'Maybe they were just unlucky; maybe it was another...' But Tomlinson let that thought trail off. Only a few months back his team had had to investigate a case of care-in-the community that had gone seriously wrong – a former mental health patient had run amok in a bingo hall with a samurai sword. One person had been killed –

beheaded – and seven others had been injured. Although the death and injuries had been tragic, what annoyed Tomlinson most had been the fact that, the more questions he'd asked, the more the senior echelons of the health authority had closed ranks; had sought to hide the truth. But Tomlinson had put two and two together for himself – the assailant had been judged a low risk, no doubt to ease budgetary pressures, and he'd been released back into an unsuspecting public. But the man had failed to keep up his medication and the results had spoken for themselves.

Peters seemed to know what the superintendent was thinking; cut him short. 'Let's keep an open mind, shall we?'

Tomlinson knew better than to push it. Instead he asked, 'Have the next of kin been informed?'

'Not yet... still trying to contact them.'

'And who found the bodies?'

Peters turned to the second page. 'A neighbour. Local CID and forensics are still at the scene. And uniform have started making house-to-house enquiries.' He flipped the top sheet back, replaced the briefing note in the folder and passed the pack to Tomlinson. 'I'd like you to take *personal* charge of this one, Ray.'

'Of course,' Tomlinson replied, wondering why Peters was singling him out. The commander knew full well he already had a heavy workload, and there were at least half a dozen other senior officers – arguably with more resources at their disposal – who'd be better placed to lead this new enquiry. The superintendent decided to risk an old psychological trick, one he'd learnt years back and had since used to good effect during interviews with suspects. He hoped Peters wouldn't notice. He left a deliberate silence, waited to see if the commander would take the bait; would feel obliged to speak, to fill the uncomfortable, verbal void.

It worked.

Peters cleared his throat, almost apologetically. 'The Home Office are scrutinising our clear-up rates. It's all linked to a new funding initiative from on high. There'll be an announcement in due course, but I'd like us to steal a march; to have a good story to tell. Off the record, given the cuts we're likely to be facing, these murders are the last thing we need...'

Tomlinson felt his jaw tighten, always a sign he was getting irritated. He saw it clearly then; understood where Peters was coming from. Not quite performance-related pay, but near enough. He could just see the headline in the *Standard*. *Cash for Clear-Up Rates*. That was what it amounted to. He wondered how long it would be before someone leaked this gem to the Opposition. The more the idea sank in, the more uneasy he felt. The clear inference was that a quick arrest was needed. But that was risky. You only had to look at the bad old days to see that – the days when convictions had been secured under duress; when there'd been frequent miscarriages of justice; and significant sums had been paid out in compensation to those later cleared at appeal. He wondered cynically if a quick arrest would benefit Peters – guaranteeing the much-rumoured promotion to DAC.

'You're one of my most experienced officers, Ray, and I know I can count on you –'

'– to do as I always do, sir.' It was Tomlinson's turn to interrupt. Somehow managing to keep his rising anger in check, he continued in a level voice, 'It goes without saying, I'll try to uncover the truth and make evidence-based arrests as soon as I can.' He could have been quoting from a text-book. But he figured he'd outmanoeuvred his superior, at least for the time being. It was a gamble, but he didn't like his professionalism being manipulated – no matter how senior the officer.

'Yes. Quite.' Peters stood up. It was obvious he wanted to bring the conversation to a close, as it was now starting to stray into uncomfortable territory.

Tomlinson rose, too. He tucked the incident folder under one arm. Just for a moment, he considered the commander's position – caught between a political rock and a self-promotional hard place, the other man really did have an incredibly difficult job to do at times; but the challenges were of his own making; came with the territory. For his part, Tomlinson was happy to stay firmly outside the politics. He just wanted to get on with good honest policing. It's what he'd signed up for all those years ago.

'A final thought; where are we with the media?' asked the superintendent.

'A reporter from a local paper was on the scene very quickly. I expect she followed the response vehicles in the hope of getting a story. Either way, she won't be getting a scoop. I've managed to get a news blackout until 13:00 tomorrow, but after that it's likely to be a free for all. I've taken the liberty of arranging a press conference for 12:30. You'll lead, of course?'

Tomlinson nodded his agreement, recognising the rhetorical question for what it was. He quickly checked his watch. 'If Sally can arrange a car, I should be able to get over to Croydon in the next half hour. I'll call you tomorrow morning with an update. Around 11:00?'

'That would be helpful, Ray. Thanks.' Peters seemed to have regained his composure; his friendly, yet assured, character on display once more. 'Until 11:00, then...'

Tomlinson retrieved his coat from beside the table, and took his leave of the commander. He was grateful to get away; to get some breathing space. He went downstairs to his own office then paged his right-hand man, detective sergeant Paul Riley. Riley telephoned in within a few minutes and arranged to meet the superintendent at the murder scene. Then, before taking the lift down to meet his driver, Tomlinson put in another call to Brenda to let her know that he wouldn't be home tonight.

The sound of the latch made him start.

His whole attention was drawn to the *second* door, the one beside the luggage cradle. Instinctively he let the curtain fall back into place and the room enveloped itself in darkness. As the door slowly opened, a wall of bright, fluorescent light flooded in. He shielded his eyes, squinting through half-opened fingers.

And there, silhouetted in the doorway, he saw the unmistakable frame of a woman. Young. Medium height. Shapely.

'Sorry, didn't mean to wake you.'

He heard a pull-cord snap and the light went out. He was aware suddenly of the jasmine scent, stronger now than ever; and, then, soft arms were circling his hips. The woman's head pressed against his chest, nestling close against him; her delicate fingers pulled lightly on his shoulders and, as he lowered his head, a warm kiss greeted his lips. Her whole body seemed soft and inviting. His reaction didn't go unnoticed.

'Well, lover boy, since you're *up*, what say we both stay up a little longer?' Taking his hand, she led him back to the bed.

His mind was racing.

Who is she? Where am I?

She laid him down and sat astride him.

How did I get here?

She was leaning forward, nuzzling an ear.

Where is here?

She was kissing him deeply now. He could taste a sweetness on her breath.

Baileys... We've been drinking? That explains the glass.

'Hey, come on,' she chided. 'You seem a little... *distracted?*'

He had to have answers – but he knew, too, he had to have *her*. He so wanted to enjoy the moment; wanted to immerse himself totally in the pleasure. It had been so long...

He made to speak, but she pre-empted him, touching a finger to his lips, 'Later. We can talk later.'

Desire flooded his body; his mind, his senses. He wanted – needed – this woman. He reached up to caress her hips, ran searching fingers tenderly up towards her breasts.

'Someone's eager,' she teased, pushing his hands gently away. 'Lie still. Let me set the pace. We've all night...'

He raised his hands a second time and stretched to kiss her; tried to pull her down onto him.

'No,' she said, still the tease. 'My speed, not yours.' She straightened up.

He tried for a third time.

'No.' This time, there was an edge of insistency in her voice. Her shoulders swayed gently in front of the amber backdrop and a faint orange misting streamed through her long hair. The shimmering effect made her all the more beautiful. 'No,' she repeated, as she began to buck her hips.

The glow was increasing now, starting to light the whole room. He was confused. Consumed in the moment, and yet... Hadn't the curtain fallen back into place? Hadn't he released it when she'd startled him? He looked round, but there was no illumination coming in from the street lamp outside. He switched his attention back to the woman; gazed up at her face.

An aura of light – golden, reddish, orange – was arcing around her head...

Percy and Ivy Wilson had owned a substantial Edwardian property in one of Croydon's more desirable suburbs. Set well back from the road, the house had a long driveway and was screened from view by well-established trees. The rear garden adjoined a members-only golf course. For a property so easily commutable to central London, it was unexpectedly private; pleasantly secluded. It was here, Tomlinson thought to himself, that the wealthy bought to stay – city traders, footballers, an occasional ageing rock star; all rubbing postcode shoulders. He knew he'd never be able to afford such a house – at least, not in Britain, and that was why he planned to make his pound go further with the move to Portugal.

The detective in him saw immediately that such privacy also had drawbacks. Already he suspected there'd be few, if any, witnesses to provide much-needed information. During the ride over, though, he'd noticed that many of the neighbouring properties had CCTV at their entrances. He'd made a mental note to ask Riley to get the footage checked for potential leads.

A uniformed officer came forward to meet Tomlinson's car and was about to lift the blue-and-white tape to let it through. The superintendent gestured that there was no need. He got out, thanked the driver and sent the car back to the Yard. When he needed to leave, he'd travel back with his sergeant.

The scenes of crime officers, together with other forensic teams, had pitched temporary camp. The house was a hive of activity – but all of it methodically orchestrated to ensure no-one got in anyone else's way. It was essential that procedures were followed, that everything remained free of potential contamination. Successful prosecutions depended on as much and Tomlinson knew how quick a skilful defence lawyer would be to point the finger of doubt at a flawed evidential trail.

'OK for me to go through?' he asked one of the white-suited staff. He received a nod and entered a central hallway. He heard Riley's voice in a room off to the right and went to find him. 'Jesus...' Tomlinson muttered under his breath. He'd had time to read through the report on the way over, but it hadn't prepared him for the actuality of what he now saw.

The scene was grim; and strangely surreal. *Beaten to death*, that's what Peters had said. But *beaten* didn't even begin to describe the savagery of the attack. Neither of the victims had anything left that resembled a skull. Instead, there was just a mass of congealed blood and matted hair; irregularly shaped bone fragments jutting out of pulped body tissue. Whoever had murdered the couple had placed them in armchairs, then arranged them in the centre of the room facing one another. But for the butchery the Wilsons could have been discussing what was in the day's papers, or deciding what to watch on TV.

DS Riley came over.

'Got to be one of the worst cases I've seen, sir.'

'*The* worst,' Tomlinson replied. 'What have we got so far?'

'Dead for around six to ten hours. The murder weapon is believed to be a hammer, or some other similar object. Nothing's been found yet, here or in the garden, but we're still looking. The pathologist's first thoughts are that the couple were killed with one or two blows to the head over there,' the sergeant pointed to the far corner of the room. 'You can see the blood trails on the carpet leading this way.' Tomlinson noted the discolouration. 'They were then dragged over here and put in the chairs. Only then did the murderer really get to work on their heads.'

'I don't get it. Why mutilate someone once they're dead?'

Riley shrugged. 'Your guess is as good as mine, sir.'

'And nothing's been taken?'

'It doesn't seem so.'

'*Any* sign of theft?'

'We've found a safe, but it's still intact. Mrs Wilson's purse was in her handbag and Mr Wilson's wallet was in one of his jackets. Both had cash and credit cards inside.' Riley nodded in the direction of a sideboard. 'I'm no expert, but those pieces of porcelain and silver look as if they cost a fair bit. And there are others round the house. There's absolutely no sign of anything being disturbed,' he turned his attention back to the bodies, 'but for the... carnage... in here.' He shook his head in sympathetic disbelief. 'No, the house is clean, sir. Absolutely no sign of any struggle. I'm guessing whoever he was, either he must have taken them by surprise...'

'... *or* been known to them?' ventured Tomlinson, following Riley's line of thought. 'In which case, the Wilsons wouldn't have had any reason to be suspicious. And there was no sign of a break-in?'

'None.'

'So they must have let him in. An acquaintance? Or maybe a tradesman?' He was remembering the cameras he'd seen on the way over. 'That reminds me, can you check the CCTV from nearby properties?'

'Already in hand, sir. I've also asked for copies from petrol stations, banks and offices within a three-mile radius.'

Tomlinson nodded appreciatively. His DS was as reliable as ever. 'Any luck yet with the next of kin?'

'Miss Woods...' Riley began, but noticing the superintendent's blank expression added '... Margaret Woods, sir – she's one of the neighbours.' Given the size of the house and grounds, Tomlinson suspected neighbour meant she probably lived at least a quarter of a mile away. 'Apparently, she'd come round to see how the couple were. She knew their son and his family were away for a few days; off in France, she thought. So she just wanted to check they were alright.'

'How's she bearing up?'

'Still in a state of shock. They've given her something to help her sleep and I've stationed a WPC at her house. I've also informed the local CID that we'll take a statement when she's feeling up to it. But we did get a mobile number from her for the son – Geoff Wilson. I've tried calling several times, but it just goes onto voice-mail. I left a message, asking Mr Wilson to contact me direct. I've also alerted CID at Gatwick, Heathrow and the Eurostar Terminal just in case he approaches them first.'

'Peters has agreed to a press conference tomorrow lunch-time. We can't risk Geoff Wilson finding out second-hand, so we'll have to reach him somehow...'

'Doing our best, sir.'

Tomlinson hadn't meant any criticism. 'Sorry, didn't mean to sound like I was having a go. I know everyone's doing everything they can.' He ran a hand through his hair, thinking through the next steps. 'How are we placed for an incident room?'

'I've managed to get us several rooms in the local station. The tech guys are coming over from the Yard, so we should have dedicated phones and computers shortly.'

Tomlinson looked at his watch. It was 10:40 am. 'Well, I don't think there's anything more we can do here for the time being. Let's make our way over there. We can get a hot drink and something to eat. Then we can review priorities before the press conference. I need to update Peters late morning anyway.'

Tomlinson was in the passenger seat when the sergeant's mobile rang. Riley pulled over and answered.

'DS Riley.' He stayed quiet, then just said, 'Right.' He looked over at Tomlinson then added to the voice on the other end, 'Let me pass you over to the Super. He's sitting here with me right now.' He handed Tomlinson the phone. 'It's CID at Gatwick. Geoff Wilson is with them.'

'Tomlinson.' The superintendent listened intently. 'We're en route to the incident room right now.' He paused suddenly. 'OK.' Another pause. 'Look, let me call you back in ten minutes.' He rang off and passed the mobile to Riley. He sighed heavily.

Four words had just changed everything...

Are the twins safe?

Serena.

He'd remembered her name. He'd seen it on her lapel badge often enough.

'No!' she shouted.

He stopped moving; let his hands fall to his side. Was he hurting her? He looked up into Serena's eyes. The amber glow intensified and he saw fear; watched as pain etched itself across her perfect features. Her whole body began to take on a pearlescent quality; seemed to be lit from within. Only then did he notice the small white dot that had appeared just beneath her rib-cage. Its intensity grew with every breath she took – her lungs acting as bellows, fanning a destructive, internal fire. The dot was more pronounced. Resembled a molten rivet. It hissed; radiated heat to her adjacent flesh.

'No!'

Serena's scream sent an icy shiver through him. Blades of numbness stabbed into his heart. But the chill, born of her fear, vanished; and so suddenly – for in an instant the temperature in the room went off the scale. He felt his throat go dry, as a searing wind swirled around him; began robbing him of breath. He needed water. Air. To escape. In desperation he tried to roll Serena off him, but she was like a dead-weight pinning him down. More and more of the white dots were breaking out all across her belly, like a strange luminous rash. She screamed uncontrollably as her whole torso erupted into flame. He could smell her charring flesh. He felt sick. His stomach heaved but nothing came. Then, something warm – innards, almost liquefied – poured out of her abdomen and spattered down onto his chest. His whole body tensed, recoiling in horrified disgust from the corporeal flood. He really was going to vomit now – but again nothing came. Spasms wracked him as he retched time and again. His ribs began to hurt. They felt bruised. His senses heightened, he was instantly aware of a sickly-sweet aroma as Serena's body began to disintegrate all around him. He tried to brush the warm, bloodied remains away. Her entrails dripped down his sides, staining the once-welcoming bed-sheets. As if in slow motion, he watched her hair catch light; strand after strand, it shrivelled away as the greedy flames welcomed the new source of fuel. And in place of her come-to-bed eyes, sulphurous flashes filled the now empty sockets –

He struggled against her weight. This time, what was left of Serena's weakened frame crumbled and her torso fell backwards to the floor – but her legs still held firm, vice-like, trapping his thighs. Panicking, he beat at them, fists hammering wildly until the lifeless grip was finally released. He snatched a breath – but the putrid smell brought on the nausea again. He hurled himself from the bed –

Something crunched under his bare feet.

It was Serena. Or what was left of her. He made for the bathroom door. Water. He had to get water. Had to cool her down. Had to cool himself down.

SHC.

The door wouldn't open. He slammed a shoulder into it. It didn't budge. He turned back to look at Serena, now little more than a smouldering pile of ashes on the floor in front of the bed.

SHC.

Three letters that pointed to a half-remembered theory. Somewhere in the back of his mind, a little voice was telling him to get out. He had to get away before the whole room went up. But why should he run? But for Serena, the room was unscathed. Then, he remembered. SHC. *Spontaneous human combustion* – when bodies mysteriously burned; with little or no damage to their surroundings. But how could that be possible? And how could it be happening to Serena?

His legs gave way and he sank down onto the carpet. He didn't know whether to cry, or to scream as Serena had done. He wiped a bloodied hand across his face and hacked repeatedly, trying in vain to expel the taste of burnt flesh from the back of his throat. It was all too much. He just wanted to disappear. He wanted the dark cloud back. He

wanted to give up; to go quietly. He'd even have gone into the cave...
But that time had passed.

Must wake up. He needed to get back to reality. *But this is reality. I am awake.*

His palms were sticky with Serena's bloody residue. He wiped them on the carpet. An image of Lady Macbeth, scrubbing at the indelible spot, came to mind. English Lit. Fifth form. His memories were all over the place. He looked down. His hands were still unclean. He looked again –

His gaze was drawn to his own torso. He blinked in disbelief. *No...* He couldn't bear to watch. *This can't be happening...* But he had to look a second time; he couldn't help himself. *No! Not me!* An identical, single white dot had just appeared. It, too, was hissing; glowing brighter with every passing second. *Please, no!* He felt tingling pin-pricks of heat start to well up deep inside him...

The circle appeared almost instantaneously, bearing painful testament to the damage being inflicted on his skin.

It took his brain a moment longer to react, temporarily confused as it was by that peculiarity of the human sensory system – at once so complex, and yet so unrefined – that sees the burning and freezing sensation initially registering as one and the same. And then, as electrical impulses finally leapt across synaptic gaps, completing circuits of mental recognition, his hand shot back in alarm; a fraction of a second too late. Even as he cried out, the flesh was already beginning to weep.

Riley swore then threw the cigarette to the ground, angrily stubbing it out with his shoe. He put the injured finger to his mouth and sucked, hoping to ease the pain.

'Told you smoking was bad for you,' Tomlinson quipped.

'I only drifted off for a second...'

'You're tired. We both are...' It was hardly surprising. The detectives had been up now for well over twenty-four hours, and Tomlinson judged it would be at least another twelve before they'd be able to get any sleep. 'Here, you could use this.' He passed the other man a hot drink. Riley had gone outside for some fresh air – or, at least, as fresh as his smoke-filled lungs would allow.

'Thanks.' The sergeant took a mouthful. Even vending machine coffee tasted good at 5:00 am.

Riley and Tomlinson had glassy-eyed expressions and their faces were covered with a light sheen of city grime. They would have given anything for a shower and change of clothes, but they knew they were up against it as they still had much to do before the press conference.

Although the media was still due to gather at lunch-time, investigative expediency had required Tomlinson to release certain information in advance of the meeting. As soon as he'd been told about the twins' kidnapping, he'd had to rethink the operational priorities and had effectively been forced to launch a public appeal for help in the small hours. Time was of the essence; the twins' very lives depended on it. He'd put in a call to Peters straight after Gatwick CID had made contact; and he'd also alerted the Yard's press office.

Capabilities had come a long way in the past decade and it was precisely to take advantage of these new technologies that Tomlinson had decided to pre-empt the conference. The growth in 24-hour digital TV and radio stations meant saturation coverage of any subject could be achieved in a relatively short period of time. Every viewer, every listener was a potential source of information. From night owls – such as long-distance lorry drivers, power station workers and security guards – to early birds – like postmen and corner-shop owners – many would listen to the radio to while away the small hours, or catch a news update before setting off for work. Each could feed in anything suspicious they'd seen – or, equally importantly – anything they'd now be primed to notice over the coming hours and days. Even the most unlikely report could hold the key to unlocking the investigation. The important thing was getting the public involved from the word go.

By 2:00 am Tomlinson and the press office duty staff had made the necessary calls to ensure that the appeal went out. Soon scrolling messages alerting people to the twins' abduction had begun to appear at the foot of late-night TV screens – everything from live-feed reality shows to tele-shopping programmes; from personal ads to job-finder services. The appeal was simultaneously broadcast at set intervals on national and local radio. The superintendent had even arranged for a pre-recorded telephone message, seeking the public's assistance, to be dialled out automatically at 9:00 am. It would target all the houses and business premises within a 25-mile radius of the crime scene.

By Tomlinson's calculations, if Percy and Ivy Wilson had been murdered even as late as 4:00 pm, then he'd already lost upwards of thirteen hours. That was easily long enough for the perpetrator to have made good his escape and to have concealed the children somewhere out of the way – perhaps in a lock-up, or an isolated house. But even so, assuming he hadn't killed them yet, he'd be under pressure to maintain some semblance of a normal routine. And that would become increasingly difficult to achieve as more and more people became aware of the appeal, and took a greater interest in what was going on around them. Even the slightest deviation from the norm could give him away.

Geoff Wilson and his wife, Anne, had arrived at the station just before midnight. Tomlinson had introduced himself briefly, before seeing them settled into a quiet room with a counsellor and Family Liaison Officer. He'd also asked the on-call Forensic Medical Examiner to look in on Mrs Wilson. She'd been offered a mild sedative, but had refused. Mr Wilson had been supportive for his wife's sake, but otherwise hadn't said much; instead, he'd left the superintendent to get on with it. The couple had given Tomlinson a photograph of their eight-month-old twins, Harry and Emily – one that Geoff Wilson carried everywhere with him in his wallet – and by 3:00 am the image had been included in the TV coverage. Tomlinson was conscious he needed to stay on top of all the reports coming in, so he could offer the couple regular updates. Understandably they'd be desperate for news, advice and support.

Only some of which he'd be able to give them.

'Mr Bryant?'

The sound of his name drew him back from the brink; saw him rescued from the inferno in the gloom.

Almost.

'Mr Bryant?'

He still couldn't quite make the break. *Something* wanted to keep him there.

She spoke his name again. 'David?'

He felt a soft touch on his shoulder and this time the physical contact, the link to the real world, did bring him back to the land of the living. Gone was the burning in his chest. Gone too the smell of carbonising flesh.

Water.

He needed water. His mouth was dry. He could feel the beads of sweat trickling down his face, catching in his eyebrows, before running down the sides of his nose. He tasted the salt on his lips.

Water.

He needed water more than ever. Water to douse the flames. *Don't let me go back there again.* He feared he was slipping away...

'David?' A further touch of his shoulder. 'Everything's fine; it was just another of the bad dreams.'

He was back. Back to stay this time. He felt the bed beneath him. Was reassured that she spoke in that same comforting tone that he'd grown so used to. They'd been through the same process day in day out for several weeks now. Some days had been better than others. But overall, with *one* recent exception, progress was encouraging. Full recovery, though, was still some way off. They both knew as much – though neither ever discussed it. Even after the physical wounds had fully healed, the mental scars would remain. For how long, though, depended on how well the experts worked their magic.

He was calming down now, his breathing growing steadier. A cool towel was being wiped across his brow.

'Here, try to drink a little.'

A beaker was pressed gently to his lips and he opened his mouth, inclining his head slightly. He took a couple of sips, let the water run over his tongue. He swallowed – too soon – and choked on the liquid. Then a hand was patting him firmly on the back.

'Here, you'll find the next one easier.' He drank again, and found she was right. 'It's nearly seven. If you're hungry, I'll order you up some breakfast.' But he didn't feel like eating. 'Maybe later then?'

She was eternally patient. Years of practice had made her so. Gently coaxing trauma victims back to health. Being there for them throughout the rehabilitation process, no matter how long it took. She'd always make time for the patients in her care, often staying on long after her shift had finished. She'd sit with them and talk about whatever took their fancy; any subject under the sun. But with David Bryant she felt it was somehow *different*. He needed reassurance but, more, a positivity and stability had to be reintroduced into his life. Intuitively, she'd always shy away from mentioning anything current on the news. He'd catch the occasional headline when left in the day-room – that couldn't be avoided – but she wasn't about to add to his burden. And if he asked, she'd lie and say she hadn't seen the news that day. Besides, everything was just so depressing – only today it all seemed to be about those awful murders and the missing children. No, David Bryant could stay shielded a little longer.

'Now, let's sit you up.' He felt her plumping the pillows behind him. 'Is that better?' Her hand was on his dressing-gown. 'Oh, you're soaked through. Here, let me clean you up a bit. I'll get you a change of clothes in a moment. At least the bed-sheets aren't that bad.' She kept up the gentle commentary as she worked.

He heard water running in a sink nearby. She removed his gown, then his pyjama top. After a quick rub-down with a flannel, she helped him put on the dry clothing. 'We've a busy day ahead. There's talk of someone important coming to visit. But they haven't told us who.' Her hands were moving down his body. But there was nothing sensual about the physical contact this time. This woman's love was altogether different – a love for her patients, born of a passion for her job; a desire to make the sick better. 'I don't think they'll be coming here. They'll probably be shown round the new children's ward...' she paused, suddenly recalling the children on the news. 'There. Nearly done.' He felt a dry gown go on top. 'I'll let you sleep now. I'll come back a little later. Maybe then you'll feel like eating something.'

Sleep –

As if he could find solace there. Sleep just let the nightmares return. He felt a final touch on his shoulder.

'Bye.'

He opened his eyes and turned to look at her. 'Thanks, Jane,' he said quietly.

'You're welcome.' She smiled appreciatively.

But the gesture was lost on him.

For the plane crash had robbed him of his sight...

CHAPTER THREE

COMMANDER PETERS HAD originally intended that the press conference be held in Croydon but, given the new direction in which the investigation was heading, he'd subsequently agreed with the Met's director of communications that New Scotland Yard would be a more appropriate venue. The Yard's briefing room was state-of-the-art and Peters felt Tomlinson would get the message across more effectively from there.

Although its relationship with the media was often fragile, the Met really did need to keep it on side now. There could be no underestimating its power, its reach into every home in the land – everyone bought a paper, or watched TV or listened to the radio. The media's support would mean thousands of extra eyes and ears on the street; potential surveillance resources that far outstripped idealistic budgetary wish-lists. No-one doubted there'd be the usual round of hoaxes – idiots hell bent on wasting police time, as well as the mentally deranged who'd genuinely think they'd be offering vital clues – but, for all the chaff of distraction, the wheat of investigative opportunity could still be sieved out. It just needed that one call.

In line with the commander's instructions, Tomlinson was about to deliver the briefing. The director of communications had, however, insisted that an experienced press officer be on hand to offer advice; to help ensure the event ran smoothly. *Professional*. That had been Peters' watch-word. The image the Met needed to portray. For his part, Tomlinson had reservations; major ones at that, but he was doing his best to keep them hidden. He'd work with the press team, but he wasn't about to put his trust in them. He knew full well that many of their now-senior number had started their careers at one or other of the Capital's papers; either that or they'd come from middle-management positions in regional newsrooms. His suspicious mind couldn't help wondering why they'd passed up the better career prospects, the guarantee of greater pay, to come and work for the police. He'd long harboured a nagging doubt about their loyalty – only too happy to believe that some had been planted as long-term moles; their instructions to lie low, to snoop around and embarrass the great and the good when the time was right. Those of his ilk with whom he'd shared such thoughts had jokingly labelled him paranoid but, then again, hadn't the inquiry into phone hacking revealed just how underhand certain media elements had been in their pursuit of a story; and hadn't it also exposed the web of corruption that existed, with trusted officers – some extremely high-ranking – found to have been lining their pockets with dirty money? Tomlinson had no doubt there were others involved too;

only so far they'd escaped detection; had kept their heads low, while probably destroying incriminating evidence. Tomlinson judged the media to be a double-edged sword, one that needed to be handled with extreme care.

Concentrating now on the facts he needed to get across, the superintendent put these misgivings to the back of his mind. He forced himself to view the sea of cameras and journalists arrayed before him as a means to an end, a tool that would allow him to reach the public, to ask for their assistance. Seated behind a table, he leaned in closer to the microphone and introduced himself.

'Ladies and gentlemen, welcome to this afternoon's press briefing. I am Detective Superintendent Ray Tomlinson. Thank you for coming.'

For the next few minutes he outlined how he intended to proceed – he would detail the key facts, the nature of the crimes being investigated, the relative timings involved, the lines of enquiry that his team were focussing on, and he would sum up by explaining how the public could help. He would then take questions. The press conference would end with Mr and Mrs Wilson being brought out to read from a prepared statement. He underlined the fact that the couple would not be taking any questions. Rules of engagement understood, he began the briefing proper.

Ten minutes in, the superintendent felt altogether more relaxed; satisfied his presentation was going well. Every so often, as he'd emphasised a key point, he'd caught the tacit nods of approval from his press office minder.

Fifteen minutes in, Geoff and Anne Wilson made their appearance. The couple had decided beforehand that Anne would read out the statement. Geoff would be there at her side to offer moral support. Tomlinson noted the reversal of roles, the change that had occurred in the pair since early that morning; with Anne Wilson growing increasingly stronger, becoming somehow better able to cope with it all – in marked contrast to the behaviour displayed by her husband. Geoff Wilson had retreated into himself, to such an extent that he'd barely spoken to anyone. Tomlinson had seen it before, and not just with murder inquiries – men who, while at first brave, later found their stoical façade crumbling away to expose their inner helplessness. He couldn't help thinking how childhood conditioning had so much to answer for.

With the couple now seated to his left, the superintendent quietly announced, 'Ladies and gentlemen... Mrs Wilson.'

It was one of those embarrassed, awkward situations. Nobody knew quite what to do, how to receive her. Just how were they meant to react to someone whose world had been thrown into such turmoil?

Whose children – whose in-laws – had been so cruelly torn away from her? The press pack stayed quiet, a protracted silence filling the room. But all attention was focussed on Anne Wilson – eyes, human and electronic alike. As she readied herself, breathing deeply for extra composure, live feeds streamed through the ether to communications satellites overhead, before being bounced earthwards again to the TV studios' editing suites. Anne Wilson began to read. She tried to remain calm but, word by word, the strain began to show. First, tears welled up in her eyes. Then, her voice rose noticeably in pitch. But she persevered.

'... So... we would like to ask anyone with any information to come forward. Please call.' She paused, took a sip of water, then pointedly continued; her appeal now directly to the perpetrator. 'To the person who did this, I ask you to release our children and give yourself up. The police are here to offer you the support you need.'

From his vantage point behind the table, Tomlinson noticed Geoff Wilson's arm shoot suddenly out at waist height to take hold of his wife. An instant later, he guessed why – her ashen face indicating she'd been on the verge of fainting. Pushing his chair backwards, the superintendent stood up.

Determined to get the pair of them out of the spotlight as quickly as possible, he said forcefully, 'That concludes the briefing, ladies and gentlemen.'

Only it didn't.

Not by a long way –

David Bryant had managed to catch a few hours' uninterrupted sleep.

The bad dreams had not returned, and for that he was thankful. But even as he lay awake in his world of enforced darkness, it seemed his brain was not averse to playing the occasional trick; lending his nostrils a waft of burnt flesh every once in a while.

Eau de mort – fragrance of death; the perfume favoured by the lost Serena.

But he knew the stench was gone. Recognised the recurrent sensation for what it was – a figment of his over-stressed imagination. For Jane had brought him back to reality, had assured him he'd just been having another one of the nightmares. Nightmares. They could have been daymares for all he knew – day and night having long since become one and the same.

For a moment he dared to think the unpalatable; wondered whether he'd be better off losing his mind completely. At least then he could stay forever in the nightmare land. And at least there he might yet wake up one day to a different life – to one in which he could see again. Like the life he'd had before. But he sensed that life was gone. Ahead of him now lay only challenges – challenges that were born of change. He wasn't sure he'd have the strength, the determination to cope. He doubted himself; doubted there could ever be light – literally – at the end of his tunnel. What he wouldn't give to be able to see again.

Sight – mother to the other four senses.

Sight – the vital faculty on which all the others depended for survival.

What use to hear the falling tree if he couldn't see to get out of the way? True, he found himself reasoning, the body could compensate up to a point, but none of the remaining senses were really so precious. He could live in a silent world; would happily never hear another sound. So too he could forego the taste, the texture and aroma of his favourite foods – accepting that from thereon in they would become nothing more than fuel; sources of bodily energy. But to lose the gift of sight – that was too much for him. Sight was the very window through which he observed – engaged with – the world beyond his self. That allowed his every perceived experience to become a lasting memory – a remembrance that was ordered, catalogued and filed away in his very own library of life. Images available on request; 24/7.

He'd been no different to so many others, scarcely giving sight a second thought. When he could fit it into his busy work schedule, he might visit an opticians once every couple of years. And he was always lucky. 20:20 every time. Maybe it had made him complacent. But not anymore. Not since the crash. Now he'd have to learn a whole new set of life skills. And on top of that, there was the depression to overcome–

Only temporary, they'd assured him. *Perfectly normal. PTSD – post-traumatic stress disorder.* They'd told him he was going through the same as soldiers who returned home from war, who'd been struck down on the battlefield of the mind; or civilians who, against the odds, had survived natural disasters; maybe even a terrorist attack. It was just the body's way of dealing with it. First there was the numbness – the lack of comprehension; next came the gratitude – that you were still alive; followed by the guilt – that others had died in your place; feelings of self-reproach weren't far behind – asking yourself why you should have survived instead of others who surely would have had so much more to give; and, finally, as all the feelings rolled together into a mental storm of confusion, the self-doubt would grow; would show itself as an unwillingness to go on.

Those blessed with an inner drive would finally escape the confusion – the gift of life a second time round spurring them on to achieve greater things. But for the apathetic, it was a different story. They just wanted to lose themselves in a world of self-pity where they'd allow fear to hold them firmly captive. Afraid to face up to their own mortality, they didn't want to run the risk of recovery – for that would again entail being exposed to the dangers posed throughout life.

Though he hated himself for doing so, Bryant had found himself falling into this second camp; siding with those paralysed by self-pity. It had come as something of a shock to him. It had been so unexpected. For before the crash he'd been a real go-getter. Self-confident. A self-starter. Risk-taker *par excellence* in the international business world. His mindset had seen him fit comfortably into the money-driven, status-conscious twenty-first century society. He'd measured his worth almost exclusively by material wealth – the executive home, the sports car, the foreign holidays. And had his marriage survived longer, he knew he would have faced pressure to get his son into the right schools. Not a pressure that would have come from his wife, but from his business peers; those who would have looked down on him if he'd failed to toe the expected educational line.

He suddenly found himself growing angry – with himself; at himself; at the shadow of his former self. Just what *had* happened to him these past few months? Why had he allowed it? He certainly couldn't explain it. He'd always thought himself impervious to stress. Had always enjoyed the cut and thrust of business. For him, adrenalin had been his life-blood. But he *had* changed...

More importantly, *The Company* had noticed it too –

He'd expected to be let go, had anticipated a handshake and a cheque to accompany the goodbye – no longer judging himself to be an asset that The Company would want to keep. But he'd been wrong. And misreading the situation hadn't helped. It had served only to make him even more unsure of himself; had made him repeatedly question whether he still had it in him to be a success – not just in business, but in any aspect of his life. Against the odds though, The Company had told him it was prepared to be patient. It would play the long game, would keep a job open for him. *But* – and he'd at least known there had to have been a but, even in the confusion and uncertainty that daily swamped him – in exchange for such corporate charity, it had every intention of capitalising on the miracle of his survival. When the time was right, it would go public with his incredible story; would exploit it round the world; would generate astronomic publicity for itself – and likely boost profits into the bargain. That would keep the shareholders happy, guarantee re-election for the Board. Everyone loved a caring employer, one that looked after its staff – paying their medical expenses and guaranteeing a job to return to. The Company was the sort of company everyone aspired to work for.

But he knew all that was going to have to wait – until he got better...

Bryant had been provided with counsellors and psychiatrists almost straightaway – only the best, and flown in from all over the world. Despite money being no object though, his progress had been slow. And just when The Company thought its man had finally turned a corner, he'd relapsed. He'd self-harmed. Had cut one of his wrists with a razor blade. The medical staff had found him in time and had bandaged up the wound. They'd explained away his action as a cry for help. They'd labelled it a positive step, marking the beginning of his long journey to come to terms with his blindness. He couldn't help wondering though; questioning whether they'd *really* be able to help him. He knew they could oversee his body's physical recovery. But that still left the mind, with its accompanying mental scars and that, he thought, must surely be something altogether different; must represent an unknown quantity over which they couldn't have any direct control?

It was at that point that Jane had come into his life.

Jane Reynolds. Staff nurse. *An angel descended from the heavens.* At least, that was how most of the other patients described her. They'd always refer to her as *Our Jane – Our*, because she somehow managed to introduce a feeling of ownership, of closeness between herself and those in her care. They said she had a talent for getting through to them, no matter how great their trauma; and that she was gifted in the way she was able to personalise their care, could always find time for each and every one of them. Without their realising it at the time, she was able to overcome the defences – whether conscious or subconscious – that they'd erected. And they said too that, once under her wing, you knew you'd soon be on the mend. She really was the best. Especially when presented with the worst. Her speciality seemed to be caring for those whom the psychiatrists had abandoned; not for her their blinkered response of prescribing medication; keeping the fragile of mind suppressed with a ready supply of pills. For her, the approach was altogether different. For her it was a question of perseverance. Of knowing there *was* a way through. Recognising that she just needed to keep on until she found the right key. Jane Reynolds had that indefinable quality found in all who came to nursing as a true vocation; that special *something* that couldn't be taught; that had to come from within. She displayed compassion, and kindness; and had the innate desire to help the sick get better again. In short, she touched them with love.

And though he wasn't yet consciously aware of it, in the weeks to come David Bryant would also find he'd been taken under that healing wing...

The young female reporter smiled to herself. She'd already decided what she was going to do. Her eyes, full of mischief, peered out from beneath the fringe of a blonde bob. Today would be the day she made a name for herself. Escaped the drudgery of parochial news; the boredom of local interest stories. Today she meant to come to the attention of the nationals. And for all the right reasons...

By doing wrong –

She stood up, her pink denim jacket – a deliberate choice from the wardrobe that morning – intended to make her even more distinctive.

'Mr Wilson?' she called out. Having failed to attract the man's attention, she tried again; louder this time. 'Mr Wilson?' Now he looked up, his eyes empty; seemingly devoid of emotion. She knew this was her one chance. She'd have a matter of seconds before they tried to silence her. She rattled off her words like a burst from an Uzi. 'I'm really sorry to speak out of turn.' She wasn't. 'I know we were told there wouldn't be any questions, but...' In her peripheral vision she was aware of a blurry form coming towards her. She knew it would be the press officer. She loaded another clip, fired another burst of words, '... I wondered if you had a personal message for our readers...' She hoped she'd done enough; had hit the mark. A moment later, she knew she had. Bullseye.

The press officer's failure to impose order immediately was seized upon by others in the room. Just as she'd planned, it became a free for all.

'Mr Wilson!' A voice from the very back of the room.

'Mrs Wilson!' From somewhere off to one side.

'When did you last see your children?'

The questions were coming all at once.

'How are you taking the deaths of your parents, Mr Wilson?'

'*Enough!*' Tomlinson didn't need a microphone. His voice boomed around the room. His authority carried a force of its own and the staccato questions ceased as quickly as they'd begun. He glowered angrily at the press officer. The message clear – *I shouldn't be doing your job for you!* 'You were told... no questions!' He forced himself to lower his voice, to regain control of the situation – and of himself. 'Your behaviour is just *not* acceptable.' He looked directly at the young reporter who'd started it. She blushed, tried to look apologetic; a quick shrug of the pink shoulders and she turned her eyes away, no longer prepared to meet the superintendent's gaze. 'You'll appreciate this is an *incredibly* difficult time for Mr and Mrs Wilson. When they feel better able to cope, they'll speak to you. But not before. Now, *please*, be sensitive to their feelings and respect their privacy...'

Mrs Wilson rose and Tomlinson put a protective arm around her – not touching, but close enough to create a barrier between her and the rest of the room. He steered her towards the exit. Mr Wilson pushed his chair back.

Then stopped –

'Yes, I have a message,' he said, sitting down again, in answer to the blonde's question. He leaned in closer to the microphone his wife had been using. 'But it's not for your readers...' his voice was steady, quiet – but determined. '...it's for... the bastard who's done this!'

All eyes were on Geoff Wilson. The reporting pack rooted to the spot in astonishment. This was dynamite. They all knew it. Some of the cameramen had been caught off-guard, but those who hadn't yet begun stowing away their kit carried on filming, capturing every moment of the unexpected scene.

'We both know they're dead, don't we? You've already killed my children. Doesn't matter what the police tell me, I know you've already done it.' Then, turning his attention away from the blonde, he looked straight into one of the cameras. 'So, it really doesn't matter what you do now, where you go. Just know this...' still no fluctuation in Wilson' tone '... I'm coming after you. For as long as it takes. And when I catch up with you, *I'm* going to kill *you*...' His expression said it all. Eyes burning into the camera. *Through* the camera. As if seeking to make a link to the murderer. No ranting. No rash words. Just a statement of intent.

'Geoff, no!' Anne Wilson had come back to the table. 'Please, Geoff, no!' She was sobbing, trying to get close to him. To get him to talk sense. To support her. 'Geoff, I need you. Come away... Please!'

But her husband brushed her aside.

'Geoff!'

He wasn't listening. Still he stared straight ahead into one of the camera lenses.

Tomlinson swore under his breath. What the hell had just happened? How had it gone *so* wrong? He was about to try to recover the situation when the press officer intervened belatedly.

'It's clearly a distressing time, ladies and gentlemen. Mr and Mrs Wilson are tired and need rest. If you could all start making your way out, please. As the Superintendent has said, this briefing is now over. We'll contact you when the next one's arranged...'

But no-one was going anywhere. They didn't want to miss a second of the unfolding action. Their readers and viewers would be in for a treat. At once tragic, and morbid; and fascinating. Ratings and sales would go through the roof.

Tomlinson wasn't prepared to wait any longer. He couldn't afford to let the briefing get even more out of control. He waded in, physically man-handling Geoff Wilson from the table – but as gently as he could. He had to get the man out of there. Had to get the couple out of the spotlight. And quickly.

'Mr Wilson, this way, *please…*'

A final, concerted push and Tomlinson had the pair through the exit. Once more, they were sheltered from the glare of the media. He, though, was still on the *wrong* side of the door. For he *still* had to bring the conference to a *professional* close.

'Superintendent?' It was the female reporter *again*. 'One *final* question?' He didn't even try to hide his annoyance from her. '*Please?*' Butter wouldn't have melted in her mouth.

He responded with an exasperated, 'Yes, Miss…?'

'Norman. Becky Norman. Addington & West Wickham Observer.'

Something clicked in the back of his mind. He recalled Peters saying a local reporter had been quick on the scene. He'd bet anything *she* was that reporter.

'Yes, Miss Norman?'

'I was just wondering…' the mischievous look was there again, '… if you'd be taking any action against *Mr* Wilson?' She revelled momentarily in the superintendent's obvious confusion, knowing the headache she was about to give him. 'Unless I'm mistaken, he did just threaten to kill someone… and that is still a crime?'

Trauma –

That's what they'd said. That trauma was behind his loss of sight. That blindness was the brain's way of dealing with the horror he'd witnessed. But why then, he wondered, could he still *see* those final moments so clearly? Replayed over and over again in the perpetual Odeon of his mind. A disaster movie without end. If this *was* the brain's way of dealing with it, then it made no sense. Surely he'd have lost his *memory*, not his sight? But they'd remained insistent – trauma was the culprit, right enough; they were sure of it. All he needed to do was consider the facts. They'd found nothing wrong with his optic nerves, they'd run their tests and each and every one had come back showing everything was A OK. There was no physical reason why he shouldn't be able to see. *Give it time* – that had been their considered view – *and your sight should return.*

Should?

For Bryant *should* wasn't good enough. Just how long would he have to wait until the time might be right? No, he wasn't convinced they were helping, and didn't rate their clinical professionalism highly. And as for Jane, despite all her kindness, he knew she couldn't restore his sight.

Fact.

But then, just thinking about the nurse seemed to calm him; helped him keep the doubts and fears at arm's length. Bryant reconsidered. Perhaps he was being unduly critical of her. Jane was a scintilla of light in his world of darkness, a lone star glimpsed fleetingly on a cold winter's night whenever the clouds parted. And though she might remain hidden from him, just like that lone star disappearing behind the misty veil, he sensed she'd still be around; watching over him, unseen, for as long as he needed her.

Unlike his family –

Not that he really blamed his father. He knew he had enough on his plate, caring for a wife now ill with cancer for the third time. It never really had gone away. Two remissions in five years and twice they thought she'd beaten it. But this time it had come back more aggressively than ever and the prognosis had not been good – the consultant doubted she'd even see out Christmas. No, blaming him would be unjust. As it was, his father had already made time to visit him on several occasions soon after the crash. And now, it was only right he spend the remaining days and months with his ailing wife.

But as for the rest of them –

His wife, Luisa – or rather his soon-to-be ex-wife, for the divorce papers were almost finalised – why hadn't she made the effort? No calls. Not even a message of support. And little Paolo – did he even know his father had survived? Bryant seriously doubted it. He could just imagine Luisa's unrestrained joy, callously profiting from the news of the crash; in years to come, telling their son how his father had died. He remembered the last time they'd spoken – *shouted* – face to face; his bags discarded in the lane outside their home and Paolo already spirited away to the grandparents. And then, once back in England, he'd tried again to make contact; to come to an arrangement over access. He'd spoken to Luisa on the phone – only to be told he'd never see Paolo again. He'd considered taking legal action, but what prospect was there realistically? Deep down he knew it would be pointless. Luisa's family was from the south. Things were very different down there. For all the veneer of modernity, its leading voice in Brussels, Italy was still a country divided. Where Luisa came from, everything depended on influence – the contacts you had; the people you knew; your position in the community. The law, the courts – they meant nothing. And if he really were foolhardy enough to press his luck, certain individuals within Luisa's family would see to it he didn't remain a problem for long. He guessed there'd be an unfortunate *accident* – his car going over a steep mountain ravine; or maybe he'd fall victim to a tragic stabbing on some quiet back-street. Who'd miss one more *Inglese*? That's just the way it was. The way things were done. Had been for generations. And would be for years to come.

But he only had himself to blame. He'd known at the time what he'd been marrying into – that Luisa's family were *connected*. At first though, it had served him well; had allowed him entry to another set of lucrative markets. So he'd not thought through the potential downsides.

He'd naively believed he could take her away from all that, to settle her and Paolo deep in middle England. He'd even shown her his house – *their* house – on a weekend back to see his parents. And for a while she'd considered it, until family pressure had finally won the day. An ultimatum had not been far behind – the clear message that *he* would stay with *her*; that he should remain there in Italy with the extended family. The in-laws' meddling had finally taken its toll and by degrees he and Luisa had grown apart. So too his local business contacts had become increasingly unavailable. He'd recognised he was being excluded. And with fewer money-making ventures open to him, he'd had to look elsewhere. Over the border. Overseas. Eventually he'd come to regard his increasingly frequent business trips as a welcome distraction, for they'd meant a breather from the disharmony at home. But he'd known that such behaviour on his part had just been an avoidance tactic, and too late in the day had he finally realised what he'd be losing; too late had he tried building bridges to span the emotional chasm that had grown between them. But that life was gone now. And his only real regret – Paolo. That's just how it had to be...

No – maybe he *was* being unfair to Luisa.

He pondered the thought. What if she *didn't* know he'd survived? That could be it. After all, The Company had taken steps to ensure his survival had remained a secret. The Company wanted him to recuperate in peace, at his own speed, and away from prying eyes. And, so far, it had been successful. He didn't know how it had managed to do so, but he suspected pay-outs big time had been offered to the hospital; boosted by the promise of funding for drug trials, and maybe more specialised wards. Perhaps The Company had dangled the carrot of sponsorship for cutting-edge technology – provided no-one spoke out of turn. The Company's money could certainly buy silence. But so too it had a stick of economic oblivion with which to beat those who failed to march to its tune. If the hospital transgressed, compromised the planned, long-term advertising opportunities – and he *was* that opportunity; of that he was in no doubt – the screws would be turned. Overnight, top management would be removed, and those displaced would find themselves black-listed from getting jobs anywhere else. The senior managers were players though. They'd know the score;

would know only too well what was at stake – and they'd have toed The Company's line. But he couldn't help thinking of those lower down the pecking order. How had they been controlled? News of his survival could so easily have netted a cleaner or porter a significant sum of cash. He suddenly pulled himself up – ashamed of himself for being so judgmental. Just because he and his business ilk had so often sold out, it didn't mean everyone else would follow suit. People might not enjoy the trappings of wealth he'd accumulated, but they still had standards; their own sense of right and wrong.

Maybe even Luisa –

No, he *had* judged her fairly. Was sure of it. She *must* have known of his survival. Yes, he remembered now. Recalled that his father had been apologetic the day of his last visit. For he'd explained how he'd called his daughter-in-law, leaving a message in his best broken Italian; the words picked from a pocket dictionary. There'd been no call back, and he'd thought maybe he hadn't been clear enough...

Bryant could feel the despondency coming on again. Without even realising it, he was touching a finger to his wrist. The one he'd cut all those weeks back. The gash had nearly healed, but it remained tender in places, as his finger retraced the line of the blade.

He wouldn't be doing that again...

Next time – if there *was* a next time; if he attempted a repeat performance – he'd be sure to use tablets; to pop a few pills. Far less painful. And far less chance of their discovering what he'd done; getting to him in time...

He knew it was the coward's way out. But what else was he? A coward. Afraid to keep his family together. Afraid to live life, disabled. Afraid to face a life of perpetual darkness.

'That all seemed to go rather well, didn't it?'

The commander's understated sarcasm wasn't lost on Tomlinson. There wasn't really a lot he could say. Someone else in his position might have tried to pre-empt the criticism that he knew was coming his way; might have tried a diversionary attack on the ineffectual press officer. But that wasn't in the superintendent's nature. He meant to take it squarely on the chin.

Peters had summoned him to his office the minute the shambles had ended. Both men were now watching the TV in the corner of the room. It was tuned to one of the 24-hour news channels and Tomlinson could see himself on the screen pushing Geoff Wilson towards the exit. Less than ten minutes had elapsed in real-time and already the pictures were being beamed nationwide. Tomlinson had to admire the station's speed; *its* professionalism – a far cry from his own.

48

'And in extraordinary scenes today...'

Peters angled a remote and muted the news-anchor's running commentary. He sighed, shook his head, then turned to face the superintendent. 'Just before I called you, I had a call from the Commissioner. He has... concerns. He wanted to know if I still thought you were the right man for this job.'

'Sir.'

'Now, I've offered him my *personal* assurance you're the best detective to lead this inquiry.' The commander went and sat down behind his desk. Steepling his fingers, he continued, 'My trust *is* well-founded, isn't it, Ray?'

'It won't happen again, sir.'

'Because if this all goes pear-shaped, it's not just your head on the line.'

'No, sir.'

From the moment he'd walked into Peters' office, Tomlinson had guessed exactly what would be coming; had known it would have nothing to do with the farcical press conference – the verbal sparring with the media and the unexpected outburst from Geoff Wilson, that was all par for the course. An embarrassment yes, but nothing the Commissioner hadn't seen a hundred times before. No, Tomlinson judged the Commissioner's concerns to be far more practical in nature; to relate to procedure – or, rather, the spectacular lack of it. It was a miracle the press hadn't already latched onto the oversight.

'Just *how* could we have missed the children, Ray? Why in heaven's name weren't they included in *any* of the initial reports? Just how incompetent does that make us look? *Well?*'

It was time for the superintendent to close ranks, to try his damnedest to defend his colleagues. 'Sir, to be fair, it *was* only after SOCO had been there long enough to...'

Peters cut him short. 'I know the facts. But, come on! The first responders ought to have done a better job. And even if we excuse them... for someone with your experience... it just beggars belief. It's not just you, you know –'

There it was again.

Tomlinson heard it at once, the repeated, flawed priority in the commander's hectoring diatribe. It was nothing to do with his procedural failings. But it was everything to do with performance assessment and related funding packages. He found himself writing another headline for the *Standard*. After Monday's *Cash for Clear-Up Rates*, he'd give Tuesday's readers *Cash for Competence*. Whatever next for Wednesday? He didn't much care for what he was hearing; nor the conclusions he was reaching. Clearly, it *was* all about the politics now. Justice had been firmly relegated, had become the after-thought. The hours they'd lost – the head start the killer would now have on them – yes, it was inexcusable; albeit it had been operationally unavoidable. But to suggest a potential loss of face for the Met warranted greater concern, that was just untenable.

Egg on the face he could live with – but not dead children.

He decided there was no point trying to fight his corner, as Peters obviously wasn't in a listening mood. But at least *he* knew it wasn't the local squad's fault. To blame them was to do them a disservice. For the killer had been meticulous. Every trace of the twins' presence had been removed from the scene – or, at least, the visible signs had. Their toys had all gone. So too their clothes. Even the kitchen bin had been emptied of tell-tale signs – packaging, foodstuffs – of anything that would have pointed to meals being prepared for anyone other than the murder victims. It had only been *after* Gatwick CID had made contact that he'd asked SOCO to cast the net wider, to try a different panel of forensic tests.

And that was when the twins' hidden world *had* started to appear. Juice spilled on the carpets. Smears of anti-rash cream on the kitchen worktops. Tiny fingerprints dotted along skirting boards. There'd simply been no reason to look the first time round. And they'd missed it all.

'I'm going to be under extreme pressure to report something positive to the Commissioner, Ray...' Peters left his words hanging momentarily, while he eyed the superintendent expectantly; '... so,' he concluded, 'I'm counting on you.'

'Sir.'

In other words, any further lack of progress and Peters would make sure Tomlinson became the fall-guy.

As soon as he was out in the corridor again, Tomlinson felt the pressure begin to drain away. Not for him the politics of it all. He undid his top button and loosened his tie. He poured himself a drink from one of the nearby chiller-units and gulped down the cool liquid.

Duck out of water. That's how he felt. Time to get back to the pond – muddied though the waters undoubtedly were.

CHAPTER FOUR

'DAVID?'

The familiar warming touch of her hand was there on his shoulder, and immediately his spirits were lifted. Just how *did* she do that?

'Good, I see you're sitting up. Can you eat something now?' Jane was back at his side and everything felt better again.

He wished he could see her. Just once. He'd tried to picture her over and over again in his mind but, without even the briefest of visual references, it was an impossible task – the make-believe faces he conjured up forever shifting, like sand beneath the waves. The frustration he felt reminded him of the guessing game he'd played as a child, imagining what his favourite radio DJs looked like. It had been long before the advent of the web; before he could snatch data from the ether with the click of a mouse. Back then those who never appeared on *Top of the Pops* remained a mystery. He'd done the same as everyone else, writing in for the grainy black-and-white publicity shots. And like so many others, he'd been just as surprised that the faces never seemed to match the voices. He wondered if it would be the same with Jane.

It wasn't even as if he could rely on other patients to paint the picture for him. He'd already gone down that route, asking for descriptions of the nurse. But he'd got nowhere. No two descriptions ever tallied. He'd put that down to their medication – probably so doped up they wouldn't even have recognised themselves in a mirror. It seemed stupid to him now to recall one of his more leftfield thoughts – when he'd briefly considered the possibility that Jane *was* an angel, who appeared to different people in different guises; and that maybe that's what had accounted for the discrepancies.

The one and only time he'd actually asked her outright, she'd just said, 'You'll see...'

He'd taken that as an indication of her confidence in his recovery. He'd found such optimism welcome, particularly as his thoughts had again begun to focus on the bad things in his life; and, in particular, the breakdown of his marriage. With Luisa growing more distant, he'd taken refuge in his work; had purposely clocked up every hour going. There'd been no point in his returning home. *Home.* Wherever that had been. As the rift had deepened, he'd returned to Britain's shores, back to his expensive detached property on the well-heeled, private estate. But for all its monetary worth, his executive pile of bricks and mortar had remained a soul-less living space – devoid of the love that comes with a family, the memories of happy times spent together, and the hopes and fears every parent has for their child as it grows. And without Luisa and Paolo's company, the house remained just that. A house – but never a *home*.

The constant flights had proved a welcome distraction from his domestic troubles. As had Serena. Instantly, she was there again, foremost in his consciousness. Serena Marshall, a vision of loveliness; mid-twenties, five-six, a size ten, with long dark hair; her make-up immaculate each and every flight. He remembered again how her rosters had coincided with many of his trips. Short-haul. There and back the same day. Europe mainly. Denied a loving relationship, he'd found himself fantasising about the stewardess – conjuring up images of how they'd have made the perfect couple. She'd come to recognise him, smiling every time he'd boarded. She'd helped him stow the hand luggage in the locker overhead. He'd stood close at every opportunity, breathing in her exquisite floral perfume. She'd chatted about the usual – his work, the trips, and how they must have worn him down. But she'd never mentioned families. Maybe she'd known, had seen enough separated executives to spot the signs – no toys for the kids on the return flight; no perfume or jewellery for the wife; no rush to get off the plane at the other end. But for all the smiles and small-talk, that was as far as it had ever gone. She'd always been the professional. Never a hint of anything personal. His had been the unspoken love of the pubescent schoolboy, watching the girl in the class from afar; desperately wanting to make the first move, but afraid of rejection – badge of the loner; that led to isolation for the remainder of one's schooldays.

Serena. The professional. Just doing her job.

He'd always assumed she'd have had a boyfriend. But he'd never spotted an engagement ring. Maybe she'd been playing the field. Enjoying herself while youth was still on her side. As suddenly as he'd been recalling her to mind, he pulled himself up sharp. Just who was he to judge her so? He'd never really come to know anything about her. But what he *did* know – what he felt now as the embarrassment rose within him – was that he'd been defiling Serena's memory through the lustful, intimate dreams he'd been having of her.

Dreams? Nightmares! Daymares! Every one as inescapably wretched as the next.

And yet... amid the fear and shame, there'd been guilty enjoyment too. Serena had been his. And he'd no longer been the loner. But the embarrassment of the fantasies – the erotic thoughts he continued to hide from the doctors; from Jane – all burdened him. Weighing down on his conscience every night, as he once again met Serena's memory in that same hotel room – that same glass, toppling from the table; that same curtain, amber light flooding in; and that same feeling of lust as she came out of the bathroom.

In real life, though he had given free rein to his imagination, his desires had been altogether more restrained – picturing himself and Serena as a normal, happy couple; going to the movies; attending parties; holding dinners for friends.

No – the carnal emotions had only come on since the crash. And they were at their worst when he was asleep. When his subconscious was free to direct his mind.

He could smell burning again.

Just thinking about Serena was allowing the nightmare to encroach on reality once more; to enter his waking world afresh. His stomach felt suddenly warm. He knew if he couldn't break free, the fire would rage again from within; devour him a further time.

It had to be a message. It just had to be – that he was *tainted*; that he deserved to be consumed by the very fires of hell – for such was his iniquity, desecrating the very memory of the dead in this way. Night after night; after night. And as soon as Serena's charred remains had crumbled away, then he had to endure the feeling, the pain he felt himself of catching light...

Only then did he wake.

And not always to Jane's tender touch –

Jane.

He was back in the present once more. Felt the nurse's hand still there on his shoulder. But just as quickly, he was gone again. Returned to the Sisyphean torture chamber of his mind. In place of the onerous rock, his fate was instead to be forever snatched between reality and nightmare. Then, the comforting warmth increased. Jane's touch stronger than all else. Causing the fear and confusion to ebb. And once more he was rooted in the here and now, Jane's presence allowing calmness to flow through his veins. A saline drip for the soul.

'Can you eat something now?' Her question was still there, hanging over him.

He did feel hungry. 'Maybe some toast?' he suggested.

'I'll get some for you. Tea?'

'No, water will be fine, thanks.'

Water.

It was only Jane being there that prevented him slipping back to the torment of that now so familiar hotel room.

'I'll just be a minute, and then I'll refill the jug for you.'

Time.

He pondered its complexity again. The increasing speed with which the years flew by the older he got. He knew he'd never again experience the interminable nights before Christmas that had so frustrated him as a child. Now he was swimming with the tide of adult time; being borne along on the crest of its wave. But another thought occurred to him. In the same way he'd reasoned there must be a time for adults and for children, what of time *seen* and *unseen*? What were the differences there? Would blindness also affect his perception?

And had it already started he wondered? For even now as he awaited Jane's return, it seemed to him as if an hour had passed before she came back. Maybe it had only been a few minutes…

He heard her set a plate down, then position the wheeled bedside-table above his legs. It was toast – but not *burnt*. He was so pleased it hadn't been burnt. He detected the occasional waft of melting butter. Then a tap briefly running, before the water jug was placed in front of him. A plastic scrape as its lid was balanced in position. She filled a beaker and closed his hand around it.

'Here you are, David. And the toast's on the plate in front of you. I've already cut it in half.'

'Thank you.'

'Now, I must get on. I'll have to leave you to it, I'm afraid.'

'Oh?'

'Yes, sorry – I've got to double-check everything before the visit.' *Visit?* Then he remembered. She'd said earlier. They were expecting someone important. But he was sure too Jane had said they wouldn't be coming to his ward. 'An e-mail's come round. The new Health Minister's making a surprise visit.' In reality, the appearance had been scheduled weeks ago – with every photo opportunity being carefully planned in advance. 'I understand she's coming to see where the new investment's gone. To find out how we're doing. Apparently, we're a…' she paused, remembering one of the lines she'd read in the e-mail, '… a *pathfinder*.'

Bryant knew all about those. Pathfinders. Innovative projects intended to spearhead longer-term change. He'd been instrumental in setting up similar schemes in Germany, only his had been private sector; manufacturing; prototype production lines to increase capacity and reduce overheads in the steel industry. They'd proved a great success. The Company's reputation had grown. And he'd done very nicely out of it – the bonus alone had paid for a new Maserati –

Suddenly, that one memory caused his brain to pump out a serotonin fix. He felt high. On top of the world. And, as if someone had pushed a neurological re-boot button, his self-doubts at once receded. He *was* the businessman again. He knew he wanted to get back into the fray. He felt sure he could overcome the blindness; even turn it to his advantage.

The calculating mind was at work now.

The blindness would open doors for him. They'd all want to

meet him. *The* survivor. They'd heap praise on him for his fight; his determination, and courage; for coming out the other side. He'd lead new pathfinders. Would make The Company proud. Would sell consultancy expertise to a whole new generation of customers – private firms, government departments, and local authorities alike. They'd all tried it their way – and failed. Whereas he – and The Company – would be the magic bullet they all needed. Just so long as the money was right. The Company didn't come cheap; nor would his services.

The *crash* was just as sudden.

And all the more soul-destroying, because it was unexpected. The new-found confidence vanished – as if it had never made an appearance. Bryant the mental cripple was back in the driving seat. A failure as a husband. As a father. Even as a suicide. What hope now for the blind man? All thoughts of pathfinders disappeared and the once-successful businessman slipped quietly back again into his despondency. He began to feel uncomfortable. The internal voice of panic becoming louder. He couldn't face visitors; they *knew* that. So why put him through this? It was too much. Too soon. He needed the quiet. No-one to disturb him. He just wanted to be left alone. He didn't want anyone to see him –

Other than Luisa; other than Paolo.

'They won't come *here*, will they?' He was the rabbit, caught in the headlights.

Jane sought to reassure him. 'It's alright, David. They'll only be around for an hour and the DHC…' she paused, 'Sorry, the Director of Healthcare, is taking them to the new cancer-care unit; over in the children's ward. So, no, they won't be coming here. Trust me, they won't have enough time…'

He felt confused, because what she'd just said didn't make sense. She'd said she had checks to make. What checks? And why make them if they weren't coming here? His fearful mind was racing ahead.

'But, the checks… you said…'

She didn't need to let him finish; saw at once where he was coming from. 'David, it's OK. Really. I've just got to make sure everything's clean; that the ward's tidy. Just in case they *do* take a short-cut.'

'A short-cut? But you're sure; they're *definitely* not coming here?'

'No. *Definitely* not.'

He knew Jane wouldn't lie, and the panic began to subside.

But visitors *would* come. He didn't doubt it for a minute. *Other* visitors. Eventually. Once The Company decided the time was right. He'd done a stint in marketing. Knew how it went. He'd be hot property and The Company would exploit him to the full. News of his survival timed perfectly to coincide with some product launch; to promote The Company's image. The subtle message – buy our services; we have blessed staff; our good-fortune can rub off on you; we can save *your* life. The madness of it all. What if they made a film about him? His escape? His return to health? The whole story would have to be exaggerated – portraying his survival as a battle in the face of adversity.

A far cry from the truth.

For, in reality he'd escaped lightly – if being left blind counted as such. But compared to the others, he *had* had it easy. Not for him the pain of being burned alive. Not for him the loss of limbs before death. Not for him the absolute terror of the final minutes. But he'd seen it all, first hand. A blonde hostess, not even twenty, being sucked out of one of the plane's windows. Just like in the Hollywood movies. But the reality of her death had been far worse than the make-believe of the big screen. He'd actually heard her bones cracking, breaking internally into disfigured shards as the unrelenting air pressure had dragged her through a hole only big enough for a fist. Her screams of agony had been momentary – but they'd be a soundtrack to a horror film he'd remember for life. And then Serena – the object of his distant affection – her clothes, hair, face all alight; a human spinning-top of suffering personified; arms flailing as she staggered disoriented down the fractured central aisle. And then there'd been the *smell* of fear. Something you just *had* to experience first-hand. Something the movies would never be able to capture.

He'd seen it all.

But, strangely, he'd *not* been afraid. It had been as if he *had* been at the movies, watching the action from afar. Safe in the knowledge he could get up and leave any time. But he hadn't left. He'd been there when the plane had slammed into the ground. Had felt the tell-tale rush of warm air, the flames following instantly behind as the fuel tanks had gone up... Only to wake in hospital. To his new world without light.

'David, sorry,' Jane continued. 'I *really* do have to go. I'll be back soon.'

'Yes, I know. I'll be fine. See you –'

See.

The stupidity of what he'd just said. Old habits.

'... *soon.*' Jane finished the sentence for him.

Jane. The kind of person whose glass was always half-full. That was his first thought. But he recognised it was more than that. As if there was certainty in her voice. He drank some of the water and placed the beaker on the table. He felt around for the plate. He was hungry. He'd eat the toast. Jane's certainty. It must have had a deep-seated, instantaneous effect on his psyche because, without his consciously realising it, the earlier feelings of hope and acceptance of the future were suddenly back with him again.

Not that they'd last –

For, though he couldn't know it, a visitor *was* coming.

A *special* visitor.

Who'd arrive shortly.

Who'd delight in making him feel distinctly uncomfortable...

'I'm telling you, I heard a child's voice. And there was crying earlier. *And*... he was bundling something out of a van last night.'

'I didn't hear anything, Howard.'

'Well, you wouldn't, would you? You're always jabbering on so. Now, shut up and listen...'

'Howard, I *won't* be spoken to in that way.'

'Quiet, woman! Just listen!' He'd got the window open, had his head angled to catch the slightest sound coming from the neighbouring property.

Marjorie Latham sighed heavily as she put down her *Times* crossword. She knew she wouldn't get any peace until she'd at least humoured her husband. She cocked her head to one side, deliberately exaggerating the whole movement.

'No, still nothing,' she said matter-of-factly. She picked the paper up again.

'Shh! Quiet! *There*... you *must* have heard that?' The only thing she could hear was the ticking of the grandfather clock in the corner of their sitting-room. She shook her head. 'Oh come on – you can't be *that* deaf!'

'My mother was right, Howard. I should *never* have married you. Far better to have remained a spinster.'

'What?'

'Oh, nothing.' Ironic that he accused her of being deaf. No, selective of hearing; that was all – the *real* secret to a lasting marriage. And with fifty-two years behind them, who could argue? She *did* love him dearly, but he could be *so* infuriating at times. She folded the paper and put it on the side-table. 'I'm going out.'

'What? Where?' he asked indignantly.

'*Don't* take that tone with me, Howard.' There was no need for her to raise her voice; she just added that certain edge, as if speaking to a troublesome – but inconsequential – child.

'I really can't believe you sometimes, Marjorie. The whole

news is about those poor little children. There they are, still looking for them... and they *could* be next door... and what's your answer? You're *going out...*' He tutted to make a show of his disappointment in her. 'Don't you care any more? What about doing your bit?' She knew he'd play the trump card in a moment. And then there it was. 'We wouldn't have got through the War with that attitude.'

The War.

Her dear Howard – nothing, if not predictable. His talk of the War always amused her. He hadn't even seen active service. Logistical support in the land-locked Midlands was the closest her husband had got to the front line. But she'd been there. Not just on the front line, but also deep *behind* enemy lines. For she'd been part of the SOE. Special Operations Executive. One of Churchill's very own; one of his finest. A secret she'd proudly take to the grave...

'Howard, I'm going out. And that's an end to it.' She rose from her chair.

'It's *him*, you know. I can *feel* it.'

Him.

Karl Nicol – their neighbour. The bane of Howard's life. *And* vice versa.

'Howard, I really don't think Mr Nicol is a murderer. Nor is he likely to be a kidnapper.' She half added to herself, 'He simply wouldn't have the time.'

Karl Nicol was a dynamo of a man; an entrepreneur forever on the go, with fingers in many pies, who was always looking for the next big thing. Entirely self-made, he'd become rich early on. He'd moved into The Avenue – *their* Avenue, as Howard referred to it – just under a year ago and had been friendly enough to begin with. He'd invited all the residents to a garden party. There'd been a beautiful floral display in the marquee erected on the rear lawn; and a classical ensemble had been brought in to serenade the guests while they ate their way through the upmarket nibbles. Marjorie liked flowers; and classical music; but she declined the *vol-au-vents* and cheap caviar...

Relations between Mr Nicol and her husband had, however, taken a turn for the worse. Their neighbour had decided to have his house totally redesigned. He'd moved out temporarily, and the builders had moved in mob-handed to begin the transformation. All the 1930s' rooms had been knocked-through to make way for contemporary, open-plan living. More and more tradesmen had arrived as each month went by and everything had been fine – *until* they'd blocked Howard in one morning. He'd gone mad; had just sat there beeping the car horn incessantly; had shouted expletives at the top of his voice. Marjorie had been furious with him, demanded that he come in. But for Howard, it had all been about a point of principle and he'd refused to back down. In the end, Marjorie had been so embarrassed she'd taken matters into her own hands and had gone to speak to the builders direct. They couldn't have been more polite. They'd moved their vans at once, promising not to block the access again. The next morning a sheepish-looking foreman had called round to give her some flowers by way of further apology. Marjorie had genuinely been touched by that simple gesture – and even her suspicion that the wilting display had come straight from the seconds' bucket at the local petrol station had done nothing to dampen her gratitude. For her, that had been an end to it.

But not so Howard.

No sooner had Mr Nicol moved back in, her husband had been round there banging on the door to complain. Only to have it slammed in his face. Howard's already short fuse had become even shorter. For Howard it had at that point become *personal*. And he meant to make sure Karl Nicol would pay. Not long after that, the parties had started; people coming and going until the small hours. And then there'd been the girls; a different one visiting every night. And all the while, Howard had been patiently observing his foe, logging the facts; compiling his dossier; preparing to go to the council to complain when the time was right. But Marjorie, she'd just let Howard get on with it. For her part, she didn't really mind what their neighbour got up to in his private life – just so long as it didn't disturb her. And to be honest, it was Howard who always complained about the music from the partying. She'd only ever heard anything once – and even then the disco had ended before midnight. Live and let live. That was her motto.

'Fine, you go out, then,' Howard continued. 'I don't care what you say, I'm calling the police.'

'Very well, Howard.' Marjorie walked through to the hallway to put on her shoes and coat. 'Oh, just one thing,' she called back to him.

'Yes?'

'Don't get arrested for wasting police time.'

'You're *unbelievable*...'

'Goodbye, Howard.' She pulled the front door to behind her.

He woke with a start.

Someone was in the room talking to him.

'Hello?'

A woman. *Who*? *What*? He guessed he must've drifted off again.

'Mr Bryant?'

Another voice. More than one person there with him.

'Hello? Mr Bryant? Can you hear me?' The first voice again.

But the woman wasn't Jane.

'Mr Bryant?' The second voice was a calming, soft baritone. 'This is Gerry Grainger, Mr Bryant. I'm the Director of Healthcare. I'm here with somebody very important who wants to meet you.'

Important?

'Hello, Mr Bryant.' The woman's delivery was measured, precise; an attribute of someone used to public speaking. 'I'm Carol Slater, Mr Bryant, the Health Minister.' Realisation suddenly dawned on him. *They have come here.* 'I'm visiting this flagship hospital today and I just wanted to tell you how sorry I was to hear of your terrible –'

He cut her dead.

'Go *away*! Leave me alone! I don't want you here! I don't want to see anyone!' There – he'd used that word again; without even thinking. But he didn't have time to dwell on it.

'Everything's fine, Mr Bryant.' Grainger again. 'You're quite safe. We won't let anyone bother you...'

'*You're* bothering me! Go away!'

But they persisted, his protests falling on deaf ears.

'I was just saying how sorry I was to hear of your accident, David. May I call you David?' the minister carried on unfazed. 'You must feel very lucky to have survived. And I know you couldn't be in a better place to get well again...'

Lucky? Get well? He heard the words echoing in his mind. Wave-like, the panic was swelling, rising up again. It crashed forcefully down. Temporarily deafened his awareness. Then, its force spent, his own anger swelled – suddenly; defiantly...

'Can they cure blindness, then?' he shouted at Slater.

The woman's voice caught in her throat, her composure thrown by the new revelation – a glaring omission from her briefing. '*Blindness?*' Someone would be for the high jump.

Gerry Grainger quickly intervened, desperately trying to hide his embarrassment. 'I'm *so* sorry, Carol. I thought you knew.' He was talking to her as if Bryant wasn't even there.

'*Owen?*' The tone was curt, as Slater beckoned her aide over. *Three of them in the room* he realised.

'Yes, Minister?' The private secretary spoke up. He was a young fast-streamer, doing his first stint in a Private Office. It occurred to him suddenly it might be his last.

'This *simply* isn't good enough.' Suppressed irritation in her voice. And then to Bryant, quieter once more, ever the consummate politician, 'I *really* can't apologise enough, David. You must think me incredibly unfeeling. I genuinely meant no offence.'

Since the crash, in so many aspects of his life, David Bryant had become a living dichotomy. Fear and anger were ever present by degrees, uncomfortable bed-fellows that fed his overall confusion. And though not suffering a split personality, he was increasingly experiencing an ever-changing psyche.

And here was a case in point.

For the Bryant of old had always enjoyed his politics, had made time to grill whichever parliamentary candidates came knocking at his door at election time. And every week he'd watch the verbal sparring on offer as modern-day gladiators fought it out in the arena of late night TV debate shows. But *this* David Bryant – the Bryant *after* the crash, the Bryant now being scrutinised by the Health Minister – was but a pale shadow of his former self. For him, politics now held no interest and he just wanted the visitors gone.

'Leave me alone!' He was still buoyed up by anger, but he sensed it was weakening; knew it could only be a matter of time before the panic attempted another assault.

Panic and anger – a battle royal, that would rage forever on.

But Bryant no longer had it in him to continue the fight. He wanted to get inland, far from the shore; to escape the lure of the cave that still called to him when his guard was down; to find a place where life could be so much simpler.

Slater had lowered her voice, intending that Bryant didn't overhear what she was saying to Grainger. But she hadn't counted on his *improved* hearing – a faculty all the more acute since the crash – and he heard every word.

'I thought you'd cleared this with Pierfranco? The man obviously doesn't want us here.'

'I'm sorry, Carol. I did. Pierfranco promised us full co-operation. *Joint announcement*, that's what he said.'

'Well, someone clearly forgot to tell our Mr Bryant...'

Pierfranco.

A director in The Company.

So, Bryant concluded, the decision *had* been taken. Time to go public with him. Nothing he could do if that's what The Company had decided.

'Yes, well... I'll leave you to get some rest now, David...' Slater clearly on the back foot now. 'Once again, I'm so sorry...' She couldn't get out of there quickly enough. The visit had definitely *not* gone to plan. Still, it could have been worse – at least the press hadn't been there to witness the sorry state of affairs. No, she'd go and see the sick children instead. They'd be more receptive. And they always made for a good picture. Nothing like a politician kissing a baby – especially a sick one.

'Can I ask what *is* going on?' Jane back on her ward. 'I could hear the noise all the way down the corridor.'

'Ah, *nurse…*' Grainger paused, reading her name badge '… *Reynolds*. I'm Mr Grainger, the Director of Healthcare.' She knew who he was. She'd seen his carefully-posed photo on the Who's Who board in the main foyer. Clearly he didn't know her from Adam. 'I was just showing the Minister around.' Carol Slater pushed her way past Jane, nothing forceful but rude all the same. 'We… er… decided to see how Mr Bryant was getting on. Just an informal visit.'

'Oh?' Jane was annoyed no-one had deigned to tell her. Besides, she'd made a promise to David, and she didn't like having to break them. 'I must have misunderstood, Mr Grainger. I thought your party was going to visit the children's unit… over in Selsey ward.'

'Indeed. As I said, just an informal visit. Head round the door. That sort of thing. Otherwise, you know,' he feigned a nervous laugh, 'our politicians *do* tend to think we're trying to hide something from them.' He looked round for Slater. But she'd already gone. He coughed awkwardly. 'Ah, I see the Minister is *very* keen to go and visit the children. Mustn't keep her waiting. Right.' He rubbed his hands together nervously, subconsciously washing away the embarrassment. 'Well, er… thank you, Mr Bryant, for your time. I, er…' And with that, Grainger was gone.

For Bryant, the relief was palpable. 'Jane, I thought they'd *never* go…' His breathing began to stabilise now she was back. He felt the angry panic slip away, her presence acting as a soothing balm for the soul.

The nurse cleared her throat. 'And *you* are?'

The aide was still there. He'd failed to make good his escape. But he saw no need to give her his name. She was, after all, a *nobody* in his world.

'The Minister's Private Secretary,' was all Owen said.

'Well, Mr… *Minister's Private Secretary*.' Jane was happy to play him at his own game. 'Isn't it about time you went as well?'

'Are you being facetious, nurse?' he challenged.

Jane refused to rise to the bait. 'I need to see to my patient. Excuse me.' She turned her back on Owen and attended to Bryant. 'Given the stress Mr Bryant seems to have been put through, he needs rest. Perhaps you should leave now.' She reinforced the rhetorical request. '*Now*.' And before the man could answer, she added, 'I expect your Minister needs you.'

The aide feigned a cough and mouthed some obscenity towards her. Bryant caught it, but let it pass. He doubted Jane would have heard it and he wasn't ready for a confrontation. Owen paused just outside the door. This time, Jane *could* hear him. Talking quietly in the corridor.

'Sorry! No mobiles!' she delighted in shouting at him.

Owen was forced into being polite, given the person on the other end. Ever-comfortable in his duplicity, he volunteered, 'Yes, thanks, nurse... I'll *just* be a moment...'

'No – *now!*' Jane replied forcefully.

The aide had to bite his lip. 'Look, let me get back to you... Yes, OK... Bye.' He ended the call, then leaned in to Bryant's room spoiling for an argument. 'I don't know what your *problem* is, nurse, but I don't like your attitude.' Jane remained silent. She'd handled enough of his type before. 'You've been obstructive, rude and unhelpful in the extreme. I'm going to report this behaviour to your Director. Do you understand?'

She understood all right. Understood he was nothing more than a pathetic little man; forever playing second-fiddle; forced to stand in the shadow of his powerful female boss. Jane knew right enough who wore the trousers; and who the skirt... An impotent bully, he was too afraid to answer back to his minister; and instead he chose to latch on to those he saw as soft targets.

'You do as you please.' She wasn't going to waste any more time on him. 'Now, if you *will* excuse me...' She picked up the folder at the end of the bed and began checking that her patient's notes were up to date.

Bryant felt he ought to stand up to the aide, to show his support for Jane. He so wanted to do his bit. He made to speak – but couldn't. All of a sudden, he felt woozy; an aching seized his limbs, and his chest began to heave. The nausea was returning.

'Jane?' he said weakly.

'I'm here, David.' She put her arm on his shoulder, but this time the magic was gone; instead of the calm reassurance he'd expected to feel, there was nothing.

'Jane...' his voice was barely more than a whisper. 'I don't feel good.' He spasmed and lunged forwards, the force of the abdominal contraction lifting him off the pillows. 'I feel sick, Jane. It hurts. It *really* hurts...'

He retched.

Nothing.

He retched again and the part-digested toast spewed down his front. Bile. Water. All mixed in.

'Alright, David. Go with it.' She was there, holding him. 'You'll feel better.'

The uncontrollable spasms seized him for more than a minute, until his sides ached with the pain. Time after time, there was nothing left to come up. The taste of bile hung in his throat. And then, when

Jane was sure the attack had passed, she eased him gently back against the metal headboard. She raised the incline and plumped up the pillows to make him more comfortable.

'Come on; let's get you cleaned up again.'

As she was walking the few feet to the tap, something caught her eye. There was someone in the corridor.

Not the aide.

Someone else.

Dressed all in black, who had their back to her.

'Excuse me, can I help you?' She heard the beginnings of another attack, as Bryant started to make guttural sounds. She was torn in different directions; knew she had to get back to him.

But *something* held her interest.

Something about the stranger in the corridor.

'Hey, wait!' she shouted. '*What* have you got there?'

'*Jane...*' Bryant again.

But she wasn't listening.

'What are you doing!' Her attention was focussed entirely on the newcomer. 'Stop –'

Bryant didn't hear anything else. The pain was so intense, he considered it a blessing when he finally passed out...

'Yes. Thank you, Mr Latham. You've been very helpful. Thank you. Goodbye.' The WPC put the phone down and called over to DS Riley. 'Sarge, one here I think might interest you...'

Riley was perched on the edge of a desk in the incident room. Or, more accurately, the *satellite* incident room in West Wickham – for the *main* room had since been moved to the Yard. The Met's technical squad had worked their usual magic, allowing the central and local switchboards to be linked – so calls to the dedicated incident line could be handled at either location. They'd similarly networked the electronic incident logs, so staff at either end had immediate access to the same, real-time information.

Riley put the folder he'd been reading back into the in-tray.

'What have we got, Penny?'

'Well... I'm not sure, but I've just got a *feeling* about this one. Too many things don't seem right...'

Copper's nose.

Riley liked that – an invaluable tool, even in today's world of modern policing. It had been copper's nose – intuition, gut-instinct; call it what you will – that had saved the Met from a car-bomb attack back in '73. Although before his time, he'd heard the story often enough – how a detective had chanced to look through an upstairs window and had seen a young woman below putting money in a parking meter opposite the Yard. She'd walked off, leaving the car parked quite legally in a metered bay. There'd been nothing untoward about that – but for the fact it had been a bank holiday, so the parking had been free. Still, thousands of other motorists could've made the same mistake. But *something* had just seemed wrong to the detective. He'd gone outside to take a closer look – and had noticed the licence plates didn't match the car's year of manufacture. It was *then* that he'd become aware of the unmistakable smell of explosives coming from the boot...

'Tell me more.'

The WPC scanned through the verbatim notes she'd taken during the call.

'That was... a Mr Latham from Orpington. He's a retired civil servant; not given over to exaggeration... and he was quite calm. He wanted us to know he's suspicions of his neighbour, one *Karl Nicol*...'

'What, that he's got the twins?' Riley interrupted.

'No, he didn't go that far. But what he did say was that he's heard a child crying next door, sounding very distressed. But the thing is, his neighbour doesn't have any kids.'

'Now that *is* interesting. What else?'

'Let me see... yes, here it is... he also saw his neighbour getting something out of a van yesterday night. And...'

'Let me guess – his neighbour *doesn't have* a van?'

'*Correct.* And... get this... he – Mr Latham – wanted me to know straight away that he's not on speaking terms with the neighbour...'

That also interested Riley. For the caller to have been so upfront only added to his credibility in the sergeant's eyes. It showed a well thought-out, rational line of argument.

'Have you got his number, Penny. I'll give him a call back myself.'

She wrote it down for him. 'There you go.'

'Thanks.' Riley went back over to his desk and tapped in the number on the phone. Someone answered almost immediately.

'854221, hello?'

'Mr Latham?'

'Yes...'

'Good afternoon, sir. This is detective sergeant Riley. I understand you just spoke to one of my colleagues?'

'Oh, yes, sergeant.' Howard Latham cleared his throat. 'That was very quick. I didn't expect anyone to get back to me so soon. My wife said I'd be wasting your time, but I told her...'

With well-practised ease, Riley gently steered the other man back on course. He didn't have time to listen to the man's domestics.

'Would you mind going through the details once more, please, sir?' He had his pocket book out, ready to jot down anything salient.

'Yes, of course.' Howard Latham covered the familiar ground – the van, something being bundled out the previous evening, and the crying he'd heard.

'And was it *a* child you heard, Mr Latham – or *children*?'

'To be honest, sergeant, I can't be sure – but there definitely *was* crying.' He was emphatic on that point.

'OK, that's fine, sir. And when was the last time you heard the crying?'

'Well… about three-quarters of an hour ago; it was just before my wife went out. She said she hadn't heard anything; but I told her she must be deaf…' He was off again.

'And… anything since?'

'No, sergeant. All quiet, I'm afraid.'

'And,' Riley was scribbling away as he spoke, 'any other unusual behaviour you've noticed?'

'It's been quieter than usual; overall, I mean – other than the crying I heard…'

'*Quieter*?'

'Well, yes – I mean the man's an absolute pest; always having late-night parties; music on until god knows when. But that's all stopped. And there have been no girls…'

'Girls?'

'Yes – you know…' he sounded a little embarrassed, '*floozies*, sergeant; probably brought in to make him look good; or when he needs to… ahem, close a deal…'

For one fleeting moment, Riley began to question his earlier assessment of the man – maybe he *was* a neighbour with a grudge, and with an over-active imagination; but then, just as quickly, he dismissed the doubts – as his *own* copper's nose began to twitch. He was half-remembering something – but couldn't put his finger on it…

'Look, Mr Latham, can I ask you to sit tight. Not do anything to alert Mr Nicol. I'd like to come round. Check out a few things for myself.'

'Oh, *yes*, sergeant; that would be very welcome. Rest assured, I'll be very discrete. And I'll make sure my wife is, too.'

'OK, sir. Well, I'll be round in the next hour.'

'Thank you, sergeant. I'll see you then.'

Riley hung up.

There was *definitely* something playing on his mind. And before he went round, he'd first do a full check on the police national computer for one Karl Nicol…

66

CHAPTER FIVE

THE PAIN HAD stopped and the nausea had passed.

But his ribs ached; and his internal muscles were sore. Bryant couldn't be sure if he'd emerged from his latest nightmare. For a moment he wondered if, perhaps, he *was* still dreaming. Hadn't he just heard a young girl's voice? But why would a child be there? It didn't make any sense.

Suddenly, he remembered; recalled he'd been having another one of his turns – the debilitating bouts of retching that he couldn't shake off. He felt down his front for evidence that he *had* been sick again, but he was clean. And dry. Only the faintest trace of bile in the back of his throat. He concluded Jane must have cleaned him up. But, no, that couldn't be right. She *had* been going to, but... His sense of time was all confused. Then, yes, it was coming back to him. The aide – Owen. And Grainger. And... there'd been *someone* outside. There had, hadn't there? And Jane had got into an argument. He'd heard her shouting –

'*Hello?*'

The unexpected, verbal intrusion into Bryant's dark world caught him unawares. Or partially so, as he suddenly joined the mental dots, realising he *had* heard a girl's voice. She was there, in the room with him now.

'Hello?' he answered cautiously.

'I'm looking for my *mu*-mmy.' She sniffed loudly and Bryant heard a tell-tale rattling in her chest. It sounded like she had a cold. As if to reward his deductive powers, on cue she coughed all over him. He felt the burst of warm breath on his face, but resisted the urge to wipe her germs away. He just smiled inwardly to himself. A typical kid. He could imagine the child's mother repeating to no avail, *put your hand over your mouth*! just as his had done all those years ago. 'Have you seen her?' she was asking him.

Seen.

He actually found the word strangely amusing.

'No,' he replied. 'I'm sorry, I haven't.' He swallowed hard in quick succession to try to remove the last traces of bile. 'Do you want me to get someone to help you find her?' From the young-sounding voice, he guessed the girl was around eight or nine.

The girl seemed then to lose interest in her mother, and instead turned her attention on him, asking, 'Why are you here? Are you ill as well?'

Bryant didn't even realise he was dodging her question, as he said, 'She'll be worried. We should try and find her for you.'

But curiosity had got the better of the girl, and she wasn't going to give up that easily. 'Why are you in bed?'

This time Bryant's subconscious must have decided the child posed no threat, that there was no subterfuge involved. Even so, it made sure he chose his words carefully, so as not to frighten her. She didn't need to know about the crash; about how everyone else had perished.

'I'm in bed because... I've not been very well.'

'*Oh.*' His visitor considered this for a moment then, with a candour unaffected by adult sensibility, carried on the gentle interrogation, wanting to know more. 'So... why aren't you well?'

Bryant *sensed* the girl was looking him over.

The bandages had gone, now his broken arm and ribs had healed. Gone, too, was the dressing that had bound his injured wrist. But under this child's gaze his attempted suicide played suddenly on his mind, and he found himself tucking his hand under the covers to avoid her scrutiny. He could understand her questioning him further because, to all intents, he showed no outward sign of injury; he looked fine.

But, then, emotional scars *weren't* visible.

Nor was blindness.

And yet *he* saw the dark. Saw it clearly. Inside, looking out. The nothingness, where once there had been a world of light.

'I had an accident,' he offered. 'But I'm nearly better now.'

The girl grew suddenly animated, her chest rattling as she said excitedly, 'Did your *car* crash?' She didn't give him time to speak before adding, almost proudly, '*My* daddy's car crashed. A fireman had to come and put it out.'

'Oh, I'm sorry. I hope he was alright?'

'Yeah, but mummy says he can't drive *her* car.'

'That's probably very sensible,' Bryant replied. 'It can take time to get over a...' a pause before he said the word, '...*crash.*'

'*No*... mummy says he drives too fast.' The girl changed subject again. '*I'm* not well,' she announced casually.

'Oh? What's wrong?'

'I don't *re-ally* know.' She sighed. 'Sometimes I'm *re-ally* tired... and then I can't go to school. But that's OK because mummy teaches me at home.'

'That must be nice?'

'Hm – yeah; but then I don't see my friends...'

'Do they come round?'

'Hm, sometimes... but...' she was thinking again, 'mummy doesn't let them, not if I'm sick...'

'Oh, that's not so good.'

She was racing ahead again. 'Mummy says I've got to go

inside a *big* doughnut. And, like, if the doctor says so, I'm going to lose all my hair!' Her voice had gone up and she was giggling. 'I'll look *re-ally* funny!'

Bryant smiled – but he didn't laugh.

He remembered then. Carol Slater had been going to the children's cancer ward.

The poor girl was a patient.

Then he heard the girl's words echoing, *Are you ill as well?* It all made sense.

How he pitied the girl's mother at that moment. How, he wondered, did you even begin to tell your child they might die? That there'd be months, maybe years, of pain and drug-induced sickness ahead? That there was no guarantee they'd get better at the end of it? At least with his own mother, she'd had a full life; which was some compensation. But to die so young, that was *so* unfair.

At least, he thought, he'd never have to face that with little Paolo...

Bryant did his best to sound reassuring. 'Maybe you *won't* lose your hair. Maybe the doughnut will squeeze out extra jam. You could use it to cover your hair.' He knew the moment the words came out he was talking nonsense, but he didn't care; it just seemed right in the circumstances.

'Don't be silly!' Another playful giggle. 'It's not a *real* doughnut. It's like a... hm...' But her childhood vocabulary wasn't up to describing the workings of an MRI scanner.

'I *am* silly, aren't I?' He laughed at himself, enjoying the freedom of stupidity – a welcome breath of fresh air after all the months of institutionalised health talk. He continued the nonsense. 'Of course I am, because if you go in the middle, there won't be room for the jam!'

'You're *funny*.' He felt the bed judder slightly as she jumped up. 'Would you like to see my book?' He hesitated. 'Oh, go on, it's really good.'

'OK.'

She wriggled to get comfy and, in doing so, pulled the sheet tight over his injured wrist. He left it where it was. He didn't want her to see the scars.

'Here!' she said excitedly.

He felt the corners of a hardback press into his chest. One of the edges jabbed into his ribs and he winced slightly – although the fractures had healed, they were still tender; and the latest bout of retching hadn't helped. He used his free hand to hold the book. It was heavier than he'd expected – the cover more like a thin piece of wood than cardboard.

'So... what's the story about, then?'

'*Der*...' she was telling him off. 'It's *this* way up!'

'So it is. Silly me. Here, help me turn it over.' Self-conscious, he persisted in keeping his other hand under the covers.

More fidgeting from the girl. 'What's...' she was looking for something; then found it, '... *that* word?'

'Where?'

'*There*.' He felt her tap the page.

The game was up.

He knew he couldn't keep pretending – but he tried one final time to hide his disability.

'I'm not very good at reading, you know.'

'Hm... what about... *this one*?' Again, she tapped a finger on the book.

'No, don't know that one, either.'

She grew all excited again. 'I can teach you! I've been teaching my little sister. She's not as good as me...' The girl took a deep breath, as if preparing to make an important announcement. '*D...O...*' she began spelling out the word.

'*Dog!*' Bryant interrupted.

'No, *der*. It's... *donkey!* Look at the picture.'

'Oh, I see now.'

The light was dawning for the little girl.

'The donkey's not *there*.' Unknown to Bryant, she waved her little hand in front of his face, noticing his lack of response. 'He's on *this* page...' He heard her leaf through the book. Then, after a moment, she asked, 'Hm... can you *see*?' Nothing accusing. Just a straight question.

'*No*,' he answered softly.

'Hm...' she was trying to figure something out for herself; for him. Then she asked, 'Have *you* been in the doughnut?'

He'd had several MRI scans, while they'd tried to work out what had been going on in his brain. They'd even asked him what music he'd like in the background – though it had been drowned out; totally inaudible once the machine had been turned on.

'Yes, I've been in there.'

With innocent ignorance, she suggested, 'If you go in again, maybe you'll get better...'

He was going to answer *No, I won't* but suddenly thought better of it – not wanting to risk undermining whatever hope the little girl might already have for the scanner. It couldn't do any harm for her to believe it might help with *her* treatment. He knew positivity counted for so much where cancer was concerned, so he just said, 'Well, let's hope so...'

70

She had another question for him. 'What's the doughnut like?'

'Small,' he replied, without even thinking. Even though he'd been unable to see its size, visually judge its confines, still he'd found it claustrophobic; almost suffocating. In fact, they'd had to take him out until a panic attack had subsided. But, again, he didn't want to frighten the girl so he added, 'But it'll be much larger for *you*... because you're smaller than me. So there'll be *lots* of room inside.'

'Hm... I guess.' She could see the sense in that.

She fell quiet for a moment, so Bryant tried to turn the conversation back to her mother.

'Don't you think we should try to find your mummy now?'

He felt the girl kicking her legs backwards and forwards over the edge of the bed. It rocked slightly. She jumped down, taking her book with her.

'Your nurse is pretty. I hope mine is.'

'Oh, I'm sure yours will be *even* prettier,' Bryant replied.

And then, perfectly logically, the girl asked, 'How do you know your nurse is pretty if you can't see her?' A valid question.

'I just... *know*,' he replied. That seemed to satisfy the girl. He was tempted to ask her what Jane looked like, but let it pass, for fear he'd get yet another different answer to all the others anyway. But, then, something inside him made him reconsider. *Out of the mouth of babes...* So he asked, 'why do you say she's pretty?'

'Coz she *is*.' No deliberate evasion. The girl just didn't understand the point to his question.

'Oh, right.' He decided he'd try one final time – but the girl moved the conversation on.

Dramatically.

'Why was she telling that man off?'

She.

The girl meant Jane.

Man.

What man?

Wait... it was coming back to him. When he was being sick, Jane had gone out. He'd heard her shouting something. He had to know more.

'Er... this *man*... Where was he?'

'Out *there*.' He thought the girl must be pointing.

'What, in the corridor?'

'Yeah... *just* there.'

Bryant guessed it must have been Owen, carrying on his argument with Jane.

'Was the man young; wearing a suit?' He assumed Owen

71

would have been dressed for the occasion; full jacket and tie.

The girl's reply surprised him.

'*No*,' she answered, as if it was obvious. 'He was *re-ally* old; like my granddad.'

Not Owen – then who?

An image of the cave on the shore suddenly flashed into Bryant's mind. Before he could make anything of it, it had gone again just as quickly.

Inexplicably.

The girl tried to be helpful, to answer her own question and suggested, 'I know... maybe the man had been naughty... my daddy tells me off when *I've* been naughty...'

'*Jessica!*' An adult's voice – but not her father's. It was her mother. She had a clipped, posh tone. Bryant heard her footsteps as she walked into the room. '*Darling*, I've been looking for you *everywhere*! Come on, we're going to be late.' Then, catching sight of Bryant, the mother continued, 'I'm very sorry. I hope she hasn't been bothering you.'

'*Mummy!*' Jessica couldn't contain her excitement. She wanted to let her mother in on the secret. '*Mummy – he* can't see us. Look!' She waved her hand, as she'd done before.

'*Jessica!* That's *not* a nice thing to say! Apologise at once.'

'But... *Sorry*....'

Jessica's mother was *so* embarrassed. She wanted to get away as quickly as she could – but knew she needed to salvage what little remained of her dignity. 'I'm *so* sorry about that. She just doesn't think sometimes.'

'That's alright.' Bryant hadn't been offended.

'We've got to go...' then, in a determined tone to her daughter, '*Come on, Jessica!*'

'*Oh, mummy...*' Jessica didn't seem too keen to leave her new-found friend.

'Come on. You know you're having your picture taken with the Health Minister. You'll be in all the papers. We're very excited, aren't we, Jessica?'

'Yeah.' Jessica didn't sound convinced.

'*Come on*, darling.'

'*Bye...*' Jessica's farewell hung in the room as she and her mother left.

Bryant heard the door close behind them.

All the talking must *really* have worn him out, because he genuinely felt tired now. But he was determined to fight it, not to go to sleep just yet – for he wanted to stay awake long enough to talk to Jane.

He needed to know who the man was. And why Jane had been arguing with him. Something about the whole episode *disturbed* him. But he didn't know why.

And where *was* Jane?

She ought to have been back by now...

Riley's suspicions had been well-founded; his intuition spot on.

He'd spent the past ninety minutes urgently calling up dormant files and speaking to team members from his past.

And then – he'd found it. The link.

He'd phoned Howard Latham to apologise that he'd be arriving later than anticipated, but he was now, finally, nearing the man's house. He pulled over and rang Tomlinson; began briefing him on what he'd uncovered.

'I knew *something* was ringing alarm bells,' Riley began. 'The PNC had a flag against Karl Nicol – actually, against *Matthew* Karl Nicol. He's dropped his first name, you see, after declaring himself bankrupt a few years back. Seems he starts up and closes companies like they're going out of fashion. It's got to be a tax fiddle, I reckon. Anyway, Nicol himself has no convictions – the flag *actually* relates to his being a known associate of the *primary* target, one Peter Maurice Schilling. And *that's* where I must have come across him before. When I'd been investigating Schilling. Don't know how the hell I remembered though – that was more than five years ago.' At the time, Riley had been working in the vice squad.

'Well done, you. This could be just what we need.' Then Tomlinson added, by way of a deliberate after-thought, 'I guess the next round's on me.'

The superintendent's praise was genuine. For his sergeant to have remembered such a distant, tenuous link was impressive; and all the more so, considering Nicol hadn't even been the main subject of the vice squad's enquiry. It wasn't the first time Tomlinson had come across such instances, where officers had recalled some half-remembered fact – but he knew such cases weren't *that* common. And when they *did* happen, it was usually because those doing the remembering had previously had dealings with someone so evil, the crime had touched a nerve; had left an indelible trace in their subconscious.

Acts of brutality against the old.

Abuse of the young.

Such crimes were often the common strand. And Tomlinson had yet to meet *any* police officer who didn't regard such crimes as the lowest of the low. He knew that even the *decent*, average criminal considered those guilty of such behaviour to be complete scum. He also found it particularly galling that successive governments chose to label such perpetrators *vulnerable prisoners*. Once inside, all the stops were pulled out to keep them safe from harm; to keep them segregated from a mainstream prison population that would gladly give them a beating as soon as the time of day. It was just a pity, he reflected, that the many victims hadn't enjoyed the same level of protection...

Brutality against the old

Abuse against the young.

They were the *truly* vulnerable. At opposite ends of their life cycles, but each, equally, the least able to defend themselves against the scum.

The old.

The young.

Easy pickings – just like the Wilson family...

And for all the increasing reliance on faceless databases and ever-changing technology, all it took was a simple *hunch* – one small, electrical impulse in the cortex of a living, breathing human being like Sergeant Riley. That was something no computer could ever replace.

Riley was continuing to pass on the background. 'Schilling – he was a self-employed electrical engineer. Repairing white goods, TVs. And... he'd started branching out into computers. Well, we'd been investigating reports he'd been kerb-crawling. You know the thing – residents taking down the car numbers; getting us to check them out. So, we were adopting a softly-softly approach; visiting people away from their homes; protecting the family and all that. I went round to see Schilling. Let him know we'd received complaints. Nothing heavy – just a quiet talk; it was more for deterrent value than anything else. But he got *really* jumpy ... So, anyway, to cut a long story short, we took him in; searched the place; took away some of his gear – and found he'd got a substantial amount of child porn on his computer. And not the sort of thing you accidentally click on, either. We went back and seized *everything* in his shop... and *that's* when we established the link with Matthew – *Karl* – Nicol. One of Nicol's laptops was in the workshop; supposedly in for repair – but it *also* had several files containing hard-core stuff; including children. Now, Schilling's computer was pretty easy to get into apparently – but Nicol's laptop, well, that was something else. The technical guys said he'd got all sorts of password protection on there; and some sort of software to hide the files; really advanced stuff.'

Steganography.

That's what Riley was alluding to.

Tomlinson had come across that in Special Branch, when

investigating Islamic extremist support networks. Ostensibly, you saw one image – but concealed within it was a whole different picture. One click in the right place on the screen and the proverbial scales fell from the eyes. It hadn't been a tool just for terrorists; the more technically-minded criminals had soon latched on to the possibilities. And those who peddled pornography – the child pornographers in particular – were nobody's fool; one look at the generic profile of those serving time revealed extremely bright individuals with a good education behind them; head and shoulders above the run-of-the-mill offender; often they'd be white-collar workers, holding down respectable jobs.

'So why wasn't Nicol brought in?' Tomlinson asked.

'You're going to love this...' Riley's tone was nothing if not ironic. 'He *was* brought in. But his solicitor – Barry Hazeldine – was there straight away. And every question was met with a *no comment*. And... Hazeldine was then apparently instructed to represent Peter Schilling as well. Up till then, Schilling had been using the duty solicitor. Well, that's when he *also* started with the *no comments...*'

'Smart guy, then, our Mr Nicol.' Tomlinson ventured. 'And generous to a fault – paying for his *repair-man*, too. Presumably didn't want Schilling taking him down with him.'

'Seems so.'

'But what about the evidence? They surely couldn't have denied having the images on the computers?'

'The CPS decided not to prosecute...'

'*What?*' Tomlinson was incredulous. '*Even* they ought to have been able to make a water-tight case out of that.'

'One *smart* Nicol,' Riley repeated the superintendent's assessment, 'but a *smarter* Hazeldine. Get this, he managed to persuade the CPS their case would be thrown out of court if they decided to press ahead...'

'How?'

'Well, Hazeldine argued their line of defence would be that *neither* man was actually *aware* of the offending material; and that neither had downloaded the images... because... both of them were using *re-conditioned* computers...'

Re-conditioned.

In other words, a legal *convenience* that meant the content, the passwords, the encryption – all could be laid squarely at the door of a *claimed* previous owner. Tomlinson didn't for one minute believe there *ever* had been anyone else; it was likely all just a deliberate fiction. But he could see how it was a clever defence. *Innocent until proven guilty.* That was the law. The onus of proof resting with the crown. And how could you prove something potentially un-provable?

The pornographers.

Always the first to exploit new technology.

Always one step ahead of the law.

He could just imagine the trouble they'd gone to, to ensure they'd be able to use that defence in the event of being discovered. Just enough faked details conveniently left on the computer to suggest a previous owner – but nowhere near enough for the police to trace the said individual. And as for the offending material, no doubt the file information would have been altered in some clever way to make it impossible for the police to prove beyond reasonable doubt that Schilling or Nicol *had* created them.

The superintendent was thinking through the potential scenarios now, some of which were distinctly unpleasant. He *had* to consider the possibility that Nicol might be involved in the twins' kidnapping; that they could be about to stumble on a paedophile ring. Clever bastards the lot of them. And who was to say there wouldn't be a solicitor – this Hazeldine – in their number? There was plenty of precedent. You only had to look at the chaotic investigations in Belgium – and the publicly-avowed suspicion the guilty had been protected from *on high*; from within government; from *inside* the very bastions of justice – their protection, a further necessary evil, to safeguard those in positions of power; those who considered themselves untouchable...

'Then we'd better tread carefully,' Tomlinson concluded. 'If this trio *is* behind the abductions, we might only get one chance...'

Jane didn't know if she was coming or going.

She was still trying to make sense of what she'd seen – the man, there, in the corridor; barely fifteen minutes ago. But such things *just* didn't happen. Not in real life. Maybe in the movies, but not in an NHS hospital in the south of England. She'd wanted to go and look in the bin, to see if she could find *it*. To prove to herself she hadn't imagined the whole thing. But the ward sister had appeared out of nowhere, all red-faced and flustered, and had told her to report to personnel at once.

And that *had* taken her by surprise.

So there she was, on her way up, taking the back stairs. She'd chosen not to use the lift, as she wanted the extra time to compose herself; to get ready for what she thought was coming. She guessed it would all be Owen's doing. He'd gone and complained, just like he'd said he would. She turned another corner as she climbed, her shoes squeaking – rubber soles on linoleum echoing all around the stairwell. And from far below, as if not wanting to be outdone, there came a response – a crash as a door slammed noisily shut, its faulty closing-mechanism yet another item for inclusion on the maintenance crew's to-do list.

Before she knew it, she'd reached personnel. She gave her name, and the nondescript secretary, more interested in reading her glossy magazine than typing the ream of papers on her desk, waved her through.

Fiona Healey.

That was the name Jane read on the door as she entered. Ms Healey asked Jane to be seated and closed the door behind her.

Ms Healey was just what Jane had expected, someone as far removed from herself as it was possible to get – power suit, styled hair, fake tan; and fake smile to match. Ms Healey was every inch the career woman who didn't care how many people got trodden underfoot, just so long as she came out on top. Jane suspected the other woman wasn't all she tried to appear; as if there were insecurity buried deeply away, for which she was always seeking to compensate.

Jane was aware of Fiona Healey speaking to her, but all of a sudden, none of the words were registering consciously. For, while she was there in body, her mind was back in the corridor outside David Bryant's room. Once more running through every second of the surreal scene that had unfolded before her eyes...

There'd been the aide, Owen. He'd been on his mobile. She'd told him to end his call, and he'd wanted to argue with her. But she'd ignored him, had gone to refill David's water-jug.

And then, she'd seen *him*.

Only it *hadn't* been Owen; not the aide, for he'd gone.

No, she'd caught a fleeting glimpse of someone *else* out there—

Someone dressed in dark clothes, almost a living silhouette against the backdrop of the pale walls. She'd challenged the stranger, had gone to see what he was up to. He'd had his back to her. And she remembered now there'd been a small girl off to one side. Then the man in black *had* turned towards her. Only briefly, but enough time for her to take in the grey hair and deathly-pale, lined face that hinted at advanced years; as had his crooked frame. She'd thought he looked slightly eastern.

Then, he'd turned away. But not before she'd seen what he'd been holding –

'Nurse Reynolds!'

'Yes?' her response automatic, her mind still preoccupied.

'I don't think you appreciate the *seriousness* of this matter.'

Jane still wasn't in the present. Fiona Healey, meanwhile, continued explaining how the hospital would *have* to take action. Jane just nodded, her mental autopilot engaged.

'… suspend you.'

Suspend – even that didn't get a reaction from her.

'Did you hear what I said, nurse Reynolds?'

But all that Jane was focussing on was the voodoo doll she'd seen the man holding.

The doll with a pin sticking out from its chest –

The doll he'd discarded into the nearest bin…

Bryant had grown impatient of waiting for Jane to return and, wanting a change of scene, had decided to make his own way to the day-room.

Change of scene.

Albeit swapping one dark vista for another.

He knew he could have asked for help, but Jane had walked him there so many times now he felt confident he could make it under his own steam. He'd just passed the patients' toilets and wash-rooms, and was adjacent to the door that led to a small kitchen. As he went, he kept himself an arm's distance from the wall; every so often letting his fingers brush lightly against the paintwork to help guide his step.

His slippered left-foot suddenly collided with something; only briefly, but he heard a hollow ring. It was something metal. Just a bin. He wobbled slightly, regained his balance, then carried on.

Just a bin.

But a bin with a waxwork doll inside –

Shrouded in blind ignorance, Bryant didn't know anything about the doll. Nor did he know that, a little further down in that same metallic container – beneath the figure, but lying on top of an empty crisp packet – there was a single copper pin.

A pin that had become dislodged from the doll's chest.

Knocked free by the impact, when the man in black had had to discard the tools of his trade; to make a quick escape, before the interfering nurse had had a chance to stop him. But the man had been confident he'd done enough…

Bryant paused for a slight breather. Without realising it, he was touching a right hand to his ribs. It was then that he *did* notice something.

Consciously.

For the first time in weeks, the dull aching had stopped…

Tomlinson had parked up a few streets away from the Lathams' house and had called Riley to come over and get him. Too many cars and he feared Nicol might become suspicious. The back-up vehicles were likewise well out of sight, although stationed nearer to the target property.

The two officers sat in Riley's unmarked saloon at the end of The Avenue. The sergeant had already been in to see Howard Latham, making Marjorie's acquaintance at the same time. He felt more confident now, judging them to be reliable; not given over to exaggeration, nor attention-seekers. He'd noted that Marjorie Latham didn't share her husband's suspicions. He wondered if she would have changed her mind if she knew about Nicol's choice of *friends*, but then Riley knew he wasn't free to divulge *that* information...

'Mr Latham's said another van's been round. About twenty minutes ago. No livery – just white. He couldn't really see anything, but he's given me the VRN.' He flipped his notebook open and read out the vehicle registration number. 'I've already traced it – *Crossfire Distribution and Freight Company*; based up at Wapping. Nothing recorded against them or any of their drivers other than the usual – speeding fines; parking tickets.'

'Do we know if they were delivering or picking up?' Tomlinson asked.

An officer less experienced than Riley might not have thought to follow that up, but he'd already set the wheels in motion.

'I've got people going over there now, sir. Thought it best we get it checked out in person, just in case...'

Just in case.

Just in case an unsolicited telephone call from the police resulted in records being destroyed, or criminal associates being tipped off. There was always a degree of risk attached to police enquiries, routine or otherwise, and Riley's caution wasn't down to paranoia; just sensible investigative procedure. Something both he and the superintendent knew was all the more important now, given the high stakes involved.

'Good call. Anything else happened? Children crying?'

'No. All quiet.'

'Right. I say it's time we go pay Mr Nicol a visit...'

Earlier on, Tomlinson had agreed his plan with the leader of the armed response team. They'd be going in mob-handed, with the officers effecting a forced entry, securing every entrance, restraining everyone found inside, and preserving whatever evidence existed. Everything all carefully orchestrated.

His decision had been informed by the psychological profile he'd received from Jim Marsh, senior lecturer in criminology at the University of West London. Dr Marsh had been assisting the Met for more than a decade. And he'd justifiably acquired a reputation for excellence. Granted, he might look every inch the stereotypical academic – crazy hair, pens in his top pocket, even socks under his Jesus boots – but there'd never been any doubting the man's credentials, nor his results.

Nor his bravery.

For in 2001 he'd been at Stansted, negotiating with the plane hi-jackers; looking up at the barrel of a gun from the steps below. No way of knowing then that the presumed terrorists were just Afghan refugees seeking a better life, driven by despair to such extreme action. Jim Marsh had been rewarded with an OBE for that little adventure.

The profile given to Tomlinson suggested they were dealing with a white male in his late thirties to early fifties, someone with an incredibly *tidy* approach – the steps he'd taken at the crime scene to conceal the presence of the twins confirmed as much; as did, in a macabre way, the arrangement of the bodies in the chairs. There was an underlying neatness running through his actions, notwithstanding the anomaly of the bloodied scene he'd left behind. Even now, Jim Marsh was predicting, the perpetrator would be going about his business as usual, thanks to his equally tidy *mind* – with its different compartments; one reserved for the killer, another for the regular guy who held down the day-job. All of which was necessary to prevent dissention in his mental ranks – letting him maintain the upper hand, keeping him free from suspicion.

Tidy.

And *precise*.

Precise, because he'd obviously planned the murders carefully. There'd been no sign of a break in, nor of a struggle, so he'd probably succeeded in building a rapport with the victims over a period of time, having cast himself in a position of trust.

But one thing *had* troubled the profiler.

Something Dr Marsh couldn't answer. In his opinion, to have built up that level of familiarity would have meant repeat visits to the Wilson family home over several months. So, he wondered, why then had no-one seen anything? Why had no-one come forward yet? How could the man have gone unnoticed all that time? Surely Percy or Ivy Wilson would have mentioned their new *friend* to their son?

Something about it just didn't add up.

Jim Marsh had, however, been more certain about the final stage of his assessment; the conclusions he'd drawn. The killer was supremely confident in his ability to stay one step ahead of the police; a confidence that was almost verging on arrogance. And linked to his violent, psychotic nature, that meant they couldn't afford to take any chances. One moment he could appear quiet, unassuming, *compliant* even. But in an instant he could easily become violent, bringing the full force of his killer mentality to bear against whoever had him backed into a corner.

One choice – kill or be killed.

And *that* fact alone now justified Tomlinson's decision to use overwhelming force. Even so, the superintendent himself still had some reservations about the assessment. He just couldn't see the *whole* profile fitting Karl Nicol, at least not based on what he already knew about the man. Elements of it, yes – the self-confidence, the arrogance; but there was nothing to suggest a murderous nature. When pressed, Marsh had conceded that point, but had insisted his wider profile was accurate. They'd concluded Nicol might only be part of a bigger picture. And though he might not be the actual killer, he would be linked to him somehow. Maybe he was harbouring him. Either way, it called for the swift, hard approach they were about to take.

The roads around The Avenue had all been cordoned off. Tomlinson was in position. He spoke into his radio.

'On my signal...'

He gave the command –

Three officers dressed head to toe in black – body armour and balaclavas protecting torso and identity – were at Nicol's front door. The lead man swung the heavy-duty *persuader* against the lock and it gave way with little resistance. The two others rushed in, semi-automatics at the ready. The third ditched the lump of metal, swung his own weapon into position, and followed quickly on their heels. The same scenario was played out simultaneously all round the house – officers smashing their way in through the back door; through the patio; through the integral garage.

'*Armed police! Stay where you are!*' came the shouts from the assault teams.

Tomlinson ran across the lawn to the front door. As he got there, two officers were already dragging Nicol out – his feet hardly touching the floor. They halted in front of the superintendent.

Tomlinson took firm hold of the man's arm – the contact deliberate, reinforcing the intention to arrest – and, looking into a pair of shocked eyes, began, '*Matthew Karl Nicol, I am Detective Superintendent Raymond Tomlinson of the Metropolitan Police. I am arresting you on suspicion of involvement in the murder of Percy and Ivy Wilson; and in the abduction of Harry and Emily Wilson. You do not have to say anything. But it may harm your defence if you do not mention, when questioned, something which you later rely on in court. Anything you do say may be given in evidence. Do you understand?*'

CHAPTER SIX

DO YOU UNDERSTAND?

Fiona Healey's words were still ringing in Jane's ears as she made her way across the staff car park at the rear of the hospital. She understood. Knew only too well that fifteen years' unblemished service counted for nothing; that they were taking the word of a political nobody at face value; and that he was jeopardising her whole career. She felt *so* angry. And that just made it worse, because it wasn't like her at all.

She reached her car, fumbled in a coat pocket for the keys. The anger made her hand shake and she missed the lock, the key scraping a little half-crescent into the fading paintwork. She sighed, exasperated; did her best to let the emotion go. Her eyes felt gritty, began to sting, but she stubbornly refused to let the tears come; refused to give them the satisfaction. She breathed in through her nose, out through her mouth; several times over until she felt calmer, then tried the key again. The door unlocked, its familiar double-*thunk* a strangely comforting sound; a token of stability in her now-changing world.

It was the unfairness of it that hurt her most. Ms Healey's instruction that she go straight home. No chance to give her side of the story. She'd had to surrender her pass, and had then been escorted by security to get her things from the locker room.

And that was it.

But she was jumping ahead. Fiona Healey had only said *suspend*. Not *fire*. *Suspend, pending further investigation*. That was it. And she *was* still on full pay. No, she was sure it would all blow over. They'd find in her favour. They'd have to... Her optimism had returned, routing the unfamiliar anger. She was feeling more like her usual self again. Without knowing why, she suddenly looked up at the wall of windows, mentally counted along until she reached her ward. David would be in there. She guessed it wouldn't be long before he heard what had happened to her. And he'd been there. He'd witnessed – *heard* – the whole Owen thing. He'd be the first to stick up for her. Wouldn't he? And then she'd be back to work before she knew it.

She'd make sure she'd see him get well again...

Inside the car now, the engine came to life on the third turn of the ignition. A cursory check in the rear-view mirror, and she began to reverse. A loud, raucous horn blast froze her to her seat as her foot instinctively stabbed at the brake. The car stalled. Alarmed, she craned her neck to the right to see where the other vehicle was; to gauge how close she'd come to rear-ending it. But the path was clear. Confused, she turned the other way. A flash of movement registered in her peripheral vision, off to the left. And then she saw them – *two* motors, just the other side of a low fence that separated the staff area from the hospital's link road.

The first pulled away, and she caught a glimpse of the Health Minister sitting in the back. Off to her next photo-opportunity. A little way behind, the second vehicle began to move. It drew parallel with her, came to a halt.

Owen was sitting in the driver's seat, a wide grin etched across his smug face. He waved a mock greeting. Sarcasm personified. And then, altogether more menacing, he drew a finger slowly across his throat. He pointed the same finger directly at her and mouthed what she took to be *ciao baby*. With that, he floored the accelerator and tore away.

The smell of burning rubber was suddenly there, in the car with her. Even as she wrinkled her nose, she felt an anger rising in her; an emotion stronger than she had ever experienced before.

Watching the whole scene play out from a little distance away was the old man dressed in black. He smiled to himself.

Pleased with how everything had gone...

The gentle rolling of the waves on the beach had become hypnotic, a steadying anchor of calm against the drifting currents that sought to pull his mind first this way, then that. Bryant felt completely at ease, with not a care in the world. The heat of the sun warmed his face, its temperature pleasant, moderated by the lightest of breezes. He'd quite happily have stayed there for the rest of his life.

But he knew he couldn't.

He got to his feet, brushed the sand from his trousers and walked back up the beach. Ahead of him stood the towering rock-face, an unassailable wall that rose defiantly to meet the sky above. He had the sense it was goading him on, daring him to attempt a climb that he already knew would be beyond him.

But he knew, too, *that* was not the *real* challenge. It was now all about the *cave* – the small, dark crevice set at the base of the brooding monolith. It was time he conquered his fear. Found the strength to face down the eyes that watched him from within...

'Cup of tea?'

The sound of the cup, rattling gently, unbalanced in its saucer, caught his attention – more so than the auxiliary nurse's question.

Snatched back from his reverie, the mysteries of the cave would have to wait for another day.

Bryant sat up in his chair.

'There you go.'

He felt the woman's hands take his own, place them round the cup – as if he were a potter working the clay. But instead of a damp, malleable column, he was suddenly aware of a heat, burning into his fingers. He loosened his grip, raised his hands to the rim of the cup. He heard the trolley being wheeled to the far side of the day-room, the rustling of a newspaper and the scrape of chair legs on the floor as someone else accepted a welcome brew.

Bryant lifted the drink to his lips, blew gently, took a sip. It was still too hot. He felt a tell-tale sting on the end of his tongue; a burn from the liquid. He set the cup back in the saucer.

He'd tried to stay awake, had wanted to think through what he could do to help Jane. But he'd been tired and had nodded off. Now he was back on the case, thoughts of the unfairness of it all foremost in his mind. He'd overheard the other nurses talking about her. How she'd been summoned to Fiona Healey's office, and how she'd been sent home. He couldn't believe it. He knew she hadn't been rude. He'd been there, had overheard everything. He wondered why no-one had come to speak to him; to hear his side of the story. He came to a decision. As soon as he'd finished his tea, he'd ask to speak to that director who'd been there – Grainger. He'd put him straight. Make sure they allowed Jane to come back. It was the least he could do for her. And, besides, he realised he still needed her.

The more he thought about it, the more the anger rose in him. He found it a real tonic. Refreshing. As if someone had turned a key and let the real David Bryant out again. He couldn't explain it, but that whole morning he'd been feeling *so* much better. Physically. Mentally. Emotionally. And his whole outlook seemed to have improved. He was looking forward to telling Jane.

And, for the first time since he'd arrived there, he'd even considered something that just a week ago he'd have thought impossible. As impossible as the climb he'd have to make to scale the rock-face. But now, thanks to this injection of new confidence, he was seriously considering asking if they'd let him get away for a few days.

He wanted a change in environment, to escape the clinical claustrophobia; even if it was only for a few days away. And he already knew the line of argument he was going to try – he wasn't *really* sick anymore; he didn't have any life-threatening condition requiring round-the-clock care. So what was stopping him? Stopping them? And, he knew, in return, they'd insist on some form of monitoring; maybe they'd want someone to be with him twenty-four seven. Why not Jane? If she agreed. And they'd have to let her go back to work now, wouldn't they?

The devil's advocate in his mind raised an objection. What if they refused? So what if they did, he shot back. He wasn't a prisoner. He could discharge himself. They couldn't keep him there, not even if they...

He suddenly thought about the razor blade; the earlier attempt he'd made.

No, he'd fight it if they tried to level that against him. His mind was made up. Before contacting Grainger, he'd give his father a call; sound him out. See if he could stay with him. Just as soon as he finished his tea –

'*Hey, I was watching that!*' one of the other patients suddenly snapped. The afternoon movie disappeared, was replaced by a final round-up of the news. '*I said... I was watching that!*'

The objection fell on deaf ears.

Bryant had already caught the main story at the head of the programme, before the grumbler had first flicked over for his afternoon film. His heart went out to those poor parents. He couldn't begin to imagine how they must be feeling. If he was honest with himself, he didn't think the children would be found alive. In cases like this, they rarely were. But it made him all the more thankful for having Paolo. Granted, Luisa might not want him to have any further contact with their son, but at least he *was* alive; at least Paolo had a future ahead of him.

That thought caused Bryant to reflect on his brief meeting with Jessica, the little girl who'd come into his room. What of her future? Years of treatment that would make her ill; her mother gambling that the drugs would destroy the cancer before her body became too weak to recover. And what were the odds of remission, even if the course was successful? But, he had to admit, at least it *was* a chance; and that was probably more than those missing children had...

The tea was cool enough to drink now.

Savouring the taste, Bryant's thoughts began to focus elsewhere. He considered things for a moment. Reviewed how he was feeling. It seemed strange, but he knew now his mind was *truly* opening up, as a new-found sunlight of recognition streamed through the oppressive cloud that had blanketed his existence for so many months. He was enjoying a rediscovered awareness; a realisation that despair and insecurity no longer had a place in his life.

He'd been given a second chance, something so many others – and all aboard the plane – had been denied. And for that, he *was* grateful. He meant to take *full* advantage of this new start...

First, then, his father.

Just the thought he'd soon be speaking to him lifted his spirits. He could hear his father's voice clearly, saying in that distinctive Midlands accent of his, '*Hello, David.*' He could almost have been there in the room with him.

Which he *was*.

For he'd just arrived.

To give his son the sad news he'd just lost a mother, and *he* a loving wife...

The shocked expression had been replaced with a steely-eyed determination. Cautious, but determined all the same.

Tomlinson knew he'd have an uphill struggle on his hands. There was no way the man was going to talk. He was far too shrewd for that, far too devious, and far too accomplished an operator; whether in business, or in his seedy little private life.

Karl Nicol was holding the officer's gaze, waiting for him to make the next move. But Tomlinson wasn't fazed. He was more than ready to play the mind games that lay ahead.

'I'll ask you again,' he repeated calmly. 'Where were you on the night of...'

'*No comment...*' the man interrupted, stray drops of saliva arcing onto the table.

Tomlinson shielded his hand as he quickly penned himself a reminder to double-check the DNA results from the crime scene. For good measure, as soon as he concluded the interview, he'd take a swab of the spittle that Nicol had just so helpfully provided.

The man glanced at the clock on the wall. He would have checked his watch, but they'd already taken that from him; as well as the rest of his clothes; everything carted off for immediate testing in some forensics lab. And they'd put him in one of the white paper suits. If he got cold, he knew there'd be a nice warm blanket for him back in the cells – not that he planned on being there *that* long. He checked the clock a second time. He'd already made his one call, so he knew Hazeldine would be rushing to get there.

The repeated action wasn't lost on Tomlinson.

'Somewhere to go?' he asked, a playful taunt to see if he could ruffle the man's feathers.

It looked like he was about to, but Nicol composed himself, and replied with a predictable, '*No comment.*'

There was a knock on the door; a moment later, Riley came in.

'DS Riley has just entered the room...' Tomlinson added for the benefit of the tape. The sergeant passed him a note. The superintendent looked at it, mouthed *typical* under his breath, then placed a finger on the tape recorder's stop button. '... Interview suspended at 15:34 hours.' There was a *click* and the tape stopped rolling. 'Seems your solicitor's downstairs.'

Nicol just smiled.

One nil.

'Shall we take a break?' this to the WPC who'd been present

with them. 'Thank you for sitting in. Sergeant Riley and I can take it from here.' The female officer nodded and left the room. 'Well, Mr Nicol, I imagine you'll want some time alone with your legal representative? Maybe you'll be a bit more talkative with him?' Another dig, but still no response. 'So, let's say we reconvene at 16:30?' The superintendent shuffled his interview papers and slipped them inside a folder. 'The sergeant will take you back to the cells. Then you can see Mr Hazeldine.'

Riley went round to stand behind Nicol's chair. He waited while the man got to his feet. Still hand-cuffed, he shot the sergeant a look of utter contempt. He stepped backwards, deliberately invading his personal space. Riley moved to one side and held out an arm, seeking to re-establish dominance, to direct the suspect to the door. Nicol just snorted in disgust and, ignoring him, suddenly made for Tomlinson. Instinctively, the superintendent pushed his own chair away and stood bolt upright in a single motion, his body already tensed, anticipating an attack.

But Nicol pulled himself up short, his movement a deliberate feint. He laughed quietly.

'Bit jumpy, eh?'

'Get him out of here!' Tomlinson had had enough of the man.

But even as Riley made to place his hands on Nicol's shoulders, the prisoner edged in closer to the superintendent and, whispering so only he could hear him, asked, *'Do you think the kiddies are having a good time?'*

Bryant didn't need eyes to see his father's grief.

He could *feel* it in his very soul.

Not that his father would have had any truck with *that*. For as far as Thomas Bryant, the down-to-earth retired accountant from Walsall, was concerned, death was just that. Final. The end. No Pearly Gates. No afterlife. And if Bryant was honest with himself, he did lean more towards his father's way of thinking.

More – but *not* entirely.

For where his father was an out and out atheist, he remained agnostic – still not able to dismiss at least the possibility of there being *something* out there. He probably had his mother's genes to thank for that. Ellen had been a firm believer – God-fearing family background, Sunday schooling through her early years, and regular church attendance for the remainder.

Atheist and the believer.

Each accepting the other. The one, firm in her confidence they'd eventually be together again. And the other, reasoning no harm would ever come from humouring his wife's misconception; allowing her to enjoy her faith, no matter how illogical he considered it.

Bryant remembered a story his father had told him, that demonstrated how easily he'd worn his irreligious heart on his sleeve. The Masons had approached the accountant, seeking to recruit him to their Lodge. His father had been open to the idea, thinking it might open new doors, and two local businessmen had duly arrived. But in place of the barrage of questions that his father had expected – to assess his social standing, his suitability for inclusion in their privileged number – he had just been asked *Do you believe in God?* He'd had to decide there and then whether to lie in the hope of self-advancement, or to remain true to himself. He'd wavered, but only for a moment. The answer he'd given would have won King Solomon's approval –

I believe there's evil in the world; and where there's evil, there must also be good...

The inference clear enough. Good equates to God. Close – but no cigar. The men had made their excuses, and had politely left. And doubting Thomas – he'd joined the Rotarians instead. He'd still made the contacts; had moved up the management ladder – *and* helped raise thousands for deserving causes over the years. But, even more importantly for himself, he'd known he could go to his grave satisfied he'd led an honest life. True to himself. Immaterial there'd be no *Maker* for him to meet...

The Bryants – Thomas, Ellen and David – had never been a *close* family, not in the traditional sense of touching; of readily sharing emotions. But love had been there in abundance. Bryant recalling how his mother and father – despite their both working – had always made time to play with him, to encourage him in pursuing hobbies, sitting down to steer him through even the most challenging homework. He'd never wanted for anything; not emotionally.

And now, in his father's greatest hour of need, he so desperately wanted to repay that kindness. More, he was determined to do so.

The nurses had helped him pack his bag for the few nights he'd be away. Of necessity, new clothes had been bought in to extend his limited wardrobe; only so much he could do sporting the *hospital look*.

So, the morning after his father had come to break the news, Bryant had found himself back there in his childhood home. He'd barely entered when his senses had been flooded with a maelstrom of memories; everything coming at once. Wrapped up in the fabric of the place were the smells of birthday cakes from years past – *Cadburys* chocolate fingers edging a home-made sponge, creating the best cowboy fort a nine-year-old had ever seen; and there'd been fairy cakes, the hundreds and thousands' magical dust sticking in his teeth. And forgotten sounds, now remembered so clearly once more – *Popcorn* spinning forty-five times a minute on the old record player in the corner. And the favourite album he'd take from his parents' black LP case that always jumped on track two. And then there was that feeling of annoyance – that the two halves of the model Spitfire's fuselage hadn't joined together properly. The sensation of stickiness, as the escaping glue sought to weld his fingers together. But a quick wipe on the newspaper underneath and the glue was gone; the only trace left the black-ink-stained finger-tips. And the sight of all those presents, arranged neatly at the foot of the Christmas tree; and then, one year, the *Raleigh* three-speed bike that had been wheeled in from its hiding place in the garage – his mother going frantic at the muddy tyre-marks left on the carpet.

Separate events. But linked memories. Each slotting into the jigsaw of himself. Stamped forever into that happy childhood home. A place that was now quiet with sadness. That mourned the loss of its mother. *His* mother. His father's *lifetime* companion.

Presently, when Bryant felt he'd mastered the memories, felt sufficiently detached, he'd offered to help with the funeral arrangements; but things had already been decided, the course of the disease having given his parents fair warning. The service. The hymns. The absence of flowers. The request that donations instead go to the local hospice. Everything predetermined right down to the last detail.

Wise even in death, Bryant's mother had anticipated the stress her dear Tom would be under; and she'd rightly sought to make it all as easy as it could be. Her final request, when she knew she had just weeks to live, was to ask that he plant spring flowers in her memory at the foot of the willow tree in their garden – so she could mingle, in spirit at least, with the primroses in her very own, living garden of remembrance. And every year, as her flowers bloomed beneath the tree's still-bare canopy, she'd be there with the primroses – the brightness of their yellow petals mirroring the radiance of her smile…

As they sat on the pews in the little village church, waiting for the service to begin, Bryant knew his father was putting on a brave face; sensed he was bottling up the sorrow. But it was for his father, and he alone, to decide when to surrender to his emotions. Then, and only then, would his father open up to allow him in. And whether that time was days, weeks or months ahead, Bryant would be there for him.

The church doors closed and, for a while, the organist filled the building with wave upon wave of echoing sound. The notes faded, as did the respectful, muted background chatter, and everyone stood up as the vicar opened the service.

'Please be seated. We are gathered here today...'

Bryant found the service moving, truly poignant; and it was all the more so, given his father's beliefs. But he knew his father wouldn't have had it any other way. This was Ellen's day, not his, and he would never do anything to detract from her special moment. His love for her *was* – *remained* – too pure; too deep; too sincere for that. Heart-felt tributes accompanied the various readings, and Bryant recognised that all his mother's favourite hymns were there – *Jerusalem*; *When a Knight Won his Spurs*; *Love Divine*... He'd overheard someone discussing the order of service, and knew they'd close with *Morning has Broken*.

The vicar was inviting those assembled to think of Ellen's passing as a timely, kindly act from God. Letting her slip the shackles of pain to be with Him; to enjoy the eternal life. He was painting a vivid picture. Likening the physical body to a caterpillar that can experience only an earth-bound existence – until set free by its butterfly-soul.

A simple, yet beautiful, image.

Bryant was aware his father was crying. Instinctively he edged in closer to place a loving, reassuring arm around him –

Only to stop.

Caught unawares by the sudden thundering noise.

A noise that grew instantly louder. That seemed to him to be so forceful it must be shaking the church's very foundations. And yet his hand, resting lightly on the pew, told a different story. For outside himself, nothing else was moving. The noise, the power he felt, was coming from *within* him; was there, *inside* his head.

Still the noise grew, its frequency, its pitch intensifying.

Bryant squeezed his eyes tightly together, his head now beginning to throb. His teeth were on edge, a dark-tinged pain burrowing down into his jaw. More pressure behind his eyeballs, as the surrounding muscles began to contract – vice-like, with no release. His whole cranium felt like it was going to explode. He was sure he must be screaming now, but couldn't tell if anyone else was aware of his suffering – for too great was the sonic distortion that had seized him.

And then his eyes were burning, as if being assaulted by an acrid smoke. He rubbed at his eye-sockets. Dug his knuckles in hard. But they were bone dry. No tears, no evidence of watering.

Then, stranger still, his tongue felt raw, as if its surface was being pierced repeatedly by pins; each stab increasingly unbearable. At once his mouth flooded with saliva, a calming river to quench the rawness.

A sudden fear.

That he was being dragged back to the hotel room. To Serena. To her burning form. To the panic. He so wanted the darkness to envelop him. To let him hide, be concealed from the searching eyes in the cave. He wished it could all be over. That he could just disappear. Be free of the mental, the physical torture being inflicted upon him. He needed Jane. To take it all away; to make him better.

But the pain.

The sensations.

It all meant just one thing –

At school Tomlinson had never been much of a history buff but, thanks to a persistent teacher, he still remembered two key facts. First, he knew Alexander the Great had cut the Gordian knot; and, second, Caesar had crossed the river Rubicon. Over the years he'd cut through a few Gordian knots himself – slashing red tape he considered pointless; shunning niceties when a direct approach promised better results – but he'd never risked his whole career on the outcome of a single action.

For Tomlinson, there'd never been a Rubicon moment.

Until now –

He'd so wanted to hit Nicol back there in the interview room, to teach him a lesson. Only supreme self-control had prevented him doing so. When the man had taunted him about the children, something had snapped. An anger had flared so suddenly within him, unlike anything he'd experienced before. At that moment, Tomlinson had thought the world would be a better place if Nicol wasn't there to pollute it...

As Riley led the suspect back to the cells, the superintendent was fighting a losing battle. A civil war of mental confusion was already drawing to a close. With rationality slain, emotion emerged victorious, free now to command the legions of his mind as it saw fit. He tried one final time to break free. And failed. The anger had returned, its strength reinforced by hatred. Anger and hatred – each closed in from the wings, capturing Tomlinson in a text-book pincer movement.

The superintendent took a deep breath, mentally prepared himself for what he was about to do. And then, following in Caesar's footsteps, he waded into his very own Rubicon.

'Riley – hang on!' he shouted, running up the corridor. 'Change of plan!' He caught up with the pair just as they reached the lift lobby. The holding cells were on the floor above. 'Look, on second thoughts, no point delaying this. You go get Hazeldine now, and I'll take our friend here back to the interview room. Hazeldine can see him there.'

'Makes sense.' Riley clearly didn't think anything of it.

Which suited Tomlinson just fine, because he didn't want any of this coming back on his sergeant. No point throwing away *two* careers.

With a *bing*, a lift arrived. A few seconds later, Riley had gone. Now it was just the superintendent and Nicol.

'Right. This way...' The superintendent took hold of the man's hand-cuffed arm and marched him back down the corridor. 'Wait...' Tomlinson tried the handle of a door to his right and it swung open. 'This'll do...'

He pushed Nicol inside. It was a small office, dark because the window blinds were closed. Tomlinson flicked a light switch and a fluorescent tube fired up to reveal the interior – black-topped desk, three chairs, and a filing cabinet over in one corner. He sat Nicol down on one of the chairs. The man eyed him suspiciously, but didn't say anything. 'Now, I'm going to leave you here for a minute while I go back to collect my papers. Sit there and don't move. Riley will bring your solicitor up shortly. Understand?' He didn't wait for an answer.

Once out in the corridor, Tomlinson only took a few steps before he stopped in his tracks. He scanned the corridor and, satisfied no-one else was around, patted his jacket pocket to check something.

Calmly, he walked a few further feet to the fire-alarm point on the wall. He picked up the little hammer and broke the glass...

The alarm sounded instantly. The noise was deafening. Tomlinson moved away, went back to stand beside the door to the office. He didn't want Nicol coming out. Officers and civilian staff began to appear, shared hesitation in their eyes; waiting a while longer to see if it was a test alarm. Satisfied it wasn't, some began making their way down the stairwells while others darted back to their offices to secure classified material. The pattern was repeated throughout the whole building, as workstations were locked, visitors were escorted to the nearest exit, and staff spilled out onto the pavements.

Tomlinson had just bought himself time.

The valuable time he needed to get Karl Nicol to talk; to tell him what he knew ...

As he was about to go back into the office, a fire marshal appeared from round a corner. He had to think quickly. The man might jeopardise his plan.

'That one's clear!' Tomlinson shouted, pointing to another door. The marshal looked blankly at him, unable to hear what he'd said above the noise of the alarm. Tomlinson pointed again and gave a thumbs-up signal. Next he indicated the rooms nearest him with a finger, then gestured to himself, then to his eyes, then back to the rooms. The marshal understood – Tomlinson would check them for him before leaving.

The other man mouthed a *thanks* as he sped past.

Tomlinson waited. No-one else came into the corridor. He turned and entered the office. Nicol was already on his feet. But still not talking. Even with all that was going on outside, he remained supremely arrogant; waiting to be led to safety. He knew his rights. And if he so much as bruised a toe getting out, he'd seek hefty compensation. He knew Barry would see to that. Nicol stood there expectantly, waiting for Tomlinson to lead him away.

But instead the officer walked round behind him.

Nicol still wasn't worried. He thought the cuffs were being removed. The burning sensation against his wrists as the restraints were pulled downwards told him otherwise. Off balance, he fell back onto the chair.

Suddenly he felt something going over his head.

A second later, his whole face was covered. There was a gentle pressure to his neck. He made to stand up, but couldn't. Strong arms pinned him down to the chair underneath. Though he couldn't hear it over the noise of the alarm, something brushed against his ears. Then he *did* hear another sound. The thumping of his heart, rhythmically pounding away in terror as adrenalin kicked in.

And that's when he realised what was happening.

That's when he suddenly wanted to talk. To shout. To scream at Tomlinson. To tell him what a bastard he was. How he couldn't do this. How he wouldn't get away with it. But the words didn't come. He was starting to hyper-ventilate. Using up what little oxygen he still had left.

Tomlinson felt strangely calm as he kept the pressure on the man's shoulders. He'd opted for one of the larger exhibits bags. Air-tight. With an elastic band slipped over to hold it snugly in place. It was a trick from the old days. Used by all sides during The Troubles – RUC; Provisionals; even the Garda, south of the border. And people always thought the Garda were a soft touch where the IRA was concerned. But he knew that was far from the truth. The Garda could often be more ruthless, especially when one of their own had been injured. They did what they needed to get their man – and the Provisionals knew it.

The superintendent looked down at Nicol's head. The gelled, dark hair was no longer as distinct as the bag misted up. The man was still struggling, but his movements weren't so co-ordinated now; his brain becoming increasingly confused.

By spreading his weight through both hands, the superintendent knew there'd be less chance of bruising showing on Nicol's shoulders. And the band wouldn't leave any lasting mark. The tell-tale sign always used to be cuts on the wrist – where the prisoner had struggled against the hand-cuffs that had been secured to the arms of a chair. But such abrasions could easily be sustained at any time...

'There's no-one coming to get you,' Tomlinson shouted into Nicol's ear, making sure the man heard him. 'They'll all be outside till the fire brigade gives the all-clear. So... I want you to tell me what you know...'

Nicol made a last ditch attempt to get free. But it was no use. He made rasping sounds inside his polythene prison.

'You'll probably lose consciousness within the next minute. Stamp your foot when you're ready to talk.' Then, Tomlinson added grimly, 'Just be sure you don't take *too* long...'

CHAPTER SEVEN

SUDDENLY, IT ENDED.

Bryant held his breath. Steadied himself for another round of the pain, the mental assault on his senses.

But there was no fresh attack. Nothing. And that neither his father, nor anyone else, had said anything to him during those tortuous moments convinced him the whole episode had been played out internally. He gripped onto the pew beneath him, desperate for something tangible to link him to reality. Still he feared he might be snatched away again.

It was his father's crying that anchored his psyche.

But he felt awkward now, couldn't bring himself to offer the supportive embrace he'd intended. He sighed, risked swallowing, fully expecting to feel the pain in his tongue – but, again, nothing. He released his grip on the seat, the movement tentative; still not convinced there wouldn't be more surprises in store for him.

He felt a gentle rush of cooling air. He wondered if the service was over, if the church doors had been opened. But straightaway his conscious mind registered the sound of someone continuing with a reading, *Loveliest of Trees* – another of his mother's favourites. *But of my three score years and ten* – the words spoken nervously, hesitant; clumsy embarrassment echoing off the old building's walls, its vaulted ceiling. And then, the coolness gave way to a calming sound that seemed to Bryant to overlay the speaker's words.

He heard the lightest of breezes spiralling round in his mind. It was like pressing an ear to a shell, focussing on a distant, swirling sound seeking a way out. The feeling could not have been more different to the pain and torment he'd experienced just seconds before. But this, now, he found completely welcoming, relaxing; something that enfolded him softly in a blanket of mental comfort.

And against the dark projection screen of his blindness, there appeared before him sudden flashes of colour, each extraordinarily beautiful, that became more distinct, more fixed in time under his inner gaze – shape-shifting chromatics, fusing purples with greens, seeing rounded blues cascading into elongated ribbons of yellow; each display falling and rising in time to the sound of the poem that was being read.

Bryant wanted to stay there, fixed in that moment in time; observing, being part of, the ever-changing light show – the mesmerising lava lamps in his mind's eye.

Then, abruptly, it went dark again.

But he felt suddenly at ease; knowing in his very soul *this* was the start of something important.

And the wall of darkness – that had for so long stared back at him, its surface a polished, mirror-like ebony – began to change.

At first he barely noticed the change in texture, as the glassy blackness began little by little to take on a pitted appearance. Small white flecks of light appeared, pushing their way through the burnished dark expanse. And then, just as if someone was tuning-in an old-style TV, a monochrome image began to appear – slowly; indistinct; ghosting; jumping; but then growing in strength, in intensity; holding its own against the backdrop wall of buzzing static.

Then, Bryant realised –

He could see again...

Tomlinson couldn't believe what he'd just done.

How could he have been so stupid? He'd compromised the whole investigation; knew he had. And more, he'd compromised *himself*; stooped to their level. It went against everything he believed in – the way he'd been raised, his values; society's values.

But he'd got his answer...

He dipped his hands into the basin and splashed cool water over his face. Tiny rivulets streamed down his cheeks, collected for a second on his jaw-line – held captive by the stubble – until gravity pulled them free. He let the water out and grabbed a handful of paper towels from the dispenser. He dried himself, sighing as he gazed at the reflection of someone he no longer recognised. All he saw now was someone who made him sick...

But that someone, he knew, had managed to establish that Nicol hadn't been involved. At least not in the murders. Not in the abductions. There was no way the man would have lied; not under that amount of pressure.

Pressure?

No, it had been *torture* he reminded the face in the mirror.

But it saved us weeks of interviews; no more games; and no paperwork the reflection answered silently.

But there'd be mountains of paperwork now. When the complaint went in. When internal investigations got involved. When he was suspended. And when personnel wrote to tell him he'd lost his pension. All those years, and for nothing. No early retirement. No comfortable life in Portugal.

What *had* he done?

He tidied himself up. He'd have to go back in there; face up to his actions. Get something sorted out before everyone was allowed to return to the building – before Hazeldine got to see his client. He wondered if he should let Riley know; tip him off, just in case. But no, that wouldn't be fair. He couldn't tell him, then expect Riley to keep quiet. And worse, what if his sergeant tried to cover up for him? No, he couldn't risk letting that happen.

He really didn't know what to do.

He'd crossed his Rubicon, but he was no Caesar...

Nicol was still in shock.

He'd nearly died.

Jesus Christ – the man was a psycho. The police just *didn't* do that. He'd have to tell Barry. *He'd* know what to do – he always did. But what if the psycho took it further? Barry could get him suspended, or fired; get compensation – but what if he then came after them; after *him*? Someone who could do *that* must have a screw loose, could be capable of *anything*... And the police, they always looked after their own, didn't they? What's to say there wouldn't be a cover-up? Or they'd start picking on him? Him – and Barry? Police harassment at every turn? They'd be watching over their shoulders for the rest of their lives. And what of his businesses? If they wanted, they could make life really difficult for him.

But he had to tell Barry. He just had to. *Didn't he?*

His mind was still racing when Tomlinson came in the door.

'Don't come near me!' Nicol tried to push himself away from the policeman; the chair scraping, its legs reverberating on the floor as it juddered unsteadily into the corner. Chair and prisoner collided with a filing cabinet. No further he could go. 'Get away from me!'

Tomlinson held out a reassuring hand.

'I'm *not* going to hurt you...'

For the first time since the crash, David Bryant was able to focus on a world no longer hidden from him.

Now he could observe the unfamiliar – familiar once more – with *second sight*...

His breath caught in his chest. He couldn't believe it was finally happening. After all the tests. All the uncertainty. He *had* to tell someone – his father; Jane; Paolo... He wanted to cry out in excitement, but instantly a little voice of caution sounded within. He had to keep it to himself. At least for now.

He was confused. He felt guilt that he should now be so elated at a time of such deep sorrow – set against the anguish, pain and loneliness his father was experiencing. And then a sudden fear knocked the wind out of him –

What if it was only temporary and he found himself plunged back into the darkness again?

But then, that same little voice of inward knowing, of certainty, spoke in calming reassurance; promising him this *was* the turning point. He just needed to be patient a little longer...

Bryant's attention was fixed on the image coming slowly into focus. Muscles that had lain unused for months tensed and released in quick succession. He felt a mild straining round his eyes.

And then, *it* appeared –

Sharp. Solid. *The* most interesting sight *ever*...

In a place so holy, it ought to have been only fitting that this miracle – this epiphany – should have drawn its inspiration from something truly hallowed. But instead of a word – *The Word* – appearing before him on a page in the Bible, he found himself gazing truly in awe at something so insignificant, so lowly, that its new-found importance in his life couldn't have been any more understated. For there, spot-lit under the intensity of his close scrutiny, was the object of his fascination –

A *flagstone*...

Simple. Humble. Unnoticed by everyone. But *noticed* by him. *Visually* worshipped by him. As if it had been the *first* thing created on Earth.

Bryant marvelled at its intricacy. The uneven lines of its contours. The areas of light and shade. The microcosm of mountainous ridges that collided with one another – peaks cresting rough summits, vying for eternal dominance, holding sway over the little valleys below; dark inclines; lands full of forgotten debris – dust from people, their clothes, and motes of dirt left by shoes over centuries past. A miniature world that counted for nothing. With no intrinsic value.

But now, observed for the first time with Bryant's new eyes – it was *the* richest sight *ever* seen...

He drew breath, composed himself, then dared to let his gaze wander. First, to his shoes – cheap, his immediate thought; not at all what he'd have bought. He pulled himself up, laughing silently at his reaction, realising just how little importance it held. He *knew* he'd now see everything in an altogether different light. That from now on he'd see the *true* value in the myriad sights he thought he'd lost forever.

Then – he was inspecting his hands, worthy substitutes for eyes these past months. His nails were shorter than he liked. And then there was the faint welt of skin on his wrist – silent witness to the razor's cut. But not even *that* could dampen his rekindled optimism; his interest in life. Those days were gone.

Gone repeated the little voice.

And turning to his right, there was his father. The face familiar, yet strangely *new*. Its shape more rounded than he'd remembered; the brow high, furrowed deeply with age; and the silvering hair, still thick; ever defying the threat of baldness; and the eternally-patient brown eyes, their edges now tinged red from the crying.

All the embarrassment disappeared.

The decades of denied emotion were as nothing.

And son embraced father, hugging him for all he was worth...

Nicol had decided not to say anything to Barry Hazeldine.

At least, not yet. Not until he was safely out of there. He was still absolutely terrified, convinced Tomlinson *would* kill him if he opened his mouth. Not that he'd been threatened. The man had just come back in, casual as anything, and said they'd go back to the interview room; would await the solicitor's arrival. Calm. That's how Tomlinson had appeared to him. As if nothing had happened...

But appearances were deceptive.

And though Nicol couldn't have known it, the superintendent had been panicking behind his mask. Trying to work out how he could get himself out of this one. The feigned composure just his way of making sure he didn't dig the hole any deeper.

Both men were sitting in the interview room, each flanked by their respective second. For his part, Tomlinson found it surreal; bizarre that he was actually going through the motions – but he had to; to protect himself; and to cover Riley. So, he proceeded to ask the questions to which he already knew the answers.

'My client has already told you, superintendent – the noises were from the dolls.' Hazeldine looked at Nicol, nodding reassurance he'd soon have him out.

'These *dolls*, Mr Nicol – life-size replicas of babies; young children, you say?'

'My client has already explained that, superintendent. I can't see why you're persisting with this line of questioning.'

It was true. Riley and Tomlinson had listened to Nicol's account of his latest get-rich-quick scheme. How he'd seen a gap in the market; had watched a TV programme about women who wanted babies – childless mothers; and grandmothers who just wanted a toddler in the family again; to let *them* feel needed; still to have a role to play. So the market had responded with *re-borns*; designed to order; hand-painted facsimiles on whom the women could dote, could share every waking moment, could satisfy their maternal longings. And Nicol, he'd taken it a stage further. He'd had prototypes made in China, full of fancy micro-circuitry. To all intents, you had a living, breathing new-born – that needed feeding; tending to every hour of the day. He'd envisaged a national contract – maybe international one day – selling them to schools, social services, health services. So the kids could experience what it really was like to have a baby to care for at their age. And he had even bigger plans – ideas for other models, of differing ages, to be programmed with specific requirements; special needs', disabilities; something to challenge parenting skills at every level.

Had he been unaware of Nicol's previous connections, Tomlinson might have had some respect for the man – doing his bit to help reduce teenage pregnancies. But knowing what he did, he couldn't help but feel there was something altogether sinister – morally wrong – about letting a man like that near the classroom...

'You'll understand that I still need to see details of the delivery and collection notes, Mr Hazeldine,' Tomlinson replied. They'd been told that *Crossfire Distribution & Freight Company* had sent two vans – one to drop off the prototypes, and one the next day to collect them again. Nicol claimed he had been unhappy with the dolls' quality and had sent them back. Tomlinson had already speculated that it was the dolls' crying that Howard Latham had heard.

'My client is very happy to provide the paperwork...'

'Already in hand, Mr Hazeldine. We've someone over there right now.'

'Then perhaps you could speed them up, superintendent?'

'You'll appreciate these things take time, Mr Hazeldine...'

And so it went on. Every investigative thrust met with a legal parry.

Nicol's solicitor folded his arms. He looked at his client and shrugged his shoulders; nothing for it now but to sit and wait. And then, ten minutes later, a WPC finally brought the confirmation Tomlinson was waiting for. The recorded drop-off and pick-up were just as Nicol had said. The superintendent knew he had no legal justification for holding Nicol any longer. Tomlinson so wished he could – but his hands were tied.

'Thank you for your time. Mr Nicol is free to go.'

Suspect and solicitor rose as one.

'You'll be hearing from us, Superintendent. My client maintained his innocence from the start. I consider this wrongful arrest.'

But Tomlinson wasn't listening.

He was wondering who to tell first – Brenda, or Peters – that he'd be resigning...

Bryant sat there, an arm still around his father, until the service began to draw to a close. As he'd expected, the organist played the introduction to *Morning Has Broken* – allowing the assembled mourners to pay their final respects in song. And then, it was all over.

Song. Service. His mother's life.

Bryant *heard* the sound of people preparing to leave – standing in the pews, putting on their coats, waiting patiently to file out – *before* he consciously *saw* them doing so. That confused him for a moment but, on thinking it through, he understood why it might be the case. For his now was a mind that had grown so used to by-passing vision, to relying instead on audible cues, that it would need time to re-balance itself; to learn to see again.

The little voice was suddenly there. Cautioning him. Telling him not to make himself conspicuous. Otherwise people would see him – *seeing them*. He had to keep this a secret. Absolutely had to.

Bryant had a problem. He simply didn't know who had been told what about him, about the crash, his blindness. As casually as he could, he glanced round, taking in the faces nearest to him. Some he thought he ought to recognise seemed to take longer than he expected to register – his brain overwhelmed now by optic overload. Then, names started to appear, half-remembered; and others of which he was more certain. Here and there an uncle, a nephew or niece all grown up. And people he simply didn't know – friends, he presumed, of his mother's, from different stages of her life.

As feelings of self-consciousness began to take hold, he wished he'd been wearing dark glasses – easier then to have hidden behind others' reflections when coming face to face with them; engaging in small talk – but not doing so had been a deliberate choice on his part. It had been his way of rejecting the disability, making a statement; leaving the door open for his sight to return. Not that he'd *really* expected it to do so...

He made a mental note. He'd need to ask his father who knew what. And to broach the subject, it followed that he'd need to tell him.

He summoned the courage to do so.

Right now. I'm going to do it right now.

Still the inner voice was there, telling him not to do so; that he was making a mistake –

Bryant turned, intending to exit by the aisle – and felt a hand on his sleeve. It was his father, selflessly offering *him* the support he believed he needed.

'Can you manage, David? Here, let me...'

Bryant felt deeply uncomfortable. Forced to maintain the fiction. To take the fragile man's support when their roles so clearly ought to be reversed.

'Dad, there's something I *need* to tell you...'

But before his father could answer, someone else spoke.

'Mr Bryant?' Father and son, each turned as one. 'Thomas,

ah... and David, I am *so* sorry for your loss.' It was the vicar. 'So sorry for the *both* of you.' And then, before Bryant had a chance to say anything, his father was being taken from him, off to one side. 'Are we ready now to press on with Ellen's burial?' the vicar continued.

Bryant realised he'd have to wait until his father was free again now. He couldn't really intrude upon their conversation. To reduce the chances of anyone coming up to him, he returned to the pews, feigning uncertainty as he went. Only as he sat down did it occur to him how stupid that had been. For somebody might have approached him to offer help. But no-one did, as nearly everyone by then had left the church. They'd be waiting outside for his mother's interment. And they'd want to speak to his father.

And, then, to *him*.

He still didn't know if he could face that; the pressure; the social etiquette required at such a confusing time. He needed to talk to his father. Now. Figure out what to do. Get his advice. He was sure his father would understand. He'd explain everything to him – the shock of his sight coming back; and he'd say he needed more time; would ask him to slip him out by a side door. He'd stay away from the wake. And then the two of them, they could catch up properly that night.

Bryant could see that the vicar and his father were still deep in conversation. He'd have to be patient. He sat there quietly, waiting for the time to pass. Just then, his subconscious decided to bring out another photo album of memories. And by far the brightest image was that of the clandestine games of hopscotch he and his best friend, Toby, had played right there in that very same church. His mother would pick them up from school and, on the way home, she'd often drop by to talk to her friends in the Women's Institute – they took it in turns to change the flowers and polish the brass. And while the adults ignored them, he and Toby would make their own entertainment. Flicking a rubber onto the stone floor. Shoes off – otherwise, too noisy – and then they'd skip and jump down the temporary path; a one-eighty at the end, and back again. More than once they'd been caught. He got a clip round the ear. And Toby, the threat of his own mother being told had seen the terrified boy apologise, promise not to do it again.

At least, until the next time the pair had gone there again.

And Bryant remembered, on really sunny days they'd add a new element to their game. For there was a stained-glass window, set high up in the wall, that shone down its rainbow lights almost perfectly onto the central aisle. They'd each pick a colour and agree the challenge – to hop from stone to stone, but with every footfall, they had to land on their chosen colour; otherwise, victory went to the other the moment one of them slipped up...

The vicar was finishing now, his father was turning away; coming back to join him. Bryant was about to stand, intending to go over to the two men. He stopped himself just in time, realising how that would seem. He had to be patient a few moments longer.

And at that *precise* moment, in an example of perfect religious symbolism not lost on Bryant the agnostic, the sun came out and streamed through that remembered window – for he saw that the vicar was suddenly illuminated in waves of multi-faceted light. Beams that overlaid his face, irradiated his cassock – rendering it, Joseph-like, his very own coat of many colours. Bryant found the whole scene beautiful. A fitting end to the service. And the part-*believer* in him thought, just for a moment, his mother *had* made a last appearance; had come to bid him – and his father – a final farewell.

A second later, and the iridescence was gone…

Sorry, sir, I screwed up. Big time.

Riley was holding himself personally responsible for the latest turn of events. And so far, Tomlinson hadn't been able to talk him round. It would take time; he knew that. He also knew that hindsight wasn't always the wonderful thing it was made out to be – especially not when it led to one of his most accomplished officers questioning his own judgement. There was absolutely no place for self-doubt in their line of work, for that meant the next time a lead – possibly *the* lead – came up, they might not act quickly enough; worse still, they might discount it.

No, the fact was it *had* been a promising lead. The call from Howard Latham. The crying. The vans. The previous PNC traces against Nicol.

Right pieces, wrong jigsaw…

Tomlinson focussed on himself. If Riley thought *he'd* screwed up, what the hell did that say about his *own* behaviour in the whole sorry affair? *Screwed up* didn't even come close to describing what he'd done; how he'd compromised the investigation through his treatment of Nicol.

He'd sent Riley back to the incident room, thinking it best to keep him busy. Besides the calls that were coming in, they still needed to trace all the known sex offenders in the area to make sure they were all accounted for. It was slow, tedious procedural work – and just what Riley needed.

Tomlinson pulled open one of the drawers in his desk. The moment had come for him to type his resignation letter. He'd take it round to the commander's office, just as soon as he'd put in a call to Brenda to explain everything. He knew he'd have to come clean with Peters about his handling of Nicol, before the man made a formal complaint and sought damages for the way he'd been treated. He reached in for a sheet of paper, and stopped –

He lifted out the colour photo.

Harry and Emily's beaming faces shone back at him. A lovely, natural shot. Not posed, just a picture snapped by the parents as the twins had played. He remembered asking Anne Wilson to provide photographs that they could use in the appeal, and this was one she'd given him straightaway. She'd promised to get him others as soon as she could.

He looked at the children's faces again. Their happy, care-free smiles. And it changed everything. No matter what he thought of himself just now, his actions were as nothing compared to those of the monster still at large out there. He knew what he had to do. Where his priorities lay. He owed it to those children to find them. To see the man responsible brought to justice – whether it be *his* brand, or the courts'.

Only *then* could he deliver that letter.

Bryant's courage was wavering; still unsure how to tell his father; and he knew any chance of escaping the horde of mourners waiting outside by taking a side exit was rapidly disappearing. Father and son were almost there at the front doors. Indecision suddenly gripped Bryant; heart pounding, breathing rapid, his legs refused to take another step.

'Do you need a moment, David?' his father asked, aware suddenly of his discomfort. Bryant nodded, desperate to buy himself more time to think. 'Wait here, then. Look, you don't need to come outside right now. When everyone's gone, we'll go back to the graveside and you can say a few words then. Would that be better?' Bryant hated himself for what he was doing. How low did it make him, not even going to see his mother buried? His father guided him to the end of a pew. 'Don't worry, I'll make your apologies. I know you've had a long day. You must be tired. Rest now, and I'll be back as quickly as I can.' Bryant nodded again, not trusting himself to speak. His father walked out into the light – leaving him alone.

Echoes sounded from further back in the church; the slamming of wood, a shrill metallic crash – the organist packing up and leaving.

With no-one else around, Bryant began taking in his surroundings; studying afresh what he saw – the dimensions of the church, the structure, its arches.

It was then he noticed the appeal board.

A crudely-painted totaliser, like a thermometer; with a red line that rose vertically up a scale indicating how much money was needed. It sat just below the halfway mark; still a long way to go before they reached the total.

Bryant went over to have a closer look. There was a laminated card affixed to the wall beside the base of the totaliser. Reading it, he learnt the church had suffered recent vandalism, and that the vicar was trying to raise enough to –

Restore its stained-glass window.

He spun round. The window was no-where to be seen. In place of the centuries-old coloured glass he'd remembered, all he saw were roughly-hewn planks that boarded up an arch shape in the wall.

He felt a sudden sickness rise in the pit of his stomach.

But he'd seen them – during that *very* service – the colours from the window, cast on the vicar...

Then, a hammer-blow realisation hit him.

Whatever the origin of those lights, they'd *not* come from the window.

CHAPTER EIGHT

THOMAS BRYANT LET the tears run freely.

Tears of joy. Genuine. Heartfelt. Springing from the relief he felt for his son. Happiness, at a time of such deep sorrow. The sense of spiritual irony was not lost on him.

'David, I am *so* pleased for you,' he offered, as they were being chauffeured back to the house. 'If only your mother had lived that little bit longer, it would have been a great weight off her mind. She was thinking about you the whole time...' Bryant felt guilty. Next to his mother's suffering, his had been as nothing and, yet, throughout the later stages of her illness, her only concern had been him. She'd been no different her whole life, always putting others first. 'So, what next?' his father continued. 'You'll have to tell your consultant. He'll want you back there as soon as possible...'

'Dad – please, no! Look, you're my priority right now. You're the one who's going to need the support, and I want to be here for you. I mean, there'll be all the practicalities – mum's clothes, her belongings... you'll have to decide what you want to keep; if you want to give anything to charity...'

'David – it'll all be fine. Your mother and I planned it. We had *plenty* of time to talk through the arrangements. I'm grateful – *really* I am, but you've got to think about yourself now. If not for me, then for your mother...'

'*But* –'

'No *buts.*'

It was one of those arguments Bryant knew he just wasn't going to win. His father had made his mind up, and that was that. He wondered if it was his way of dealing with the shock – as long as he kept busy, he could keep control of his emotions.

'OK,' Bryant conceded, 'what if I telephone the hospital and say I'll go in tomorrow lunchtime? Just for a couple of days? Then, once I get the all-clear, I'll come back again...'

'Hm,' his father considered the proposition. 'Alright – but *only* if they say so. Your health's the most important thing here. We can't bring your mother back...'

They both fell silent at that, neither wanting to be the first to speak; content to share each other's quiet company as the car continued its journey.

Bryant judged it would be another twenty minutes before they reached the family home. His earlier worries weren't so prominent now – his father already having reassured him that only his closest relatives had actually been told about the accident; and that he and his mother had taken care only ever to have mentioned *a crash*. They'd purposely not offered further details, leaving it to others to fill in the blanks. Most assumed it was a car-crash. Luisa *might* have known more. His father thought he'd mentioned the *plane* crash in the message he'd left her; and possibly the blindness, too. But he couldn't be entirely sure; couldn't remember exactly what he'd said – she'd never called back anyway...

So, Bryant considered, just the wake to get through. And if no-one was any the wiser, it would make it easier for him; he'd just play along. His father didn't think anyone had noticed him being led into the church either; and, if they had, they'd probably have thought it had been the other way round; the younger Bryant offering the older one a shoulder of support. Bryant would wait and see.

And if anyone asked about his accident, he'd keep it simple. *Car-crash – one broken arm, several ribs.*

He began to mull over what his next steps should be. First, he'd need to satisfy himself his father really was alright; that he'd be able to cope without him. He knew it took time to get over grief, and he meant what he'd said about being there for him. But after that? What should he do next? He knew he didn't want to stay in hospital any longer than he had to. He guessed they'd try and convince him to stay while they ran their tests. But he already knew what his line of reasoning would be – if his sight *had* returned for good, why then should he stay? And if it *was* only temporary, then he'd cross that bridge when the time came; would book himself back in with them...

No, Bryant knew he had much to sort out, personally *and* professionally. And he wasn't going to let himself become distracted.

There was his divorce. The inevitable division of assets. Custody of Paolo. And his job. Could he go back to his old position? Would The Company let him? He'd have to talk to Pierfranco; see what he thought. Maybe they'd want to move him into marketing? Use *him* as a publicity tool? That would see his story out in the open. He'd be plagued by the media. There'd be no privacy. Not for a very long time. If ever. He thought through his options. Maybe he shouldn't contact Pierfranco. Maybe he should cut his losses and resign; send The Company a letter? But what if they wouldn't let him go? There were just so many questions...

Tomorrow, he decided; everything could wait till –

A sudden thought.

An idea plucked from the back of his mind. Something he'd been meaning to do for years, but had somehow never got round to doing.

Until now...

It made for an impressive garden feature.

The stone circle.

And while it was no Stonehenge – measuring just eighteen feet in diameter, with six of its original nine stones standing – to Sam Girvan it was no less spectacular, no less magical, no less important.

He'd been fascinated by stone circles ever since he'd come across his first one, aged eight, during a family holiday in the Lake District. And while most kids begged their parents to take them to theme parks when school had broken up, Sam had instead scoured maps to see if there were any circles near where they'd be staying. No holiday was complete without a visit to try and find a new one. He'd read many books on the subject over the years, but he remained as keen as ever to know more about the iconic structures – how they'd been built; by whom; and for what purpose. Especially the *why*...

Perhaps it was due to the remoteness of so much of its landscape, but scores of circles could still be found in Scotland – from recumbent examples across Aberdeenshire, to the multiplicity of stone structures that had been built in the west, running the length of the Kilmartin valley. And while the most impressive were signposted – formed part of the tourist trail – the majority lay undisturbed; visited only by the most committed of circle hunters.

Sam's circle fell into the last category. Which suited him just fine. Other than the occasional guest who showed a passing interest, he was free to enjoy his little piece of history in private. And because it wasn't marked on any modern map, he hadn't even known of its existence when he and his wife, Neve, had bought the house. He'd discovered it by chance when he'd been digging over the grass, intending to put in a new vegetable patch. The rotovator's blades had sparked and come to a juddering halt. He'd got his spade out and dug round what he'd thought was a boulder. But the more soil he'd removed, the more granite had kept appearing. At first, he'd just decided to let it be, move on elsewhere – but, with each new furrow, he'd continued to unearth more of the strange features. He'd cleared away the topsoil, and had revealed the crowns of six stones; three others – those that had fallen – finally seeing the light of day only when he'd dug further down. He'd tried lifting one back into position, but had soon given up; especially after Neve had overruled his suggestion they get a JCB in.

All in all, the clearance project had taken him around a year to complete. Far longer than he'd have wished, but he'd *had* to fit it around the more pressing business of renovating and extending their home – the *Achavanandra* guest-house. And as Neve had kept reminding him, that was their business; their priority; for without its income, they wouldn't be able to get by. So Sam had knuckled down, had helped her create their haven of peace and tranquillity. And the bookings showed they were making it work...

The whole idea – the decision to move – had come about four years earlier. When Sam had had his midlife crisis. Had decided there had to be more to life than the daily commute. Working in the dead-end London job he so hated. It had taken a couple of weeks staying in B&Bs in the Highlands to sow the germ of the idea; for Sam to begin to see the light; to realise there *was* an alternative. So, after a year in the planning, he'd decided to make a break for it. Escape the rat race before it wore him down. And with Neve's unwavering support, they'd done the sums, had agreed it was a risk worth taking...

And had packed it all in.

He, his wife and their then-nine year old daughter, Katie, had upped sticks and headed for the Scottish Highlands. True, money was tighter now. But they were *far* richer in so many different ways – in their freedom to live life at a gentler pace; in the healthier environment; in the better upbringing they could offer Katie; in the rediscovered sense of community they'd encountered, long since lost to the millions trapped in crowded southern isolation; and in their house, with its views to die for – sapphire seascapes rolling seamlessly into verdant pine forests; the evergreen canopy snaking its way across an undulating landscape; until the trees finally petered out at the foot of the wilder heath-lands; with jagged mountain ranges rising steeply beyond – earthly masters that dared challenge the supremacy of the sky.

The guest-house was doing quite well – the year's takings up fifteen percent on the previous twelve months. When they'd first taken on *Achavanandra*, business had been fairly slow – a few repeat bookings from the previous owners' regulars, but otherwise Sam and Neve had had to rely on the unplanned over-nighters; those looking for a place to stay before they cut across to the west coast. But the pair had come on leaps and bounds since then – thanks in part, they believed, to their decision to advertise on the internet; but also, and perhaps more importantly, to the seemingly-coincidental upsurge of interest in the area that television had generated. There'd been a succession of programmes all homing in on the counties of Caithness, Sutherland, Easter and Wester Ross; every one praising the natural wonders of the Highlands. There'd been everything from the most challenging mountains to climb; to where to find the best views in Britain; to where the chances were greatest of seeing bottlenose dolphins; when was the best time to see the Northern Lights. The programmes must have touched many of the armchair tourists at some deep, emotional level – for significant numbers had then voted with their feet, journeying north to experience the wonders for themselves. And even now, the Girvans still had bookings right up until late-November; then a few weeks respite, before the Hogmanay season would be upon them. Friends who'd come up to visit had asked when they got away for their own holidays. And Sam? He'd just pointed out of the breakfast-room window at the one hundred and eighty degree panorama. With scenery like that, he'd said, why ever *would* they want to go anywhere else? For them now, every day was a holiday – living life on their terms; enjoying their own little piece of heaven. They'd never been as happy – and they wouldn't change their new-found freedom for anything in the world...

'Sam – tea!' Neve was outside the back door, holding a mug and waving at her husband to get his attention. He signalled he was coming and she heard the strimmer cease its high-pitched whine. Sam walked down the slight incline and flopped into one of the chairs on the patio.

'Thanks, I could do with that.' He had the cloying aroma of unleaded petrol mixed with oil, and was glistening with sweat. He wiped a forearm over his brow and bits of cut grass stuck to his forehead.

'Very appealing,' Neve chided, giving him a playful kiss. 'Look at the state of you.'

Sam pulled at his tide-marked, heavy metal T-shirt, exaggerating his need to cool down. 'What do you expect? It's *hot*.' It had just gone midday and, although it was the last week in October, the Highlands were experiencing a late burst of summer – the complete opposite to the cold front that had moved in to assault south east England. He gestured towards the circle. 'If you want to take over...' He'd already mowed as much as he could; now he just needed to finish removing the long tufts of grass that grew tightly round the base of the stones. He'd already decided he might give it all one final cut in a couple of weeks' time if the weather held – but, otherwise, that would be it until the spring.

'Oh, no – they're yours. *You* look after them.'

Sam drained the last of his tea and held the mug out.

'Right, better finish off,' he said, standing up. 'Listen, do you want me to do the cooking this evening?' He was talking about the meal they'd need to prepare for tonight's incomers. Ordinarily, they only offered breakfast but, if guests gave them enough notice, they were happy to prepare something simple for dinner.

Neve nodded. 'That'd be good – means I could get on and wash a couple of extra loads of sheets and press the ones in the dryer.' Washing – bane of their lives. They should've set up their own laundrette. They could've made a killing from all the other guest-houses in the area. It wasn't so bad when people were booked in for several days – but those in for just one night meant a quick turn-round on the linen front; time consuming and wasteful on resources – but necessary; everyone wanted fresh sheets.

'What time are they arriving?'

He meant the party of Danish bikers. Seven of them. Booked in for two nights. Bikers – most hotels down south would've run a mile, but here it was different. They were usually fifty-somethings, couples whose kids had grown up; and who now wanted to enjoy their own lives again; taste the spirit of freedom. And for the Danes particularly, touring the Highlands offered that escape. While they might look like a hell's angel convention rolling into town, they were never any trouble. They were polite, and paid in full up front.

'Six; sevenish…'

'OK. Give me ten minutes, and I'll come in, grab a shower; get a quick bite to eat and then see what we've got in for this evening …'

They heard the phone ring.

'I'll get it,' Neve volunteered.

But it stopped – daughter Katie had obviously picked it up. There was a brief pause, then she appeared at the back door.

'Dad, it's for you.'

'Who is it? If it's a booking, your mother can take it.'

'No, dad; it's a man for you. He says he's a friend.'

'Alright, hang on, I'll come in now.' Sam started to unlace his boots. 'Did he give a name?' But Katie had already disappeared.

Gone to find out.

A moment later, she returned. 'Dad, he says his name's *David…*'

Bryant had his address book out, his splayed fingers holding the pages open. Just below *Garage – Westway Engineering*, there was an entry for *Girvan, Sam*. And then, in brackets afterwards, he'd at one time pencilled the words, *Gone Native*, followed by an exclamation mark.

Earlier in the day, before setting off for the hospital, Bryant had taken a taxi back to his own house – a little over a half-hour's drive from his father's – to get the book for the number. Sam, like so many others who received the annual Christmas card, hadn't yet made it into his electronic world; the phone-cum-organiser still largely reserved for business contacts.

He heard Sam taking the phone from Katie at the other end.

'Hello?'

'*Sam*?'

A split second, and then realisation. 'David *Bryant…* Long time no speak. How the hell are you?'

'Good, thanks. And yourself?'

'Yeah, fine. We're doing OK. So, to what do we owe this

pleasure? You finally thinking of coming to join our commune; share a bowl of lentil soup?'

Bryant knew he only had himself to blame for that one. Ever since he'd heard that Sam had packed it all in, he'd taken great delight in winding the man up every time he sent through the seasonal greeting. First, it had been asking him if he knitted his own shirts; then, if he recycled his own bodily waste; and this year, he'd planned to send him a spoof advert for umbral panels, like solar ones – but powered by rain clouds; just perfect for a hippie tucked away in the wilds of Scotland...

Deep down, though, he *did* have a healthy respect for the man. To have had the courage to break free from the increasingly-demanding treadmill of southern work life – that had taken some doing.

They'd known each other for more than twenty years, since first meeting at Edinburgh University in the eighties. Bryant had been reading accountancy and business studies, Sam archaeology. Bizarre as it sounded, they'd actually met *inside* a wardrobe. There'd been no Turkish delight; no Snow Queen; no fawns; no lion. Just a merry Sam and a cloudy flagon of serious-looking cider. Bryant had gone to see one of his friends further down the corridor and, while the latter was in the communal kitchen making them both a coffee, he'd heard giggling coming from the wardrobe. Opening the door, he'd found Sam. And the cider. For reasons he never could explain, Bryant had acted on impulse, climbing into the already tight space with the inebriated Sam. From that moment, they'd hit it off.

They'd kept in touch after leaving university. Sam had gone to work for the government – he'd always liked the great outdoors and had applied to join the Forestry Commission, but the nearest he'd got to trees was a desk job in the Department of Environment. And Bryant, he'd landed himself a graduate traineeship with one of the big five accountancy firms. He'd worked hard, had played to his strengths, and had stayed *just* long enough to see his reputation established – before greedily setting his sights elsewhere. He'd known even then that his future lay in management accountancy and he'd wanted to find an employer for the long haul; one with a strong global presence, and enough avenues to accommodate his boundless, driving ambition ...

And that was when *he'd* been head-hunted. When he and The Company became one. He a living, breathing part of the greater, corporate entity.

He'd always thought Sam would stay chained to his Whitehall desk until retirement – or death; whichever came sooner – so it had come as a real surprise to learn of his premature escape. But he'd wished him well. The last time they'd actually seen one another had been years ago, at a reunion bash in Edinburgh; a decade after they'd left the world of academia behind. Bryant remembered the scene clearly. He'd arrived at the Royal Oak, just off Chambers Street, mid-afternoon and had sat there in the upstairs lounge with two-dozen faces from the past. He'd chatted with those at his immediate table, and had then moved on to another; happy to circulate – *and* to have got away from one particular bore. Nothing untoward at the second table, until something had prompted him to do a double-take. He'd suddenly found himself peering at a vaguely familiar set of eyes; eyes that glinted knowingly – and perhaps a little mischievously – from behind a tangled barb of facial hair. *Sam Girvan*. Sporting the whole Grizzly Adams look, and years before he'd done the whole get-out-of-London thing.

And now Bryant would be seeing him again.

'*Lentil soup*, you say? Hm, you know, that sounds quite appetising...'

Bryant snapped his phone shut.

The arrangements were in place. First, the appointment with his consultant later that day; then, back to his father's that night; two days, then he'd catch the train to Edinburgh, and from there continue north to Inverness.

Train. *Not* plane. It was too soon for *that*.

And even if the hospital agreed he *could* drive himself – and he suspected they'd never do that until they were absolutely certain his vision had returned for good – he wouldn't have felt comfortable attempting such a long car journey. The distance he'd need to cover would take at least ten hours, even with regular breaks and clear roads. No, he'd take the train. And he'd book the ticket later that afternoon.

He looked at his watch. 12:08 pm. He'd already been in to the hospital earlier that morning for an MRI scan. They'd sent him away until the afternoon consultation, so he'd spent the past few hours killing time in the local shopping centre; idly browsing the window displays of electrical and wireless gadgetry – each one promising technology that would change his virtual life. But he'd not found anything he didn't already have; and, besides, his toys were always top of the range – not like the inferior brands he'd seen on sale there.

At 12:30 pm he was due to see Mr Markland. He figured he had just enough time to freshen up before reporting to the ophthalmology department. He looked right, then left to check there was no traffic coming, then crossed the road and went into the Royal County's main entrance for the second time that day. It was busier than it had been before. There were people everywhere. He deliberately stayed focussed on following the corridor signs. He feared if he looked at all the sights – the faces, the colours, the commotion around him – he might overload his brain. After all these months of darkness, he knew he had to take it slowly; one step at a time.

He waited while an automatic door opened, then made his way towards a bank of lifts at the far end. He hadn't noticed the elderly man dressed in black who had been sitting out there. But the man had noticed him. Had been patiently awaiting his return all afternoon.

As Bryant headed off down the corridor, the automatic door opened for a second time and the man entered; followed after him.

The man was acutely aware of the importance of his mission. This time there could be *no* room for error...

Chris Markland wore two hats – consultant in both the ophthalmology and neurology departments.

When Bryant had first walked into the consulting room, he thought the man had seemed less interested in him than in the abstract art that hung at irregular intervals around the walls. Or, at least, that's what he'd concluded from the way Markland kept moving his head aimlessly around. He'd wondered for a moment if the man had been testing him, seeing if he'd follow his gaze; checking he really *could* see. But he'd finally just decided Markland's mind must have been on altogether higher things, like when he'd maybe get off to lunch or escape for an afternoon's round of golf – the clue to his sporting interest being the set of clubs that nestled in the corner of the room.

Bryant had met Markland several times before, but now he could actually *see* him. Put a face to the voice – literally. The man was in his early fifties; of slight build; thinning hair with frameless glasses. He looked tired – as did his clothes; the creases most pronounced around his eyes – mirrored in the crumpled material of his jacket. It was not at all the image Bryant had conjured up after hearing the man's voice in their earlier sessions. He'd always sounded far more dapper than he now appeared in the flesh.

Markland had stopped inspecting the artwork and had turned his attention to the scan results lying on his desk. Bryant took a seat opposite him.

'It's a difficult one...' the consultant began. 'We'd like to run some more tests, David; just to be completely sure. You understand...'

'Why?' Bryant shifted uneasily in his chair. 'Is there a problem with the scan?'

'No, no – just routine,' Markland reassured him. 'Nothing to worry about. Really...'

Bryant was confused. It didn't make sense.

'So...' he countered, 'if everything's OK, surely the other tests can wait till I get back?' He soldiered on, knowing how important it was to him that he could still get away. 'It's just... I've already made plans...'

'*Plans...*' The consultant drummed thoughtful fingertips slowly on the desktop. 'Well, we'd rather you didn't go anywhere...' He could see from Bryant's face there was irritation there. 'But...' he didn't want a confrontation; that would altogether ruin his appetite so close to lunch, 'if you're determined to go, I guess we could defer the tests for a few weeks.' Bryant seemed happy with that. 'But... you *will* need to give us a contact number for the duration; and if *anything* seems wrong, you must seek medical advice at once. I really can't emphasise that enough.'

Bryant nodded.

They'd given him the green light, albeit temporarily.

Almost...

'I would, however,' Markland continued, 'advise that you check in with Mr Sommer before you go.' Vincent Sommer the consultant psychiatrist; the one who'd attributed the blindness to the trauma of the crash. Markland swung round in his chair and scanned the notice-board on the wall. 'Ah, here we are...' He swung back again and picked up the phone. 'No time like the present. I'll just give his secretary a call; see if he can spare us a few minutes. Then we can have you on your way; off to all your... *plans...*'

Bryant was starting to feel distinctly *odd...*

Not unwell. More, uneasy. Strangely unprepared. But unprepared for what he wondered. He was aware of the other man talking – but couldn't see him clearly any more. Something was happening.

Something was interfering with his vision –

Great horizontal bars of colour, their edges growing more and less distinct by degrees, began to flash across his line of sight; pulsing with an inner life of their own; their vibration increasingly destructive – until they shook themselves apart; at once to be replaced by yet more energetic waves of the visible light spectrum. The room behind Markland was receding; more and more visual distortion overlaid the hitherto-focussed, discernible, physical world. He tried to fight against it. Willed himself to see clearly again. He'd made the breakthrough once before – knew he could do so again. *He had to.* But the lateral blurring became more intense; and there was a droning noise growing in his ears; steadily becoming louder like a swarm of bees approaching. He stared back to where Markland should have been. The voice still there – *just*; though growing less audible – but, otherwise, the traces of the man were disappearing. He scanned the wall for the modern art – again, *nothing.* Instead, an ever more confusing sight greeted him, imprinting itself on his optic nerve; challenging his brain to decipher the images in some perverse, tortuous game of *magic eye*. Myriad coloured dots were suddenly everywhere – reds, purples, greens, yellows, browns mixing into blues; like *hundreds and thousands* exploding, before raining down in his mind's eye. Each mote, animated, dancing to an unseen tune. And then, as one, like a flock of starlings wheeling across the evening sky, the disparate flecks began to join together in a rapidly expanding blanket of oblivion. Instantly, the colours all disappeared and the pitch-black screen of *nothing-ness* – his constant companion these past months – was back; a shutter drawn down on the camera of his perception; with no way to press the release.

And then – even the darkness changed.

Strangely so. It was like fainting in reverse. For instead of dot after growing dot of ebony appearing, obliterating his sight, he found pin-prick after pin-prick of white punching its way through the backdrop of the gloom – until he was looking at a screen of vivid, intense, bright white light. And still, the incessant droning noise increased. Now, the final traces of Markland's voice had gone. Bryant felt he was being imprisoned in a mental cocoon of *exclusion*; tied up and left *apart* from the rest of the world; apart from his sense of *self*.

This was something *altogether* different. It wasn't his blindness returning.

He was aware the whiteness was hot, as if he was being heated from within. The memory of Serena burning; the molten pin-pricks in his own abdomen all tried to come to the fore – but this time, even *that* memory was different. This wasn't the recurrent nightmare either. And then, he was suddenly short of breath, as if someone was squeezing his rib-cage – trying to break the healed ribs.

The droning stopped –

Then, a moment of silence – but only short-lived. For his heart went into overdrive; beating in his ears – the *bump bump bump* rising to a hypnotic crescendo. And then he *did* feel a panic rise within him; a queasiness beginning to grow in the pit of his stomach.

He wanted the white light gone. Willed the darkness to return. At least that was something he understood. For it had been his constant companion.

But the *brightness*...

What if this wasn't his sight? Worse, what if he was losing his mind? He truly thought he *was* reaching the end of his sanity – a neural vanishing point; but *white* – not *black* – was the colour of the rapacious, cosmic hole that was drawing *everything* into its inescapable vortex...

And it was *then*, like someone flicking a light switch – but this time to turn the *darkness* back on again – that the little voice of internal calm spoke to his whole being; removed the blinding light and restored

116

the familiar black screen. Urged him to let go. Of everything. Not to offer any resistance. Just to go with the flow.

He wanted to argue – to tell the voice it was wrong; but its message, its assured insistence was so persuasive; so pleasantly welcoming... He was *just* about to give way; to trust the voice; to cede control of himself to the unknown, when he had the strongest *feeling* it was all a deception; a trap. That the voice was lying to him. That its goal was to see him buried in oblivion once and for all. With no escape. Ever.

He was torn – not knowing which way to turn.

Unsure which to heed.

The *feeling*.

Or the *voice*.

And then, even the freedom to choose was denied him – as *everything* just seemed to stop; ceased to exist there and then.

The darkness became nothing. Nothing gave way to oblivion. And oblivion disappeared into its own realm of non-existence...

The first thing Bryant saw when he regained consciousness was the hazy silhouette of an old man – his dark frame moving slowly against a brightness that streamed in from behind. He blinked several times, tried to improve the focus – but the silhouette had gone. In those few seconds, Thomas Bryant had walked over from the window and now stood beside his son's bed.

The younger Bryant registered the father's presence in his peripheral vision; caught sight of the older man's faded overcoat – brown suede with the sheepskin collar; favourite fashion accessory of all seventies football reporters; and the occasional dodgy second-hand car-dealer. A flash of sudden memory – he remembered the coat as a permanent fixture; lying unused for years in the boot of the family Vauxhall Cavalier – just in case his father had got caught out in the snow; even in the middle of June...

And, then, his father was there. The solid paternal smile looking back at him.

'Oh, David – you had me *so* worried.' He tried to joke, to lessen the seriousness of what had happened. 'And there was me thinking *I'd* be the one who needed *your* help.' He placed a hand on his son's shoulder. 'Don't worry – I'm here for you as long as you need me.'

Worried? Help? What *was* his father talking about? Bryant was confused. He made to sit up, but found he couldn't. The restraints that tied him to the bed denied him that freedom. Questions raced through his mind –

Where am I? What's happened? Why's dad here?

Then he began to remember.

The meeting with Markland... His room. Sommer... And then there'd been the colours. No, wait – the darkness. No – the bright light. The noise. A voice in his head...

'I wish I'd known, David – really I do. I'm sorry I missed the signs. I've let you down; I've let your mother down. I promised her I'd look after you, no matter what.'

'Mr Bryant?'

Instinctively, Bryant mouthed *Yes?*

But it was his father that Vincent Sommer was addressing.

'If we might get on?'

'Yes, of course.' A pat on his son's shoulder and then Thomas Bryant said, 'I'm going to leave it to the doctors, David. They know what's best. But I'll come and see you soon, once you've settled in...'

Know what's best... Settled in... What was going on?

'*Dad!*' Bryant shouted the word. '*Don't go!*'

But his father had already moved away, his place instead taken by Sommer, the clinical psychiatrist.

'Now, David, let me just reassure you – everything's going to be fine. We're going to take very good care of you.'

'*No!*' Bryant was desperately trying to sit up; he wrestled against the restraints, rocking the bed with the force of his struggling. All he could see was a blinding white light.

'Nurse – some help, please.'

'*What are you doing to me? Get off! Dad, don't leave me!*'

'David,' Sommer again. 'For your own good, please lie still. We'll soon have you comfortable.'

A needle went in. The sedation worked within seconds – the intense light disappeared and Bryant felt himself tumbling away. But his hearing, his primary sensory vehicle these past months, hung on for longer; as that part of his cortex fought against the drugs. He heard Sommer talking, and his father seeming to accept what was being proposed.

A mention of pills. Suicide. Something about relapse. *Sectioning* –

And then, even *that* part of his brain finally shut down...

Bryant drifted back into the now.

His eyes flashed open – and he found he could *still* see...

The blinding light was gone. He didn't think he'd gone mad...

He remembered the restraints. He looked down and saw straps pulled tightly over the bedclothes, holding him fast. He gazed around the room. It was a place he didn't recognise. Pastel colours. All very relaxing. He guessed it must be the room they reserved for the mentally deranged. He was going to cry out, see who came running – but the little voice was there again, talking quietly to him in his head.

Please – just stay as you are ... Trust me ...

Bryant was confused, wondering just who *me* was. Surely *me* was... *him*? The little voice that part of the self that everyone has inside; that appears from time to time? The voice of reason? The occasional moral compass? Gut instinct? Call it what you will. He found himself silently asking the voice to identify itself – the question amounting to little more than a thought; a fleeting feeling; not an internal dialogue.

But the question went unanswered.

Instead, he just heard the voice whisper *Trust me ... Now stay quiet!*

Suddenly there were other voices. External. Real people talking. A man and a woman. Just outside the door. He heard the man saying,

'... quickly as I could. Is he in there?'

And then the woman reply, 'We need your second opinion, Mr Graveley. He can't be sectioned otherwise.'

'And his father?'

'He's happy to go along with whatever you suggest.'

'I see. And where is he now?'

'I think he went home to wait for our call.'

'Hm...' There was the sound of pages being turned.

'Should I see if we can transfer him today?'

Then, the man's composure changed; agitation suddenly audible in his voice.

'We're on *really* weak ground here. I don't know what Sommer was playing at. He should've known better.' A pause and then, 'No, I'm sorry; I simply can't sign up to this. Where's the evidence? It's one thing for Sommer to say he *heard* our man talking about popping pills; but I can't find anything to corroborate the fact. At the very least, I'd have expected Chris Markland to have offered confirmation. And look – the progress he's been making under Nurse Reynolds...'

'But we can't just let him go. Not if he's a threat to himself. To others?'

'No – I *don't* accept that. There's nothing in his history to say he's a threat to others. And as for himself, the previous attempt could be seen as a one-off. Look here, even Sommer wrote *it was a cry for help*. No, I simply don't agree with his diagnosis. And what about here...' Further pages being leafed through at speed, '...he was *clearly* on the mend.' A sharp intake of breath, and then, 'Do you know how much trouble this could cause? If we get hit with a case of negligence? It wouldn't be the first time Sommer got it wrong... No, I think the best thing's for him to be with his family. His father can give him the stability he needs just now. Home will be a familiar environment in which he can complete his recovery.' There was a pause, then the man called Graveley cleared his throat. With an air of finality, he announced, 'I'd like him discharged.'

      'But –'

      'No buts. I have seniority over Sommer in these matters. Do it, please. *Now...*'

An hour later, Bryant found himself standing back in the hospital's car-park. Apology upon apology heaped on him by a flustered-looking nurse as he'd left the unfamiliar ward; leaflets on his right to appeal thrust in his hand.

      He hailed a taxi.

      He'd head to his father's house.

      No – go home. It was the little voice; reading *his* mind – *their* mind. *Home* it repeated. *Then Scotland. Tell no-one...*

Des Graveley looked hot and bothered. Clearly out of breath. He'd been running. He screeched to a halt at the nurses' station.

      'Sorry. Got held up. Emergency... just couldn't get away any earlier.' He took a handkerchief from his top pocket and wiped his brow. 'Right,' he was still panting, 'where's this patient Sommer wants me to assess?'

      The earlier-flustered nurse looked even more discomfited now as she said, dumbfounded,

      '*But...* you asked me to discharge him over an hour ago...'

CHAPTER NINE

AFTER DECIDING NOT to resign, Tomlinson found himself battling his conscience every day. His only real saving grace had been the photo of Harry and Emily that he'd found in his drawer. He'd taken to carrying it around with him and, every time he felt the self-recrimination or loathing grow, he'd look at their faces, remembering the promise he'd made to himself, to them – that he wouldn't leave, not before he found them; had brought their grandparents' killer to justice...

Days had passed since the superintendent had had to release Karl Nicol, and they were no further forward with the investigation. The CCTV that Riley had obtained hadn't yet provided any clear leads, but a dedicated team continued to sift through the remaining footage, taking vehicle registrations – including the partial ones – and cross-checking them against the police national computer. It was a time-consuming process, but one that had to be completed.

'Any joy?' Tomlinson asked.

Riley pushed himself away from the desk and rubbed at his tired eyes. He'd been working through the list of known sex offenders in the area. He'd just finished speaking to the probation service and every person of interest had now been accounted for.

'No, sir. Sorry...'

Tomlinson sighed hard. 'Damn. We're running out of options.' He wasn't wrong. He'd already asked forensics to revisit the initial SOCO results, as well as the second wave of tests carried out at the Wilson's home – but nothing new had come up on the DNA front either. He'd hoped it might have produced *something*. All he could do now was wait for someone to call in with the vital piece of information they so desperately needed. And there was no way of knowing when that would be. If ever.

The superintendent was acutely aware of one fact – that in the modern, digital age of twenty-four hour news, there *was* a real danger of apathy setting in; with people just watching the media reactively; conditioned to observe events from afar – thinking they could leave it to others to pick up the phone, while they just enjoyed the free entertainment.

Every day, the networks carried stories of death, rape, mindless violence, cruelty, and suffering from all over the world – and people's morbid appetite for real-life horror seemed to have no limit; true revulsion at such crimes now largely a thing of the past; the continuous, twenty-four-seven exposure to such stories somehow brainwashing the majority into seeing such evil as the norm; nothing to get unduly worried about; little more than a filler before the next article on the latest divorce between an overpaid footballer caught with his pants down and his glamour-model wife.

Tomlinson knew he *had* to jolt the public back into action; needed to inject a new urgency into the investigation. Because someone, somewhere held the key. They just didn't know it yet.

'I'm going to see Peters...' he announced.

Tomlinson was back at the incident room more quickly than he'd expected. At least *something* had gone right. He'd thought he was going to have a fight on his hands, but the commander had agreed to his proposal straightaway – in no small part, he suspected, because Peters had been looking out for his *own* interests; unsolved case – maybe no promotion. But whatever the reason, Tomlinson didn't care. He'd got what he wanted and that was what mattered.

'Paul, can you get me a summary of the incident log?' he asked, as he swept through the room. 'I'd like everything since the press conference.'

Riley looked up from the computer screen. 'OK...'

'And... we need those other pictures of the twins; the latest ones...'

'Right...'

'Oh, and you'll need to get them put on a disk...'

'OK.'

'And I need it all in the next half-hour...'

Before the sergeant could answer again, Tomlinson was out the door, heading for his office to get ready. In his short meeting with Peters, he'd put it to him they needed to maintain the investigation's momentum – and the best way he thought they could do that was by an appearance on the national *Crime Alert* TV show. It aired every fortnight and the next programme was scheduled for the following evening. It would be tight, he knew that, putting together something at such short notice that could re-focus the viewers' interest so soon after the earlier appeal; and, yes, he knew there'd be no time to film a reconstruction; but he'd been adamant that was the way they needed to go. The commander had called one of his personal contacts at the TV station direct while Tomlinson had waited in his office. A few pleasantries later, and he'd given the superintendent the news he'd wanted to hear – air-time promised... *if* he could get over there to see the executive producer in the next hour. The editors were already finalising the scripts and would need to decide which of the other stories they'd have to drop to make way for the Wilson case. And before committing to that, they first wanted to talk to the officer leading the investigation. In person.

As he reached his office, Tomlinson realised this would be make or break. For him. For the investigation. If he messed up again, there'd be no more chances. Someone else would be brought in to take over, preventing him keeping his promise to the twins. And he knew any later failings would be blamed on him.

He'd got just under thirty minutes to get himself fully up to speed and to work out how he was going to handle everything. He knew it would be too risky getting Geoff or Anne Wilson up there again in front of the cameras – so he'd have to stick to a straight interview; provide an update and answer the presenter's questions.

Live TV. Nerve-wracking. But necessary.

He consoled himself with the thought that at least there'd be no female reporter in a pink jacket to hi-jack him this time...

For two days, Bryant had kept a low profile at home.

He'd ventured out only once to get money from the hole in the wall, and to buy some food. He'd expected his father to call; to come round; to try to talk him into returning to the hospital. But he'd not been in touch. Bryant had wondered if perhaps his father thought he *was* still in there; in a secure ward, out of harm's way. He'd even considered calling *him* – but, again, the little voice had intervened; had urged caution.

Tell no-one it had repeated.

And this time, he hadn't questioned it.

Worse still – he'd expected the hospital staff to descend on him. To find himself snatched away by men in white coats without warning in the early hours; strait-jacket applied and a needle in the arm to keep him quiet. But, like his father, they'd not come either.

And now, on the third day, he was ready to put his plan into action. He'd already packed his clothes and was checking the rest of what he'd need one final time. Credit cards, money – all there in his wallet; the mobile's battery was topped up; the charger was in his bag; the hard-copy address book was there too. He was ready for the off. Time to book a taxi to the railway station. He dialled a local firm. ETA, ten minutes. Just enough time for a last look round the house.

A few minutes later, he was waiting outside. He gazed around at his neighbours' houses. The well-maintained gardens. The expensive cars on the drives. A slice of suburbia – *superior* suburbia. One he'd been more than happy to buy into for all these years. But now, as he stood there, he realised it all felt strangely *empty*. Devoid of any *real* meaning. That none of it mattered any more...

He was about to question himself – question the *voice* – to see if *it* was responsible for the feelings he was now experiencing but, before he could even attempt an internal dialogue, *something* made him turn to look at one particular house down the far end of his estate. He'd seen the owner a few times, but never spoken to him. He'd guessed that, like himself, the man must have lived alone; out of a suitcase – for there'd never been any sign of a family awaiting his return.

Bryant set his bag down on the pavement at the end of his drive. He stared more intently at the other house. He felt strangely drawn to it; sensed it almost *calling* to him – not with words; but *emotionally*; softly; quietly. It was completely illogical – he knew that. But still he felt somehow compelled to go and see why he felt that way. He began walking slowly up the road towards it. The man's house was similar in style to his own – they all were on the private estate – but at the same time he could feel it was totally different; alien almost. There was just *something* about it; something that didn't feel right. He scanned round at the other properties – but he didn't get the same feeling from any of the others. He kept walking, almost as if he was being pulled there by some magnetic force. Something reeling him in...

Stop! The little voice was suddenly shouting at him. Bruising the insides of his skull with its intensity. *Don't go on! It's a trap!*

But Bryant couldn't help himself. One foot after the other, he kept walking until he reached the gates. His hands had already opened them and suddenly he was there, striding up the block-work drive. He began to feel nauseous, light-headed. He thought he was going to faint and decided to sit down quickly; placed his head between his knees.

Don't let them see you! There was urgency now in the voice's tone. *Don't look at them! Don't –*

But the voice was abruptly cut off. Whatever its intended final warning, Bryant remained in the dark. As well as alone –

He *knew* he shouldn't go any further, but still the house kept calling to him; promising him a place of refuge; somewhere he could just sit back and let everything else disappear. He'd have no more cares. No more worries. No need for a future... He breathed deeply for a few seconds, contemplating the attraction of what was being offered. He stood up; still unable to resist the house's strange appeal. He approached its front door, watched as his hand – almost in slow motion – edged forward to ring the door-bell.

But, before his finger had pressed the button, something strange happened –

The mahogany door became less distinct. The more he looked at it, the more translucent it seemed to become. The wood giving way to a glassy surface; frosted – pitted; but with an image coming into focus on the other side...

He'd been there before.

It was...

The cave –

The place he'd feared. Had not been prepared to enter. And yet, here it was, in broad daylight; so near his own house.

A new thought began suddenly to form in his mind. What was there to be afraid of? The cave had been there all the time. Familiar. Comfortable. Just waiting for him to find it. It all felt so natural...

David...

The cave was calling his name; inviting him in.

He *so* wanted to go inside. He guessed *they* would still be in there. But this time he knew he needn't be afraid; for they'd look after him; they'd help him; do whatever needed to be done. It could all be so simple...

Don't! A final, last-gasp warning from the little voice. Somehow evading their best defences to get the message through.

David... come now... We can help you... came their reply.

Bryant was aware of eyes. Pair upon pair, all suddenly revealing themselves in the gloom; stretching away in every direction as far as he could see; pupils floating in their sea of white; piercing flashes of awareness; scrutinising him; watching his every move; willing him to let go and join them...

A loud noise caught him off guard –

He felt his muscles tense. His shoulders hunched up defensively. And, then, there it was again...

The noise.

The strident, angry-sounding *beep* from the taxi that was waiting beside his house. It was the lifeline he needed.

Immediately, the cave was gone. The eyes disappeared. And the glassy portal to the other-world returned once more to become the indistinct, dark wooden door.

What the hell? Bryant looked – *was* – confused. *How did I get here?*

Go now... The voice was suddenly back again.

The driver lowered his window and shouted up the road to Bryant, 'Hey, mate? You order a taxi?' He'd noticed the discarded bag. And Bryant was the only person he could see on the street.

Instinctively, Bryant gave him a thumbs-up. 'Coming...' he shouted back.

He started running back towards his own driveway. He still didn't know what he'd been doing. How he'd got over there. One moment he'd been outside his house – and, now... He just wanted to get away. Knew he had to. *Now.* Everything else could wait. He grabbed his bag, opened the car's door and climbed in behind the front passenger seat. He stowed the bag quickly in the adjacent foot-well.

'Station, isn't it, mate?' Bryant nodded to the pair of inquisitive eyes that now stared back at him in the mirror.

Eyes. But not *their* eyes.

The driver accelerated slowly away. 'You saying goodbye to someone?'

Bryant ignored the question. A sudden thought uppermost in his mind.

'Actually – sorry, could you make it the *bus* station?' He'd originally booked the taxi for the *train* station. The two were only about a quarter of a mile apart.

'No problem, mate. Bus station it is. Hah – you roughing it ?'

Again, Bryant ignored the question. He fell silent and the driver got the message.

The coach turned out to be more comfortable than Bryant had expected. He'd thought the leg-room might have been a problem, but he'd been lucky. Mid-week, there hadn't been many other passengers, so he'd managed to get a double table by the window; all four seats to himself. He switched off the table-light and stretched out; settled back. He'd not had a chance to buy any drink or food before getting on, but it didn't matter now as he could see there was a trolley service onboard; he'd get something when it came round. He knew he had a long journey ahead – several hours more than the train to Edinburgh would have taken – but he expected it would actually turn out to be an easier trip, because the coach continued on from Edinburgh to Inverness direct; as such, he'd have no connections to worry about.

He unfolded the mini-timetable he'd picked up in the booking office and double-checked the details. Overall journey time, two hours' more. He'd wait until later, then ring Sam to give him an update. He still hoped to be there by mid to late evening. He took out a pair of ear-phones, connected them to his mobile and searched for a radio station to help while away the time. Nothing too demanding – he didn't want news; maybe some easy listening; or a play. He closed his eyes and settled down for a sleep.

He woke to the gentle touch of a hand on his arm. He looked up and saw a waitress with the trolley. He took out his earphones, smiled and asked for a couple of sandwiches, a chocolate bar and a coffee. While he was paying, he also asked for two bottles of mineral water. Still a long way to go – and he could already feel the drying effects of the air-conditioning. He sat up straight and unwrapped the food. He ate half the sandwiches, washing them down with mouthfuls of coffee. Next, he started on the chocolate. More coffee. The rest of the chocolate. And then he was pleasantly full. He decided to save the rest of the sandwiches until later. He was just about to return to his solitary audio-world when something caught his attention – a flicker of recognition in the corner of his eye. He stared out of the window. The coach was labouring slightly, climbing a long steep hill on the motorway, and off to the left in an uncultivated field he could see one of those advertising boards that had become all the rage in recent years; where enterprising farmers had found new ways to make a little spare money – towing an old trailer into position, and letting some shiny ad-man use it to extol the virtues of their client's latest product. Motorways and railway lines the prime locations – and all at a fraction of the cost of hoardings in the cities.

Bryant knew the advert instantly.

It was one of *theirs*. *The Company's...* At its most persuasive. The scene showed a caveman chasing down his quarry – but instead of a spear, he held a laptop. And underneath the picture was the tag-line –

Still the same killer instinct; only the tools have changed...

He'd always liked that advert. Thought it worked well. And on the back of it, he'd secured a huge contract in east Europe. The Company had been happy – and he'd earned a nice little bonus...

But now, this too seemed somehow empty; hollow almost – the same kind of feeling he'd experienced seeing the neighbouring houses on his estate.

He didn't think anything more of it.

He adjusted his ear-phones to get a snug fit, then tuned out, hoping the coach would have eaten up another few hundred miles by the time he woke again.

When Bryant came to, the coach was stationary – surrounded by bumper-to-tail traffic. He looked out the window, craned his neck to see what the problem was. Bored, frustrated and angry faces stared out of their own vehicles all around him. No-one was going anywhere fast. The traffic was completely backed-up.

The coach had been leaving the motorway and had come to a halt half way up a slip-road. He could see rows of vehicles in front being held at red traffic lights; everyone waiting for green; to be on their way again. Bryant had a thought. He pushed a few icons on his mobile's screen and searched for the latest traffic reports. After a few seconds, he found what he was looking for. While he was scrolling down the lines of text, the coach driver made an announcement over the speakers.

'Ladies and gentleman, sorry for the delay. I've just heard from our control room that the police have had to shut the motorway two junctions further on. That's why we've had to come off here. As soon as I have any further information, I'll let you know. Thank you.'

But Bryant *already* had that further information. Being beamed straight to his mobile by satellites overhead.

The 9:50 am Edinburgh inter-city service had been de-railed; roughly ten miles north of his current position. Coaches had been strewn over the tracks, and down onto the adjacent motorway below. Emergency services were at the scene. The motorway had been closed. Hundreds of passengers were believed to have been injured, and many were feared dead...

His heart skipped a beat as the significance of what he was reading began to sink in...

9:50

Edinburgh.

That was the train he would have been on –

Tomlinson was eating the last of the biscuits to which he'd helped himself before leaving the producer's office. He wiped the crumbs from his stubble with the back of a hand. He pushed the call button for the lift and waited, rocking up and down on his heels. There was a *ping* and the doors in front of him opened. He stepped forward without even thinking– and bumped into a familiar face. The other man seemed taken aback just for a second; then, as one, each spoke the other's name.

'*Ray?*'

'*Mick?*'

Both men laughed, broad smiles breaking out on their faces. Tomlinson edged backwards, giving the man room to exit the lift. They shook hands warmly, patted one another on the back, and then both started to speak; again talking over one another.

'What are you...?'

'Small world...'

'Wait, now – on you go...'

'No, Mick; *you* first...'

'Well... my God, Ray.' The man's estuary English was as pronounced as ever. A rough diamond, but a policeman worth his weight in gold. Tomlinson stared into his dark, inquisitive eyes. The man's short hair was still jet black; the only tell-tale signs of stress the deep lines carved into an otherwise youthful-looking face. 'Good to see you. It's been what? Five years?'

'Six.'

'*Six?* Jeez – where does the time go?' Mick shook his head. 'Hey, you know what?' The man started to laugh. 'I saw you on the news the other night. Hah, what a balls-up. That reporter, though; she was a bit of alright... Pushy, though...'

Tomlinson spread his hands in mock apology. 'What can I

say? Guess I'm not a natural-born performer...'

Mick was suddenly very serious, all traces of levity gone. 'I'm sorry about those kids. Grim, what with the murders as well. You've got your hands full there, no mistake.' He looked knowingly at Tomlinson. 'And let me guess, Peters is on your back, yeah?'

'No surprises there.'

'He's just worried he's not going to get promoted.'

'Well, Peters, aside, I'm running out of leads. And *that's* why I'm here. Been in to see the *Crime Alert* team. We're doing a fresh appeal tomorrow...'

'Then we're partners in crime...'

The penny dropped. 'You've got a meeting, too?'

'Yeah – got to see a... Richard Foster...'

'Right, that's who I was just with.' Mick raised an inquisitive eyebrow and, in reply, Tomlinson offered, 'He's OK. Not much for small-talk; but seems to know what he's doing.'

'Suits me just fine.'

'So, what's your case? Must be important if you're getting air-time for it.'

'Serious assault on a WPC. Lucky for me, the DAC's agreed we should take a stand. You know, send out a message to the public – and the scum responsible. If we let them get away with it, where do you draw the line? It's already bad enough the sentences the courts hand out. Not like the old days, is it?' Mick sighed heavily. 'There's just no respect for the uniform any more...'

'She's one of yours?'

'Yeah – only finished her training six months ago. Good team round her. Plenty of experience there. It was just supposed to be routine crowd control at the football...' A wave of anger suddenly washed over the man's face. He spat out the words... 'Some bastards got her separated from the others, cornered her and then gave her a right kicking.' He shook his head, as if blaming himself. 'No intel from the football unit; no reason for it. But I *should* have been more careful...' Mick's face had absolute determination etched into it; the worry lines ploughing ever deeper into his ridged brow. 'She's in intensive care. Touch and go. And if she *does* make it, she'll probably have brain damage. And for what? Because some kid wanted to make a name for himself...' He punched the wall hard. 'I'll get them, Ray! You watch if I don't!'

Tomlinson didn't know what to say. They'd all been there at one time or another. If not you, then it was your partner...

Occupational hazard – risk of the job.

Mick took a deep breath and regained his composure, glad to

have been able to vent some of his anger. At least for a while. For he knew it would be back; his unconscious fixated on nothing else. 'Hey, but listen,' he continued, 'you free to stick around for a bit? Be good if we could get a quick pint? Catch up?'

'Yes – we can do that. Let me think, now.' Tomlinson tried to remember if he'd seen a pub on his way there. He couldn't recall one. But he asked, 'there's a hotel isn't there? Out the front of the building; then turn left? Hundred yards?'

'Yeah – you're right; I know where you mean. It's the *Springfield*.' Tomlinson nodded; he'd seen the name; silver on a blue background. 'Used to be the *Lowesmore* before that. Next door to the copier shop. Yeah, that's got a bar.' Mick clearly knew the area better than Tomlinson did. And rightly so. For that's where detective inspector Mick Bancroft had started his career with the Met twenty years earlier.

'Alright. Well, I'll go and wait for you there.'

'Yeah – OK. And, Ray?'

'Yes?'

'Mine's a pint of bitter. You get them in.'

Same old Mick...

'I'm *so* sorry I'm late...'

'That's alright.' Sam Girvan wasn't at all bothered. These days, he had all the time in the world. He shook his friend's hand. 'Here, let me take that for you.' Bryant passed him the bag. 'Travelling light?'

'Oh, you know, the basics. Sure I can buy anything else I need up here. I take it they do have shops?'

'Well, just the one...' Sam replied, leading his visitor to where he'd parked the car.

They stopped beside a blue Land Rover Defender. Bryant wasn't going to say anything at first, but then couldn't resist it.

'Hey, this isn't very eco-friendly is it?' He patted the roof with one hand. 'Or are you going to tell me it runs on bio-fuel?'

'No. Diesel. Guilty as charged.' Sam opened the rear door and placed the bag inside.

'I'm *very* disappointed in you.'

'Well, eco-friendly's one thing. But heavy snowfalls are another. It's all a question of balance. You should see Neve's car, though. That runs on hot air...'

'Hm – right.' Bryant did his best not to sound convinced. 'I'll tell her you said that...'

'She won't believe you. She's blinded by her love for me...'

There was the word again.

Blind.

He'd tell him later. Sam *and* Neve. Tell them everything. He half-expected the little voice to chip in; but all was quiet.

'You thirsty? Hungry?' Sam asked. 'There's tea and home-made cake in here somewhere...'

'Wouldn't say no.'

'Now... where is it?' The rear of the Land Rover was full of kit and the small back-pack containing the food and drink had somehow buried itself away during Sam's drive down. He pushed a pile of blankets and an assortment of breakdown paraphernalia to one side; moving a pair of mud-encrusted walking boots out of the way. 'Ah, here we are... Sorry about the mess. You never know when you're going to need something. So, I find it best to carry everything, just in case...' He handed over the back-pack and gestured that Bryant should get in up front; he then closed the rear door and a few moments later settled himself into the seat next to his friend. 'Help yourself... plenty more cake in the tin at home.'

Bryant unscrewed the thermos' cup, opened the lid and poured himself some tea. He placed the drink on the dashboard while he looked for the cake; the windscreen steamed up immediately. He wiped at it with the back of his hand.

'Sorry, I'll just be a minute.'

Sam smiled and waited patiently while his friend found the food, ate a few mouthfuls and drank the tea.

'OK, now?'

Bryant nodded. He screwed the lid shut again and replaced the cup. 'Right, let's go.' He glanced down to the clock in the console. 11:29 pm.

Noting his interest in the time, Sam offered, 'should be home... one-ish; quarter past. It's the A9 all the way. Good fast road – and there won't be much else this time of night.' He started the engine and turned on the radio.

They'd been driving north out of Inverness for about ten minutes and had just crossed over the Kessock Bridge when the travel news came on.

'... *Police say they expect the motorway to remain closed for at least another twenty-four hours...*'

Sam pushed the mute button.

'Don't suppose you've seen the pictures, have you?' Bryant hadn't. He'd deliberately avoided calling them up on his mobile. He'd had his fill of carnage, and didn't want to see any more dead bodies. Not yet. Not ever. He shook his head. 'I caught them on the lunch-time news,' Sam continued. 'Those poor people. What a mess. They might get the motorway open in another day, but the main-line, that'll be out of action for weeks, I'd say...'

Bryant suddenly felt he needed air. He lowered the window. A cold blast shocked him, made his eyes water. He waited a few moments, then put the window up again. He tilted his head back slightly and blinked rapidly to dry his eyes.

'And *you*... you had one hell of a lucky escape. Till I got your call, I thought you'd been on there. As soon as we saw the news, I tried calling you – but there was no answer.' He fell silent, then added, sombrely, 'I really thought the worst, you know...'

'Sorry, Sam. Didn't mean to worry you. I meant to call – but kept putting it off. I was just so tired. I didn't think. It didn't even occur to me you'd be worried.' He apologised again. 'Sorry.'

'Well, I'm just glad you're alright.' Sam waited a moment, then asked, 'Was the train full? Couldn't you get a seat?'

'What? No – I just...' Bryant knew he could hardly mention the voice he was hearing in his head; his friend would think he'd gone totally mad; so he offered, '... thought it'd be quieter; an easier journey; that's all.'

Sam seemed to accept his line of reasoning. He pushed the mute again but accidentally spun the volume dial in doing so. Deafening music suddenly pounded out. 'Whoa – *too* loud!' He quickly turned the dial again and the decibel level fell away.

'What, too loud even for you, Mr Heavy Metal?'

'It is this time of night.' Sam fiddled again, then gave up on the radio. Instead he selected the CD. 'There, that's better – bit of local Scots rock.' Bryant heard a melodic, rocky guitar instrumental kick in. 'This track's by a friend of mine; based up on the north coast, near Thurso. What do you think?'

'Hey, that's not bad...'

'*Not bad*? It's bloody brilliant, you Philistine!'

'Alright, it's *bloody brilliant!*'

'Thank you.'

Bryant listened until the track finished. The music certainly had an edge to it; you could hear its Scottish overtones through and through; rhythmic drumming mixed with lilting, soaring notes.

'Yes, that *was* good. What's it called?'

'*Eagle Watching Over Me*. Apparently, he was up walking in the mountains one day, and just sat there watching this eagle circling overhead. Melody came to him straight away...'

Watching Over Me.

Bryant fell silent.

Tomlinson had only bought himself a half, knowing he'd have to get back to the incident room before too long. And while he'd have loved to go on an all-nighter with Mick, he couldn't afford to.

'You going soft on us?' asked Mick, seeing the half and throwing himself down into the seat opposite the other man. 'Cheers!' He drained three-quarters of his pint in one go. He exhaled loudly. 'Ah, needed that.' He undid his tie and fumbled in a pocket for a packet of cigarettes.

'Now, you *know* I'll have to arrest you if you light up in here.'

The man snorted in disgust and put the pack away. 'Bloody government!'

'Ah, come on – you know it's good for you...'

For the next hour, the two men talked about old times; and let each other know what they'd been up to since last working together. Mick Bancroft had still been a detective sergeant back then. He'd learnt a lot from Tomlinson. Knew he'd been lucky to have worked under him.

'So, that's the plan,' Tomlinson was saying. 'Head off to the sun...'

But Mick didn't want to hear about his retirement. He was more interested in something he'd heard on the grapevine.

'So what's all this about you digging up bodies in Scotland? Busman's holiday, was it?'

Tomlinson shook his head in mock disbelief. 'News travels fast – even to your far flung corner of the empire... And just *where* did you hear that?'

'Ah, sorry, Ray.' Mick tapped his nose and winked. 'Can't reveal my sources...'

'Hm – well, then... Met canteen?'

'Maybe... maybe not...'

'Alright, at least let me set the record straight. *I* didn't dig up *any* bodies. They were *already* there. No, see... Brenda and I were touring the west coast. We'd driven the Road to the Isles; a few other day trips; and we were staying in Oban. She'd been flicking through the hotel brochures one night and saw this place, *Kilmartin*. A whole valley packed with ancient monuments. Greatest concentration in the UK, apparently. Anyway, so off we go. And there's me, expecting a nice quiet day out; coffee shop; museum; stretching the legs... and what happens? A bunch of archaeologists have come across three bodies. So I'm left holding the fort...'

'Dare I say it, if they *were* murdered, I think the killer's long gone by now...'

Tomlinson nodded, letting the other man's humour wash over him. 'I know, should have been routine. But you know what? There *was* something odd about it. I said there were three bodies. Man, woman and a child. Well, the last two were pretty badly decomposed... no flesh, just bones; as you'd expect after all this time. Although, having said that, I remember some of the clothing had survived – and the archaeologists couldn't really explain that. Bodies decomposed, but fabric still there. Odd. Something to do with anomalies in the soil conditions was their best explanation. Anyway, the man, *he* was *much* better preserved. That's why they felt it necessary to get us involved. In case he wasn't old at all; you know, someone murdered recently and just dumped there; made to look like he was some historic corpse...'

'And was he?'

'*No*. Mind you, I didn't know that at the time. What happened was, I got a courtesy call from one of the local sergeants a few weeks later. He confirmed there was no need for any further enquiries. Foul play, *yes*... but a *very* long time ago! And the archaeological group also confirmed that in a subsequent e-mail which he also forwarded to me. Apparently, all *three* bodies were carbon-dated to around two thousand BC.'

'Interesting. You know what, Ray? You're in the wrong job...'

'Oh?'

'Yeah – you should've been an archaeologist...'

'Right?'

'... or a grave-digger...'

Tomlinson laughed. 'No, I'll stick to the day-job, thanks. Speaking of which, I do need to get back.'

'Sure you can't stay for another?'

'Can't, sorry.' Both men stood up. 'Right, guess I'll see you at the studio tomorrow...' Tomlinson shook his friend's hand.

'Yeah – see you then, Ray.'

Watching Over Me.

Bryant focussed on the significance of the words. It certainly seemed someone was watching over him. Keeping him out of harm's way. First, the *plane*. And now, the *train*. But –

No, he wouldn't allow himself to dwell on it. He was being stupid.

It was just chance.

Nothing more. Nine lives, that was all.

But nine had become eight. And eight seven...

Six...

From somewhere in his mind, there was a distant echo of the voice. Not quite there with him; out of reach; but not altogether gone.

Six?

He pondered the thought for a moment. Why six? He couldn't recall anything else happening to him... And then, he was suddenly *there* –

The ground thick with fresh streams of browns, russets and gold; the river of leaves blown free from the branches overhead; his boots slipping on the ground beneath; muddy, damp earth stains on his trousers' knees where he'd fallen; the dormant, decaying smell he always associated with autumnal woodlands.

And then he remembered...

A vivid flash of panic. The prison of his own making. No longer fun. But *deadly* instead. No way out. And his father's sudden appearance; towering above him – strong hands pulling him to safety. Lifting him out of the hole. The underground den he'd created collapsing all around him.

Seconds away from being buried alive.

The care-free seven year old.

Who otherwise would never have reached eight...

CHAPTER TEN

BRYANT SLEPT LIKE a log.

Maybe it had been the change of scene, his new-found freedom after months of hospitalisation, or the restorative powers of the clean Highlands air – possibly a little of each – but either way his body had taken the rest it needed and he only surfaced late into the afternoon. He looked a little sheepish as he wandered into the kitchen. He found Neve and Katie busily folding sheets in the adjacent utility room. Katie, not long back from school, was still in her uniform.

'Hello,' Bryant said quietly.

'Hello,' Katie called back.

'Someone slept well. Would you like something to eat?' Neve asked, leaving her daughter to finish putting the laundry away. Neve had already been fast asleep when Sam had arrived with Bryant early that morning. 'It's lovely to meet you at long last, David.'

Although the two of them had spoken briefly on the phone over the years, they'd never actually met before.

'Yes, please – I'm famished.' He genuinely did feel hungry and, as if to reinforce the point, his stomach rumbled of its own accord.

'Let's see now,' Neve glanced at the clock, 'Sam shouldn't be much more than an hour, so, if you don't want to ruin your appetite before dinner, I could make you something light – soup, or a sandwich?'

'Anything, whatever's easiest. Really I don't want to put you to any trouble.'

Neve picked up on his awkwardness and tried to put him at ease; and succeeded. 'Here, have a seat.' She gestured to one of the chairs round the kitchen table. 'Katie could probably find room for a sandwich as well, couldn't you, darling?'

'Yeah!' Katie abandoned the last of the sheets, and made a beeline for the fridge. She yanked the door open and peered inside. 'There's cheese... ham... chicken... beef... coleslaw... salad...' She rattled through what seemed to Bryant to be the entire contents, then turned to await his order. Bryant noticed the slight Scots lilt in her accent.

Neve caught his eye. 'So, what's it to be?'

'Alright, well, how about some cheese?'

Katie nodded her approval. A good choice, it seemed. 'Brown bread, white or rolls?' she asked.

'Brown will be fine, thanks.'

'Mum, can I have some chicken?'

'Yes, but don't take too much.'

'OK.' Katie set about her creations, taking over the work surface next to the sink.

'Would you like a tea or a coffee?' Neve asked.

'A cup of tea would be good, thank you.'

'Coming up.' She flicked the switch on the kettle.

'Chip off the old block?' Bryant asked, indicating Katie. 'She'll be running this place before long.'

'Yes, she's very good; aren't you, darling?' Katie beamed back a smile.

'Listen, thanks for the room,' Bryant began. 'As I said to Sam, I'm more than happy to pay...'

'*No*, don't be silly; we wouldn't hear of it. And you know you're welcome to stay as long as you like. Besides, it's only the old box room. If we weren't full, you could have had one of the guest rooms...'

Bryant knew she was being modest. *Box room* certainly didn't do it justice. While there *was* only space for a single bed, it was a lovely room; tastefully decorated – and with the most amazing views to the mountains and sea. But more than that, it was part of their personal space. Sam and Neve had invited him into their own home. He was *family* – not *guest*. He knew money was tight for them and it was clear they wouldn't accept payment from him. But he resolved there and then to do something to repay the kindness; one day, when the right opportunity arose.

Cup of tea and sandwich duly arrived within a minute of one another.

'Thank you,' he said to Katie, as she set a plate down in front of him. 'That looks *filling*.' She'd not been sparing with the bread – two huge chunks surrounded an equally generous layer of cheese.

Katie sat down opposite Bryant to tuck in to her own pre-dinner snack. Bryant couldn't help smiling. The girl's obvious contentment was infectious. He saw that she'd inherited her father's height and his – *once* – dark hair; that, and her mother's good looks. In the years to come, he guessed she'd break a few hearts. But pretty as she was, it was something else that caught Bryant's attention. It was her *eyes*. Deep pools of grey – light, bright, and so full of life. But there was more to it even than that –

And, then, he was suddenly reminded of the eyes in the other-worldly cave...

The taxi driver staring back at him in the rear-view mirror...

Instantly, he let the thoughts go; refused to allow his psyche to dwell on them. He let *himself* go; allowed himself to slip free from the memory of it all. For he'd left *that* world behind. A world of anxiety, uncertainty; and a faltering – *his* faltering – mind. No place for any of it any more...

He was free now. Wasn't he? At least, for a little while.

He felt at once self-conscious, as he realised Katie was staring at him. No, not *at* him – but *through* him. No, it wasn't that either – she was staring *into* him. And that's when he thought he understood it. Realised what that *something* was. Her eyes – it was as if they were observing another dimension; looking beyond the physical. He began to feel awkward again; thought his very *soul* was being subjected to scrutiny under her intense gaze. He looked down at his plate, breaking eye contact, fearing she might uncover his secrets; unearth his troubled months of recovery. He dared a fleeting glance – but the girl's only interest now lay in wolfing down the last of her sandwich. He wondered if he was being stupid, paranoid; if he'd just imagined it all. He quickly concluded he *was* being paranoid; an understandable mental fall-out from recent events. Only natural he still needed more time – to get back to *normal...*

'Mum, can I leave the table, please? I want to go and get changed.' Her mother nodded and Katie left the kitchen. Footsteps thudded on a stairwell, crossed the ceiling above them, then grew fainter as the girl headed off to her bedroom.

'She's great. You and Sam must be really proud of her.'

'Yes, we are. And we're lucky... she loves it up here as much as we do. Oh, you always worry, don't you? I mean, it's one thing for us as adults, but it's harder for kids to leave the world they know behind... but she's fitted in really well; made lots of new friends at school. Getting good reports. And there's always something to keep her busy – dancing classes; sleep-overs; trips away.'

'You don't ever worry? You know, running the B&B? All those strangers under your roof?'

Neve shrugged her shoulders. 'No, not really. It's not like down south. Everyone who's stayed has been really friendly. We always get their home details in advance – more for cancellations than anything else. Touch wood, we've never had any trouble. And...' she pointed to a door over in the corner, 'that leads through to the breakfast room. Our bit of the house is self-contained anyway; we *can* lock the connecting door if we want.'

Bryant nodded, intrigued at the sudden insight that he'd been conditioned into accepting such a southern-focussed mindset. Maybe in a few days' time, he'd be able to experience the difference for himself. Be more open. More trusting. He hoped so.

'You're pleased you made the break, then?'

'Best thing we ever did.' Neve looked reflective for a second. 'And the best thing for Sam, too. Oh, he never made a fuss about it, but I know all that commuting, the long hours, the endless demands at work

– they were all wearing him down. He's had a whole new lease of life since we moved. And he's lost a couple of stone since getting away from his desk. He looks ten years younger; don't you think?'

'*Ten years younger?* Then he'll be a match for you now...'

'I wish...' Neve laughed. 'No, I've still plenty of worry lines; it's just the slap on top that stops you seeing them...'

'Never...' Bryant thought Neve looked radiant. She didn't need make-up. Her shoulder-length brown hair framed her pretty, oval face; and light freckles added to her youthful look. Before today, he'd only ever seen the photos of her – and Katie – that Sam had sent over the web; not forgetting the obligatory wedding snap that had come through the post with the boxed piece of wedding cake. He suddenly regretted not making the time to get to their wedding – but work, as always, had dictated his life. 'I envy you, you know; and respect you both.' He was being entirely honest. 'Not sure I could be that brave. Wouldn't want to miss out on all my home comforts...'

Neve smiled. 'It's surprising what you don't miss when you can't afford it. Makes you appreciate what's *really* important in life.'

'Wise words. I'll drink to that.' Bryant raised his tea. 'Long may your good life continue...'

'Right, better get the dinner on. Pork chops and vegetables OK?' She took his plate and cup.

'Sounds great.'

'It'll be about an hour. Have a wander round outside if you like. Take in the scenery. Sam won't be too long, and I'll give you a call in plenty of time anyway.'

'I will, thanks.'

Bryant followed his nose, out through the utility room to the back door and then on to the patio beyond. He noticed a gravel path curving away in front of him, climbing a slight incline, bordering a neatly-mown lawn. He decided to take the path, see where it led him. Its length was deceptive, and it continued up the slope further than he'd anticipated. He turned back to look at the house, taking a moment to breathe deeply, to fill his lungs with the air of freedom – a freedom he had every intention of enjoying to the full. He exhaled slowly, letting go of the recent months' tensions as he did so. He felt momentarily light-headed, but not in an unpleasant, dizzying way. Rather, it was more of an ethereal experience, as if he was acclimatising to his new surroundings; becoming one with the place.

Turning on his heel, he continued up the path – and discovered just what a place it was...

He'd been to many countries in his life. Had seen many different landscapes. But none were a match for the living canvas on which nature had seen fit to paint the scene before him. The vista was nothing less than stunning. Sam and Neve's plot was perched high on a flat plateau that afforded uninterrupted views, stretching thirty – perhaps fifty – miles out, in whichever direction he looked. Rough pasture merged with woodland on the slopes below, but gorse was conspicuous by its dominance – the invasive plant voraciously eating up any spare land that man had failed to tame. And, beyond, the hillsides fell by increasing degrees to join the lower-lying terrain where tree-lines snaked their way, following unseen water courses. Browns and greens carpeted the valleys, their colours ever-changing – at once vivid, then dulled – as bursts of sunlight occasionally streamed through the scudding clouds. And to the east, where the earth simply ran out of land, the sea took over – a vivid blue, edged with faint beaches of gold; a blanket of sparkling sapphire; a natural infinity pool, where the sea met the sky. Bryant could make out small villages, the houses dotted along the coastline – every so often, plumes of drifting white smoke suggesting someone was home. He turned and looked north, then north-west to the higher lands; to the serried ranks of mountain tops, some of which already wore mantles of snow.

Bryant felt intoxicated by the beauty of it all...

Had one of *those* moments – so rare, so precious, and yet so completely overwhelming... Understood that Nature herself was speaking to him – not with words; but that she was now reaching deep into his being; reconnecting him at some profound level to an awareness he'd long since forgotten even existed; that had seen itself first marginalized, then locked away when adulthood had taken over his life; when he, like so many others, had reached a point of exclusion; had shut himself off from further inter-action with the natural world. Long gone the care-free days as a child, playing in a summer garden; walking through the woods with a favourite grand-parent; or building a dam in the stream on a holiday in Wales. Nature no longer *there*; but relegated instead to something he only saw on television, or read about in a Sunday supplement...

Bryant closed his eyes to enjoy the feeling *inwardly*; allowing Nature's voice to continue its unspoken dialogue, to immerse himself in its primeval potency.

Life without – now beating within.

His whole body felt strengthened, invigorated, filled with a boundless energy. He wished he could stay there forever, just enjoying the moment.

But a low pulsing broke his concentration –

His eyes flicked open. The physical beauty of the landscape was still there, mountain ridges fixedly returning his gaze – but the *connection* had gone; and Nature's voice had fallen silent once more. *Unlike* the pulsing.   Short bursts of sound.   Repetitive. Hypnotic. That grew louder. Then quieter. Then louder again. That seemed to bore deep into his body, causing vibrating at his core.

Bryant looked – *listened* – to find where the sound was coming from. He moved several paces to the east. Nothing. He turned quickly back to the north. The pulsing was there again, but it seemed to be *off-centre* – like someone adjusting the balance on a set of speakers. He ran back down the path, reached the patio. Intuitively, he tried to focus on where he thought the mid-point *ought* to be...

He set off again, uphill once more, scrambling up the lawn but this time heading further away from the house. He picked up speed. Ran, until the lawn stopped. Until the grass thickened, became more coarse.

And then he saw it – a derelict building.

Still he ran.

Only Bryant realised straightaway that it wasn't a building; but it *was* part of a structure – that he could see, and one that, while seemingly ill-defined, soon took on a cohesion of form under his gaze. One by one, the pieces fell into place. Tall slabs of stone. Weathered. All similar, yet universally different. Arranged. Set out in a pattern at the brow of the hill.

He had it.

He was so nearly there now. Lost his footing on the grass. Recovered from the fall. Kept going. Threw himself into the centre –

Of the stone circle.

Instantly, the rhythmic pulsing ceased.

He spun round, confused...

The only sound now Sam Girvan's voice. 'So, what do you think?' he asked.

Sam had finished work early, keen to get back to spend time with his friend. His arrival had put out Neve's timings, so she'd sent the pair away for another half hour until dinner was ready. The two men had sat on the patio, a glass of island malt in hand, toasting to friendship, new beginnings, the quiet life.

Or, rather, Sam had.

For though Sam didn't notice, Bryant had actually said very little; nodding on autopilot; raising his glass on cue. But Bryant had been seriously distracted, his mind elsewhere, trying to make sense of what was happening to him. The sounds – the pulsing; the droning. And the things he'd seen – lights at the church; the blinding whiteness. The fears he still held for his sight – there one minute, gone the next.

Quite apart from the strange visual distortion he'd experienced – sounds and vision blurring one into the other. He remembered then what they'd said to him. That he *must* contact them. Immediately. If *anything* untoward happened. If he took a downturn. He felt a fear rising in him. So sudden. Draining him of confidence, of the new-found calmness. He didn't want to tell them. They'd lock him away again. He knew it. Was sure they would. And then there was the little voice that lived inside his head. What would they make of *that*? Even he was beginning to doubt himself, but they'd take it as proof he'd lost his sanity. He couldn't go through more treatment. He simply didn't have the strength for it.

But the train –

The three words slammed headlong into his mental confusion, momentarily derailing his doubts.

Wait. Yes, he reasoned, the voice had *warned* him. It had. And that *proved* it existed. It must do? Mustn't it?

So many questions. But no answers.

His mind had still been buzzing when they'd all sat down to eat. He'd managed to feign some semblance of normality during the meal, but it had been a real struggle. He'd made casual conversation, asking Katie how she liked her new home, what she wanted to do when she left school. And Sam, he remembered, he'd been talking about work. And about how modern-day crofters had to have other jobs just to make ends meet. But all the time, his attention had been elsewhere, focussed on his own questions; trying to fathom out what was happening to him.

Then, a *single* question. One he *could* answer.

'Refill?' Neve asked, fresh pot of coffee in hand.

She'd set out a plate of shortbread on the table. Bryant had resisted so far, the meal more than filling.

'Please,' he answered, holding his cup – and wandering mind – steady, as Neve topped him up.

'Help yourself to milk. And *do* have one,' she nodded at the biscuits. 'There's plenty more where they came from.'

'She buys them by the forklift-load,' Sam chipped in. 'Now, I know the guests expect them – trappings of Highland hospitality and all that – but I keep telling her, it's selling out to consumerism; making *The Man* richer. What she should be doing is the home-baking thing...'

'As if I don't have enough to do?'

'Just saying...'

'Well don't.'

Bryant didn't really want anything else to eat, but he took one of the pale, sugared fingers anyway so as not to offend. He balanced it on his saucer as he leaned forward for the milk. He added a dash, stirred his coffee, absently gazing round the small sitting room.

The three of them – Katie had already gone to her room – had taken up position for what remained of the evening. It was all very homely. All very Neve and Sam, he thought. Understated comfort. Hand-painted water-colours on the stone walls. A fireplace as the central feature. Two sofas that had seen better days given a new lease of life, thanks to a pair of matching throws. Assorted tables positioned carefully, and wherever gaps presented themselves, eclectic reading material piled at their bases. *Who'd live in a house like this?* Sam Girvan, that's who. Books on healing, crystals, and earth energies comfortably rubbing shoulders with a popular tome on the history of the universe. Not forgetting the pamphlet on quantum mechanics awaiting the hand of an interested reader. And to lighten the cerebral load, a glossy hardback of Scottish landscapes – one of Neve's, Bryant guessed; that, and the accompanying guide to woodland trees. Several walking maps and a week-old local paper completed the informal, *ad hoc* library of their life.

Something for everyone. Everything for no-one person.

A clock chimed quietly in the corner, signalling another hour passed. Sam got up and went over to the TV.

'Do you mind if I put the headlines on?'

Bryant shook his head. Not like Sam, he thought to himself. He was sure his friend had told him years back he'd given up watching the news, or reading the papers – too full of the horrors of the world; bad news story after bad news story; all far too depressing.

'You've changed. Thought you didn't watch any of this nonsense anymore?'

'Well,' said Sam, 'it's not quite so bad... not now they've brought back the *And Finally* section. You know, bit of good news to round off the gloom. Gives us all a bit of hope, doesn't it?' He shrugged his shoulders then said, 'Besides, I suppose even I realised you can't cut yourself off completely. Now,' he was on the mock defensive, 'I don't watch *that* much...' He looked across at Neve. 'There's your *real* newshound. Always got something on. No, you can't escape it, not even up here in the wilds ...'

The TV was small by Bryant's standards – a far cry from the monumental flat-screen that took up almost an entire wall in his lounge – but adequate for the size of his friends' room. He didn't recognise the brand name. It certainly wasn't flat-screen. And there was no chance it would be HD. But there was a set-top box attached, so he guessed they received at least some digital channels. He couldn't see a video or DVD player. He wondered if they even had time to watch any programmes they might record.

He suddenly felt uncomfortable, aware he was being

judgemental, snobbish even; comparing his own living standards to theirs. To the very people who'd so generously opened their door to him. As he thought about it, he wondered how many others in his contacts list he could have counted on in that way. Not many. And maybe not any...

He felt a flush of shame. Tried to bury the vestiges of the old Bryant who still lay within him. The Bryant who avoided insecurity by thinking instead about the size of his pay-packet. Whose self-validation came from being financially better off than his peers. The same thought, he knew, that surely filled the minds of a million other executives the world over.

Echoes of that Bryant still wanted to get back in the game, wanted to be a player once more, wanted to do The Company's bidding.

He drew a long mental breath. Wanted a few moments respite from it all. Focussed instead on the television, where a man and woman were on screen. The man was older, *gravitas* in his voice. Bryant noticed straightaway how every other sentence had been verbally choreographed to allow the younger newsreader, an attractive blonde, to pick up from where the man left off. A double-act worthy of the old music halls, peddling their routine to an expectant crowd. The only difference that the grease paint and lime-light had been exchanged for satellite coverage and Wi-Fi.

Without consciously being aware of what he was taking in, Bryant suddenly realised he'd reached a decision.

He had to trust someone.

And who better than Sam and Neve? It felt so... *right*.

He was going to tell them his whole story – the crash, his blindness, *three* lucky escapes, and the strange experiences he'd been having...

Including his friendly little voice –

Besides, what had he got to worry about, he reasoned? They were open-minded. And look at Sam – he'd been into far stranger things for a very long time. Next to his crop circles, Mayan calendars and spirit orbs, a few neural tricks of the brain weren't going to faze him. The man had his very own stone circle for goodness' sake...

And maybe – just maybe – they could shed light on all this...

Bryant paused, expecting the little voice to pipe up; thinking it would warn him off. Waited for it to say that *telling no-one* must include Sam and Neve. But there was nothing. He waited a second longer. Silence.

He exhaled purposefully, and prepared to dive in...

Tomlinson was seething.

Inwardly angry at the realisation he was being manipulated. But he was managing to keep his emotions in check. Just.

Not that it was an easy thing to do with the camera on him. As soon as this was over, he meant to give the production team a piece of his mind. So much for their promise to drop a story to make time for his case. They'd done no such thing. Instead, they'd knocked a few minutes off the time-slots for the other stories and had shoe-horned his investigation into the closing moments of the programme. He'd spent longer in make-up...

'So, Superintendent,' the presenter was saying, 'can you tell our viewers what it is you need? What can they do to help with your investigation?'

He wondered if the host was playing to the cameras, or being entirely earnest. He hoped the former, otherwise it took dumbing-down to a whole new level. He felt like saying *Call! Call, stupid!* prefaced with several expletives, but he knew the case was far too important – even if the TV station didn't seem to think so – to let his pride get in the way. So, he swallowed his irritation, loosened the tightening in his jaw, and prepared for his moment. He cleared his throat.

'Thank you. Yes Er... as you know, we held a press conference earlier this week to appeal for information into the deaths of Ivy and Percy Wilson; but the priority remains finding their grand-children – Harry and Emily....'

Tomlinson caught a movement out of the corner of his eye. It was the floor manager trying to wind-up proceedings. He was running out of time. He knew it. The pressure was on. Uncharacteristically, he suddenly felt flustered, started to stumble over his words. He feared this was going to be as *professional* as last time.

The presenter, though, *was* a pro and stepped in to help him. 'So, I think what you're saying is... you still need the public to call?'

'Yes, er... that's right.' He could feel his face going red. 'Please don't leave it to others. Please, make the call yourself.'

He could hear the programme's theme tune being played. God, how could he have made such a mess of it again? He'd had it all worked out. Had done his homework. Had been fully up to speed.

'We'll be back with an update after the late film. And remember, *your call counts...*'

As the lights faded throughout the studio, the editing suite quartered the viewers' screens and put up stills from the evening's main cases. Tomlinson glanced at the stage monitor – no sign of the twins' new picture he'd so insistently been told to bring with him.

'OK, everyone, we're off-air; take a break.'

People started to mill around, unclipping microphones, moving cameras, gathering up the stand-by scripts. But for the police, the evening was only just beginning. Time for the storm after the calm. Each team of detectives hoping they'd get the breakthrough they needed. And Tomlinson was no different.

But there were no caller-waiting lights showing on his console...

Neve sat quietly still as Sam returned Bryant's gaze. But where his friend's face showed expectant anxiety, Sam's seemed blank, as if lost in thought. Which, he was. For Sam, it wasn't that he found Bryant's revelations unsettling. More, it was the *change* he was seeing in the other man. That the narrow-minded Bryant he knew from old was prepared even to *begin* to contemplate the possibility that *something else* was going on, that factors outside his control – seemingly beyond rational explanation – might be affecting his life, *that* to Sam was the real shocker. And that he *did* find disconcerting.

Sam steepled his fingers, searching for the right words to break the silence. For someone usually so easy-going, he was finding it remarkably difficult. It was just *so* unlike his friend. All the years of playful ridicule he'd endured at Bryant's expense...

He suddenly had a nagging doubt.

His *own* little voice of reason hinting at a question he didn't really want to consider. But he did so all the same. What if all this was a pretence, some well-crafted wind-up? He couldn't entirely put it past the other man. He'd had his moments before. But even as he sat there, watching his friend, he knew this was different. He could read the sincerity in Bryant's eyes, as well as the confusion; a look that was asking for help; that was reaching out to him for the answers...

'David,' Sam said at last. 'From you, that's quite something...' Still Bryant studied him, not even a smile of irony, a raise of the shoulders. 'Well, I can't pretend to have all the answers... because I don't. But,' he continued, hoping to offer reassurance, 'I think there's someone I know who might be able to help you. If you'd like, I can fix up a meeting. His name is...'

But Bryant wasn't listening.

His attention had switched elsewhere. Away from Sam. To the TV. Seemingly transfixed now by one of the four stills. An image from a football match. Date stamped in one corner. A shape – a person – being attacked, there on the ground. A crowd of onlookers behind.

Bryant stared at the screen, stunned.

The timing, he thought, it *had* to be wrong. He re-read the numbers. But he wasn't imagining it. The evidence was there, right in front of him.

'The date…' he mouthed silently under his breath. 'But how?'
It defied belief.
And then, there, in the background was a face.
The face of someone he'd never forget.
The face of a *dead* man.
The man who'd been sitting next to him on the plane –

CHAPTER ELEVEN

TOMLINSON LEANED BACK in his chair, craning his neck to look past the divider screens to the far side of the studio. There, the phones were all busy. People milled purposefully around. Eager hands snatched papers as soon as they were offered. Mick Bancroft's island of desks was a hive of activity.

Unlike the superintendent's.

It was fifteen minutes since they'd gone off-air, and still there'd been no calls.

'Just need to give it time,' offered Riley.

Tomlinson sighed hard. 'I hope you're right.' He pulled himself closer to the desk. 'If this doesn't generate a response, I don't know what else we can do.' He steepled his fingers, gazed at the phone; willed it to ring. Silence. 'Oh, come on!' He slammed a hand down. Angry. Frustrated. Powerless.

A number of eyes flicked up from adjacent islands – but the heads were soon down again, busily engrossed in their own investigations.

Tomlinson needed a break; something to ease the tension; the waiting; the not knowing. 'Do you want a coffee, Paul?' he asked.

'Prefer a tea, if there's any going.'

'I'll see what I can find. Back in a few minutes.' As Tomlinson stood up, he half hoped – *expected* – the phone would go as soon as he made to leave; like some hackneyed Saturday-night comedy sketch. But there was no canned laughter, no ironic timing, no punch-line.

The temporary catering area just outside the studio was practical, though not particularly inviting – self-service the order of the day; a few easy-chairs and tables positioned on rugs that had seen better days. But at least the food seemed to hit the mark. There was a selection of good old-fashioned stodge – guaranteed to appeal to coppers – with chips, bacon and eggs, sausages and beans, and toast laid out under the heat-lamps. Tomlinson got a plate, piled on several rashers of bacon, then found a couple of bread rolls; knife, butter, tomato sauce – and he had a feast fit for a king. He grabbed a handful of serviettes, squashed them under the edge of the plate and went over to the coffee pot.

Riley looked up as Tomlinson came back and sat down opposite him.

'Here you go...'

The sergeant took a quick sip. 'Coffee? I asked for tea...'

It had been a genuine oversight. Tomlinson rolled his eyes apologetically. 'Sorry... here, maybe this'll make up for it?' He handed over the plate, then added, seeing the hunger on the other man's face, 'Just the one, mind...'

'Now you're talking.' Riley dug in, barely letting the food touch the sides. He swigged down a mouthful of coffee then half added under his breath, 'I'd still have preferred tea.'

'Then you know what you can...'

But Tomlinson fell silent.

His phone was ringing –

Bryant was on the mobile.

'Pick up... What are you waiting for?'

He'd excused himself, had gone back to his room. He'd just needed those few extra moments of quiet to compose himself.

He'd *had* to call.

Had felt compelled to do so. As soon as he'd seen the face. But it was only now, with the line ringing at the other end, that he suddenly had doubts.

'What the hell am I doing? Oh, this is stupid. What am I going to tell them?'

Yes – what are you doing?

The little voice was back.

Loud and clear.

Louder.

Clearer.

More prominent. As if someone was sat right there beside him. In the room. On the bed. Speaking directly into his ear. No longer just inside his head.

Tell no-one. You can't...

'But –' he interrupted, wanting to protest; at least, to get some answers. Get the voice to explain more. This was all too one-sided.

But he wasn't going to get anywhere.

No-one. The voice emphasised the word. *It's that simple.*

'But – '

But... it repeated back to him... *you can't even do that.* It was playing with him now; taunting him; its tone full of derision.

'No... Listen... Wait...'

But the voice was gone.

And then... *another* voice, there in his ear. 'Hello? *Crime Alert* Incident Room. Can I help you?'

Bryant panicked. Thoughts flashed through his mind. Instant. Disjointed. Protective. They recorded the calls, didn't they? And they could trace you. Fear. Paranoia. He needed more time. Rationalising. Had to think this through. Properly. He reacted instinctively.

'Erm... sorry. No... Wrong number...' *Wrong number.* How stupid did that sound? He quickly pushed a button; ended the call. And for good measure, turned off his mobile as well. They couldn't trace you if your phone was off, could they? *Could they?* Paranoia again. 'What *am* I doing?' He tossed the phone onto the chair, then sat on the edge of the bed, head in his hands. *'Well?'* He was doing the accusing now; demanding that the little voice answer him. His breathing sounded loud; an internal, syncopated accompaniment to the heartbeat pounding in his ears. Again, for a second time, he demanded of the voice, *'Well?'*

But it wasn't his to control.

Silence.

He waited. Determined. Still nothing. Then –

A gentle knock at the door.

'David, are you alright?' It was Sam. 'Neve's putting the computer on...'

He'd seen Bryant stood there, totally immersed in the image on the screen. They both had. Talking to himself. Saying over and over, *Can't be. He's dead...* They'd sat him down, had tried to get sense out of him. *Who's dead* they'd asked? But Bryant hadn't been forthcoming. He'd got up and walked off. Sam had gestured to Neve that they let him be, at least for a while. And then, when Bryant had gone, Sam had had a thought. He'd asked Neve to go and log on with the laptop. They could get the programme back. Watch it again on-line.

He knocked again, 'David, I'm coming in...'

The Saturday-night comedy sketch was alive and well.

'Superintendent Tomlinson speaking...'

But the phone carried on ringing.

Mobile.

Not the studio land-line.

An easy enough mistake to make. They'd all had to turn them off while they'd been on-air. Tomlinson *had* at least remembered to turn it on again – but his subconscious was still clearly a quarter of an hour behind. In the rush to locate the mobile in his jacket, he cack-handedly dropped the receiver back into its cradle. Again, eyes flicked up around him, disapprovingly. But he didn't pay them any attention. He was already listening to a voice on the other end. Familiar, but not instantly recognisable. He couldn't quite place it. And, then – realisation.

A voice from the past.

Not unwelcome. But unexpected.

Tomlinson reached for a pad and pen; the biro-lid skittering over the desk towards Riley, dislodged by an over-eager thumb. 'OK, I'll find it,' he was saying, jotting down an address, 'just give me fifteen…' Then, 'Hello? Hello? Nick, you still there?' But the caller had rung off.

Riley could tell by the look on his senior officer's face that this was important. *Nick?* The name didn't ring any bells. 'You're off, I take it?'

Tomlinson tore the paper from the pad – not just the top sheet, but several from underneath too. It was a habit from the old days, to prevent others seeing what he'd written. Too few and the indentations might still be visible. It was an act that didn't go unnoticed by Riley, but the latter kept the observation to himself. He'd worked with Tomlinson long enough to know there must be a good reason for such caution.

'Look… got to go.' Tomlinson swung his jacket on. 'Sorry to leave you in the lurch, Paul…' Riley laced his fingers behind his neck, nodded acceptance. 'I'll try and be back in an hour. Listen, if it starts getting busy, ask Mick Bancroft to lend you a body; say I asked…'

And with that, the superintendent shot out of the room.

Some of the disapproving eyes followed him; before seeing Riley smiling knowingly back at them…

'Nearly there,' said Neve. 'I had to download some software and do a re-start. I'll put the kettle on while it's warming up.' She left Bryant and her husband huddled round the laptop while she went to make the drinks.

'Look, you know you can tell us *anything*,' Sam offered, hoping to reinforce his earlier reassurance.

Bryant was still distracted; his eyes darting meaningfully; deep in internal thought; processing information; recalling names – or, to be precise, *one* name; to go with *that* one face. And then, he'd got it.

'Anything. Really.' Sam was saying.

Bryant was back with him. He smiled appreciatively. 'I know. Thanks.'

Sam nodded briefly in acknowledgment. 'Right, here we go. Looks more promising, doesn't it?' Sam tapped the mouse up and down as the icons arranged themselves neatly on the desktop.

'I saw that.' Neve was hovering in the doorway. 'You know it doesn't make *any* difference.' She disappeared again.

'No, but it makes me feel better,' Sam said quietly to himself. He tapped the mouse again, just to labour the point.

'May I?' Bryant leaned forward and Sam moved to one side. Bryant's fingers danced lightly on the keyboard and, after several clicks of the mouse, the screen filled with the TV channel's familiar logo. 'We follow the link… *Crime Alert*… today's show… OK, here we are…'

'I made us some tea. And there are a few biscuits as well.' Neve came in with a tray that she placed on the table between the sofas. 'David?' Neve handed their guest his tea.

'Thanks,' he replied, setting it down beside the laptop. 'There...' he took a long in-breath. '*This* is the still.'

He fell silent. Stared for the second time at the face in the crowd. At the man's eyes that were fixed on the scene in the foreground; watching the attack on the police officer. He stepped aside to let Sam and Neve inspect the image. Picking up his tea, he walked over to stand by the fireplace. He gazed back at the laptop, then at his two friends.

'I just don't understand... he's there... but he *can't* be...'

Even with the heat from the fire behind him, Bryant felt suddenly cold.

Deathly cold.

Despite hailing a taxi, it had still taken Tomlinson over twenty minutes to get there. He'd half expected the door to be shut, a *closed* sign in the window, but the lights were on; someone was definitely at home. He closed the door carefully behind him.

'Good evening, sir. Table for one?'

Tomlinson sized up the waiter. Attentive. Overly so. Probably with time on his hands – the rest of the bistro's patrons already having eaten. A quick glance round at the tables confirmed his assessment. The remaining handful of diners were well onto their coffees and liqueurs.

'I'm...' he scanned the room for a second time; purposely, taking in all he needed. Bingo. There. Corner booth to the right. Over by the mirrored glass panel – perfect for seeing who came in. And beside the kitchen swing-door. Convenient for getting out the back way. And then, a glimpse of an elbow. 'I'm... actually meeting someone.'

'Oh, I see.' The waiter nodded and went off to check on the other tables.

From the carefully-selected vantage point, the caller was able to see Tomlinson's reflection as he approached the booth. 'Thought you might have stood me up. I was about to pay the bill and leave,' came the soft voice.

'You know I wouldn't dare.' Tomlinson eased himself into the seat opposite the woman. Petite to look at, she exuded a great inner strength.

'Bit too snug? You must have put on weight. You should get out more.'

Tomlinson patted his stomach. 'I'm sure they just make the

seats smaller these days. You know, cram more diners in.'

'Hm, maybe.' The woman smiled, then raised a hand to signal the waiter. 'A filter coffee, black...' she paused for a moment, until Tomlinson nodded confirmation, 'please, for my friend.'

'You're looking as good as ever...'

'From anyone else, I'd take that as a sexist comment... but you're right.' She was only joking, and Tomlinson knew it. 'Good genes, that's the secret.'

'And doing well on the career front, I hear...'

'I *am* honoured. Wouldn't have thought I'd register so highly on the Met's radar.'

'Well, I like to keep my hand in. Good to know who's doing what. Never know when you might need something...'

'Contacts? Yeah, I know. Contacts are everything, aren't they? Especially in our game.' Despite the false modesty, she was genuinely touched he'd bothered to take an interest in her.

Nick – *Nicola* – Lennox had not long been appointed a desk officer at the Security Service when Tomlinson had come into her working life. It had been the late nineties, when he'd been seconded there as a liaison officer. On the face of it, to help the flow of intelligence between Thames House and the Yard. But they all knew it for what it was – a political appointment. He, the safe pair of hands; to help keep the peace. There'd still been bad blood between the two organisations back then, following the government's decision to give MI5 the lead role in tackling Irish republican terrorism. And it *had* been getting in the way of operations, no matter what the respective heads had told the Home Secretary.

'You've gone on to better things?' He'd heard on the grapevine she'd been promoted several times. From general intelligence duties; to overseas liaison; and then the move to the technical side – something he knew she'd always hankered after. 'Bugging and burgling your way across London... or so the libertarians would have us believe?'

'Let's just say I found my niche. Anyway, enough about me.' The shields were suddenly up – *need to know*, even between those *in* the know, the eternal guiding principle. 'To business –' She paused as the waiter set down Tomlinson's coffee. When he was out of earshot, she continued, 'I think I might be able to help you... and you're going to owe me *big* time.'

'I'm listening...' Tomlinson raised his cup.

'Now, what I'm going to tell you can't be used evidentially.'

The old bug-bear. The Service wanting – *needing* – to protect its sources. Couldn't risk anything being disclosed in court; cross-questioning; staff being called as witnesses. That would mean public interest immunity certificates – and tiptoeing carefully through one hell of a legal and political minefield.

'So, as far as my investigation goes, I received an anonymous tip-off?'

'Correct.'

'And your call to my mobile?'

'You'll find it came from an unregistered pay-as-you go. It can't be traced.'

He'd expected as much. 'Right. Oh, and here – you'll want these.' He handed Nick the sheets of paper he'd torn from the pad in the studio.

She saw he'd written down the bistro's address. 'Impressive – good to see you've not forgotten your tradecraft; not bad for an old timer.' And then, pre-empting his next thought, she added, 'No, don't worry about this place. We've got an *understanding* with the owner.' Tomlinson nodded his own understanding. Probably meant the place employed the occasional illegal; papers maybe not quite what they ought to be; but with the Service's help, any over-zealous officials from immigration or the council could be persuaded to turn a blind eye... in the interests of national security; not that it would be put to them quite so bluntly.

'OK.' He got comfortable in his seat. 'So, what have you got for me?'

'At the time your murders took place, we were running a surveillance operation. You'll understand I can't go into too much detail, but what I can say is we were following a person of interest – a suspected intelligence officer from one of the embassies. We'd received information to suggest he might be visiting a key contact. Now that contact lives...' she was choosing her words carefully, aware she might be disclosing more than she should be doing, 'in a postcode area broadly consistent with that of your victims.'

'*Broadly consistent*? Not the *same* street?'

'So,' she continued, pointedly refusing to answer, 'we'd set up an observation post, and had cars, vans, officers on foot out there. All of which, it turned out, was a complete waste of time. Our target visited no-one and just kept driving round. What we think now is he knows – or more likely suspects – he's being tailed, and possibly this was a set-up. You know, he's put the word out, expecting something to reach us. And he was carrying out his own anti-surveillance; seeing if he could spot us.'

'And did he?'

Her look said it all. 'You know we're better than that... Now, I said it was all a waste of time. Well, for *us* it was. But, for *you*...'

'You've got footage, haven't you? Hours of the stuff?'

'We have, yes. But don't go thinking I can just pass it all over to you. You'll appreciate there are limits. However, that said, I did begin wondering if we'd actually picked up anything that might help with your investigation.'

'*And*?'

'By the way, meant to say well done. Great interview. I've never seen you so eloquent. I really enjoyed your fifteen minutes of fame...' Tomlinson was visibly cringing, thinking back to his TV appearance, '... but *not* as much as I enjoyed finding *this* when I played our recordings back...' She'd brought her handbag up onto the table. She reached inside and passed the superintendent a folded *Post-It* note. 'It's the registration number of a small van that was parked-up at your murder scene. Actually, let me clarify that – parked-up *before* the murders. Our surveillance car didn't go back that way afterwards, so I can't say what time the van would have left. But the timings fit, near enough. And they'd have needed some way to get the kids out of there unnoticed. What better than in the back of a van?' She shrugged. 'Might help, might not.'

'And what do *you* think?' Tomlinson knew Nick Lennox would already have run the number through the computer. 'Suspicious?'

She spread her hands. '*You're* the detective... but it's certainly an unusual one...'

Bryant finished washing his hands and shook the excess water into the basin. He looked at himself in the mirror, trying to decide whether he needed to freshen up. His short hair was still neat enough; and a few hours' sleep would tone down the redness in his eyes; only the sheen on his nose was letting the side down. He wiped at it with the back of a hand. The shine went; replaced by a thin line of water. The attendant noticed and offered him a warm towel – in exchange for the customary tip. Bryant touched the towel to his nose; cursorily patted his hands – before fumbling in his pocket for a selection of coins. The attendant feigned indifference as he took them but, with well-practised ease, noted the amount in his peripheral vision. No smile; no nod – but no disdainful sneer either, Bryant noticed. He couldn't be sure how much he'd given him; but he didn't intend to prolong the agony. He wanted to get out of there before the final judgment came.

Businessman and washroom attendant. Polar opposites. Yet here the balance of power lay firmly with the latter. Enabling him to bestow favour, or remove grace as he saw fit. The decision now only seconds away... Bryant caught the slight movement. The attendant was going for one of the bottles on the shelf. Which would it be? Eau de...

cologne; ... or *toilette?* The door swung open and caught the attendant off guard. A temporary distraction, giving Bryant the chance to escape. Which he took. A quick burst of the pump – but the newcomer took the hit; coughed loudly as the fragrance went to the back of his throat. A raised voice. Spluttered shouting. The beginnings of an apology... but Bryant left the commotion behind him. Freedom within reach. Just the outer door to go.

And then he was there.

Back in the executive lounge. God – how he hated running the gauntlet. Even there, cocooned in his preferential microcosmic world, it was impossible to avoid the one-upmanship and backstabbing. He slumped down in one of the leather armchairs and smiled as a young waitress came over.

'May I get you something to drink, sir?' she asked, her accent indicating mid-west origins.

'I'll have a beer, please.'

'Certainly, sir.' A few moments later, the waitress returned with a tray. She placed Bryant's drink on the table and set down a bowl of peanuts beside it. Then she handed him a menu. 'If you'd like something more filling, sir?'

Drinks; snacks; three-course meals; newspapers, or even a massage while you waited – all were complimentary; benefits that the high-powered frequent-flyers expected. *Demanded.* And with competition among the airlines so fierce, they had to oblige. Couldn't afford to lose out to their rivals. Not that any of it was really complimentary. The ticket price easily covered the overheads. All paid for by The Company; and others the world over. Or, rather – ultimately – by their customers...

'No, this'll be fine, thanks.'

'Enjoy your drink, sir. Have a nice day.' The waitress left.

'Sure you won't try the rainbow trout?' The rustle of a newspaper from a sofa beside Bryant. 'I can thoroughly recommend it. Cooked to perfection.'

The paper sagged in the middle and a pair of blue eyes appeared over the crease. Businessman. No – correction. The air of confidence. The easy charm. That approachability. And the accent; English, long rounded vowels; posh. An MD at the very least. Bryant couldn't help it. He was in automatic mode; assessing the man; unconsciously looking for the next sale; his response conditioned; trained to perfection by The Company. But Bryant needed a rest; *more* than another sale. He'd met – exceeded – his targets for this month. And this *was* down-time after all; switching off on his journey home. He flicked the mental switch to *off* and he was plain Bryant again.

'I might have something on the flight. But thanks, anyway.'
The man had put the paper down.
'Long way from home, too, eh?' Bryant nodded. 'Kindred spirits. We ought to stick together.' The stranger was holding out his hand. 'Edward Graysbrook...'

'Edward... Graysbrook...' Bryant repeated the name out loud. *Double hand-shake – and be sure to remember their name. Know your client. Know their needs. Inform their needs.* Chapter one, page one, line one of The Company's sales' manual. He'd spent two weeks having the same message drilled into him at a training centre. He'd also been taught the all-important technique for remembering names; committing them instantly to the long-term memory. *Double hand-shake – and be sure to remember their name.*
It had worked all right.
'Sorry?'
'There. In the crowd. The man. His name is Edward Graysbrook. He was on the plane with me...'
'*He's* the one who should be dead?' Sam asked. 'The man you've been talking about?' Bryant nodded. 'OK, well, look...' he was thinking on his feet; trying to rationalise an explanation for his friend. '... he obviously *didn't* die. I mean... from what you said, everyone thought there were no survivors... That's what they said, yes? But *you* lived. So he obviously did, too.'
'But they said I was the *only* one.'
'Well, we don't know that. You can't know that. Maybe they just wanted to keep it quiet, like they did with you. Maybe there are others, all in different hospitals.'
'But look – you can see he's not injured. What are the chances of that?' Bryant did have a point. He himself had escaped with little more than a few broken bones. But for someone else to have walked away unscathed – that really was pushing the boundaries of probability. 'I'm sure it was difficult enough for The Company to keep me out of the media. But if you're now saying there are others all over the place, why hasn't the story broken? And...'
'Hey, come on...' Sam hadn't meant to stir up memories of the crash. He tried to calm the situation down; lowered his voice. 'I know as much as you...' he corrected himself, '... *less*. I'm just saying... maybe you weren't the only one.'
'I'm sorry.' Bryant knew he'd over-reacted. His friend was only trying to help.
'Which one is he, David?' said Neve, peering at the laptop's screen.

'There,' Bryant pointed. 'Next to the couple. Just in front of the guy with the T-shirt...'

Sam was still trying to come up with a sensible answer. 'There's you; and there's him. Now let's suppose for a minute that you two *were* the only survivors. That's possible as well, isn't it?'

Bryant nodded slowly, following the logical line of argument. 'He *was* sat *next* to me. So... yes, it could have been a fluke; a one in a million chance.' He looked at Sam for support; carried on where his thoughts were taking him. 'You always hear of miraculous escapes, don't you? You know... babies surviving, their seats intact... and yet the parents – right next to them – end up dying...'

'Well, let's just suppose you *both* got lucky this time; maybe yours was the only part of the plane that didn't break up completely...'

'But there was a fire. I can remember it... vaguely. I'm sure they told me that much.'

Fire.

Bryant suddenly had to use all his will power to suppress the picture of Serena that wanted to form in his mind. He sent it back to his unconscious; waited to see if it tried again. He didn't want to re-live that nightmare. But it stayed buried...

'Look, even if it is just a fluke as you say. You and he are the luckiest guys on the planet... can't you just accept it? Just be thankful you've got the chance to do something with the rest of your life...'

Sam *was* only trying to help. Bryant knew that – but this was starting to sound like therapy; and he'd had more than enough of that. He didn't want to lose his temper, so he tried to rein in the discussion.

'Let's just leave it... We don't know – and we probably won't ever know how come I'm still here. As you say, Graysbrook and me, we're the luckiest guys on the planet...'

But he didn't mean it. There was no way he could leave it alone. Not now he knew there was someone else out there. That fact changed everything. The realisation there was someone who might be able to help him piece together what had happened. To him. To them both. *Kindred spirits...* a clear echo of Edward Graysbrook's words.

Bryant knew what he had to do. Knew what *not* to do. The police – their investigation... that *wasn't* his concern. Not any more. That had just been the catalyst. *This* was what really mattered now. Getting his own answers. Finding this fellow passenger. As soon as he could, he'd start researching the crash. He'd begin with the news reports; check the on-line accounts. And there'd have been an air-accident investigation; maybe the report had been published? Or an interim one? He could check their website. And there'd have been a coroner's inquiry. Maybe too soon for that – but he could check...

His mind was keen; alive; racing through the next few weeks; mentally logging all the leads he'd need to follow up. He *could* start right now. And he would.

'Look, I'm sorry... I know you're just trying to help.' He sighed. 'I'm tired... and... there's a lot for me to get used to... I think I'll turn in. Wake up in a better mood tomorrow...'

'Sam?' Neve tapped her husband on the arm. 'Look...'

'One sec.'

'No, look. Look now... *please*...' Clear insistence in her tone. But he ignored her; his friend too important; needing his attention first.

'We'll see you in the morning, then. Here... let me,' he went to take Bryant's cup from him.

'Night.' With that, Bryant retired to his room.

'Sam!' Neve's impatience growing; determined to get his attention now. 'Just *look* will you...'

'Alright... you could see the state he was getting in...'

He put Bryant's cup down. Neve pulled the laptop towards him, her finger squarely pointed at the screen.

'I'm not wrong, am I? Seeing things?'

Tomlinson hadn't managed to get back to the studio in time for the live update show. Not that it had mattered. He wouldn't have been interviewed anyway. The developments were all taking place on Mick Bancroft's case. Mick had done the familiar piece to camera, thanking the public for their support; saying there'd been a number of useful lines of enquiry they'd be following up.

Tomlinson had already phoned Riley to say he'd be along later – he'd wanted to go check something out first. When he finally arrived, he saw their island of desks was empty. Riley was over with Mick's team.

'You pinching my staff?' Tomlinson joked.

'Maximising available resources,' came the reply.

'Good night?'

'Think we've got him.' Mick's whole demeanour had lifted. 'Calls coming in all evening – same name; seven times. *Seven*. That's got to be a result. I've already got a team going over there. As soon as they call, I'm off. Want to see the bastard for myself.'

'Mick... do it by the book.' The DI looked taken aback; but let the feeling subside. 'I know it's personal... but don't give him any reason to get off.' Even as Tomlinson was offering his words of advice, the irony of his own behaviour towards Nicol was sinking in.

'It'll be by the book. Don't you worry.'

'Good.'

'What about you? Paul said you'd had to leave sharpish. Lead?'

'Maybe. Maybe not.' Tomlinson was playing his cards close to his chest. He wanted to get Riley's second opinion before going any further.

'Well, let me know how you get on anyway.'

'Will do.' Tomlinson heard Riley start laughing at something with one of the other detectives. 'Private joke? Or best not to ask?'

'Sorry, sir. No... just glad I didn't get a call from this one...'

'Homing pigeon,' came a voice from the other side of Riley's desk. Not the detective the sergeant had been speaking to, but one of the programme's staff. 'Calls every show. Always picks a case and phones in with something. He's totally bonkers, of course. Says he's a psychic or something. You should arrest him for wasting police time.'

Riley was reading through a print-out from the other team's log. 'Patrick Maltravers... aged 56... called to say the shotgun used in the jewellers' robbery will also be used in a drive-by shooting next week...'

'Well, it could be,' Tomlinson ventured. 'Shouldn't just dismiss it out of hand. Maybe he'll be right this time...'

'No... don't think he's rated highly on the credibility stakes, sir...' The sergeant waved another piece of paper. 'He's been flagged. See? Let me just...' he scanned the information, '... here we are... apparently, he's well known as a time-waster; but... he's never been charged as he seems genuinely to be deluded... Says here he was even the subject of ridicule on daytime TV. Claimed he'd predicted his own death. You remember that plane crash... few months back?'

'Hm... rings a bell; everyone killed?'

'Well, he claimed he saw the crash coming. He was flying that day; chose not to board.'

'If that's true...'

Again, Riley read ahead, then concluded with, 'Total fabrication. Says here the producer checked with the airline. He wasn't on the passenger list. He hadn't even bought a ticket. A total fraud. Just trying to sell his story...'

'Sounds like he's got real problems... Anyway, how did we do?'

Riley handed the papers back. 'It did get busier, sir. 'About a dozen calls... possible sightings of the twins. No two the same, though. We're following them all up. Oh, and, I asked and the inspector very kindly gave us some help...'

'Yeah, meant to ask. What's this about me owing you a favour, Ray? By my reckoning, I'm easily quids in...'

'I'm not so sure...'

'Oh, you've forgotten Lewisham, have you? Don't think you'd have got...'

The phone went. One of the detectives passed it to Mick Bancroft. 'Right. I'll be straight over.'

'Don't forget what I said, Mick.'

'Noted. Catch up soon, yeah? And I'll let you buy me that pint I'm owed.' Then, to his team, he added, 'You can call it a night...' The detectives started to pack away; Mick left.

Twenty minutes later, it was just Tomlinson and Riley. Tomlinson had explained where he'd been; who he'd met – first name only – and what he'd got out of it. He'd been late getting back as he'd already stopped in at the Yard; run the vehicle's number through the computer. He'd got a name and an address; and an occupation.

'If you don't think it's too late, I'd like to go over to the Wilsons' house. Just want to take another look...' One of the phones rang down at Mick's end of the studio. 'Leave it, they'll ring off,' said Tomlinson. But the caller was nothing if not persistent. 'Oh, I'll get it.' He walked slowly over, hoping it would go silent. It didn't. 'Hello, Superintendent Tomlinson... Right... What, my number? No, it's not my case. You want DI Bancroft... No... I just picked up his phone... Yes, try him tomorrow on his main number. Yes. Thanks. Bye.' He put the phone down. 'Some people just won't listen.'

'Should we get in touch with him?'

'No, it's routine stuff. Call-logging tonight's incoming; that's all. It can wait.'

Seeing things...

Neve's voice had dropped to a whisper.

'Look, here's the couple...'

'Yes?'

'And this is the man in the T-shirt, right?'

'Yes?'

'So... *where's* Graysbrook?'

Seeing things...

If only.

'No, that can't be right. Budge over...'

But it was the same for Sam.

Where Bryant had indicated Edward Graysbrook should have been, there was no-one; all they could see was empty space.

Just a *gap* in the crowd...

CHAPTER TWELVE

BRYANT WAS BACK in his room, the world-wide-web at his fingertips – data now streaming directly to his mobile. As a starting point he'd typed the words *plane crash*, together with the date and the airline he'd used – he'd not been able to remember the exact flight number – into a search engine. Those parameters alone had brought up several thousand hits. Too many, so he'd narrowed the list down by adding *survivors* and *interim report*. 873. He clicked on the first record, skimmed the text until he read the words *no survivors*, then realised the search was still too imprecise. He'd have to accept The Company had been successful in concealing his survival, so he'd have to try something else. He had an idea. He entered his own surname and also that of Edward Graysbrook. The search came back for a third time. 226 hits. That was manageable.

Bryant wished he'd brought a laptop with him. Mobiles were functional enough, but their limited screen size couldn't compete with the greater versatility of the laptop. Even a tablet would have been preferable. He considered for a moment going back through to Sam and Neve and asking to borrow theirs, but quickly dropped the idea; he already felt uncomfortable about the way he'd treated them and, in particular, how he'd spoken to Sam. He'd be sure to apologise in the morning.

There were just so many questions. Old ones. New ones. All jostling for position in his consciousness. No sooner had he decided what he thought the priority should be, he began doubting his judgement and the question was ousted; its position usurped – casualty of the dog-eat-dog world of a mental civil war.

'This is no good...' he said quietly to himself. 'Need to focus...' He put the mobile down, closed his eyes, took a few deep breaths. 'Now... *what*'s the priority?' His breathing more measured, increased oxygen fuelling his concentration. 'What do I *most* need?' He exhaled long and hard, determined to master the stubborn uncertainty. Then, '*Graysbrook...*' he said simply. 'Find *him*, *I* can get some answers.' He retrieved the mobile and tapped the *advanced search* icon. Deliberately, he omitted his own name, this time entering Graysbrook's alone; and linked it to the flight details. 'There, that should at least halve the number...'

Bryant wasn't wrong.

'Wait a minute... this *can't* be right?' He tried again. 'What do you mean *no matches found*? But you just said there were...' He clicked the back button. '...226...' He selected several of the links at random and each time it was *his* name that came up highlighted.

Again. And again. But not Graysbrook. Never Edward Graysbrook...

You won't find him.

The little voice. Back with him once more. But Bryant wasn't in the mood for any of its riddles, its superior tone. He challenged it head on.

'Look, why should I believe anything you say?' He was angry, irritation spurring him on. He didn't care if the voice disappeared for good. 'You never do anything for me. I don't even know who – *what* – you are. Are you... me? Go on – tell me! Are you me, or what? Just who are you?' Silence. 'Damn it, tell me who you are!' Again, nothing. 'Well, that's just great, isn't it? As soon as I ask you something, you go quiet. Useless. That's what you are! Well, if you won't answer my questions... or talk to me... then you can just go... Just leave me alone and get out of my...' he paused momentarily, '... *life...*'

You were going to say head.

'Now look!'

No, you look. The volume low, forcing Bryant to concentrate on listening. Just three words, but already he could detect something in the tone. Not threatening; nor menacing – but somehow disturbing; latently so. *You couldn't even begin to imagine what I've done for you. And still... you can't – or won't – follow simple instructions...*

'But...' Bryant was suddenly less sure of himself; his resolve wavering – as was his voice.

But nothing. It was the voice's turn to pause, waiting to hear if Bryant would come back at it again. But this time, he remained silent. And then, satisfied control had been regained, the voice's tone was at once more neutral; familiar; even strangely reassuring. *Good. Now we're getting somewhere...*

'*We?*' Bryant couldn't help himself, latching on to even the slightest of clues. 'So you're *not* me?'

Quiet – one more chance! That's what I'll give you. After that, you're on your own...

The words struck a chord. Something inside Bryant told him not to push his luck. Reluctantly, he toed the line. 'I'm sorry... I just need to know...'

The voice must have been considering its own position, for it offered an unexpected concession. *You may ask one question...*

'And you'll answer?' Bryant fired back straight away. Then, realising his stupid mistake, immediately added, '... and *that* wasn't my question...'

The voice seemed genuinely amused. *That's good. You're learning... Now, your question?*

163

Bryant really could only ask the obvious.

'*Who* are you?'

'Mind!'

The two detectives were in Percy and Ivy Wilson's house.

'Sorry, sir,' Riley shouted back in the general direction of the kitchen. He'd accidentally caught his sleeve on a handle and, in freeing himself, had caused the door to swing heavily open. It had collided with the edge of the sideboard behind. 'I'll be more careful.' He continued his search of the room and, finding nothing, went to join the senior officer.

Tomlinson was half way round the kitchen units, opening each cupboard and drawer in turn. 'It's got to be here somewhere. I know it has.' He was as much thinking out loud as talking to Riley. 'If we can *just* find that link...' He knew he couldn't afford another mistake. Peters and the Commissioner were already on his back.

'Sir, I thought SOCO had been through everything...'

'They have – but they're not infallible.' And, as if to reinforce his point, Tomlinson added grimly, 'Look how they missed the twins.' He was feeling the pressure, the urgent need to find the children. 'No, we're going to check. Go over everything again. I don't care if it takes all night.' He wasn't going to argue the point with Riley so, to end further discussion, told him to go inspect the adjacent utility area.

The room was a modest, L-shaped annexe; nothing particularly distinctive about it – sink, worktops and storage to match the kitchen; white goods; and a connecting door to the garage beyond. Riley gave it the quick once-over, and was just about to begin replicating Tomlinson's methodical searching when his attention was drawn back to something.

An incongruity picked up at the subconscious level.

Translated into a hunch.

He felt the twitch of his copper's nose...

Who am I? The voice didn't answer straightaway. After a moment of quiet reflection, it offered, *We'd perhaps get further if I rephrased the question to... who are you? Yes... who are you, David Bryant? That is much easier to explain.*

'I didn't ask that –' Bryant interrupted, but the voice carried on; speaking over him; louder, to silence the complaint.

Yes... you are... me... another brief pause... *but... I...* a longer hesitation *am not you.*

'You're doing this deliberately, aren't you?'

Now, that would be a second question; and we did agree just the one.

164

Bryant didn't like being made a fool of. 'I didn't agree to anything –'

Enough. You waste time – yours; mine; ours. And we have so little left. I caution you again... let all this be; tell no-one of your survival...

'But Sam; Neve they already know...'

No-one else... And do not try to find Edward Graysbrook. He cannot help you.

'But how can I? Put yourself in my place. You'd want answers, wouldn't you? After all that's happened... I still don't know what to make of...'

Of what? Oh... the noises in your head? Or the lights that you see? Or maybe the strange voice – my voice? Or what it means that you are me? Further calculation on the voice's part, and then, *If you still don't understand what questions you should ask, how ever can you expect to find – make sense – of any answers? You won't. You can't. Now leave it...*

Bryant still had some fight left in him, the wavering resolve itself now uncertain. He didn't intend letting up until he got some answers; enough to give him a head-start.

But he was starting to feel strangely ill at ease.

The hint of a memory slowly building within; familiarly uncomfortable; it was the memory of... bile; its heated, burning ascent all set to scale his throat.

'Are you doing this? It's you, isn't it?' He felt he was going to choke, but even so managed to spit the words out defiantly. 'The same every time... always you...'

No, it's not my doing! Now be quiet! They're coming for you! The little voice sounded genuinely panicked. *Don't look at them!* No longer sure of itself; of its ability to lead Bryant where it would. *Whatever they say, don't answer them! And don't go with them! Don't! You mustn't believe...*

A sudden, deafening noise cut the voice off –

A thunder-clap of pure audio-energy. The resultant echo slow to fade. And, then, in its wake, an undulating tide of static rushed in; buzzing; crackling; possessed of electrically-charged life. The buzz morphing steadily into a hum –

Loud.

Then quiet.

Quiet.

Then loud.

Loud, then quiet.

Quiet, then loud again.

So it went on, the rhythm hypnotically repetitive; falling into step with Bryant's consciousness. And, then, with no warning, he was in total darkness –

Everywhere, the once-familiar, all-embracing nothingness.

An awareness of standing. Looking round in confusion. Room. Bed. Mobile. Everything gone. Familiarity only discernible in the darkness – former reference point for the little boy lost; seeking out the missing school-bag. Darkness – his ever-reliable, umbral companion – protectively shrouding him in welcoming oblivion. Darkness – escapee from a world of light – back now to offer him solace.

But there was something else –

Water.

All around him.

He could sense it, but not yet see it.

Warm.

In motion – just like the static; primordially animated. Waves there, below him; toying with his feet; their force increasing, causing his body to sway. It was soothing – Neptune's hand gently rocking his psyche to sleep.

Back and forth.

Back and forth.

Equally hypnotic.

Back and forth.

Calming and inviting. A hint of brine carried on the breeze; a balm for his welcoming lips.

And then, there *was* a light –

Strangely subtle in its intensity. Away to the left. Above him – but getting closer. Like a spotlight. Of awareness. Of feeling. Its shaft glimmering brightly; harrying countless motes – each ineffectual in their ill-timed attempts at escape; the probing luminescence slicing its way through the surrounding, tenebral curtain. Here, a crevice illuminated; and there, a jagged edge; stalactites growing lazily down towards the water's mounting force.

The cave –

Once more welcoming Bryant in; prepared to reveal its secrets – in *exchange* for learning his.

David...

His name carried, gossamer-like, on the lightest of winds. Cave-dwellers seeking to understand his importance; the meaning of his survival.

David...

The call of his name again, and he was walking towards the shaft of light. He felt the water level rise up his legs. Higher and higher.

Higher still it went. But he was safe. No matter it had reached his chest. *David... Edward is here. He's waiting for you...*

The going getting harder now. The natural inclination to swim; but being urged – persuaded – to reject it; just to keep on walking. The water now round his chin. And then –

Submerged.

Immersed totally in a strange new land. A world of distortions – sounds, distinctly indistinct. Screens of ebony swaying freely in the current; their curling edges – tendril-like – wrapping round his limbs. Holding him fast. A captive.

Physically.

Mentally.

Totally.

He, now, only too prepared to surrender himself fully. And the shaft of light, its natural course bent through refraction, beneath the water's surface, criss-crossing the space to either side of him; a sabre of light, carving out a path to allow *their* approach –

The eyes...

Back to scrutinise him.

First, one pair.

And, then, another.

And more still.

From single figures to double. And double to treble. Each blink spawning further multiples. Everywhere, more and more eyes opening as word spread of his arrival. So it went on; relentlessly – until the whole sub-aquatic realm was packed with the ethereal orbs.

Bryant was entranced. No longer discomfited by their presence. *David...*

'I'm ready,' he said, prepared now to become one with them; to be admitted into their number; to join the collective.

And, then –

Eyes he felt he should recognise.

There – straight in front of him. Two orbs; radiating a connection. No need for words. The unspoken message that it was his soul mate. Come to find him. That the search was over. Finally. Journey at an end. Time now for rest. To sleep. He felt his eye-lids growing heavier; wanted to let them close. But couldn't. Not yet. He resisted the feeling *just* long enough to observe the eyes assume a solidity; become fixed in place, as a facial outline materialised; increasingly defined; framing them with comprehension.

I'm ready...' he repeated.

But this time the words came out garbled; his mouth contending with an alien environment. A panicked feeling, as the air bubbles exploded. Percussing the waters just outside his airways. Realising too late his error.

Fish out of water – more accurately, man no longer on land. The coughing. Retching. Instinctive spluttering. Convulsions as his body switched to self-defence. Self-preservation now the only goal. Fighting against all that was unnatural. Canute-like, desperate to turn back the approaching tide of mortality...

As he inhaled the water –

A Lethean draught, headed straight for his lungs. Cruelly ironic, the way it engulfed him; burning the nostrils; choking the throat. And in a final moment of lucidity, though fractional his understanding, Bryant saw the face –

Of Graysbrook staring back at him.

Upon closer inspection, Riley could see there was slight damage to the lino at the base of the tall fridge-freezer standing in the corner. Scrape marks and indentations, possibly made when the unit had been moved into position. But he knew there was something else, too.

Something that he couldn't quite...

And then he had it – the penny dropped.

He'd helped shift his daughter's own fridge a few months back, when he'd gone round to see her; find out how the decorating had been going – ahead of her flat going on the market. And he'd got into trouble, using what he'd thought was a dish-cloth to mop up the water he'd found underneath. How was he supposed to have known it was one of her favourite hand-towels? But the small pool of water – continuous, unavoidable by-product of the cooling process – had rusted the freezer's rear wheels; left a discoloured tide-mark on the floor. And, now, here – it looked as if this fridge-freezer had also been moved.

But recently?

He followed the direction of the scrape marks in reverse. Scanning the lino, checking if there was a similar, tell-tale mark on the floor...

And there was.

Opposite the garage door. Indentations. Faint, but still visible. And two rusted marks. Certainly enough space over by the wall for the unit to have stood. He man-handled it, pulling it a few inches away; inclined it slightly, then jammed a foot hard in below. Just enough clearance to let him crouch down; balance its weight precariously with one hand, as he ran the other underneath along the back. He looked at his palm. Little in the way of dirt; and no moisture to speak of; and no rust. Chances were, the fridge-freezer *had* been moved.

And not long ago.

Tomlinson leaned in round the corner, watching what his sergeant was up to. 'Hunch?'

'Yes, sir.' Riley pulled his foot clear; held the sides as the unit returned to the vertical. He pointed down to the floor. 'Rust marks there. But none over here, sir. It's clean underneath. I reckon it's been moved. Recently...'

'Same day as the murders?'

'Maybe...'

'So why would you...' Tomlinson was thinking out loud. 'To hide something... They – he; she – must have been hiding something. Pull it further out will you?' The sergeant obliged and, as he did so, the superintendent noticed a small notice-board on the wall behind.

As did Riley.

'Which...' the latter continued, following Tomlinson's line of thinking, '... is where we might expect to find our link.'

'And?' Tomlinson held his breath; anticipation set to burst.

Riley tried to squeeze in. 'No good, sir; hang on...' He moved the fridge-freezer slightly further out. 'There...' He reached for several pieces of paper that had been fixed to the board. His hand passed over two, then stopped at a third. 'Got it... *Clean Sweep.*'

'Clean Sweep.' Tomlinson repeated. Riley removed the drawing pin and handed over what was an advertising flyer. 'Interesting... look here...' Tomlinson angled the paper so his sergeant could see. Someone had penned a message in one of the corners. Blue ink. The handwriting shaky, but recognisably copper-plate; a style no longer taught; a throw-back to 1930s Sunday schooling. The superintendent was already ahead of himself. Running through the possibilities. Making an *extra* link. One he'd not expected. He read the words aloud. '*Ivy – Lucy's details, as promised. Love Margaret.*'

Now he felt more confident about making that arrest.

Or, rather, *two* ...

Bryant felt the mother of all pain explode in his ribs.

Thought he'd relapsed into his nightmare world. There to remain, re-living the crash; over and over; time and again. Death and destruction on continuous, looped play-back. He braced himself, waited for the shockwave – for the wall of heat, as the fiery wind must surely tear past him again in search of its victims. Living flesh reduced to ash.

Rewind.

Play.

Fast forward to the gruesome bits.

Rewind. Play. Fast forward again.

But the heat – the wind – never came. There were no screams.

And no charred flesh. The action halted. Held in limbo. The pause button depressed. And, then, someone hit the stop button.
His mental viewing screen went blank.
Totally black.
Another detonation in his rib-cage. Further bruising to add to his war-wounds, as something seemed to slam him hard into the ground.
Voices.
Pain for a third time.
Then light –
But *not* the light from the cave. Nor the brightness glimpsed at the end of a tunnel. No Heaven awaiting his arrival – but no Hell either. And a face slowly coming into focus. *Not* Graysbrook's. Instead, someone Bryant didn't recognise. Young-looking; dark hair; eyes filled with the satisfaction of a job well-done.
'Well hello there, big man.' The Scots accent broad. Welcoming. Verbal honey for the sore of soul. 'You certainly had your pals worried.' His arm constricting now. 'Easy, there; just checking your BP. Lie still for me. A few more seconds.' The sound of Velcro being torn open, as his arm was freed. He was eased into a raised position. A softness behind his back; around his shoulders. The warmth of a hand. Then Sam's voice beside his ear.
'Is he going to be OK?'
'He's over the worst, aye. But we'll need to check him over; keep him in overnight for observation. Just routine.' And then, a warning signal. 'We'll soon have him away to Raigmore...'
No. The voice. Instantly back. With no time to argue. *Tell him no!* Insistent. *No hospitals.*
Bryant knew he had to act fast, despite his weakened state. 'No...' he repeated the voice's word. 'I want to stay here...' He felt so drained; tired. 'Please...' But knew he had to win the argument; only then could he allow himself the luxury of sleep. He used what little reserves of strength he still had left to sit fully upright. He could see now he was in the corridor outside the bathroom. He'd no idea how he'd got there. But that would all have to wait. He focussed on the paramedic; then Sam. 'Please, Sam. Just let me stay here... come on... you know me, I'm a survivor...' He'd not intended any pun. 'I'm fine; really... you can always take me in later...'
Instinctively, Sam was prepared to fight his friend's corner; take his side. 'Look,' he began, 'if one of us is here with him... you know, watching him for the next – what – twenty-four hours, then that's alright, isn't it?'
'Well...' the paramedic didn't sound entirely convinced.
But Sam knew what it meant to Bryant. And he was

determined to help him, so he reasoned patiently; persuasively; until, finally, the other man agreed.

Half an hour later, Bryant was back in his bed, Sam seated beside him. 'You must be the luckiest guy alive. I mean...'
Lucky.
Bryant couldn't even begin to know the half of it. But he would. In time.
'Do you know how close you came?' Sam still talking. 'I thought you were blessed before; but, my God, you've certainly got someone watching over you...'
Bryant didn't know what Sam was talking about.
But the voice did.
How close... He's saying how close you came to death. He thinks you were trying to kill yourself. They all do. Him, his wife; the paramedic. You can't expect them to understand...
And, as if the voice were writing the script, Sam continued gently, 'David... I need to ask you something. OK? Look, I'm not going to judge you. And, whatever's happened... that's fine. You know we're here for you... but...' He was embarrassed even to be asking, 'Did you try and... you know... end it?'
'Sam...' Bryant looked his friend straight in the eyes. 'No. Believe me; please. I can't explain it. Not yet... but no.' He held Sam's gaze, until he seemed convinced.
'Alright. No more questions. But, I did have to ask... you understand? OK now, you get some rest. We can talk later. I'll let you get some sleep. I'll ask Neve to check on you later; bring you something to eat...' He excused himself, closing the door quietly behind him.
Bryant settled down in the bed, pulling the sheets closer round him; inviting the exhaustion to set him free; at least for a while. But, again, his mind was whirring; so many questions; new ones.
What just?
Who?
Why would he think?
Why couldn't I?
You'll never get any rest. Not going on like that.
'You still here?' Bryant was too tired for all this. 'Just let me sleep, will you?' Then, a sudden reproach; barbed; so quick even the voice didn't see it coming. 'Wait! Where were you? You left me to...'
He heard you in the bath. You woke them all up. Running water at that time...
'Wait! What bath? I was in my room...' The diversionary tactic had worked. Bryant's focus was now on himself. '... looking

up... Graysbrook! *He's* behind this, isn't he?'

I've told you before, leave him alone. You really do need to listen to me...

'But...'

But nothing. Count yourself fortunate your friend heard you; reached you in time. You owe him your life.

It was starting to sink in. Bryant understood what the voice was saying. Sam must have found him and given him mouth-to-mouth before calling the emergency services.

The voice, as ever, was reading his mind. One step ahead. *Now do you see why you must listen to me? Do as I say? You... Me... Me... You... Our survival depends on it... Now sleep!*

And, with that, Bryant did sleep.

Soundly. Deeply. Restfully.

Just as the voice had commanded.

By 4:00 am, everything was in place.

Tomlinson had again arranged for armed response teams to be present at both locations – his and Riley's squads were each to effect simultaneous entry to their respective properties at 5:00 am.

His watch showed 4:59 am. The countdown now underway. Thirty-seven seconds to go. Thirty-six. Thirty-five...

He knew he still needed to be cautious. They weren't there yet, he kept reminding himself. Another half minute, though, and he'd know for sure. But he – Riley – both of them felt they'd got it right this time. And the very incredulity of the scenario just made it all the more believable.

And Nick Lennox's tip-off had been the key to it all. But for her chance call...

Twenty-eight. Twenty-seven. Twenty-six...

He'd checked the number she'd given him. It had been registered to one Lucy Tanzer; sole trader; owner of *Clean Sweep* – a chimney-cleaning firm. Lucy Tanzer, its one-woman band. He'd wanted – needed for his own peace of mind – to establish a connection to the Wilsons. And that's what he and Riley had been searching for at the murdered couple's house; had found through the presence of the advertising flyer pinned to the notice-board. That much he'd hoped for. But what the superintendent hadn't expected to find was the *additional* connection...

The relationship between Lucy Tanzer and Margaret Woods – Margaret, the neighbour who'd discovered the bodies.

The hand-penned note was what had alerted him. The old-style script. Only one *Margaret* in the frame who was known to the couple;

her name familiar to him, too. Margaret the neighbour; a young pensioner only too willing to help her less able-bodied friends.

A quick check had confirmed it – Margaret was Lucy's mother-in-law.

It had all started to fit together. He'd wondered earlier why the Wilsons had been caught unawares. He'd reasoned they must have known their attacker. Or *attackers*. But what could the pair possibly have hoped to gain? He couldn't see any obvious motive for their actions. Still, he felt there was just *something* about all this.

Eleven. Ten. Nine...

His mobile, on silent, vibrated momentarily. The final signal from Riley. Two suspects. Two properties. Two entries.

Two children –

Tomlinson was there, right behind the armed officers in the vanguard; he, their living breathing shadow; watching, as torch-lights mounted on gun barrels swept through the rooms in well-rehearsed, choreographed perfection.

Hallway and living room. Cloakroom and kitchen. *All clear* the signal. Leather boots ascending creaking stairs. Two bedrooms. Bathroom. *Clear.* Final bedroom...

Suspect found.

Contained.

Eyes, sleepy; movements, slow; demeanour – *expectant*. Surprise not even registering. Tomlinson pushing past the black-clad figures – room, to room; to room. His shouted question ringing through the house.

Where are they?

His clear instruction – *Find them!*

People milling round; checking every space – wardrobes; understairs; airing cupboard; anywhere a child could be hidden.

Tomlinson's growing sense of panic – counterbalanced by Lucy's calmness. Patient throughout; awaiting his return. Smiling as she said,

'Shh – you'll wake them; they're sleeping.'

CHAPTER THIRTEEN

THE SUDDEN COMMOTION failed to wake the children. Harry and Emily, eyes tightly shut, remained in the deepest of sleeps. The uncertainty of those first few moments – the rear doors of the van being opened; the rescuers' collective anticipation at a peak, adrenalin pumping hard and fast; then, the twins being cradled protectively close to Kevlar vests... all amounted to nothing. The lead officers already realising they'd reached their goal too late. The odour of decomposition working its way through their face-masks, even as they bore the motionless forms in Tomlinson's direction...

Several hours later, all Tomlinson could think of whenever he closed his tired eyes was failure – *his* failure. He did the only thing he could; deliberately allowed his anger to rise – hoping it would prove a stronger emotion than the self-recrimination he was feeling.

He fired off a salvo of accusations; questions – open, closed, rhetorical – each directed at their target; but none scored a direct hit. Instead, throughout the barrage, Lucy Tanzer just sat there; nonplussed; smiling at him, at everyone else in the room; and at no-one. As if she were somewhere else. With no concept of the harm she'd done; the unspeakable nature of her crimes. Two generations slain by her hand.

'Speak, damn you! Answer my bloody questions!'

The duty solicitor raised an eyebrow, but no objection; uncomfortable even to be sitting there with his client; wondering why he'd drawn the short straw.

'Oh... let's take a break!' Tomlinson scraped his chair hard on the floor, causing one of its legs to buckle under the sheer force. He swore and kicked it at the wall. The solicitor visibly flinched; but not Lucy Tanzer. 'Interview suspended 08:26.' He yanked the door open, slammed it behind him and headed straight for the toilets to cool off.

Fifteen minutes later he was back in the interview room; back, too, in control of himself. He apologised to the solicitor, to the WPC who'd been sitting in – but not to the suspect. He felt no reason to justify his actions to her.

'Let's start again...' He looked Lucy Tanzer straight in the eyes. 'Did you, or did you not murder Ivy and Percy Wilson?' The same emptiness there; a void in her comprehension; and still the unchanging smile. 'Why did you abduct Harry and Emily Wilson?' Still no response. 'Why did you have to kill them?' A slight flicker. Instantly, he followed it up with, 'What possessed you to..?'

Possessed.

A word she recognised. Felt. Deep within. And then, for the

first time since her arrest, she spoke. 'When can I see my children? They'll be missing me. I need to...'

Tomlinson shot back another question, desperate to maintain the connection, 'What do you mean, *your* children?'

'My babies... they'll be missing me,' she repeated.

'Look... do you realise what's happened; why you're here?'

Tomlinson didn't like the way this was going. If Lucy Tanzer wasn't trying to pull a fast one, there was a real risk she might be suffering from some form of psychosis. He wondered if the solicitor was going to play a trump card – diminished responsibilities; no further questioning until she's been assessed. That would mean delays. Experts. Wasted time. But the man didn't. He just sat there, unwilling to get more involved than he had to. Taking notes his way of escaping taking responsibility for his client.

Tomlinson had heard of cases where women abducted babies – either because they couldn't have children themselves, or had lost a newborn – but he'd never experienced it first-hand. A part of him, allied to his innate decency, still felt compassion and he found himself wondering if Lucy Tanzer fitted into either category; if she, too, in some perverse way deserved his pity. He'd see what he could find out; contact her GP; just as soon as he concluded the current interview.

'Oh... but, of course, it's alright.' Lucy speaking again, a quick nod in the direction of the clock on the wall. 'They'll still be asleep.'

The interview – monologue would have been a more accurate description, for Lucy Tanzer said nothing further – went pointlessly on for another forty minutes until Tomlinson called time. Tanzer was led back to the cells while the superintendent went to check what progress Riley was making with the mother-in-law. He sat outside the interview room, watching the exchange on the CCTV monitor. The woman had been crying, appeared almost broken; the pressure getting to her. The realisation that she and her daughter-in-law had been found out.

And yet...

Riley was being patient – though determined – with his line of questioning. The solicitor appointed to represent Margaret Woods was on the ball; in stark contrast to her counterpart. She stepped in every few sentences, subtly deflecting Riley's probing; cautioning her client to offer no comment. Tomlinson studied the volley keenly, as key facts, questions, inferences and counter-questions were exchanged; back and forth; with varying speed and accuracy. Neither side gaining the advantage – deuce the closing score, when poor light finally stopped play. He waited until solicitor and client had been led away, then took Riley to one side.

'First impressions?'

'I don't think she knew the first thing about it, sir.'

'Really?'

'Really.' The sergeant folded his arms defensively; as if he thought he was on trial; about to be subjected to hostile questioning. But Tomlinson just wanted to hear his deputy's thoughts. He'd worked long enough with him to trust his judgement. Riley was no fool. 'I don't think she's putting it on, sir. She genuinely seems totally... horrified... by it all. She's been holding herself responsible.'

'Because *she* introduced her daughter-in-law to the Wilsons?'

'Well, yes, but also... thinking she missed something. She's blaming herself for not going round Lucy's house sooner. You know, maybe then she'd have noticed something; maybe even have been able to save the kids...'

'Well, we'll never know.'

'No, sir.' Riley gestured towards his interview notes. 'The solicitor's offered us an alibi for her client. For the time of the murders...' The sergeant quickly clarified his last statement, '...for Mr and Mrs Wilson. I'll of course be checking that. Oh, and, don't know whether you'd picked this up yet? Mrs Woods has suggested one motive – for the abduction, at least. It might be linked to some misguided attempt at mother love...' *Smother love*, Tomlinson thought to himself. He could already guess what was coming. 'You see, when Lucy Tanzer was married to Mrs Woods' son – they're separated now – she couldn't have children so... he left her for someone who could.'

'And our Mrs Woods blames her son?' Riley nodded. 'And that's why she's stayed in touch with Lucy Tanzer?'

'Seems so. She doesn't speak to her son much now. But she's been there throughout to support Lucy. She even helped her out with money to set up the business.'

'Hm – OK; look, you go test Mrs Woods' alibi. I suspect you're going to be proved right, and it'll check out. But, also, we'll need to establish what her movements were since then; up till whenever the twins were...' He couldn't bring himself to say the word.

Killed.

They were still waiting for the initial forensic results into the children's deaths.

'Do we know when we're likely to get the first report, sir?'

'I'm hoping tomorrow, but I'll put in a chaser. And, separately, I'll see if I can find out anything more about Lucy Tanzer's medical history. You know – depression; counselling; that sort of thing. Any previous suspicions she might have wanted to abduct children.'

'Poor woman...'

'She's a murderer.' Tomlinson said, matter-of-factly.
Riley chose not to reply. The mood the superintendent was in, it didn't matter that he'd meant Margaret Woods.

'What do you think?'
  'Lovely. Just what the doctor ordered,' Bryant replied, finishing the last of the soup that Neve had brought him earlier on.
  'Here, let me take those,' she lifted the tray and its contents clear of his bed. 'Have you had a chance to look through that yet?' She nodded at the brochure that Sam had left for Bryant.
  'Not so far, but I'll make a point of reading it before Sam gets back tonight.' A note, paper-clipped to the front, read simply *D – Any Interest? S.* Bryant picked up the glossy pack to scan through it. There was an aerial photograph on the cover that showed a moderately-sized, fortified tower. It was set in woodland, with one side open to a loch. 'Well, it's not the grandest of country houses,' he noticed the title, 'this... *Castle Sorralan*. But, worth a visit would you say?'
  Neve laughed. 'You can't really see Sam doing the whole history thing, can you?'
  'What, tea and scones in the coffee shop after the guided tour? Blue rinse brigade buying the souvenir guidebook? No, I guess not.'
  'Have a read. It's not your traditional Highland estate. Sam does a bit of odd-jobbing there from time to time. Think he's quite keen to show you round, though; introduce you to a few of the locals. But don't let him bully you into it; not if you don't want to go.' She drew back the curtains with her free hand. 'Beautiful day out there.' Then left, closing his door behind her.
  Bryant rearranged his pillows and settled back to read all about Castle Sorralan.
  'Welcome to Castle Sorralan,' he began, thinking he was only taking in as much as interested him; but his long-conditioned mind had other ideas. 'Ancestral home of...' he skipped ahead, '... fourteenth century fortified tower, fully restored by its present owner, Mr Rudi Fridriksson.' He paused over the name; thought he ought to have known it. But he couldn't place it. He figured the man might be Scandinavian – a Swede? 'After many years of planning, the castle and its surrounding estate are now entering an exciting new phase of development... self-sufficiency... sustainability... diversification... archetype for the future.' Bryant clicked his tongue in disapproval, without even being aware of it. His subconscious was already busy, assessing what chance the castle had to turn over a profit in the next five years. He guessed the owner must have invested heavily; and he'd want a return on his capital. He leafed quickly through the remaining pages.

'All the buzz-words are here, but,' he shook his head, 'it could all be a complete waste of your time and effort, Mr Fridriksson; money down the pan if you're not careful.' He checked the small print, just to make sure he hadn't missed anything. But he hadn't. 'No. Nowhere here do you actually tell me *what* you do at your castle; or why I'd want to come visit. Definitely a thumbs-down. Not how I'd have advised you if you'd been my client.' He just couldn't help it; a willing wage-slave to his erstwhile life. Another extract from The Company's training manual appeared out of nowhere; a pennant waving in the mental breeze of recognition; the message all too familiar – for him; and likewise all the other executives who'd ever studied it.

> *Become the focus. Inspire the Desire!*

In layman's terms – get their attention; then get them to buy our product. Job done.

'Well, let's see, now; was I being over-critical? Is there *anything* we can salvage?' Bryant went back to basics; tried to come at the publicity material with fresh eyes. 'Hm, I suppose the photos are nice enough... so, yes, alright, I'm interested enough to read your glossy advert. But, as for inspiring desire...' a considered review confirmed his initial thoughts, 'no, doesn't do anything for me ...'

Thump –

A bird had flown into the window.

The unexpected noise caught his conscious attention; it, now, master again over his subconscious. Quietly, the analytical business mind slipped back into the boardroom and closed the door for another day. Bryant wanted to see if the bird was hurt. He re-attached the post-it and put the brochure to one side, got out of bed and went over to the window. Neve had been right. It was a beautiful day out there. He lifted the latch and pushed gently against the frame. He leaned out and scanned the ground from left to right, hoping not to find the glassy-eyed victim. But there was no sign of any bird. This time, he concluded, it had been lucky. A survivor. Just like him. Given another chance.

He came to a sudden decision.

He'd go visit Castle Sorralan after all –

Edward Theodore Graysbrook was not the successful businessman he portrayed himself to be.

Successful, yes; and businessman, surely.

But there *was* no Edward Graysbrook...

He was no more than a convenient fiction. His creator, the consummate master of re-invention – of necessity; but, equally, by design. For staying on top had forced him to assume many identities in his lifetime. Always he'd managed to keep one step ahead. And the more skilful he'd become, the greater the distance he'd managed to lay down between the pretence and the truth. His true identity was now virtually untraceable; every means at his disposal constantly updated, used to preserve his anonymity; and to maintain the fiction. Of those closest to him, less than a handful knew the truth about his origins.

So, Edward Graysbrook he would remain.

For now.

When he'd first started out – only in the early days had he used his birth name – there'd been those who'd been cautious of his potential; who'd eyed him as a threat. They'd managed to control him when he was still too young to know any better – by degrees, co-ercion mixed with reward; and when that had started to fail, with threats. But he'd soon grown dissatisfied at being pushed around; playing second fiddle; doing all the work, but for little gain. And, finally, realising his talents far exceeded theirs, he'd struck out on his own. They hadn't liked that. It had meant competition – something they simply couldn't tolerate. A challenge to their position, to their authority. So they'd given him an ultimatum. And he'd come to his decision.

Had committed murder; when so young.

Even then, he'd displayed a ruthless streak mature beyond his years. He'd planned their deaths right down to the last detail; had taken care there'd be no trail leading to his door. Perhaps, surprisingly, he'd not actually taken any pleasure from the act of killing them. Survival of the fittest – that's how he'd viewed it. No different to how, these days, he made financial killings, orchestrating the latest multi-national take-overs. The gamble back then had been immense – but it had paid off. And that had been the turning point. When he'd come of age. No going back. Overnight, established himself as a force to be reckoned with. And after that, those he'd left alive had elected to side with him; had judged it better to wait in the wings; patiently sit it out until he came a cropper; overstepped the mark...

Only he never had.

A fast learner, he'd been quick to sow seeds of doubt among his rivals; to generate paranoia; mistrust – had incited them to engage in in-fighting; to remove one another; saving himself the trouble. Equally, he'd strengthened his own hand by positioning around him those he felt sure he could trust; age no barrier to placement; loyalty and a new, exploitable skill brought to the table the only credentials needed.

Edward Graysbrook.

Acorn to sapling; sapling to oak.

And now the corporate chameleon.

But despite the passage of time, his mind and memory were as keen as ever – the details of each persona he'd used carefully compartmentalised; catalogued; filed for immediate retrieval – should the need arise. So far, he'd not been caught out – he'd always taken precautions. The stakes were just too high. And more so now, than at any other time in his career. For his was a world experienced – reserved – for but a select few. Largely unseen. And fiercely guarded. Where the wealth he'd accumulated was, to most, unimaginable – surpassing the worth of many a small country. Where he had private jets; a helicopter for the weekend; penthouses in every major world city; yachts in as many harbours; a string of villas – some he'd not even bothered to visit. All across the globe, the sun never set on one of Edward Graysbrook's properties. And his sphere of influence was extensive. With world leaders, financial movers and shakers on speed-dial; and captains of industry; press barons – all linked to his interests one way or another. His was the virtual power behind so many thrones; his, too, the hidden funding that bankrolled successive players – with plans long since drawn up to sponsor the next generation of presidents and prime ministers.

Edward Graysbrook.

The epitome of achievement. From nothing to something. From something to everything. From nowhere to somewhere. And somewhere to everywhere. Self-confident. Arrogant. Single-minded. Driven. Forever in the right place at the right time. As if he had a sixth sense. Everything he touched, always turning to gold. Possessed of the greatest luck imaginable.

He'd even cheated death –

But, necessarily, he'd misrepresented what had actually happened; conscious of the importance of safeguarding his wider interests…

For he, and only he, knew what had really happened; had seen all too clearly his own mortality – the accident that had so nearly killed him; when his whole world had so nearly ended.

Power. Status. Importance.

All could have been wiped out in an instant. And his survival; his escape – something only he could fully appreciate.

There was a knock at the door.

It was his 11:30 am weekly round-up. Directors' meeting. One by one, a string of drones filed in to sit round the conference table. For the next thirty minutes, he received updates on how his key portfolios were faring. Global recession. Multi-nationals going bust. Banking system in meltdown. Countries facing bankruptcy. A world in financial crisis. All of which was good news – his interests once again all set to benefit from others' misfortune. No matter the human cost, he just recognised the opportunities for expansion; to re-model the empty shells into the visions he wanted to see. He thanked each member of his team for their reports and sent them on their way.

All except one.

Tom Casey.

His closest friend and ally. One of those rare individuals whose ruthless single-mindedness he judged comparable to his own. Just as well the man had other limitations – or he might justifiably have needed to consider *him* a threat. But he knew Tom's innermost secrets, his own weaknesses; and should the time ever come...

Graysbrook toyed with a cuff link, a red ball of material that matched the hand-woven tie. One concern preoccupied him; nothing to do with the reports he'd just heard. Without looking up, he said, 'Why is he *still* alive?'

Casey had been expecting the question and answered calmly. 'He isn't a problem, Edward. He doesn't know anything. He *can't* know anything – you of all people should understand that.'

Graysbrook's blue eyes narrowed; grey eyebrows furrowed by another concern. 'I think someone's protecting him. What do you think? Or does he just lead an exceptionally charmed life?'

'I can't say,' Casey spread his hands, apologetically. Not the answer Graysbrook wanted to hear. He needed to recover the situation; deflect any potential anger from himself. He decided to appeal to the other man's logic. 'We've tried to have him killed. You know the lengths we've gone to. The planning alone is like nothing we've attempted before. If we go on like this, we do risk drawing attention to ourselves. And that's the last thing we want. Yes?'

Graysbrook considered the man's analysis. He began tying and untying the other cuff link. He answered Casey's question with another question. 'Where is he now?'

'Far north of Scotland. We're not exactly sure where, yet. But we'll trace him.'

'Be sure you do.' He stopped fiddling. He'd reached his decision. 'Very well. Against my better judgement, I agree – for *now*. But when you do find him, we need to be sure we can control him; where he goes; who he sees. So, I want you to give Pierfranco a call. Get him to offer him something. The man's going to need a job after all...'

'I'll get onto it straight away.'

'And... I *do* want to know if someone is protecting him. And if they are, I want them killed. We need to send a message out loud and clear. That's all.' Graysbrook swung round in his chair to admire the London skyline.

Lucy Tanzer hadn't always heard voices.

They'd only started speaking to her after her husband had left. She'd had to put up with years of his belittling comments before that. Telling her how she wasn't a real woman. How she'd let him down. How he'd never have married her if he'd known. He'd insisted she go for tests to find out why she couldn't conceive. He'd never gone with her, of course. But why would he? The problem was hers, not his, and, in hindsight, it seemed he'd been right. But the one time she'd dared suggest they could go together, he'd gone off on one. Telling her never to question his manhood again. He'd insisted he could have had his pick of the girls. He'd have had four or five kids with any one of them. She should have considered herself lucky – honoured – he'd chosen to be with her. That's when his absences had started. He'd not come home. Just the odd night here and there to begin with. He'd said he'd had to work late; had crashed in the office. But, by the end, she was lucky if she saw him two days out of every seven. He hadn't even bothered with excuses then; had just said he needed space. And that had gone on until he'd announced he was seeing someone else and would be leaving her. For good. He'd told her not to say anything to his mother – or there'd be hell to pay. He said she'd disown her. Take his side. But Lucy had gone ahead and told her anyway, not caring about the consequences. And his mother had been anything but dismissive; had been a real support to her – everything her husband never had been. And if only she'd known before; not been afraid to ask for help, maybe it would have turned out differently.

But the voices had helped, too.

Margaret had only had so much time. She'd had her own life to lead. Whereas the voices had always been there when she'd needed them. Always a kind word for her. Ready to offer a verbal helping hand; to raise her self-esteem whenever she hit a particularly low patch. She'd always found it hard walking past mothers with prams; toddlers walking along the street. And she'd made a point of avoiding schools at going-home time. Too many sad thoughts. Of what might have been…

It had been *their* idea – the voices' – for her to break away; to branch out on her own. And they'd been really supportive of her idea of going into business. Maybe they'd planted the idea – she couldn't remember now – but she'd seen an opening in the market; had noticed there were still a lot of houses with working chimneys. And mostly older folk – like Margaret – who liked to sit by a real fire. Feeling the natural warmth; the glow; the feel-good memories it invoked. Nothing could compete with that. Fire equated to safety; protection; comfort. An instinctive memory, programmed into the psyche long before the Stone Age. So, she'd gone on a business course; learnt about market research; sent out questionnaires; conducted a *vox pop* in the high street;

and the feedback had been so encouraging. Many had commented how they'd feel safer with a woman in the house; especially at their time of life. And finding an apprenticeship – that had just fallen into her lap; proof if ever it were needed the whole thing was just meant to be.

She'd been working for around three months when Margaret had mentioned her neighbours. Nice old couple, Percy and Ivy Wilson. Getting a bit slow, but still liked to sit round their fire. Would she be able to go round? She'd intended to go... but the voices had dissuaded her; had kept telling her the time wasn't right. The couple would keep. She'd made her excuses; said something about all the work she had on; and they'd been really accommodating, telling her just to let them know when she was free. No rush. They'd get by.

She remembered she'd been in the supermarket car-park when the voices had told her to go round. Didn't matter she hadn't made an appointment. The pair knew Margaret and so, through Margaret, they knew her. Decent, trusting folk. They'd let her in; no bother. And did she also know, the voices had asked her, that the couple needed other help? With the kids? They were too old to look after children. She could do that for them. They'd be really grateful. So she'd gone round. And like the voices had said, they'd let her in; been really welcoming when she'd introduced herself. She'd seen the twins. Oh, they were gorgeous; just how she'd imagined her own children would have been. And the voices had been insistent – no need to ask; just take the children. They were hers now. Yes, they had another mummy and daddy; but hadn't they abandoned them? What sort of parent would put their own interests before the happiness of their child? And to leave the vulnerable with those no longer able to care for them? It was wicked. It was abuse. Whichever way you looked at it. So she did as the voices had suggested. Had decided to become the twins' new mummy. They'd be much happier with her. She'd give them the love they were missing.

The rest of it was a blank, really. She'd been moving furniture; tidying up... there'd been mess; blood everywhere. She couldn't recall from where though. No wonder the voices had said the couple were past it – if they couldn't even keep their house tidy... She remembered she'd done her best to clean up for them. Surfaces... and she'd emptied the bins... she remembered that much. And the twins, they'd been crying – needing their feed she'd guessed. She'd locked them in the van. Not too long a drive. She'd been sure they'd be alright. And she'd got home. Had been about to take them indoors. But the clever voices had helped her again; offered her the benefit of their experience. Moving them would have meant waking them; so she'd followed the advice and kept them in the van; taken them blankets to keep them warm. And had made up a special milky drink to help them sleep. She couldn't remember exactly what she'd put in, but the voices had guided her. There'd been something she hadn't readily had to hand – but with the voices' prompting, she'd found a suitable alternative under the sink. And it had worked – and so much better than she'd expected. She hadn't heard a peep out of them since. Honestly, she didn't know why other mothers didn't have it as easy...

Tomlinson was sat in Commander Peters' office watching a recording of the latter's press conference from earlier that day; he'd still been busy interviewing Lucy Tanzer. Despite their best efforts to buy time – in particular, to allow them to break the terrible news to Geoff and Anne Wilson; and to get them safely away to see a counsellor so they could begin their grieving in private before the media intruded – someone had leaked word of the arrests. Consequently, their whole arrangements had had to be adapted; and quickly. Tomlinson had had to begin his interview early; with Riley not far behind. And he'd had to leave it to others to contact the Wilsons; something he bitterly resented not being able to do himself. That – he considered – should have been his responsibility, and his alone. So, Peters had decided he'd needed to regain the initiative. He hadn't even consulted Tomlinson – something the superintendent found particularly galling. As it was, the only saving grace was that Peters had kept the statement short and bland. At least no damage done there.

'I didn't alert the press, but we've lined the women up to appear at the magistrate's court first thing tomorrow. I take it you'll have enough evidence by then to charge them?'

'Er... no.'

'What do you mean?' Peters sounded distinctly irritated.

'I mean... Lucy Tanzer, yes – I'm sure we've enough there; the forensics should only add to that. But, Margaret Woods... Riley doesn't think she's guilty...'

'I don't care what your sergeant thinks. What do *you* think, superintendent?'

'I agree with him... we'd need more time to...'

'Well, you haven't got it. Tomorrow, first thing.'

'And the CPS are happy with that?' Tomlinson had serious concerns. Usually the fast-track was reserved for the terrorists. Or – *embarrassing* cases. Peters had gone to the top. Pulled strings. He was certain of that.

'I did what I felt was in our best interests. There's no point prolonging the agony. The children aren't alive. The sooner the press lose interest the better. And the Home Office, there's a storm brewing there. They're already raising concerns about our profiling abilities...'

Tomlinson couldn't believe what he was hearing. He'd thought the commander insensitive before. But this, this was the final straw; proving his senior officer was only interested in two things – protecting the Met's reputation, as well as his own promotion outcome.

It wouldn't do to attract any undue negative publicity. Nor to upset the Home Secretary. And never mind the four dead bodies. Nor the remaining family. Two pitiful souls torn apart by grief; about to be thrown to the media lions. The superintendent knew he had to get out of there, before he said something he'd regret forever. He rose from his seat, excused himself; claimed he had an enquiry that couldn't wait; pointedly looked at his watch for added effect; happy to leave Peters – as well as the man's vacuous pronouncements – behind him as he went.

Tomlinson made for the rear stairwell. His heart was pounding. Anger and disbelief threatened to overwhelm him. He started to feel giddy; had to sit down on the steps. He tried to calm himself; took long, deliberate breaths. Several minutes passed before he felt composed enough to face anybody else.

He felt disgusted by what he'd just witnessed. Found himself thinking if that was what policing had come to, he no longer wanted any part of it. He'd only delayed resigning for the twins' sake. Now, he didn't care anymore. He'd go first thing in the morning. And the magistrate's court? The evidence? Not his problem. Peters could take care of that. They could dock his pay; do what they wanted. But he had no intention of doing any more; and there was no way he'd serve out his notice. If they caused trouble for him, he'd go sick.

He'd go tell Brenda.

Then give Riley a call.

Other than that, no-one else mattered.

Not any more.

'Tomorrow then?'

'I've said yes.'

'Good.' Sam was happy. 'I'll give Rudi a call after breakfast; see what he's got on.'

'You do *really* want to go?' Neve asked Bryant.

'Yes. I'm actually quite looking forward to it, especially after what Sam's just said. It'll be entertaining, if nothing else...'

CHAPTER FOURTEEN

'THE DEFENDANT WILL be remanded into custody, pending full medical assessment and provision of psychiatric reports...'

Lucy Tanzer didn't hear the magistrate's words. Her attention was elsewhere.

Since being interviewed by Tomlinson, she had retreated further into her fragile psyche; withdrawn even deeper into her private world of personal confusion. To the point that, during her brief court appearance, she'd not even been lucid enough to speak to confirm her name and address. Her solicitor, instead, had had to offer confirmation to the bench.

Throughout the proceedings, Lucy had just remained blissfully ignorant of the storm brewing all around her – of the disbelief and contempt directed towards her from the public gallery; of the fires of hatred spreading outside, their flames being fanned by a greedy, zephyrous media wind as reporters jockeyed for position – tabloid space and air-time their coveted finishing post; and of the feelings of helplessness and anger being fostered in homes across the land. Unknown to her, as the hours passed by, radio phone-ins and TV programmes would variously be debating her macabre story; their switchboards alive with calls for the re-introduction of the death penalty.

And even as she was being escorted from the dock, Lucy was already a lifer; sentenced to see out the rest of her days in a prison of shifting awareness – where time, comprehension, engagement followed a different set of laws; where the rules of existence were governed by a separate reality; one reserved for those in psychological solitary; and where the cacophony of voices that she heard would be her only cell-mates.

She tilted her head to one side, straining to make sense of the garbled messages that were bouncing from ear to ear; the words disjointed; by degrees louder; quieter; truncated; or eliding; each rolling separately into the many. She persevered, waiting for the relative clarity to emerge – as it had done so many times before over the past weeks. Patience the watchword; she knew that. She tried humming. She'd found that that usually helped, too; somehow reducing the intensity of the sonic interference; levelling the vocal wave-front. And then – yes, it was working. The more she listened, the clearer some of the words became; repeated messages, that stood out from the background noise. That were different in tone and accent – sometimes even in language. But there was a pattern emerging. Joining the audio dots...

And then she had it.

Understood what she needed to do.

Tomlinson felt completely at ease as he walked into the office. He'd sat down with Brenda the previous evening and run through it all. And she'd taken the news in her stride, had supported him – just as she had done his whole career. As he'd expected, she'd asked how they were going to manage until he retired, and he'd reassured her – had said he'd find something; would maybe go freelance, do a bit of private investigation, or see if there was any security work on offer with the multi-nationals. He still had contacts – he'd put out a few feelers. Either way, they'd get by until he received his lump sum; until they made the break and headed for the sun.

Tomlinson looked around for Riley. He wanted to let him know first. Break the news that he'd be going.

He checked his watch, guessed Lucy Tanzer would be out of court by now; probably on her way to the nearest local prison – or maybe en route to a secure psychiatric hospital. He could just imagine how annoyed Peters would be when he did finally get to see him. There'd be the official rebuke, the posturing, the feigned incredulity he'd been let down. And that would be followed by the attempted guilt trip – that he'd let his colleagues down; that others had had to take his place at court at such short notice that morning. What had he been thinking of?

He wondered if Riley had been ordered to attend in his place. If the sergeant had, he'd be sure to apologise to him for not having given him the heads-up beforehand. But Tomlinson knew the court appearance would have just been a formality; not really that much that could have gone wrong. And so what if it had? So what that he'd not been there? No – he'd be sticking by his decision. This was no longer his case. None of it his concern any more. And he wasn't going to be rail-roaded into changing his mind. Peters, the Commissioner; the whole lot of them – they could just go hang.

His pager vibrated again. It had been going constantly all morning. He'd not even checked it once. And, likewise, he'd deliberately kept his mobile switched off, just to make sure they couldn't reach him.

He saw Riley was there, standing by a row of filing cabinets. Maybe he'd not had to go to court after all. He walked slowly up to him. The sergeant couldn't help noticing Tomlinson's air, more confident than usual; more assured than the situation demanded. But before the superintendent could say anything, Riley spoke first.

'Sir, you'd best go see the Commander. His secretary's already been down here looking for you. *Twice.*' The emphasis clear. 'He's not happy with you...'

'What, that I dared go AWOL?' Tomlinson shrugged dismissively. 'Listen, Paul,' he continued, 'I need a quiet word with you.'

'But, sir,' Riley persisted.

'No,' Tomlinson was equally insistent. 'Peters can wait. This can't.' A couple of minutes later and the sergeant was fully in the picture; as well as genuinely speechless. 'Right, then. Into the lion's den,' said Tomlinson flatly.

Sam had telephoned Rudi Fridriksson a little after 8:00 am. Rudi had been his usual, welcoming self and had offered to set aside several hours so they could all meet up and talk properly. He'd told Sam he'd need to leave them by 3:00 pm though as he already had a prior appointment. He'd suggested the two of them come over as soon as they could after 9:30 am. So with fifty minutes to go, Sam and Bryant were climbing into the Land Rover. Neve waved them off.

'How far is it?' Bryant asked

'Thirty miles, give or take.'

Bryant looked at the clock. 'Won't we be cutting it a bit fine?'

'No. Plenty of time. You'll see.' Bryant was still in southern-commuting mindset – where the car was slave to traffic jams, diversions and increasing levels of stress at the wheel. Sam could see the dubious look, so offered further explanation. 'It's a good fast road most of the way; then we take the single-track, but there's regular passing places if we meet anyone – although I don't think we will. It's quiet enough even in the summer, let alone now. And the visibility's good – you can see what's coming miles ahead.' Bryant nodded his acceptance. 'Radio?' Sam gestured his passenger should oblige.

Bryant turned the dial. The station was half way through a news flash.

'... *Tanzer, aged thirty-three, has been remanded into custody by magistrates. Police are continuing their enquiries and, as yet, are keeping an open mind into the motive for the two sets of killings. Our reporter at the scene, had this to say...*'

'*Not* to me he doesn't –' Sam quickly pushed a button and muted the station. 'Here, see if there's something in there you fancy.' He reached a hand down into the central console, fumbled around and passed Bryant a CD wallet.

Before he'd even opened it, Bryant asked, 'Is there *anything* in here that isn't going to be heavy metal?'

'Hm – *Driving Selection*'s probably your best bet...'

Bryant leafed through the wallet. '*Driving Selection* it is.' He loaded the CD, as Sam pressed the mute button again to restore the sound. Bryant couldn't help smiling as he heard something he recognised; something he actually liked; something that wouldn't deafen him for the rest of the journey. 'Hey, this is from the 60s.'

'Aim to please.'

With music to match, Bryant found the rest of the journey a delight. For, unlike the night drive up from Inverness, he was now able to enjoy the beauty of the scenery; taking in the landscape – the hillside colours, the way the light was continually changing. They soon branched off from the main road, heading further away from the eastern coastline to journey inland, westwards, into the heart of the Sutherland mountain ranges. To begin with, the road steadfastly accompanied its twin cousins – the adjacent river and railway line – following the line of least resistance, as it snaked its way up a succession of glens. In places, the hillsides looked ravaged; having fallen prey to the hand of man – commercial deforestation seeing acre upon acre of pines felled; wide grey scars running menacingly towards the next tree line; the respite but temporary, before the next scheduled round of mechanical carnage began. And where the rocky surfaces had once more been exposed, skeletal houses had emerged into the daylight; proud in their isolated defiance – but isolated equally now in memory; their history, stories, owners all but forgotten. The Land Rover pressed on, passing through a string of small villages. Bryant noticed larger Victorian houses set prominently on the outskirts – testament to a bygone era of incomers' wealth. But jostling for attention here and there along the valley floor were new-builds, some equally large, all cream exteriors and double garages growing incongruously out of the ancient landscape; awaiting time's weathering effects to afford them at least a partial, natural acceptance.

On they drove and, just as Sam had predicted, nothing much came in the opposite direction – a post van; a solitary oil tanker; and a courier going like the clappers. But otherwise, the road had gone unused – but for the occasional wandering sheep, and roadside buzzard sat atop a fence-post.

'Nearly there,' Sam said presently. The terrain had become more rugged the further inland they'd gone and the higher they'd climbed. Wind-bent trees crafted into demonic shapes signalled the remotest of cottages; with intervening tracts of marshland and lochans the owners' nearest neighbours for miles; man's-planted woodlands less noticeable now; and instead, the hillsides rising more naturally to meet the rougher, high lands beyond. 'Another couple of miles, then we'll strike south-west. Through that range,' Sam pointed over the dashboard, 'then double-back on ourselves and continue down towards the coast.'

Bryant called to mind the picture of Castle Sorralan from the brochure. It had been surrounded by woods and was open to a loch. Sam had said coast, so he asked,

'The castle's what... on a tidal loch?'

'Sea loch – stunning position; the pictures don't do it justice.'

Sam's estimated time of arrival had only been five minutes out. They pulled into the long driveway at 9:35 am. Gazing to either side of him, Bryant could see wide expanses of deciduous woodland, interspersed with Scots pine; and judging by their size, some as old as the castle itself.

'What are those?' he asked. Where the trees had lost their leaves, he could make out structures of some kind set back into the woods.

'Cabins, chalets; still fairly new. All part of Rudi's great plan. But I won't steal his thunder. He can tell you about them – and the rest of his vision.'

'Don't get me wrong, but I'm surprised he's even seeing us. I mean, from what Neve said – no offence, Sam – but you're only really a *handyman* of sorts...'

'No offence taken.'

'So,' Bryant continued, 'I wouldn't have expected you to be rubbing elbows with the local laird.'

Sam smiled. 'Rudi's not exactly what you'd call your typical upper-crust kind of guy. He's very warm; open; caring; and absolutely passionate about his beliefs. But, again, I'll leave him to explain. What I will say is... I didn't *actually* meet him through work. I came here last winter for a series of talks and I didn't even realise who he was. We just happened to be sitting next to one another and got paired off for the remote-viewing exercise.'

Remote-viewing.

The way Sam had casually dropped that one into the conversation didn't faze Bryant in the slightest. Straightaway he fired back, 'Oh my God – he's not another of your happy-clappy band, is he?'

'Afraid so. New Ager through and through – and very proud of it. And you thought I was bad...'

'And yet he's got all this?' Bryant shook his head in disbelief. 'Well, he can't be that simple-minded. This must have cost millions.'

'Well, he bought the estate back in the nineties – when everything was cheaper – but, relatively speaking, yes, he's spent a small fortune on it. Especially over the past year.'

They were approaching the front of the building now, but Sam veered off down a gravel track.

'It's OK, we're not going in the tradesman's entrance, or anything. Rudi just prefers visitors to park down here.' He reversed the Land Rover neatly into position, turned off the engine then tapped the dashboard clock. '9:38. That was good going.' He undid his seat belt. 'Come on.'

The media were already camped outside the front of the prison when the escort van and police out-riders approached its main entrance. Photographers swarmed round the vehicle, impeding its progress; and raised arms, holding flashing cameras aloft, ran along its length, taking frame after frame through each of the tinted windows. The chances low, but the stakes high. The first of them to get even a partial head shot of Lucy Tanzer would be able to syndicate the image; sit back and watch as the money rolled in.

The van edged slowly forwards and, after the police had finally cleared a path, it drove through the double doors into the prison's secure reception area. Once the doors had shut out the free world once again, prison staff emerged from the gatehouse to check the vehicle – hand-held mirrors sweeping along the underside; and the roof observed using the high-level, wall-mounted mirrors above. A thorough search by a dog and then, when they were satisfied nothing was amiss, the vehicle was allowed to continue further into the prison complex.

A female escort officer descended from the rear of the van, hand-cuffed to Lucy. She led her prisoner quickly through to the reception area.

For her part, Lucy was aware she'd been placed in a room; alone. Others – prisoners like herself – had been kept together in a small group, and they were banging on the adjacent glass window. But she couldn't hear them; the voices in her head blocking out all other noise. She could see their faces, though, and wondered why they were spitting at the glass. She just smiled back. Everyone liked a smile, didn't they? They'd discovered that with babies, hadn't they, some researcher or other? She remembered, it had been on a TV programme; how babies naturally smiled.

And just for a moment, her smile faded as she wondered where her babies were. She hoped they were being looked after. Still, it wouldn't be long before she could get back to them. The voices had told her as much. Had promised she'd soon be released.

She felt hands on her arm. Powerful. Dominant. Was aware of a white shirt. A black tie. And then she was being led along a corridor. Someone beside her opening a door. Pushing her through. And then she was collapsing onto the floor...

A pain in her shoulder.

Her hand hurting.

And then her left eye, cheek and nose; suddenly all on fire –

Sally, the commander's secretary, didn't even want to meet Tomlinson's gaze when he walked into her outer office.

'He's absolutely fuming, Ray. You'd better go straight in.' She buzzed through to announce the superintendent's arrival but, even before she'd finished speaking, Peters was at the door; summoning Tomlinson in; ready to call him to account.

The superintendent, though, was ready for Peters.

But not for the *other* man in the commander's office –

Just for a moment, Tomlinson's calmness wavered. He was trying to identify the third party. He couldn't put a name to the face, but he knew the man worked in internal investigation. As likely as not, that meant *he* was under investigation. But for what?

Nicol.

It had to be. Police brutality – the torture he'd inflicted on the man. Damn it, he reasoned, Nicol had reported him after all. Or his solicitor had. They'd obviously made an official complaint. But then, hadn't he expected it? And didn't he deserve it?

Suddenly, it was all happening too quickly. He didn't even hear what Peters was saying. The other man there was shaking his hand. Firm. Composed. Controlling. Tomlinson wondered how he'd escaped that long. He'd expected Nicol to blab straight away. Only a matter of time, he'd guessed. And now his actions had caught up with him. He was trying to weigh up the repercussions. Of course, he'd probably be suspended while they investigated the complaint. But – wait – what was he worried about? None of this mattered. He was resigning. They couldn't touch him.

'... *suspended* until further notice, superintendent...' The other man speaking.

And then Peters, adding, 'I'm extremely disappointed by this, Ray. Ordinarily, I'd step in; keep you here but, after this morning... well, I think the best thing is for you to have some space; take time to consider your options. I really couldn't believe it...'

He was still waiting to hear mention of Karl Nicol. But he was sure neither man had said that name. He was about to raise the subject himself, when he heard the word *fraud*. And then Peters challenging him, 'How long did you think you could get away with it? Why? I trusted you...'

And then the third man was there, a hand on his elbow; escorting him to the door; passing him an envelope. Advising he should leave at once; and that someone would be in touch when they wanted to interview him. And there was a warning about his bank account. That he'd find his assets frozen for the duration. Just a precaution.

Tomlinson was in a daze.

Confusion uppermost, as he was ushered out of the commander's room. And Sally, she was pretending to be engrossed in her typing; but he could feel her eyes in the back of his head as he walked out into the corridor. He'd not gone that far when he remembered the envelope. The letter within. He slid an index finger down the seam, nicking his skin in the process. He touched the digit absently to his lips, sucked at the thin line of blood that was appearing. A pause, and then he pulled out and unfolded the sheet of paper; noted the heading – he'd been right; it *was* the internal investigation squad. He read – re-read – the typed allegation that was being levelled against him. He stood, dumbfounded as he studied the contents for a third time. The letter spoke of investigation into long-term fraud; financial irregularities that had come to the squad's attention; and that he was being suspended, pending a full investigation. All monies obtained by deception would be recoverable, notwithstanding any charges brought against him. And, then, the final body blow; mention of the sanctions that could be imposed on him – reduced or cancelled pension entitlements; demotion; reduced years' service.

All of it to do with money.

Blood money – for his finger was even now staining the letter from underneath.

Just *what* was going on?

None of it made any sense. They couldn't suspect *he* was involved in fraud? It was ridiculous. He'd never even inflated an expenses claim – quite the reverse, in fact. Over the years he'd let so many go. Never filling in the paperwork. Always too little time. Proper policing to be getting on with. This was all nonsense. They'd have to see that. Just a stupid mistake. Wrong man…

He got back to his office. Riley came over to see him.

'How did it go?'

The superintendent's chin dropped and his eyes stared incredulously as he said, 'I've been suspended…'

The gravel crunched noisily underfoot as Bryant and Sam walked up the path towards the stone tower. Bryant could see now that the adjacent trees weren't as close as he'd initially thought; the photograph's perspective skewing the reality.

The tower measured around sixty feet square; its height was another third taller still. It sat atop a levelled terrace and there was a surrounding outer wall, although Bryant judged this to be too low to have had any defensive purpose historically; maybe it had been a more recent ornamental addition. He noticed also that the rocks in this wall were darker in colour than those used in the tower's construction; again, potentially suggesting a different construction date. There was a single wooden doorway at ground level, visible over the top of the wall; and to either side of it, but set far higher up into the block-work, were four windows; two pairs of two; each set indicating living quarters on the upper storeys. To all intents, the tower remained true to its origins – no unnecessary windows or other openings added; as defensive in structure now as it had ever been.

The building was smaller than Bryant had imagined – quite modest, in fact, given the wealth of its owner; unless, of course, there were further outbuildings, or conversions, he couldn't yet see.

Sam led him right up to the front door.

'You weren't kidding, were you?'

'Like I said, he's very easy-going.' Sam pushed a brass button for a few seconds.

They heard the scraping of metal from behind the door and then a headless man appeared, filling the entrance –

Rudi Fridriksson.

A moment later and he'd crouched down, coming forward a few feet to allow his head to clear the unforgiving stone lintel. Long grey hair framed a pale, chiselled face; with a wildly-flowing beard that wouldn't have looked out of place on a fantasy-film magician. Fridriksson was marginally taller than Bryant, measuring six foot five, with the frame and build to match. But he didn't appear overly heavy; more compact; solid. Very much like his castle. Bryant found it a little disconcerting to find himself staring up at someone – an unusual occurrence – but Rudi was instantly there, holding out his arm; the handshake firm, the degree of pressure well-judged.

'Welcome. Welcome to you both. Please, come into my home.' His voice was soft, like the man himself, but edged with a quirky vocal foreignness; shades of the Teutonic – and the pitch, a pastiche of Scandinavian and wider European all thrown into a carefree, vocal melting pot. But his English seemed very good. Fridriksson stood to one side, inviting them to go first. Sam led the way but, before Bryant could follow, an arm blocked his progress. 'You are like me,' Fridriksson laughed. 'You must watch your head; yes?' Bryant nodded. Further laughter from the other man.

The interior was altogether different from Bryant's expectations. To begin with, it was less spacious than he'd anticipated and he soon figured out why. The tower's walls were deep and encroached significantly into the usable living accommodation. But more than that, he'd thought it would be a case of small dark rooms, with little natural light coming in through the few windows. But it was nothing of the kind. The main living area was bright and airy, and the sense of space was magnified by the double-height ceiling. He saw now that the first-storey windows he'd noticed from outside had been included in the design of the room, letting additional light flood in.

Everything was open-plan; the large main living-area housing sofas, tables, easy chairs, the TV and a home entertainment system; while off to one side there was a functional kitchen; and adjacent to that, a dining area that comfortably seated six. The floor was a light marble, its smoothness contrasting vividly with the rough, uneven lines of the tower's original stone walls. And where the first storey would originally have been, a small gallery had been introduced, running a full circuit round the interior; black guard-rails keeping any modern-day sentries safe from harm. Bryant could appreciate the planning that had gone into the conversion – bookcases and other storage cleverly built into every available niche; and original features preserved throughout. The gallery's supporting framework had been concealed beneath a wooden façade; the theme of the soft tones continuing where light-coloured panelling had been added to some of the alcove walls. And high above, the ceiling had been painted white; reflecting further light back into the centre of the room. All in all, understated comfort; personal to its owner – but welcoming of guests.

Bryant thought the interior had something of a seventies feel – but if Fridriksson had only moved in during the nineties, this must all have been the taste of a previous owner. And for Fridriksson not to have redecorated must have meant he'd approved. His own furniture certainly fitted in well with the overall tone of the place – earthy colours and creams; but for the splash of loud colour in the dining area, where six red chairs screamed out for attention. He scanned round for other doors, but couldn't see any that were immediately obvious. He knew there was still a further unseen storey above – most likely where they'd built the master bedroom; as well as the guest rooms and bathrooms. He judged there'd be no more than five bedrooms – including the master. And the stairs? Maybe attached externally to one of the building's corners; or built into the walls? He guessed the latter would be more likely, given the tower's original purpose and the thickness of the walls.

Fridriksson ushered his guests towards one of the sofas. 'Please, be seated. Would you like a drink?'

'Thanks, Rudi. Whatever's easiest. David? Coffee OK?'

'Oh, er, yes, fine thank you.' Bryant replied, still taking in his surroundings.

Each gaze rewarded him with another discovery. He'd noticed a map of Iceland hanging on one of the walls. He put two and two together – Fridriksson was Icelandic, not Scandinavian. But he'd been close enough. And then he'd seen the metallic clock on the wall; impressionistic – maybe signifying the points of a compass; or a crystalline snowflake; certainly something in that style; simple – and yet intricate. It showed ten to ten.

Presently, Rudi came to join them, setting down their coffees before seating himself in a reclining easy chair. 'So, my dear Sam, thank you so very much for coming to see me... and for bringing with you your most interesting friend.'

How does he know you're interesting?

The little voice was back.

Sam was making the formal introductions. 'David – Rudi Fridriksson. Rudi – David Bryant.' The host raised his coffee by way of a welcoming toast.

What's he been saying?

Bryant almost cursed aloud as the voice registered in his consciousness. But he contained himself, and mentally willed the voice to leave.

Why? It asked.

Again, Bryant *thought* rather than silently spoke his reply. Intuitively, this meeting with Fridriksson just felt – so right; meant to be; and with Sam here, too, comfortable. Bryant just wanted to be able to relax and enjoy himself. Just for once, without any interruptions.

But I've told you before... the voice starting to argue now.

But Bryant persisted; quietly; inwardly thinking – *imagining* – it should go; urging it to leave him alone. It fired back a question at him and he replied in kind – his one concession, a promise not to raise Graysbrook. Other than that, he insisted, what he chose to tell the man would be his decision. And *his* alone. He expected the voice to offer further objections but it didn't. He paused, waiting for it to answer. But it had gone. Bryant raised his own cup in a belated, mutual gesture.

'So, David; Sam has been telling me of your incredible good fortune. You are a very lucky man, I think?'

'Hope you don't mind?' Sam ventured. 'Like I said before, Rudi might be able to help... you know, explain what could be going on...'

Fridriksson nodded. 'If not me, then perhaps we will find some answers for you...'

Answers.

Answers sounded good. Bryant was happy to make time for someone who had answers.

'I'd like that; that would be very welcome, Rudi; thank you.'

'That is what we will do, then. But first, we finish our coffee,' Fridriksson swirled round the contents of his cup, trying to speed its cooling. 'I will show you, if you like, the projects we are doing here...'

Tomlinson was rifling through his desk drawers, seeing if there was anything personal he ought to take with him. He guessed he'd have around fifteen minutes to pack up the essentials and get out before Peters had the presence of mind to send security to escort him from the building. He'd not been told to surrender his warrant card so he decided, if nobody asked, he'd keep it. Not that he planned to use it – what would he need it for, as he'd already decided to resign? No, he'd hang on to it for the time being just to be bloody-minded. Whatever was going on, he wasn't going to make it easy for them.

Fraud.

He still couldn't believe it. Just *where* had that come from? But he wasn't going to let them get away with it. Not if it meant compromising his financial security. He'd fight them all the way. And when they realised they'd messed up, he'd want not just an apology – but some form of compensation, too.

Fraud.

The word was out – and it seemed some were already prepared to believe the gossip; judging by the suspicious, disapproving looks he was getting from several people over the far side of the office. Riley was on his way back in. Tomlinson saw him stop by one of the desks, say something to one of those who'd been staring. Riley. Loyal to the end. But this wasn't Riley's battle. It was his.

The phone went on Tomlinson's desk – not that he considered it his desk, nor his phone any more. He ignored it. It carried on ringing. No-one else was going to pick up, and he could see Riley was preoccupied; remonstrating with the doubters. Tomlinson sighed wearily and picked up the receiver. He'd be polite. Not the caller's fault all this had suddenly kicked off.

'Tomlinson, hello?' He listened patiently for a moment, then said, 'No, look, I told your colleague before… that's *not* my case; I just happened to pick up the phone; that's all. No, you want DI Mick Bancroft. *Bancroft,*' he spelled out the name slowly for the caller. 'Yes, that's right. What?' A question at the other end. 'Well, if it's here, yes, of course I'll send it on to him. What? No. Well, when did you send it? Hang on, I'll have a look.' Tomlinson lifted the uppermost papers out of his in-tray. Second down. 'Yes, I've got it here. Right, will do. Yes, bye. Bye.' He put the receiver down.

Unsurprisingly, and despite his best efforts, wires had remained crossed after he'd taken that call for Mick the other night in the studio – so *he'd* been sent the call-logging data instead of it going to Mick's team.

Just for a moment, Tomlinson was tempted to put the document back in his in-tray; forget about it. But that wouldn't be fair to Mick. Wouldn't be fair to the WPC who'd taken the savage beating. So, instead, he opened a drawer and took out a transit envelope. He scribbled a quick note and was about to staple it to the front of the log when something caught his eye.

Half way down the page.

A paragraph of text.

On the face of it, no different to the others. And, yet, the content was drawing him in. He tapped a finger beside the relevant details box. Began to read the background to that one particular call.

'Wait a minute,' he mused to himself. 'This can't be right? Someone's having us on...'

He was remembering something Riley had said.

Making a connection.

A disconcerting one...

CHAPTER FIFTEEN

LUCY TANZER WASN'T the only one who'd been injured in the sudden attack. The officer who'd been escorting her to the prison medical centre had also sustained minor burns to her face, hands and torso. The injuries to both of them might have been far worse, but for the fact that the officer had had the briefest of warnings – ever watchful, noticing just the slightest of movement out of the corner of her eye before the assault had begun; before the shouting had shattered the relative calm. It had given her a fraction of a second to place herself between the prisoner and the assailant; time enough then to get a door open and push her charge to the floor while she took the full force of the shower of scalding liquid; as well as the screamed obscenities that rained down alongside.

When they came to write up the incident report – and the aggressor would subsequently be called before the governor for adjudication – the facts would show that management's carefully thought-out precautions had been found wanting. As soon as the prison authorities discovered they'd be receiving Lucy Tanzer from the court, they'd taken a gamble and had instigated a full lock-down. Never a decision to be taken lightly. For lock-downs had their own inherent dangers, and were usually reserved for the most serious of scenarios – when intelligence suggested a disturbance was planned; or if it appeared keys might have been compromised; or, occasionally, if a major drugs search was planned. Even at the best of times, prisons were potential flash points – someone always harbouring a grudge, looking for an opportunity to settle old scores; or others just wanting to flout the rules; deliberately give the screws a hard time – allay the boredom; fight the system, all part of the fun. And, so, it had been a calculated risk. To lock up more than three hundred prisoners without warning – and so soon after breakfast, when they were just starting their day's activities; about to enjoy the relative freedom of being away from their cells – and to expect them all to return quietly.

But they did.

The gamble had paid off.

In management's favour, the prison had been fairly settled over the past weeks – in no small part, thanks to the overwhelming success of a recent show that the inmates had been involved with; planning it, staging the event, undertaking the performances. And all with the help of a local performing arts' group who'd coached them; uncovered latent talent – plenty of it, just waiting to be tapped into. The group had received several grants to carry on its work with underprivileged kids, but had wanted to give something extra back to their community; to help out those they felt were being excluded; sidelined; so they'd contacted the prison. When they'd all been security-cleared, and the necessary measures had been put in place, they'd been allowed in; had begun their work with the inmates. As ever, many prisoners had at first signed up just to get out of their cells – but when they realised commitment was needed, that it wouldn't just be a breeze, they'd just as quickly lost interest. But there had been those, too, who'd stayed the course; who'd put their heart and soul into the project; had been determined to achieve something of which they could be rightfully proud. And, with the support and coaching of the arts' group, many of those had rediscovered long-forgotten feelings of self-worth; had recognised again their potential; the opportunities that could yet lie ahead for them on release; had become ever more determined to apply themselves inside, while still enjoying the enforced freedom from their former lifestyles – which, for many, had meant drug abuse and petty crime to fund the never-ending habit.

Happy inmates.

Stable prison.

So it had been. And so it would have remained on the morning their *celebrity* arrived, but for the oversight –

The *exception*.

The waiving of the rules that simply ought not to have been allowed. For lock-down meant *everyone*. But one of the senior officers, Nev Holmes, thinking he knew best, had decided to let Emma stay out. Emma was a red-band. The mark of distinction. The badge – arm-band – of trust. Red-bands were given the best jobs. And access. Access that was denied to others. He'd asked Emma to get a brew on. Just like she did every morning. He'd given her ten minutes' grace. No need to keep an eye on her. And all thanks to Nev's arrogant misjudgement, one of his colleagues had just paid the price; not to mention their newly-arrived prisoner.

Injuries. Needless. And so easily preventable.

The report into the assault would include senior officer Holmes' part in the whole sorry mess, too. Would mention the period he'd left Emma unsupervised – time enough for her to add repeated cupfuls of sugar to the tea-pot's boiling water; cup after careful cup; until she got the consistency just right; so it would no longer dissolve; but instead would be held in suspension, ready to stick to the skin; painfully exacerbate the scalding effects. And then, coming as no surprise to anyone, there'd likely be the usual one-liner, claiming no-one knew how word of Lucy Tanzer's transfer details had leaked out; the conclusion reached that it would have to be attributed to the prison grapevine. Grapevine – the inmates' very own internet of illegality.

Just one of those things.

Untraceable.

As untraceable as the pictures that Lucy was now drawing...

They'd withheld writing implements from her; and, without those, there'd been no need for paper. Too dangerous to give her a pen or pencil in her condition. So, she was using her right index finger to make imprints on the bed-sheet. Little creased ridges and troughs. Not that the end result looked anything like the pictures she was seeing in her mind. But, then, how did you portray disembodied voices?

The medical staff had dressed her burns, and had given her some painkillers. They'd also given her the obligatory once-over – physically and mentally. And, because of the notes that had accompanied her arrival from court, they'd had to book an appointment with the psychiatrist; resident at the nearest hospital. He'd be coming to assess her tomorrow afternoon – so, until then, they'd need to play it safe and she'd need to be considered at risk of self-harm; be put on suicide-watch. And that's why they'd not allowed her any sharp objects. They'd checked she hadn't been wearing lace-ups; nor a belt. They would have put her in one of the cells purposely designed for the potential suicide cases – all soft edges; electric plug sockets covered over; and no ligature points – but they were all already in use. So they adopted plan B; did the next best thing. Put her in the special cell with bars in place of a solid door; an officer stationed permanently outside, to watch and log her every move.

Great for the suicidal.

But not so great for the paranoid.

Just so long as the prison didn't fall foul of its duty of care to protect her.

It didn't take long for word of Emma's actions to get round the prison. Nearly every other inmate was a mother; and they all sympathised with what the red-band had done. They all felt the same hatred towards the child-killer. They'd had her sort in there before. And no matter how hard the authorities tried to keep such individuals out of harm's way – placing them on vulnerable prisoners' wings – there were still times, infrequent though they were, when the child-killers and mainstream prison population had to meet. Could be in the chapel; en route to court appearances – in the ante-rooms; or in the secure car-parks; and some of the cannier ones even feigned bullying – got the marks to prove it – just to be admitted to the exclusive wing, so they'd get close; get a chance to have a go.

And so it was to be this time round. Enough of them roped in.

So, two hours after they'd all been unlocked again for the day, the ring-leaders gave the signal and the diversion was underway – a small fight; seemingly innocuous, over nothing important. And the way it quickly spread. With more and more joining in. They didn't care that they'd lose privileges and visiting rights for the foreseeable future. Getting to the murdering bitch was everything. They'd teach her a lesson. Who needed the courts when they were on hand to dispense their own brand of justice?

Before heading outside, Fridriksson had given Bryant a whistle-stop tour of the rest of the house. Bryant had been shown the bedrooms and bathrooms – as he'd suspected, they'd been on the upper level – as well as a games room down in what originally would have been the dungeon. The stairs had indeed been built into the thick walls. But, as they'd moved from room to room, he'd not come across anything to suggest there was a lady of the house – no Mrs Fridriksson. No magazines by the bed. No mirror, make-up or perfume on the dressing table. And no subtle toiletries. Throughout the tower, everything had had a male voice to it. He'd guessed Fridriksson must be a widower – a fact seemingly borne out by his occasional sighting of photographs. And once he'd spotted one, he began noticing others. Always the same woman. At different times in her life. Black and white prints giving way to colour. Pictures that, strangely, seemed never to have been put fully on display; but, instead, had been relegated to the background; on display, but in private.

Bryant hadn't wanted to seem overly intrusive. Even so, as the three of them walked slowly towards the loch-side, he waited until their host was ahead of them, then turned to Sam and quietly asked,

'I saw the pictures. I take it Rudi's wife's dead?'

Sam nodded. 'Yes. Her name was Johanna. Rudi lost her not that long after they moved here. Before my time… but, I've heard it was all very sad. They came over to put down their final roots. But she'd already developed some neurological wasting disease. MND. Something like that. So, Rudi did what he could to make her comfortable. He even got in a carer – maybe I should rephrase that; he got in a *doctor* – to look after her. But it was all very quick. She got worse far more quickly than they'd expected. And Alice – she's the doctor; you'll meet her later; she's still here – wasn't able to do anything more for her. It hit Rudi very hard. He doesn't show it often, but I know he must miss her. I think that's the main reason he's doing all this.' He saw Bryant's quizzical expression. 'I'm running ahead of myself again, aren't I? Just wait and see, Rudi will explain all…'

Bryant wasn't finished yet. 'But how did they cope?' One of his late mother's closest friends had suffered from motor neurone disease. 'I mean, presumably she was in a wheelchair?' His mother's

friend had been. 'And, well, their house isn't exactly *accessible*, is it?'
'As I say, I don't really know all the details. But Alice did tell me how she marvelled – still does, in fact – at Rudi's dedication; in everything he does. And it was the same with Johanna. Apparently, according to Alice, he used to carry her up to bed; bathe her morning and night. Actually, something else she said... they'd never spent a night apart their whole married lives. Can you imagine that?' Bryant couldn't. Even when his marriage had been on track, he'd spent more time away from Luisa than with her. Work always coming first; the relative priorities in life firmly instilled in him by The Company. 'Do you want to hazard a guess how old Rudi is?'

Bryant thought momentarily, weighing up the man's size. He was still powerful; in good health. He could see that. He did a quick calculation; allowing for Fridriksson's likely early retirement; the benefit of being a millionaire.

'Hm, maybe mid-sixties?'

'Try adding another ten years. He might outlive both of us...'

'Wonderful!' Fridriksson's voice, carried back to them by the sea wind. 'Do you see that!' He turned, arms flailing like a child mimicking a windmill; encouraging them to walk faster; to join him at the water's edge. 'see... it is a bottlenose dolphin, I think. There. You see?' Sam and Bryant watched the water where Rudi was pointing. Nothing. Then, just as their concentration wavered, the big man cried out again in excitement; boyish wonder in his voice; reflected in equal measure in his wide-eyed amazement. He clasped his hands together; rocked back and forth on the spot. 'There! Again! Quick! Come! Watch there!'

They played the cetacean game of now-you-see-me, now-you-don't for several further minutes until Sam at last glimpsed the rapid cart-wheeling motion of a grey-black fin.

Then Bryant saw it, too.

Then saw *two*.

'Wait! What's that?' he asked.

The second fin, smaller.

'Oh...' there was no containing Fridriksson's delight now. 'My... We are seeing the mother with her child! Oh, this is... magical...' He sighed contentedly.

Bryant found himself caught in the moment. Had to agree. He stood there, waiting for the water's surface to break once more. His patience finally rewarded. The smaller fin arcing before him; slower to rotate than the adult's. All three men watched happily for twenty minutes as the dolphins took their fill. And then, just as silently as they'd arrived, the water-dwellers slipped away again unseen. No warning. Just leaving their audience with the innate high that comes from having watched something so special; so naturally enchanting 'You bring us good fortune, dear David.' Fridriksson came over and landed a heavy pat on Bryant's back. It nearly sent him tumbling, such was the man's force. And then, before Bryant could answer, Fridriksson was leading them back towards the woods. 'Now, we go see my work, yes? I think you will find it all very interesting?' Bryant couldn't help smiling. Rudi's strange accent; the intonation and, just occasionally, the flawed grammar. Just like a bad impressionist. Little Englander does Johnny Foreigner. But totally lovable. Endearing. He could see why Sam liked the man so much. 'This way, please. We go now...'

The men made their way back towards the tower, then continued round its side; on through a small area of enclosed garden – Bryant could see now it was screened behind the lower wall he'd first observed on arrival – and then onwards to the tree-line. The main path they were following soon came to a fork. Three options – each route marked by a rustic-looking sign-post. The first read *Centre*; the second, *Walks*; and the third, *Private*.

Centre.

Walks.

Private.

Bryant wondered which of the three Rudi would select.

But the big man must have read him perfectly; observed the anticipation in him – for he said, with a little sweep of his hand, 'Which path are you wanting to take, my David?' Before Bryant could answer, Rudi added, 'I think... yes, this is very much like your life. You have different options...' Bryant felt suddenly pressured. The feeling totally at odds with the tranquil surroundings. He couldn't decide which path to explore. He tried to rationalise what would lie at the end of each; which would yield the greatest benefit; but he just couldn't make up his mind. The acuity of the businessman gone. Blanketed by who knew what. But what did it matter? This was – literally – a morning stroll; no multi-million dollar contract riding on the answer. He knew this was stupid. And then Fridriksson was laughing at his indecision. 'It is like...' he paused, translating the word from his native tongue; and continued, 'ice-cream... when you are a child and given your choice, yes? When we have doubt, we should take them all! Excellent...'

'Yes. We should take them all,' Bryant found himself agreeing.

'Come. Now we go to my village.'

Village, Bryant thought, then said aloud, 'But it said *Centre*?'

'Yes,' Fridriksson replied, as if it was patently obvious. 'My village. My centre. Where we have our healing...'

Sam thought he ought to help out, otherwise he could see this going on a long time. 'Rudi's built a healing retreat.' He explained. 'You know, folk travel from all over... come stay for the peace and quiet; do a bit of meditation; get away from the smoke...'

'And they are coming also for our talks...' Rudi interjected. 'I have good speakers. Many more are coming from US; Russia; we are boundless...'

'Boundary-less,' Sam helped out. 'Everyone's welcome; everyone's equal.'

Bryant suddenly had his business head back on. 'So that's the new direction?' He mentally linked what he'd read in the brochure to what he was now being told. 'And the diversification is... what? Relaxation retreats? Time away from London for the stressed executive? Well, there's certainly a market there. And they'll pay high prices...'

Sam looked at Fridriksson; the unspoken question whether he should go on; explain more. The man smiled his agreement. 'Yes and no. Yes – Rudi wants to run the retreat commercially, but it's not really going to be a five-star affair. You'll see the cabins as we go on. And, yes, they come with all the mod cons; home from home – and, yes, I'm sure the execs will love them; no doubt they're even better than their Swiss skiing chalets. But Rudi's aiming for more than that. This'll be a mix of paying guests – coming for the break; the talks; the great outdoors; but also he wants it to be – well – a *healing* centre; like he said. Somewhere that can provide complementary therapies; free; for those who can't otherwise afford them.'

Bryant was starting to understand.

'What, like a foundation; or a charity?' he asked.

Sam turned to Rudi. The big man's eyes were glistening. 'It is for Johanna.' He said simply.

Bryant felt embarrassed at the man's display of emotion; by his own reaction to it; and just said, 'I'm so sorry. Sam told me earlier.'

Fridriksson nodded. 'I made her my promise. To help others, in her memory.'

'So,' Sam added, 'you'll probably find all sorts of the beardy-weirdy stuff that so appeals to you going on here next year.'

'*Beerdy weerdy*?' Rudi repeated, phonetically. 'What is that?'

Sam stayed quiet, deliberately putting Bryant on the spot; just for old times.

'It means someone open-minded; looking for the truth,' Bryant replied tactfully.

'Ah, yes? And you are one of these?'

Bryant wiped a hand across his clean-shaven features. 'Well, let's just say, I've still got a long way to go...'

Fridriksson seemed happy with that. 'Come, we will go and see more now.'

They pressed on further into the woodland and finally came to a clearing. A dozen or more of the chalet-cabins had been built sympathetically into the landscape; some partially submerged beneath the forest floor. The word hobbit was uppermost in Bryant's mind, but he dismissed it. Despite his initial reservations, he could see that Fridriksson had obviously put much thought into all this; not to mention the personal tie he felt towards it all. It might not have ticked his particular business boxes, but he knew there was a growing market out there. Glastonbury alone had been built on little more; hundreds of thousands attracted every year by the lure of the New Age.

'Is that...?'

'A *shop*; yes.' Sam answered, perhaps a little too over dramatically. 'Think of it like... where you'd go buy your bread and milk if this were a camp-site. Hm, not that I suppose you go camping, do you? Oh, and there's a *village* hall...'

'Right. Can I go take a look inside?' asked Bryant, pointing to the shop.

'You can go *buy* something... This is a business, after all.'

The shop was built in the same style as the surrounding accommodation blocks. A timber-clad affair, just starting to go silver-grey as the wood began its ageing process. Bryant walked in through a half-height swing-door; it reminded him of a cowboy saloon. But there was no interrupted piano music; no-one turning to stare as he went in. Just a friendly hello and welcoming smile from a girl on the till.

'Hello,' he replied quietly, returning her nod.

The first thing he noticed was the overpowering aroma of essential oils; candles; all the relaxation trappings that Sam had so eagerly gone off in search of during their university days – even then, the seed of alternative living just waiting to germinate inside his friend. But had it been, he reflected? Maybe he was attributing things to his friend in hindsight. Hadn't it all been a phase? Something to do with a girl? Yes, he was remembering now. There'd been that hippy chick in their second year, the one who'd been wearing the very fetching bin-liner at that party they'd gone to. Where Sam had used the window as a door. No matter they were two floors up. That was about the time Sam had got into his incense sticks...

'Careful, Tyler!'

Bryant flinched as a young boy tore round the end of one of the aisles, nearly colliding with him. The boy careered to a halt. Just beside Bryant. The boy had no interest in him. He was pushing jars to one side. Searching for something.

'I can't see them, mum. You come look?'

More of the jars being moved out of their neatly-arranged lines. The girl on the till looked up, but just smiled, not in the least worried she'd have to straighten them up again afterwards.

'Come on, Tyler; I've got to go and pay. You can look again tomorrow.' She put a hand on his shoulder; tried to encourage him to follow her.

'They're not here!' The rising voice accompanying a reddening face.

Even Bryant, with his limited experience of fatherhood, could tell it was a countdown to a screaming fit. He caught the woman's eye. Sure enough, the screaming kicked off. The boy fell to the floor; foetal position, like an upturned turtle; arms and legs kicking in every direction. A couple of blows landed on his shins. He winced and moved backwards.

'Sorry,' said the mother, her own cheeks starting to redden. 'Are you alright?' Bryant nodded. 'I don't know what's got into him... well, I do...' she corrected herself. 'It's his older brother's doing. What was he thinking, telling him honey's made from crushed bees?'

'Oh?'

'Hm... not that it's put him off honey, mind. No, he just wants to see the bits of broken bee. He thinks he'll see wings and stuff in the jars; you know.'

'Right', said Bryant, as if it was the most natural thing in the world to be standing in a shop in the middle of a wood with a kid screaming because he couldn't see crushed bees' wings.

'Come on, you. I've had enough.' The woman grabbed hold of an arm and started dragging her son across the floor towards the till.

Bryant made a quick exit.

'You didn't buy anything then?' Sam asked, when Bryant had rejoined the two of them.

'No, nothing took my fancy.' Then he added, 'Maybe I'll get Neve some honey next time.'

'*Next* time? Hm, that's encouraging...'

Fridriksson was already keen to be off. 'If we are quick, I can show you now my *big* plan. Come, please.'

Bryant fell into step beside Sam.

'So, what's his *big* plan?'

'Well, he's got two, actually. One, he wants to find a clean source of energy. Do his bit to make amends –'

'Amends for what?'

'All the pollution.' Bryant's blank face again. 'You *do* know where he made his money?'

'No.'

'Travel. Back in the sixties and seventies, he was a founding-father of the package holiday. Then he branched out into cruises round the fjords. And later, when the market started getting swamped, he still managed to keep one step ahead – selling pick 'n' mix tours; you know, people wanting to arrange it themselves, cut out the travel agents; so he sold them the various elements separately. He was probably one of the first to recognise the potential of the internet, as well...'

'And then he gave it all up?'

'Yeah – but Rudi's one smart cookie; must have had his reasons for doing so. Anyway, as I was saying... he wants to do something, save us from our uncertain future; so he's started a research project, trying to find an alternative to fossil fuels.'

'The middle east won't be very happy – not if he succeeds.'

'I think there's a way to go yet. You'll see the lab; we'll go straight past it.'

'What? Another log cabin?'

'Have a bit more faith...'

'Sorry. You said *two* plans...'

'Yeah – the second; well, again, it's research – but that's all down to Alice. The doctor I mentioned. Who looked after Johanna?'

'Right. So, she's here, too. And she has a hut?'

'You are *such* a cynic.'

'Sorry.'

'Come on. Let's catch up with Rudi.'

'Research lab; and hospital. Can't wait.'

Fridriksson didn't show Bryant round any research lab; but he did take him to see doctor Alice. Unfortunately, she wasn't there so, instead, he walked them back through the woods to the tower. Bryant's legs were aching by the time they got there. Rudi made tea, and brought out some biscuits.

'I hope you will meet Alice later? You are most welcome to come back. Sam? You are free to drive David back here. Tomorrow, perhaps?'

'Er, no – sorry, Rudi; David.' He spread his hands apologetically. 'I'm actually helping put up stock-proof fencing for the next few days. But...' he was thinking through the options, 'I guess you could borrow Neve's car, David. Don't think she's going anywhere. No big shop planned, as far as I know. I'll check when we get back.'

'Excellent, then it is settled. I will find out when it is convenient, and you are free to come and meet with Alice, yes? David?'

'Yes.' Bryant didn't know if he wanted to meet doctor Alice, but Sam gave him a covert thumbs-up. 'Yes, that sounds fine.'

'Good. And now I must take my leave of you. I am slightly late...'

Bryant looked for the silver clock on the wall. It showed it was only ten past two. Sam had said Rudi needed to be away by three. That left another fifty minutes. He wondered why Rudi thought he was late. Bryant glanced back at Fridriksson. Saw the man looking at him. Fridriksson let out another of his mirthful laughs.

'You are confused by my clock, I think?' Bryant looked bemused. 'Here, come see...' The man beckoned him over.

Bryant obliged. When he got close, he realised the clock only had *one* hand.

Not two.

A minute-hand; but no corresponding one to show the hour.

So it wasn't ten past two at all – but ten past *something*.

He checked his own watch – ten past *three*; so, Fridriksson *was* late... Something, though, was nagging at him. He cast his mind quickly back. Back to when they'd first arrived. And then he had it – remembered what it was. He'd checked the time then, too. But he'd looked at the wall-clock; not at his watch. Ten to ten. That's what he remembered the clock had shown. Yet another example of when the hour hand would similarly have been hidden on any normal clock...

'This is the *only* clock in my house,' Rudi explained. Bryant had to think for a moment. He'd seen pictures; the map; photos of Johanna – but, no; no clocks. He couldn't remember even seeing any radio alarms in the guest rooms... Rudi continued, 'When Johanna and I come here, it was to be forever; no point to time any more. So, I get rid of my clocks; and my watch...' he showed Bryant his bare wrist. 'Aha...' he pre-empted Bryant's next question, '... all except *this* one; this clock. It is for my guests...'

'The one concession,' Sam added. 'An approximation of time; nothing more.'

'Quite,' Fridriksson sighed. Then, a moment later he was doing his mind-reading thing again; or so Bryant thought. 'So, you wonder, how do I know I am late, yes?' Bryant nodded. '*Magic!*' Rudi burst out laughing again and took his leave of them.

'Magic?' Bryant asked, when he and Sam were alone.

'Otherwise known as a *pager*. Oh, and a secretary back in the Centre – the Village – who keeps an eye on his more important meetings... who *does* have a watch. Mind you, even she can't stop Rudi turning off the pager when the mood takes him...'

Tomlinson had needed time to get his head straight.

So much had happened already that morning – and none of it

had been what he'd expected. He'd had it all mapped out. Quiet chat with Riley. Ten or twenty minutes with Peters. And then he'd have been on the home leg. Tidying things up for the duration of his notice. And who knew – maybe they'd have let him go early?

But his route-planning had gone awry. The map had led him into a dead end.

Destination nightmare.

And all because of the sudden accusation – questioning his integrity; slating his honesty; doubting his loyalty. A whole career now in potential jeopardy. Thirty-plus years about to go up in smoke. The rug of financial security about to be pulled from under his feet. And none of it of his making. Not a good place to be; he'd known that. He ought to have been devoting serious grey cells to the task in hand; working out how to fight his corner; challenge the lie. But none of it concerned him consciously as he sat there quietly by the window in the back-street café, sipping the dregs of his cold coffee.

Instead, his mind was elsewhere.

The casual observer might have thought him a businessman, grabbing a brief respite; killing time; doodling to relieve the mounting pressure, before heading off to give a make-or-break presentation.

But they weren't idle doodles.

Closer inspection would have shown the paper serviette, on which all his attention was so keenly focussed, to be a living, cranial canvas. Emerging thought in motion. Low tech. 2-D. But its growing data, its expanding linkages, as meaningful as the output from any of the Met's analytical computers. Powered by the organic, micro-processor of his brain, Tomlinson was busy creating linear patterns. Boxes. Inter-connecting lines. Asterisks above the actions he needed to take. And questions. Plenty of questions. Each with their own box.

And each, in turn, linking to just one final question…

Had he not taken the call himself – re-read the entry in the call-log – he'd happily have thought it beyond the bounds of reason even to be thinking what he was now considering. But the fact was, he *was* party to the information. The seed had been sown. He couldn't let it rest. Hunch. Intuition. Call it what you would, he felt something very strange was going on. A twitch of the copper's nose that would make Riley proud.

A flick of his pen and he'd linked three boxes with a circle. Three calls he needed to make.

First, Riley.

Then, Mick's team.

And, finally, Nick Lennox.

Tomlinson felt a draught as someone opened the door. He

looked up and saw a man ordering a take-away roll. Friendly words were exchanged quickly with the girl behind the counter – he might have been a regular, but had too little time to stay longer; for him, it was lunch on the run. The man exited, then turned left. He paused almost immediately to answer a call on his mobile and, in between speaking, took several bites of his food. Three pigeons landed on a small table beside him, each puffing their chest out to try and appear the dominant bird. He tossed them a few crumbs and they flapped their wings, danced a squabbling chorus.

Idly, Tomlinson smoothed out the serviette. The pause – the interruption while he'd observed the departing man – let the morning intrude on his thoughts again.

Destination nightmare? He wasn't there yet.

Time to double-check the map and engage reverse...

Shortly before midday, the prison was in turmoil.

The diversion had proved so successful, it had gradually escalated into a full-blown riot. Not the ring-leaders' original intention. But they'd been happy enough to go with the flow. And what did it matter that they were now well and truly smashing the place up? That some of them were sitting it out on the roof-tops? It was a nice day; they could catch a few rays; no need to go in until night brought the cold. Besides, after they'd had their fun, they'd have to be accommodated elsewhere while all the repairs were undertaken; it was their right – duty of care. No, it was the prison authorities' problem. And the rich middle-class taxpayers could foot the bill. Who said crime didn't pay?

The staff had been caught totally unawares – lulled into a false sense of security by the ease of the earlier lock-down. But now, under the onslaught of a tidal wave of female fury, they'd had to retreat, locking doors as they went. Standard procedure – but not one that guaranteed everyone's safety. Several officers didn't manage to get a door open in time – some fumbling in panic; others with keys ever so slightly damaged that meant several turns in the lock were called for. Vital seconds lost. But the latter really only had themselves to blame. Wearing their key-chains too long – despite the reminders to shorten them – meant there'd been occasions when they'd dropped them; when the key tips had hit the concrete floor. Slight scuffs. Fractional bends. Barely visible to the naked eye. But enough to hinder the turn when speed was of the essence. Poetic justice that they might take a beating. But inexcusable that colleagues trapped beside them should undergo a similar ordeal...

Officers lay where they fell. At first, trying to put up a fight but then, as the anger washed over them, they curled up ever more tightly, waiting for the undertow of aggression to recede.

And when it did, their keys had gone –

Passed unseen from hand to hand. Spirited away. Criminal career-opportunists readily seizing the moment. But there was never any risk of escape for the inmates, for the keys worn inside only granted certain levels of access. Separate arrangements safeguarded the entrance to the prison. No matter how serious the riot – wherever the prison – enough time had always been bought in advance. To contain the population. To sound the alarm. To call in the national *Tornado* squads. The professionals. The specially-trained officers who dealt with such disturbances. The ring-leaders knew as much. Only a matter of time before the riot shields and batons arrived. With dogs in reserve. The full-weight of the emergency response system brought to bear against them.

But, then, escape wasn't the goal. Never had been. It was all about getting to their target.

They pressed on to where the Tanzer woman was being held. Several more officers tried to slow their progress – at first, attempts to talk the rioters down; and when those failed – valiant, selfless, albeit brief resistance. But all to no avail.

The prison radio network had been alive with confusion. Security cameras watching the action. Operators trying to call ahead with warnings.

But the rioters had had their own lines of communication – the handful of mobiles they'd managed to stockpile. Standing ready for just such an opportunity. The parts smuggled in over many months; the constant advances in technology making it easier to conceal ever-smaller units. And thanks to human rights, restrictions on the powers of intimate search had meant more opportunities for caching miniature components within the body. They'd lost several mobiles when the scanners had first been introduced – but they'd soon got wise to the screws; knew the score; knew when to turn the phones off; occasionally hide them with a red-band – the threat of violence usually enough to ensure co-operation.

Radios went head to head with mobiles in the communications battle. But the mobiles gained the upper hand – especially after radios seized from fallen officers allowed the rioters to stay one step ahead; enabled them to get advance notice of the duty governor's plans. Eventually, the authorities realised what was happening and silenced that source of intelligence. Frantic attempts were meanwhile being made to activate further emergency protocols; to ensure mobile reception within the prison was shut down.

The officer assigned to watch Lucy had received warning in

good time. Had been told to withdraw to safety. But the order had come through to leave Lucy where she was. The considered judgement that she'd be safer behind the bars – but, crucially, the decision had been taken *before* the authorities had realised several key-sets had been seized – including ones that gave access to Lucy's cell. And by the time the authorities realised that, they considered it too dangerous to send the officer back in again.

Lucy would have to wait it out until the *Tornado* squad reached her –

Internal CCTV footage would subsequently be used at the coroner's inquest to show the moment when, at 11:58am, a mob of anger-fuelled rioters swept into the corridor outside Lucy Tanzer's cell. It would also show someone opening the door and several accomplices entering. It would record, too, a brief period when nothing much seemed to be happening – when those left in the corridor stood still; an air of expectancy hanging over them. And, finally, it would capture the moment when Lucy was dragged out into the centre of the pack and every person – each spurred on by one another – took a turn at kicking, punching or gouging her.

But what the CCTV wouldn't show – what only the post-mortem would reveal – was that, when pulled from the cell, Lucy Tanzer, thankfully, was already dead.

The subsequent death-in-custody inquiry would take several months to complete. But when all sides were finally satisfied with the findings, it would state categorically that, in the time Lucy had been left alone, she'd hanged herself. There'd be an interesting observation – namely, the method she'd used had mirrored exactly that employed by a twenty-four year old male in a Welsh prison just six months earlier. A detailed annexe, linked to the main report by a footnote, would reveal in both cases the deceased had first used their teeth to tear the bed-sheet into strips. Next, these had been fashioned into a crude, short length of rope. One end had been attached to the horizontal, tubular strut of the metal bed-frame; just above the pillows. The other had been looped around the respective victim's neck. And, despite the bed-frames being little more than three feet in height, still that distance had been enough to let each take their life – the noose pulling tighter against their wind-pipe as they'd angled themselves; had held their body firm; plank-like; feet wedged hard against the opposite wall to maintain rigidity; to prevent their bodies – ultimately, their *resolve* – buckling at the last.

Thirty-three degrees of fatal constriction.

Just how each managed to fight against the innate, self-preservation impulse would remain the subject of intense speculation; though it would forever elude satisfactory, rational explanation.

Twin cases. Two counts of asphyxia. Identical in every detail – despite the Welsh *modus operandi* never having been made public...

And by ending her own life in that way, Lucy Tanzer ensured the Wilsons' suffering continued. Robbed, first, of their loved ones. Robbed, too, of the answers they so desperately needed.

The answers she'd silently taken to her grave.

CHAPTER SIXTEEN

IT WAS EARLY evening before Tomlinson got a call back from Riley. Mobile to mobile, so there'd be less chance anyone would overhear their unauthorised conversation – after all, with the superintendent suspended, the sergeant shouldn't even have been talking to him.

'You free to speak, Paul?'

'Yes, sir.' The formality still there, despite recent events. 'I'm in the canteen. No-one nearby though.'

'Look, tell me now if this is going to be a problem...' Silence, so he continued. 'I need you to check a few things.'

'You know I don't mind a spot of bother, sir.'

'Thanks. I was hoping you'd say that. Right. First – cast your mind back to when we were in the studio. You were joking about a crank call that had come in. Yes?'

'That's right. The psychic nutter guy. What about him?'

'Alright, well – and just hear me out before you think *I've* totally lost it – what was his name?'

Riley concentrated for a moment, then answered '*Maltravers*.' He'd remembered at the time thinking it had sounded like Matravers – as in Worth Matravers, the small Dorset village near Poole. He knew the place well. Had gone there many times as a lad. Day-trips with his grandparents. 'Christian name...' He didn't have as much luck with that. 'Hm... *Peter*, was it?' He couldn't be sure. 'I'd have to ask someone on DI Bancroft's squad for you...'

'You're ahead of me. That was going to be my next call.'

'You sure, sir? Probably better if I approach them. You know, things being as they are.'

'Yes, you're probably right.'

'Consider it done.'

'OK, so, if I've got it right, this man – Maltravers – telephoned to say he knew something about...' The attack on the WPC was uppermost in Tomlinson's mind. He paused, trying to recall the other case, but Riley helped him out.

'It was the jewellery robbery, sir. He said that the shot-gun was going to be used again...'

'Ah, that's right. And he also said something about a plane crash; yes?'

'I don't think he said that – not when he called in that night. No, that was earlier, if you remember. I was reading from the assessment notes. Telling you he had no credibility, and that he'd been ridiculed publicly for saying he'd foreseen his own death; and that he'd avoided taking *that* plane. His whole story was shown to be a total fabrication.'

215

'Right. Now – what if the guy *isn't* a crank?' He heard Riley's snort at the other end.

'But, sir, even the production team knew about him. I mean, that's got to tell you something.'

'Yes, but, even so... just for a second, consider the possibility he *might* actually get something right; once in a while.'

'Well, I'd need a lot of convincing.' The sergeant got straight to it. 'What's behind this, sir?'

'Like I say, go with me on this one. Now, just before I left the office this morning – and I know you won't have been aware of this, because I saw you were arguing with someone –'

'Hughes, sir. Total jerk. Said you deserved...'

'Never mind what Hughes said... Look, I took a call. It *also* links back to Mick's case. You remember I picked up the phone? In the studio? And they wanted to know where to send the call-logs? And I told them it wasn't me? Well, someone at their end obviously didn't listen so, guess what? It was there waiting for me on my desk. I was going to send it on to Mick when I noticed something. Don't ask me how. I don't even know myself. But – well, this is where it's all going to sound a bit strange... *maybe* this is where Maltravers comes back into the picture.' Riley was all ears. 'I was looking down the log. Whoever was working the graveyard shift to produce it obviously had time on their hands – or they're anally-retentive – but, either way, they're nothing if not resourceful. You know how we sometimes only get a two-liner?'

'Yes.'

'Well, whoever it was compiled this one really did a thorough job for Mick. Make a welcome change if they were all done so professionally. If they're not an intelligence analyst by day, their talent's wasted. So, anyway, what I want to know is... The caller's name I came across... Hang on,' Tomlinson consulted his high-tech serviette. '... this *David Bryant*. Have you come across him before?'

'Can't say I have.'

'Well, he called in – we presume about Mick's case; as that was the number dialled – but he hung up soon after. No message.'

'And?'

'*And*... they did the routine check on his incoming number; found it was registered to the aforementioned David Bryant. They must have gone on to search against the PNC. No trace. So, I'm guessing they then tried CRB.' The Criminal Records Bureau – linking data from the passport, as well as driver and vehicle licensing agencies. 'CRB showed he had a clean licence and a passport. *But*, cross-referenced to *them* – and *this* is the really interesting bit; where our eager-beaver struck gold – his name was shown as a person of interest against the *customs'* database.'

'Don't tell me; drug smuggler?'

'No.'

'Tax evader?'

'No. Person of interest... in case of *attempted identity theft*.'

'Identity theft?' Riley queried. It made sense, though. The authorities taking precautions; helping prevent a scam; criminals approaching the passport agency or DVLA to steal an identity. *Day of the Jackal* and all that. 'In which case, you're not suggesting... What, that he's *deceased*?'

'Seems the logical conclusion. Now, this is where I'm going out on a limb, but... you got a pen?'

'Yes.'

'Take these down.' He read out a series of letters. 'And this number.'

'Got it. What is it?'

'I think it's customs' code for a plane – and probably some kind of flight number. It was on the log next to this Bryant's name. I'm guessing the collator didn't realise the significance. I can't be a hundred percent sure myself either, so you'll need to do a quick bit of digging. But, I remember back in SB, when I was at Gatwick, every so often showing new guys round and we'd always do a familiarisation visit to see customs; say hello, shake hands; you know. Now, I'm sure I picked up on stuff I shouldn't have, but... there's just something in the back of my mind...'

'I'll get on to it.'

'If I'm right and it *is* a plane, what if this Mr Bryant was on the same flight that Maltravers was talking about? I can't remember any other recent crashes. Can you? Not unless any light aircraft – or maybe a helicopter – went down?'

'Nothing springs to mind.'

'So, my best guess is, you'll find this guy's name on a manifest; and it'll relate to the flight that crashed. In which case...'

'Is our Mr Bryant...' Riley continued the line of reasoning, '... an imposter, or is the real one *alive*?'

'I reckon the latter,' Tomlinson added quickly. 'I mean, if you'd nicked someone's identity, you'd hardly phone in to the police would you? Even the most stupid con wouldn't do that...'

'But he did ring off...'

'Yes, but even so, I've just got a feeling.'

'Should my nose be twitching, sir?'

'Hm – you let me know after you've got me some answers.'

'Will do.'

'And, if I'm right, what I want to know is – what are the chances two men, seemingly not connected, call in on the same night, on the same programme; and both of them seem to have a link to that same plane?'

'And we don't do coincidence, do we, sir?'

'No, we most certainly do not. There's something's not right about this, Paul. Not right at all. I can feel it.'

It was early evening, too, when Sam and Bryant arrived back at the house.

'Good day?' Neve asked, as they came in the door.

Bryant nodded. 'Very enjoyable, thanks. And what a place – absolutely stunning.'

'David was really taken with Rudi's plans, weren't you? Offered him some free consultancy...'

'Ignore him,' Bryant retorted.

'What did you make of Rudi?'

'He's certainly... *individual*,' Bryant replied tactfully. 'But, no, I actually liked him. Larger than life, but so full of enthusiasm. And that's always a good sign.'

'David's been invited back,' Sam volunteered.

'I know,' said Neve. 'Rudi called about an hour ago to say Alice definitely will be there tomorrow. So,' this to Bryant, 'She'll be expecting you any time after eleven.' She inclined her head, rolled her eyes; a hint of annoyance there. Then she said to her husband, 'You're working tomorrow, aren't you?'

'Yes?'

'So who's going to drive David over?'

'Ah. Rather said he could borrow your car. That is alright, isn't it?'

Neve folded her arms. 'It'll have to be.'

'Sorry. Should have checked with you first. Were you planning to go out?'

'Evidently not.'

Bryant sensed the brewing argument and tried to head it off. 'Maybe I could call her back, suggest a different day?'

'No, David, you shouldn't have to do that. This is Sam's fault. I'll rearrange.' She glowered at her husband, only Bryant's presence preventing the air turning blue. 'But I'll want *your* car for when I do.' Sam nodded his sheepish acceptance.

Bryant thought he'd better leave them to it. He didn't want a domestic ruining his day, so he took his cue. 'If you'll excuse me, I'll go change.'

'Dinner will be another half hour.'

'Right. Look, is it OK if I grab a quick shower?'

'Yes, help yourself. Sam will come and give you a shout; once he's laid the table. Won't you, darling?'

A further sheepish nod from Sam, conscious it would take a lot more than that to get him out of the dog-house.

Bryant had been quick, and was back in the sitting room before Sam had been sent to find him. He settled himself cosily down into one of the sofas, waiting for the call to the table. He hadn't seen or heard Katie, and guessed she must still be in her room. He could, however, hear Sam and Neve. They were speaking in the kitchen. Their voices were, at first, too quiet for him to make out what they were saying –

But even as that thought began to occur to him, he experienced a sudden burst of static –

So loud. And unexpected. Like a thunder-clap.

It was suddenly there again. Right between his ears. Fluctuating. As if someone was balancing a hi-fi's speakers. And, then, that same someone had turned up the dial. Had increased the volume.

Now, he *could* hear what they were saying...

He tried not to listen in. Didn't want to eavesdrop on what might be a private moment. But there was the mention of his name, so curiosity naturally made him all ears.

'... I've already said, I *do* believe you.' Neve speaking. 'I don't for one minute think he actually did try to commit suicide.'

'But...'

'All I'm saying is, maybe you should have a quiet word with Alice. Just ask her, in her professional opinion, if she thinks there's anything, you know, *wrong*...'

'Oh, yeah – you mean, is he hallucinating? Bit of a bump to the head, poor guy? Telling us he can see people who aren't even there?'

Bryant was fully alert now – but confused, not understanding what they were talking about.

'Oh, come on, Sam! You couldn't see him either! No way there was anyone else in that picture. David can say this man...'

'Graysbrook –'

'Graysbrook... was there all he likes, but you and I both know he *wasn't*. So excuse me if I find that a bit strange!'

'Neve, give him a break! You think if you went through what he has, you'd be alright? Get real. Of course it's going to take him time to adjust...'

'I'm just saying...'

'He needs rest. Peace and quiet. And I'd have thought that's

219

the least we could offer him. Don't you? Or is that asking too much?'
'You know that's not what I'm saying. He's more than welcome...'

Sam didn't intend discussing the matter any further. 'I'm going to freshen up before dinner. Then I'll get Katie, and David. And let's try and be civil when we eat, yeah?'

Bryant reacted instantly. Leapt up from the sofa and backtracked a few steps into the hallway. Pretended he was just coming through as Sam came towards him. His friend looked taken aback by his sudden appearance, but quickly recovered his composure.

'Oh, hi. I was going to come and get you a bit later.'

With Sam now in such close proximity, Bryant found his friend's voice disproportionately loud; could feel his teeth on edge. He needed to find a mental control button, to turn down the volume. Without his consciously knowing how he did it, the decibel level seemed at once to respond to the thought – and Sam's voice returned to its normal pitch. Bryant tried to put the audio anomaly to the back of his mind, but he realised then this had happened before. When he'd been in the hospital. Just before they'd let him go. But he'd have to analyse it some other time. For now, he just had to pretend he didn't know Neve and Sam had been arguing.

'Anything I can do to help? Table – all laid?'

'Er, yes, I've done that.' And then Sam's tone changed, annoyance still there. He shouted back towards the kitchen, 'Neve? David wants to know what he can do to help?'

Bryant thought he detected a *double-entendre*.

What *could* he do to help? *Leave*? But Neve wasn't letting on about their disagreement.

'Everything's fine thanks, David,' she replied calmly. 'You can just take your seat at the table.'

But Bryant knew everything *wasn't* alright. And he wasn't thinking in terms of his friends' spat. He was thinking – *Hallucinating. Seeing people who weren't there.* That's what they'd said. But why? Why would they think that?

It's because they can't see him. The little voice. And before Bryant had time to frame his response, it continued. *She thinks you're mad, delusional. Maybe you are. Who knows? Dinner should be fun...*

Tomlinson had just finished speaking to Riley. He now had the further information – and confirmation – he needed. Maltravers' first name was *Patrick*, not Peter, and he'd got an address to go with him. Also, he'd been right about the customs' serial. It *had* denoted flight details – and *had* included the flag to warn of the potential for identity fraud. And, yes, Bryant *had* been registered as a passenger on the flight. So, too, his name was included in the casualty list annexed to the air accident investigation branch's interim report. Likewise, Riley had provided a home address for the man.

Both sets of details Tomlinson had added to his serviette. It was beginning to show signs of wear and tear. He'd transpose the contents to something more durable before the day was out.

'So,' he mused to himself. 'You definitely *were* on that plane,' a light circle drawn round Bryant's name, 'and you *claim* you were.' The motion repeated round Maltravers'. 'You both pick the same night to call in... but, why? And why the different cases? Why? It doesn't make any sense...'

'Would you like anything more, sir?' From the waiter's tone, Tomlinson could tell it was a rhetorical question. The man wanted to get away home. The kitchen staff had probably already left.

'Thanks, no. I'll just finish this, then I'll be on my way.'

A half-forced smile from the waiter. 'Very good, sir.'

Tomlinson didn't recognise him. He wasn't the same waiter who'd been serving when he'd met Nick Lennox. The superintendent had gone back there as he considered it safe; away from prying eyes. *Nick.* He'd need to call her next. He'd just one final nagging thought to get out of the way.

When were the dead not dead? When you were protecting them; that's when.

He wanted to check with Nick that this guy Bryant wasn't one of theirs – or customs'. He didn't want to find this was all a cover-up. Staged death. Witness protection for an informer, or something like that. He'd enough on his plate as it was. He checked his watch. He'd only be a few minutes. The waiter would have to hang around a little bit longer. He took out his mobile and dialled.

'Nick?' He could hear a voice half-asleep at the other end. 'It's Ray Tomlinson. Listen, I'm so sorry if I've woken you.' He got an earful of most unlady-like abuse. 'I just need to ask you one more favour...'

A few minutes later, Tomlinson was out on the street, the waiter quick to shut the door behind him. The bistro lights were off before he'd even crossed the road.

Priorities.

The priority – to await Nick's reply. And if Bryant wasn't under the protection of the State – if he was fair game – then he'd start digging. He was determined to get some answers. About Bryant. And about Maltravers. Somehow, he had the strangest feeling this was all still linked to Lucy Tanzer in some way. Gut instinct. Nothing more.

But it was starting to affect him personally. He couldn't turn back time, save the twins – but he could now try to uncover the rationale for all this. If there was one. No, he knew there *had* to be one –

Practicalities.

His subconscious interrupted the flow of his conscious mind.

Money.

The word thrust uppermost into his awareness. He'd been skirting around it all day. But it needed addressing. They'd said he'd find his bank account frozen while they investigated the suspected fraud. God, he hadn't even told Brenda yet –

He'd have to call her. Tell her the news. Tell her not to worry. It didn't matter how late it was. He got his mobile out again. There followed a brief, uncomfortable exchange. He told her he'd get it all straightened out – and that she should use the credit card for the time being. No, not their joint one; the one just in her name. She mentioned his pension – and he told her nothing had been decided. It would all be fine. He said he still had a few things to take care of – and, no, they couldn't wait. Yes, he'd be away for a few days. He'd see her later. He ended the call.

Money.

His subconscious again. Just in case he'd forgotten. He knew what he had to do. Go retrieve the key…

The key.

Key to another life. The key that would allow him to access money – funding he'd set up years back as part of his contingency arrangements. When still in the Branch. Money he could now use – at least, until the mess was sorted out. And, to this day, everything was still in place. In case he'd ever needed to disappear quickly.

Not only money – but accommodation and transport, too. Even another identity, should he have needed it. He'd always imagined that, if the balloon had gone up, it would have been down to the terrorists; or one of the crime lords – maybe sanctioning a hit against him. Brenda – she'd have been safe enough. One call and she'd have been spirited away. And he could then have gone to ground, until he'd been able to get back to the protection of the Yard. And now? Not the same risk. Completely different. The danger altogether less. But the pressure coming from within – from his own side. Just how ironic was that? The disruption would be the same though.

Now, his careful planning would pay dividends. So, first – the key. Then – get hold of some money. And, finally – get some rest before the morning.

The previous evening's dinner had not gone well. It had become a decidedly uncomfortable affair. Sam had still had a chip on his shoulder and Neve's patience had been tested.

As the meal had gone on, the couple had increasingly avoided eye-contact and had spoken to one another as little as possible. Katie had picked up on it, for she'd eaten quickly, then asked to be excused even before she'd had any dessert. Throughout, Bryant had tried to keep some conversation flowing – but there'd been long silences that had left him feeling awkward; and guilty. Guilty that he'd come into his friends' lives only to cause upset. By the end of the evening, he'd been in two minds whether to pack his bags and go. But after sleeping on it, he'd decided to stay put. With all that had happened – and *still* was happening – to him, he'd be glad of the support. He knew Sam; and Neve. They'd make up. And, besides, he *needed* them. Needed to be *there*. Where he'd get his answers. He knew it. Felt it. Something deep down; deep within – *not* the little voice – something else telling him as much.

Sam had long gone by the time Bryant actually sat down to eat his breakfast. He was pleased to find the air had cleared – or, at least, that Neve was back to her usual chatty self with him. He wondered if there'd been any knock-on to the paying guests. He hoped not.

'Here you go.' She'd cooked a full fry-up.

'You not having anything?'

'No. I grabbed something earlier, thanks – after the others had all set off for the day.'

Others. Plural. He interpreted that to mean guests, not Sam. There was his answer. The guests seemingly unaware.

He looked at the size of the servings. *Hearty*. That was the word that sprung to mind.

'Thanks. This'll set me up nicely – especially if I've a long day ahead.' Straightaway he wished he hadn't said that. A long day for him would mean even longer without a car for Neve. He didn't want to rub salt into the wounds. But he needn't have worried.

'Look, David,' she wasn't about to hold him responsible. 'I'm sorry about last night. You know what Sam can be like. Always happy to help out – but doesn't think things through.' She offered Bryant the contents of a small tray. He selected the bottle of *Lea and Perrins* and shook the brown liquid over his mountain of bacon and eggs. 'You're welcome to use the car for as long as you like today.' He noticed the word *today* slipped in there. 'Don't feel you need to rush back. And there's plenty of petrol, so don't worry about trying to find a garage.'

'I really am grateful, Neve.' He placed the sauce bottle back on the tray. 'And... if I *do* overstay my welcome, you *must* tell me. I know my turning up was all a bit sudden; but I don't want to put you out. I know you've a business to run.'

'David,' an edge of finality in her tone. 'It's fine.' She beamed him one of her all-embracing smiles; and he knew the subject was closed. Just for a second, he was tempted to raise the issue of Graysbrook. Question the conversation he'd overheard. Reassure Neve he wasn't seeing things. Persuade her he wasn't losing his mind – despite what the little voice had told him about her suspicions. But what then might that say about her? And about Sam? He thought better of it. The little voice not there to warn him off this time – just a conclusion he reached by himself.

It took Bryant considerably longer than Sam to drive the same route to the castle. Not that he missed any turns – in fact, he'd been careful to check the map before setting off; visualising the few major junctions he knew he needed to keep an eye out for – it was more the unnatural driving style that, of necessity, he had to adopt that slowed his progress.

Unnatural.

Unnatural – at least – for him. But not for the locals. Nor the holidaymakers, with two weeks' intensive touring experience under their belt. Bryant, though, was far removed from his familiar urban environment, with its artificially-straightened roads and grid-iron mentality. For out here, Nature's hand was the only sculptor – unforgiving of anyone who failed to show her due respect. Her paths, temporarily on loan to man, weaved their historic way across the landscape; serpent-like, coiled around the foot of the hills; or occasionally basking in the undulating folds of the higher lands. But for anyone unwary – or arrogant enough to believe they had the better of her – the sinuous routes all afforded a short-cut. Straight to the deadliest game of snakes and ladders they'd ever play. Too much acceleration; a brake applied too late – and the driver would skew off the road; slip from the spiralling folds of the serpent; maybe over-turn; there to await the ladders of the rescue services – if they arrived in time.

Brake. Gear-change. Accelerate. Brake. Sharp turn. Brake again. Blind summit. Select gear. Accelerate away once more. Then brake hard before the next corner...

It went on like that for mile after mile. Sam had made it all look so easy; had known when to make up time on the more visible stretches. But not so Bryant. For him it was all about the constant acceleration and deceleration, throwing the car into the bend at the last minute, fighting with the wheel to straighten up before the next hair-pin; and skidding uncertainly to a halt on the chippings as a vehicle bore down from the other direction – hoping the passing place would accommodate them both. Neve's car was certainly being put through its paces. Just so long as he got it back to her in one piece. That thought uppermost in his mind.

Bryant's driving continued its stilted pattern until, at last, the single-track road finally widened again. Another fifteen minutes, a final turn and he found himself headed along the approach to the castle. The familiar sight of the trees, welcoming his return. He glanced at the dashboard clock. 11:25 am. The drive had taken him just under an hour and a half.

He parked up where Sam had done, followed the same path round the tower. On then through the walled-garden to the tree-cover, and the three signs. He chose the *Private* route and headed for Dr Alice's cabin. He hadn't actually ventured inside – the previous day, Rudi had led the way and he and Sam had remained outside while their host had popped his head round the door, declared Alice to be absent, then taken them back to the tower. Bryant wasn't sure of the form – whether he should knock or just walk straight in. But the decision was taken for him. The door suddenly opened inwards and he felt something brush past his leg. A blur of dark, tangled hair – and then the exiting boy had gone. The door started to swing shut. Bryant stepped quickly forwards – and bumped straight into a woman who was coming out.

'Hello... *again*, ' she said, not in the least flustered.

'Oh, hello...' He recognised her – the woman from the shop. The blur of hair must have been her son, Tyler.

'The doc's free now.' The woman added helpfully.

'Right, thanks.' He stood slightly to one side, holding the door while she edged past. She nodded a friendly smile.

'Come in, grab a seat. Be right with you,' came a voice from inside. A hint of the Liverpudlian discernible; but only just.

And so, Bryant entered Dr Alice Dysart's pseudo-surgery.

A world, based on recent events, he'd learned to mistrust. But, here, he felt strangely at ease, as if he were being welcomed with open arms. Almost immediately, he became aware of an all-pervading feeling of calm; utter tranquillity. Pastel shades – apple greens, offset with whites – were dominant all round her consulting room; if that's what it was – for he could see no desk, no couch, none of the sterile medical motifs to which he was so accustomed. Here, it could just so easily have been a friend's front room – sofa, a couple of easy chairs and a small table with a scattering of magazines – somewhere you'd drop in for a drink and a chat.

And then it dawned on him. Maybe that was precisely the image the doctor and Rudi wanted to promote. Peaceful. Comfortable. Above all, *natural* – fitting so seamlessly into Rudi's wider vision.

'Hello, you must be David?' A slim woman in her late thirties emerged from a side door and came into the centre of the room to shake hands with Bryant. 'Please, sit down.' She gestured towards the sofa.

He took off his coat, placed it on one of the chairs, then accepted the invitation. With the ease of someone used to dismounting a horse, Dr Alice swung over the sofa's other arm and dropped neatly in beside him. She inadvertently flashed a little too much winter-stockinged leg, and was quick to rearrange her dress. She certainly wasn't like any other doctor Bryant had encountered. But for the northern accent, he'd have thought her one of the jolly hockey-sticks brigade from the home counties.

'So,' she rested an elbow on the arm of the sofa, cupped her chin in a hand, 'what do you think?'

Too open a question for Bryant. What did he think about *what*? He gazed at the young woman, trying to gauge what he should say. What he thought she *wanted* him to say. But he found himself distracted; felt drawn to focus on her hair. Shoulder-length, autumnal in colour – browns inter-twining with flecks of gold; but warm russets the dominant colour; and all surrounding her face like some cobral hood.

Snakes.

A flash-back to the drive over. The sinuous roads.

'About all this?' Alice continued.

Bryant still didn't answer, his attention now focussed on the deep pools of hazel that were her eyes. Inviting of trust, and yet simultaneously enquiring; reading him; seeking to uncover his secrets. A sudden thought of Katie – and her piercing grey stare.

Both images reminded him of the cave's other-worldly eyes…

'Takes a very special individual, doesn't it? Money's one thing. But you have to have the vision. And the drive to see it through. It's more a vocation, isn't it?'

Like being a doctor, Bryant thought to himself. Then – no, she wasn't Liverpudlian; she was Mancunian. He'd misjudged her accent. He forced himself to stop scrutinising the woman; and consciously engaged in the polite conversation.

'Rudi's certainly an *individual*,' he said, repeating what he'd told Neve. 'Have you known him long… *doctor*…' he wasn't sure how to address the woman.

'Alice.' She answered for him. 'Just Alice.'

'Alice,' he repeated.

'And, before you ask,' she pre-empted the usual follow-up question, 'yes, I am still *technically* a GP, but I've long since moved on to other things. Medical research, mainly.'

'But Rudi, Sam; they all call you *Dr Alice*.'

'Yes, they do. And I still see the occasional patient – well, people staying here, anyway; minor stuff, that's all. But the first inkling of anything serious and it's straight off to hospital with them.'

'Oh, I thought...'

'Can I guess?' Alice interrupted him. 'You thought I'd be all herbal remedies and positive thinking?'

'I wouldn't have put it quite like that...'

'Don't worry, I won't take offence.' She patted him on the knee. Nothing forward. More like a reassuring touch from a grandparent. 'I suppose it's the stereotype that goes with places like this. I mean, people coming to a retreat – all very spiritual, *man*. It's what they expect, isn't it? Everyone else just like them?'

'Hm. I can see you're not like that.'

'Don't get me wrong. Relaxation can work wonders. A bit of down time and there's definitely a health benefit – lower BP; reduced cortisol levels. But a lot of it's just gimmickry. Sell the believers the latest line of panaceas. Definitely not what I'm about and – thankfully – not what Rudi has planned either.' She was in full flow, but interrupted herself. 'Ah, but you asked about Rudi, didn't you? Let's see...' Bryant already knew from Sam what was coming, but let Alice tell it her way, 'I first met Rudi around ten years ago. I was *on the market* and he needed someone to care for his wife, Johanna. You've heard about Johanna?' Bryant nodded. 'Lovely lady. Lovely couple. Absolutely made for one another. Well, she had MND,' that confirmed Bryant's suspicion. 'It was just a matter of time,' he could see Alice's eyes glazing over as she held back the tears. 'But, we made her comfortable, gave her as good a quality of life as we could. Afterwards, I was all set to leave, but Rudi asked me to stay on. I felt so guilty. I thought he was only doing it out of kindness. But make no mistake – yes, Rudi's altruistic, but he's first and foremost a businessman. So, I'm still doing the job I love – but I'm working slightly off on a tangent ...'

'Meaning?'

'Meaning... Rudi provides the funding and I look into the medical possibilities that interest Rudi.'

'And you're happy with that?'

'Yes,' Alice answered straightaway. 'Yes, I'm very happy with our arrangement. And, let me rephrase what I said. My job is to conduct research into what interests Rudi – *but*, I also get to research what interests me. So, although Rudi's work is the priority, often his and my interests amount to the same thing. Maybe we're just coming at it from different directions. Rudi, he's very...' she paused, thinking of the right word, '*intuitive*. Whereas, I'm logical; I want empirical proof.'

'You mean he's happy to take things on trust – and he wants you to find the science to back him up?'

'That's about it, yes.'

'Can you tell me what you're working on now? Or is it secret?'

'It's not secret. But I don't think you'd understand half of it…'
'Try me on the other fifty percent.' Bryant was enjoying this.
'OK,' she took a deep breath, focussing her thoughts; deciding how to explain the complexities in layman's terms. 'I said I was *on the market* when I met Rudi?'
'Yes?'
'I was… sort of let go. Not struck off, but I was pretty much *persona non grata* within the medical community. You see, when I qualified, I stayed on even back then to do research. All centrally-funded. I'd heard of a technology that had potential, diagnostic applications. Completely external. No need for invasive internal procedures. Cutting a long story short, you've heard of electrical skin resistivity?' Bryant hadn't, but he nodded; not that he fooled Alice for a minute. 'Look, the body's effectively controlled by electrical impulses from the brain – controls everything; so, by measuring the activity, you can determine how well someone is.' Bryant looked unconvinced. 'They use it with astronauts; think of it as long-distance *e-consultation.*'
'Alright,' he conceded.
'Now, electricity's only part of the electro-magnetic spectrum. Heat, light, radiation, microwaves *etcetera* – they're all part of the same thing. So, this technology that interested me claimed to be able to diagnose by measuring the electrical fields emanating from different parts of the body. You put it all through computers, convert the various calibrated readings into colour – think of it like a diagnostic colouring-in book. By reading the colours, you can see where problems exist. Diseased tissues, cancerous growths and so on.'
'And this works?'
'Put it this way, they were happy enough to fund my research to the tune of two million pounds.' Bryant whistled quietly. '*Until…* they didn't like what my findings were suggesting. I'd been asked to see what the applications might be for cancer patients. In summary, the results implied the radiotherapy and chemo actually caused more harm than good.'
'But that's only to be expected, isn't it? In the short-term, you'd think patients would get worse. Stop the cancer and then wait for their immune system to grow stronger.'
'Again, I don't want to be patronising, but that's oversimplifying it. What I found was that in a significant number of cases, the patients' deterioration was speeded-up. Without the chemo or radiotherapy, they undoubtedly would have lived longer.'
'Controversial, to say the least.' Bryant shifted his position on the sofa. 'I can see why they were keen for you to go.'

228

'What really annoys me,' said Alice, 'is that it's only now the truth's coming out. Various research papers; international studies; and all reaching the same conclusion. A lone voice, I was an embarrassment, easy to side-line. But now, when a whole crowd's shouting to be heard, it's harder for the establishment to ignore it. And here we are, a whole decade on. Just think how many lives could have been prolonged. Even a few extra months could have given so many more families the time they needed to say their goodbyes properly; to treat loved ones to a trip of a lifetime...'

Bryant could empathise with that – *partly*. In his own mother's case, he knew his father would have given anything to have had a few more months – or even days, at the end – with her. But, equally, the pain she'd been in, it had been a blessing when she had finally died.

'So, with Rudi's help, I'm pretty much going full-circle. Back to the research, where I started. He also wants me to look into sonic diagnostics.' Unintentionally, Bryant rolled his eyes; it sounded like an evening with Sam. But he remained polite. 'Sonics – the idea that cells resonate within certain frequencies. Think of it like a piano. One note signifies a healthy organ; if the note changes, it suggests disease. So, you play back the healthy note at the organ – like a tuning fork.' He must have let a yawn escape, for Dr Alice stopped abruptly; but she didn't challenge him. She just said, as if by way partly of passing the buck. 'I've still to be convinced on the sonics front, but I can see where Rudi's coming from; the parallels he believes are there. But, I'm happy with my own research; totally vindicated...' She stood up and walked around the room. 'So,' she turned back to Bryant, 'enough about me. I'd like to hear about you. Rudi's told me you're a very *complex* individual.'

Bryant looked up at her from where he was sitting.

Decision time. Whether to put his trust in someone else. Trust might mean answers. He wanted them. *Needed* them so desperately. To make sense of the continuing – *escalating* – confusion. Barely a day passing without something else strange happening. But Alice seemed level-headed enough. Coming at things scientifically. One thing he knew for sure, he didn't want to subject himself to tests at the hands of people like Markland and Sommer. Once under *their* care, he might never get out. But this woman was different. With her, he felt at ease. And none of this – he gazed round the welcoming room – was representative of the impersonal, clinical laboratories he'd been used to. And then there was Sam, Rudi; they had complete faith in her.

It was his turn to take a long in-breath.

Then, just as he had with Sam and Neve, he arrived at a crucial decision. He *would* share with Dr Alice his catalogue of strange events.

The crash. The blindness. The visual and audio anomalies. His escapes from death. The voice. The attempted suicide that never was. And now – if Sam and Neve were right; and Graysbrook hadn't survived – his latest ability...

Seeing the dead –

He paused, anticipation pounding inside his ear-drums; expecting the little voice to interrupt, to steer him away from further revelations. Nothing. He waited a fraction of a second longer. Still nothing. He exhaled, readying himself to begin. He fixed his gaze on Dr Alice.

And saw –

– a rainbow pattern of lights moving across her face...

CHAPTER SEVENTEEN

TOMLINSON STRAIGHTENED HIS back and shifted position in the driver's seat several times, trying to banish the aching stiffness. It made little difference. The twinges were still there in his lower muscles and he winced at a sudden, stabbing pain. Nothing he could do. He just needed rest, plenty of it. A few nights' undisturbed shut-eye would have been a good starting point.

The previous night's sleep had been interrupted by a call from Nick Lennox. Tomlinson wondered if she'd deliberately waited until the unearthly hour she'd chosen, just to get even with him. But at least he now knew that David Bryant wasn't one of hers; and nor did it appear he was an asset for any of the other agencies. Green light. He was free to make whatever enquiries he wanted.

From his inside breast pocket, he took out a sheet of paper and unfolded it. He gave it a quick, sudden flick to straighten out the creases. It was his new *aide memoire*, replacing the serviette that had seen better days. When he'd transcribed his earlier notes, he'd also taken the opportunity to sharpen their focus. Less now amounting to more – fewer words, boxes and lines; but possessed of greater meaning.

The superintendent yawned, nodded gently to himself. He'd spent long enough sitting there. Time to see if Patrick Maltravers was in.

He'd parked in a street parallel to that of his target property. He locked the car, walked back the way he'd driven in, bore right twice, then paused to get his bearings. To either side, Victorian houses extended ahead of him; their frontages set slightly back from their tree-lined road. Immediately to his right was number 201. Not just a number, though, he noticed; it had a name, too. Incorporated into the stained-glass panel above the door – *Abercrombie*. He scanned the other side of the road. 202. But he couldn't make out that property's name clearly. It was a very nice area though, the houses probably double what his was worth, and no doubt home to the upper end of society – PR directors, IT consultants, senior civil servants, the occasional magistrate; maybe a high-ranking Met officer here or there. Private – but near enough to get into town easily.

78, Frimley Street.

That was the address he needed. Left-hand side and a fair distance down he reckoned. He checked there was no traffic coming, then crossed over. A little while later he was standing outside number 78. It, too, bore a name – *Darnleydale*. He stepped forward and gave three raps with the lion's-head knocker. After a few moments, the door opened. Tomlinson was face to face with a man he took to be Patrick Maltravers.

The superintendent knew better than most the dangers of stereotyping, but in this case he thought his pre-conceptions were spot-on. From someone claiming to be a psychic, he'd expected some form of flamboyance to be on show. And the man didn't disappoint. From the way he was dressed, he could easily have been a Victorian, answering his door from a century ago. Bulging waistcoat and pocket-watch, small round glasses, white collar-less shirt; the only echo of modernity the grey goatee that elongated the face, drawing attention away from the all but receded hairline. He looked mid-fifties. Heavier build, but a few inches taller than the superintendent, Tomlinson expected him to have a deep, resonating voice, but when he spoke his tone was overtly effeminate; very discordant with the whole persona.

'Yes?'

'I'm sorry to bother you, but I'm looking for a Mr Maltravers?'

'Do you have an appointment?'

'Er, no,' the superintendent replied. 'Do I need one?'

'Well, I don't usually do readings without one. Mother doesn't like company.'

'Right. Well, I'm not actually here for a reading –'

'*Oh*?' The man was quick to interrupt. He crossed his arms defensively and fixed Tomlinson with a suspicious gaze. 'You're not press.' It was a statement, not a question. 'You're too neat. And I don't think you're from the council...' Tomlinson couldn't help but smile inwardly at the irony. Given the man's supposed psychic ability, he didn't seem to be doing very well. But then it seemed Maltravers had got it. 'Ah – *solicitor*.' He exclaimed. 'Yes, you'll be here for –'

This time, it was Tomlinson's turn to interrupt.

'Actually, sir,' he offered gently, 'I'm Met police. Superintendent Tomlinson...'

Quick as a flash, the man changed tack. 'Yes! Yes, I thought, so. Now you mention it. *Not* solicitor. *Police*. That's where I was getting confused. Easily done, I'm sure you'll agree – but it's all the law, isn't it?' Maltravers tutted to himself. 'It can be *so* confusing when they all come through at once.'

'Might I speak to you, sir? *Inside*, perhaps?' The superintendent emphasised the word.

'Oh. I'm not sure. It's mother, you see; she's not very good with strangers.' Then, almost as an after-thought, 'I'm not in any trouble am I?'

Tomlinson was quick to reassure him, 'No, sir, not at all. No, I was rather hoping you might be able to help me. I just wanted to run through something – the information you telephoned in to the *Crime Alert* show...'

'Ah, yes! I did, didn't I?' Maltravers was all interest now. 'Was I right?' He clapped his hands in glee. 'They don't usually listen, you see. Oh, yes, please do come in.' He held the door open but as Tomlinson made to step forward, he changed his mind. 'No, wait. What did you say your name was?'

'Tomlinson, sir. Superintendent Ray Tomlinson; Metropolitan Police.' He produced his warrant card.

Maltravers nodded, seemingly satisfied. 'If you'd just give me a moment, I'll go and let mother know you'll be coming in.' He disappeared inside. Tomlinson could hear Maltravers talking quietly. He reappeared. 'Good. That's that taken care of. This way, please, superintendent. To the sitting room. And, as I say, we mustn't disturb mother. That's very important.'

'Of course, sir. I'll follow you.'

The man closed the front door gingerly; led Tomlinson through the downstairs. The superintendent took in as much as he could. The house had a musty, old feel to it. Furniture, pictures, possessions; even the dust from a bygone era. Little sign of life, of daily habitation. He thought it felt somehow *sad*.

'Is it just you and your mother here, sir? No Mrs Maltravers?' He suspected he already knew the answer to that one. Before the days of political correctness, Maltravers would have been labelled a confirmed bachelor. But there was no prejudice, no malice in the superintendent's question. He was just making polite conversation, working to establish a rapport with the man.

'No, superintendent. I never married. Mother wouldn't have approved. It's just the two of us. Father – he was taken a very long time ago. Quite suddenly.'

'I am sorry.'

'Now, if you'd like to sit here?' Maltravers indicated the first of two chairs arranged to either side of a gas-fire.

'Thank you.'

The man took the other. 'Would you like tea?'

'No, thank you, sir. I don't want to put you out. And this shouldn't take long.'

'Very well, as you wish.' Maltravers crossed his legs and looked expectantly at his visitor.

'Right,' Tomlinson began, 'I was just wondering if you'd go through it all again for me, please, sir? What you said to the detectives when you called in?'

'Yes, of course.' Maltravers cleared his throat. 'I have...' he paused, building up to the moment, '... a *gift*, superintendent. I operate outside what most people consider the norm. I have...' he paused a second time for added dramatic effect, '... *guides.*'

'Guides, sir?' Tomlinson repeated, fighting to keep a straight face.

'I know,' Maltravers swept his arms wide, as if by that action he could persuade the superintendent how candid he was being, 'It's very hard for many people to accept the possibility that such *beings* exist. And I understand that. Really, I really do, superintendent. But, you see... I get messages from my guides. Very confusing, sometimes. They all go on at once. It's not like I can control them. They speak to me when *they* want to. I just have to listen. When I can, I try to interpret...'

'I see, sir. So, when you telephoned the studio...' Tomlinson tried to steer Maltravers back to the matter in hand.

'Yes? Ah, the studio. Well, it was... now let me think...' he turned to one side, cocked an ear, then nodded. 'Thank you, Seth... Yes, it was Leonora that time. Not like her at all. She's usually far more attuned to finding missing people; not crime.'

'*Leonora*, sir? Right, and what was it she told you?'

'Oh... that the robbery at the jewellery shop – you know the one?' Tomlinson nodded. '... yes, that it was staged by that gang. The... oh, no, sorry; name's gone. But... like I told the officer, they used a shot-gun. And Leonora said it *will* be used again. *Drive-by shooting.* Those were her words. Drive-by shooting; that's the term, isn't it, superintendent? You're always hearing about drive-by shootings; oh, and *hoodies.*'

'I see. And do you know when this is going to be, sir?'

'Well how would you expect me to know? I'm not a mind reader, superintendent. I can only work with what's channelled to me...'

Tomlinson stared hard at the man, felt his jaw tighten with annoyance. He couldn't be sure he wasn't being taken for a ride – an afternoon's amusement for the psychic showman. But all he saw was *belief* in the man's eyes; mistaken, misguided, deluded perhaps; but it *was* there. Not a hint of deception. He let the man's rebuke pass.

'Right,' Tomlinson wanted to draw the conversation to a close. 'Thank you for your time, sir. I'd better be off. Won't keep you any longer. But... just one more thing, if I may?'

'Of course.'

'I understand you booked yourself onto a flight a few months back; but you never travelled?'

'That's right.' The words spoken hesitantly, as suspicious eyes watched him closely. 'And what has this got to do with the robbery, superintendent?' Maltravers was on the offensive. 'If this is some sick game, I'll tell you now, I simply can't take any more of it. I just can't –

not after what that dreadful little man did to me. He humiliated me publicly. He made me a laughing stock. It *so* hurt mother's feelings...'

Tomlinson was quick to allay the man's fears. 'No – please; forgive me, sir. It's nothing like that. Honestly. I just wondered why you didn't travel, that's all. Anything you can tell me might help me...'

'What – with *another* of your cases?' The suspicious eyes now sparkled with genuine interest.

'I'm sorry; I really can't say more than that, sir. Confidentiality, you understand...'

'Hm, I suppose so.' The man clearly would love to have known more.

'You were saying... you didn't travel?'

'No. I was advised against it.'

'Right. By?'

'Seth told me not to.'

'Seth. *Seth* being?'

'My chief guide, superintendent – in the spirit world. You understand? Very knowledgeable fellow. I think he must have been around, variously advising others who've shared my gift down the ages, since the 800s. Thankfully, though, he's not as noisy as the others. He doesn't shout all the time. And I do find that most refreshing...'

Tomlinson was fast reaching the conclusion he wouldn't get anything else from Maltravers. And he certainly didn't have time to waste humouring the man's fantastical beliefs. Informants were one thing – but 1200 year-old ones; and from the *other* side? Who was the man trying to kid? He decided he'd finish up – a couple more questions, then call it a day. Sighing hard, he asked, 'So... Seth... told you not to travel on the plane *because*? What? Did he see danger? Did he know it was going to crash?' Tomlinson wondered how Seth could even have known what a plane was; not too many of those around at the end of the first millennium. Clearly an oversight in Maltravers' self-created, delusional world. Not that that seemed unduly to bother the man as he gamely replied,

'Oh, yes. Oh, he was very certain about that. They needed it to crash, you see.'

'*They*?'

'What's that, Seth?' Again, Maltravers cocked his ear; deaf to extraneous noise; to the superintendent's last question. 'Well, yes, I can tell him. Wait... say it again. Yes... and can you be more precise? No? Oh...' A nod of his head, then Maltravers announced, 'Seth says you need to be careful, superintendent.'

'Right. Thank you... *Seth*.' The policeman looked round the empty room.

'Oh, this is *very* important, superintendent.' Maltravers looked quite agitated. 'He's really insistent. Seth says you need to beware of the trees. It is trees, Seth? Yes, *trees*. He says it's the trees.'

Tomlinson nodded. The man was obviously on another planet. No wonder he'd been flagged as a nutter. 'I'll certainly look out for them.'

'Yes... Seth says that's very wise, superintendent. He just can't emphasise enough the threat they pose to you.'

'Now – can I just check... this flight? You presumably had a ticket all booked?' A nod from the man. 'My understanding is that they said you'd...' the superintendent coughed, apologetically, '... made your story up. But surely your ticket would have proved otherwise?'

'Ah, *they're* very clever. Very clever, superintendent. They'd already thought of that one. You see, I booked on-line.' It seemed an odd fusion – the suggestion of twenty-first century technology being exploited by the Victoriana-styled gentleman. 'And I was due to collect my ticket at the airport. The flight out would have been fine, of course. It was the return flight that crashed. And that's the one Seth warned me about. But, I chose to avoid both anyway, just in case there was any *confusion* in the message... No, Seth, I know you don't get...'

'Your ticket, sir? You were saying?' Tomlinson instantly there, trying to head off any further meandering.

'Yes... like I said, I'd booked it on-line. So, as I didn't fly, I wanted to see if I could get a refund. But they said I'd *never* made the booking. But I know I did. So I called the credit card company – and they said I hadn't completed any such transaction either. So, strangely, I wasn't out of pocket. But, then, well I couldn't prove it either way. My word against theirs... And, I believe, you know the rest...'

'Indeed, sir.' It was time to call it a day. Escape the madhouse. Tomlinson stood up, began to head for the door. 'Like I said, sir. Thank you for your time. I really must be going now.'

But Maltravers was also on his feet, edging round between the superintendent and the exit to sanity; extending a hand.

'My card, superintendent? You never know when you might need it. If you'd like a reading? What's that, Seth? Does *Jack* mean anything to him? Jack has a message. Yes, I'll ask him...'

Cold-reading was Tomlinson's first thought. Pick a name; seemingly at random – but, then, Maltravers could see he was in his fifties; Jack would have been a common enough name back then in his father's – or even grandfather's – time. And depending what he now replied, the showman in Maltravers would no doubt go on to offer further vague thoughts until he got something right. A good stage act – but not proof of any psychic ability.

The superintendent shook his head – first, to the suggested

name; second, to the proffered card. But Maltravers wasn't finished yet. He insisted the policeman take his contact details.

'We're very good with missing persons. Leonora's speciality. Did I mention that?'

'You did, sir; yes.' Tomlinson reluctantly took the card. He turned it over a few times. '*Monty* Maltravers...' he read aloud. 'I thought you were *Patrick* Maltravers, sir?'

'Oh, I am. It's my middle name – Montague. *Monty*. It's my mother's idea. She thinks it has a ring to it. Better for attracting the clientele. They can be quite *discerning*. And who'd choose a reading with *Paddy*, when *Monty*'s available? Just not the same, is it? That's right, isn't it, mother?'

Tomlinson did a double-take.

Felt the adrenalin rush kick in. The hairs suddenly standing on the back of his neck.

He scanned the room warily. He hadn't seen Maltravers' mother. Nor heard anyone come in while they'd been talking. Monty seemed amused.

'Oh, my fault entirely, superintendent. I keep forgetting. You must forgive me. Don't worry – *you* won't be able to see her. She's in the spirit realm. But she is sat *just* there. On the rocking chair.' Tomlinson could see one over by the window. 'It's her favourite spot. She'll sit there for hours watching people come and go.' Maltravers raised his voice. 'Won't you, mother? Yes?' Then lowered it again. 'She's a little hard of hearing, poor dear; you'll have to excuse her.'

For a second, Tomlinson wondered if the rocker would move – a concealed wire; all part of the show. But it remained motionless; maintained its silent vigil on the world outside.

'Well, I'd better excuse myself, sir. I know your *mother* will want her privacy. Don't want to intrude.' Before he realised what he was doing, he was nodding apologetically in the direction of the vacant chair. *Crazy* he mouthed under his breath.

'Well, thank you for calling in, superintendent. I hope I was able to help?'

'Yes, sir; you've given me much to think about.' More honesty there than he'd intended.

'Yes, I'll remind him, Seth. There's no need to go on. Now don't forget, superintendent – *beware of the trees...*'

Bryant tried to rationalise the irrational; work out what it was he was seeing. His first thought was that this must be a repeat of what he'd witnessed at his mother's funeral – the strange radiant lights that had briefly surrounded the vicar.

'They're nice, aren't they?'

'What are?'

'The lights,' Alice replied.

'*You* can see them?' Bryant was stunned.

'Yes?'

'But… I thought it was only me. I mean, no-one else – '

'*Complex*, indeed,' mused Alice. 'The lights we're seeing, they're from the rainbow-maker. Over there.' She pointed towards one of the windows. Bryant looked and saw a small crystal rotating near the pane, catching the sunlight; glittering brightly as it sent cascades of rainbow light around the room. The iridescent flashes caught the walls, the ceiling; and Alice. 'It's solar powered. Turns the crystal and – well, you're looking at the result. Very pretty to look at. Not sure it does anything for the *chi* of this place – but Rudi swears by them. And it does add to the relaxing ambience of the place.' She returned to sit beside Bryant. 'But you weren't meaning that, were you?' She scrutinised him, holding his gaze. 'You've seen something else, haven't you?' She took one of his hands between hers. 'Come on, you can tell me…'

So he did.

Everything.

Beginning with the crash. And ending with his new-found ability to observe people who weren't there.

'So?' he asked, anxiety uppermost in his thoughts. 'You think I'm mad, don't you?' He exhaled sharply. 'I wouldn't blame you. I mean, I don't understand any of this myself.'

Alice steepled her fingers, deep in thought for a moment, then said matter-of-factly.

'*Clinical synaesthesia*.' She raised an eyebrow, pausing to observe his reaction. There wasn't one, other than the blankness etched into his face. 'Thought not. You've never heard of it, have you?'

'No.'

'Well, the good news is… I think a lot of what you're experiencing can be attributed – directly or indirectly – to the trauma of the crash. Your episode of blindness for one thing, that's a good indicator. And there's still a fair degree of resultant synaesthesia in evidence. That's where I'd put my money…'

'And the bad news?' He had to ask.

'Hm – not so much *bad news*; more a case of… that I'll need to give it further thought. Look up some of the more unusual periodical entries…' *Unusual.* Bryant wasn't sure he liked the sound of that. 'But don't worry, I think we'll find a perfectly logical, medical explanation for everything.' She smiled encouragingly.

'I'm not going mad, then?'

'Absolutely not.'

'You said clinical syn –' he stumbled over the word.

'S*ynaesthesia*. Yes. It's a physiological anomaly. Where you sense something – but the experience occurs in a part of the body other than the one being stimulated...' Alice could see Bryant still wasn't grasping what she was saying. 'Here, try this. Imagine your senses are like wiring circuits, all leading to different parts of the brain. But whoever did the wiring got it wrong, so you ended up with *crossed wires*. Well, you might find that instead of hearing sounds, you actually perceive them as colours; or you might experience them as different tastes. Or, you end up converting tactile responses into sounds – a smooth object being quiet; a rough one loud. Does that make it easier to understand?'

'I think so,' Bryant answered. He began relating what Alice was saying to the instances he'd experienced – the meeting with Markland; the church; Sam's stone circle. He wondered if maybe she *was* on to something.

'You know,' she continued, 'what if there's a link here to...' She didn't expand on what she was thinking. 'It would certainly add a whole new dimension to...' Again, she didn't offer Bryant any wider explanation. Then she seemed satisfied by whatever it was she'd been considering. 'Look, would it be OK if we tried something?'

'Like what?'

'How about a quick spin into town? There's something I'd like you to see.'

'Alright,' he was intrigued now.

'Here,' Alice stretched across to the chair and passed Bryant his coat. 'You go on, I'll meet you at the car-park.'

Five minutes later, Bryant was still waiting for Alice. He rocked back and forth on his toes, whistling absently to pass the time. He suddenly heard a loud metallic *thwack*. It made him jump. Then another. He turned to see where the noise was coming from. A little way over into the trees, he could see a tall, skinny man in an ill-fitting, green boiler suit. Like Rudi, the man sported a long beard – but his was still black, like his unkempt hair. The man noticed him, and nodded. Bryant went over to see what he was doing.

'Afternoon,' said the man. English from his accent. West Country.

'Hello,' Bryant answered. 'Keeping busy?'

'Always work to be done.'

The man seemed to be hammering in tall, spindly canes – but made of copper, not wood.

'Looks interesting. What's it going to be – vegetable patch?'
The man laughed.

'No.' A grin spread across his face. 'Pest control.'

Bryant thought he might be constructing a fence. 'Bit small for deer,' he ventured.

'Deer!' The man roared with laughter. '*Bit small for deer* he says. That's a good one. I'll have to remember that. Deer.' A shake of the head; almost pitying, as if it was obvious it wasn't intended to keep any deer out. The man waited to see if Bryant would come back with another suggestion but, finding him erring on the side of caution, staying silent, he explained, 'This is for the *serpents*. Stop *them* getting in.'

'Oh, right.'

Bryant didn't know what to say to that. He knew Rudi's estate would inevitably become a magnet, attracting the more unconventional of society's individuals; but this really did seem weird. Especially as the man must have been working for Rudi. You wouldn't go hammering in copper pipes in someone else's land otherwise. The man didn't say any more; just kept bashing away at his snake-proof posts.

'Well, guess I'd better let you get on with it.' There was a beep of the horn and Alice was there, the engine idling as she waved at him from the drive. 'That'll be for me. Bye then. And good luck with your serpents...'

Tomlinson had left Maltravers' comfortable suburb, and had parked up in a less affluent neighbourhood. Not the worst by any means, but it still had a way to go. Semi-detached, local authority new-builds were taking on the sixties' high-rise blocks. *Regeneration* the government's priority; no matter it would take at least a decade to achieve. But it was a start. And without that, there'd never be any progress.

He jotted a few further thoughts on his piece of paper. Drew another arrow leading to David Bryant's name. Then, something suddenly jolted his memory – he turned the paper over and wrote just one word.

Attic.

Followed by a question mark. Something else to consider.

His stomach rumbled a timely reminder. It wanted feeding. He was about to start the car and drive off when he noticed a kebab van. He gave it the once over – fairly new registration plate; paint job still in good order. Decades spent grabbing meals on the run meant he'd built up a strong constitution. He'd risk buying something. He got out of the car and began walking over towards the mobile meal wagon. While he was still some way off, he heard an engine revving loudly. Kids perhaps from the local estate; showing off – all set to practice their dough-nuts;

hoping the cops with cameras would turn up and get them on the TV. He carried on walking.

Suddenly he registered movement out of the corner of his eye. He turned to look. A small lorry driving along. White. Nothing there to interest him. But then he heard the shouting. Angry. Confrontational. He scanned his surroundings to find out where it was coming from. He could see two youths. Late teens or early twenties. They were arguing with each other on the pavement. One in a hooded-top, his face partly covered; the other wearing a T-shirt.

Hoodies – an echo of the meeting with Maltravers.

The one in the hood backed away a few paces. A glint of silver. The other had pulled a knife. Tomlinson reached for his extendable baton. Not there. It was in the car. He started running back towards his vehicle. The hooded youth had fallen over; the other was almost upon him. No way he'd get to the car in time. He shouted a warning, to try and buy the underdog a few seconds to escape.

'Police!'

But the youth with the knife was only interested in one thing. Reaching his target.

Tomlinson tried again; a last-ditch attempt; an out and out bluff.

'*Armed* police! Drop your weapon!'

At that, the attacker did react; stopped what he was doing but then, seeing only Tomlinson – and no sign of any backup team – he pressed home his advantage. His victim only seconds away now from serious injury. Or death.

The gunshot was totally unexpected –

It caught the attacker – and Tomlinson – by surprise. Both were aware of the sound of screeching tyres and then a hot-hatch, windows tinted midnight-black, tore round the corner into full view. The youth with the knife looked stunned. Didn't know whether to stand or run. A split second of indecision and the car was bearing down on him. At the last moment the driver braked hard, spun the vehicle through ninety degrees; gave the passenger another chance to take a shot. The terrified youth turned and fled, desperate to increase the distance between himself and the shooter. This time with the car motionless, the sound of the gun was even louder. More distinct.

Tomlinson recognised it for what it was. A shot-gun.

Shot-gun – Maltravers, again.

Instinctively he assumed it would be a sawn-off. Too unwieldy, otherwise – insufficient space to brandish it within the car. He looked around for the aggressor with the knife. Was he injured? Dead? Or still running? He spotted him. The latter, thank God. He was weaving left to right, zig-zagging his way to freedom. The shooting had stopped. Maybe re-loading? Never mind the technicalities – that the sawn-off was inaccurate other than at close-range. The knife-wielder had survived to fight another day. As had his victim. Next time, the knife-wielder would probably come out better prepared. More guns on the streets. Just where would it all end?

Tomlinson looked at the hatch; tried to memorise as much as he could – the registration; anything he could see of the occupants inside.

'Hey! Watch out!' The kebab seller roared at him.

Turning in alarm, the superintendent had just enough time to catch sight of the lorry that was coming straight for him – the driver having had to swerve to avoid colliding with the shooter's car. Only now the lorry driver was doing his best to miss Tomlinson.

Fifty-fifty chance. Matter of life and death. Dive left or right?

Tomlinson dived right. The lorry careered to the left – the driver yanking the steering so hard that two of the vehicle's wheels lifted clear off the road. There was an almighty crash – the scraping of metal on tarmac as the lorry went over onto its side. Then, silence.

The kebab seller was next to Tomlinson, helping him to his feet. The superintendent felt shaky; his first thought that he was getting too old to subject his body to such treatment. He checked himself over quickly. Couldn't believe his luck. Nothing broken.

'I'm fine,' he panted rapidly, pointing in the direction of the overturned lorry.

The good Samaritan from the kebab van ran over to see how the driver was. He climbed up the side of the cab, opened the door and leaned in to offer his help.

As Tomlinson walked unsteadily over to join them, limbs still reeling from the shock, the hot-hatch disappeared round a corner. He shot a glance in the direction where the hooded-youth had been. No sign of him. Probably safe in the car with his associates.

Tomlinson stopped a few feet from the lorry.

'Bloody hell…'

Now he was up close, he could see the vehicle's livery. White, with a name all along the side – *Ashworth's Nursery.* And below that, a stylised logo.

A stand of trees…

Tomlinson was headed straight for Maltravers' house. How *could* the man have known? He couldn't have. It was *impossible.* There was just no way. And as for all that Seth nonsense. Come on, who had Maltravers been trying to kid?

He hit the brakes hard –

Just managed to stop in time, as a car pulled out of a side-street in front of him. Broken rear indicator light – not that the driver had made any attempt to use it. And there was a mini-cab identification plate screwed to the bumper. But he didn't have time to take the number. He flashed his lights at the car to show his annoyance, only to have the driver in front give him the one-fingered salute. His jaw tightened. Then, a few moments later, the mini-cab turned sharply off into another side-street. Tomlinson mouthed a few obscenities in its direction.

Less than a minute later, he was pulling up outside *Darnleydale*. He jumped out and ran to the door, rapped forcefully on the lion's-head.

'You were too slow,' said a voice. Tomlinson turned to see a man, late sixties, standing at the front of the adjacent property. The man was looking at the superintendent's vehicle. 'Nicer car than the other,' he said admiringly, 'but it's punctuality that counts in your game, isn't it? Otherwise, you lose the fare.'

The penny dropped.

Mini-cab.

Tomlinson would have bet a hundred to one – the cab he'd just avoided, Patrick Maltravers had been on board...

CHAPTER EIGHTEEN

THE TOWN WAS little more than a collection of former fishermen's cottages, set back from a crescent-shaped harbour. The idyllic, picture-postcard scene masked the harsh realities of making – *sustaining* – a living for the inhabitants from centuries past. Each of the white-fronted houses had their own stories to tell; their walls possessed of ears – but not of tongues; with no way to recount to future generations the sadness, hardship or suffering they'd witnessed. Many drivers sped through the settlement with neither the time, nor inclination, to dwell on its history. But some – tourists mainly – did stop and there, just before the *Haste Ye Back* sign, they found a small convenience store, an adjacent car-park and a non-descript toilet block; each providing welcome respite; a chance to stretch the legs; take in the scenery; refuel the stomach. Some might even walk the length of the cottages, pause beside the information board down at the harbour-side; read about their construction; nod approvingly at the wisdom of building them close together, end-on to the sea – affording protection against the wind-driven storms, and lessening the frequent battering meted out by the changeable sea. But even these were soon back in their cars. The next leg of their journey mapped out. On their way again.

The town did, however, have *one* major attraction.

Not that the tourists knew. And even those who dropped into the stores remained ignorant of the fact. But that was only to be expected because Angus, the proprietor, had long since fallen out with Mary, so there was no way he was going to publicise her venture. Nor had Mary persuaded the powers-that-be in the tourist hierarchy that her exhibition deserved a prestigious brown sign; and she didn't have enough money to print the glossy pamphlets for casual browsing by guests in the local B&Bs.

And so, starved of publicity, Mary's exhibition remained an eclectic oddity; infrequently visited; something usually sought out only by those in the know, who shared her passion for all things geological and who'd most likely heard about her special collection by word of mouth when visiting the marvels of *Knockan Cragg* up on the north west coast.

She hoped she might still achieve some form of recognition for her collection – her life's work – but she knew time wasn't on her side. And when she did die, there'd be no natural successor to take over. She'd considered bequeathing everything to one the universities, but she suspected her precious items would be catalogued, sub-divided and shut away in wooden drawers for the rest of their days; or worse still, the rarer pieces might be sold off to private collectors. Either way, successive generations would be robbed of the chance to gaze upon their natural beauty. But then she'd met Alice. Mary liked Alice. Maybe one day she'd ask her to take it all on.

For her part, Alice did what she could to offer encouragement. She'd mention the collection to those staying at the Sorralan retreat; would ask if they'd like to drop by. And she'd already persuaded Rudi to include a page about it, with photos, on the castle's website. Alice had also made a small donation to the cause – relatively insubstantial, but it had allowed the lighting to be upgraded, and had led to a number of new display cabinets being built. Small gestures, but they'd at least gone some way to injecting an air of amateur professionalism into Mary's grand plan.

Currently the exhibition occupied several of Mary's downstairs rooms, with a sizeable proportion spilling out into a makeshift lean-to that ought to have been condemned many years ago. And still more objects were housed in an old summerhouse.

A natural carer, a people-person, Alice had chosen to help Mary and that same altruism was even now working overtime, compelling her to offer a Hippocratic helping-hand to the newcomer in her life – the conundrum that was David Bryant. It was for that reason she'd driven him to meet Mary; to let him experience the marvellous collection. More though, Alice wanted to see if her hunch would pay off.

Mary had been busy when they'd arrived. She'd invited them in and had asked that they show themselves round. Just so long as they let her know when they'd finished so she could padlock the summerhouse.

'How did you hear about this place?' Bryant asked.

'I went to a poetry-reading evening, about a year ago now. And, you know how it is, I got talking to the others over a glass of wine afterwards... and Mary was there. We started chatting and hit it off straight away. She told me of her travels as a young woman – the adventures, the life she led; how she'd met her husband. He'd been an engineer. They'd gone all over the world together because of his work. Nigeria; South Africa; South America; the Orient. And with her love of the natural world – particularly an interest in the Earth's creative processes, the way rocks form and so on – she'd indulged herself and started a little collection of precious stones. Just something to keep her occupied while her husband was away for weeks at a time. Well, she obviously got the collecting bug and when they finally returned to the UK, Mary found she'd amassed a huge collection. It was – still *is* – very important to her. It became even more so after her husband passed away. The rocks and gemstones, they gave her a focus. She'd not had children, you see. So, I think, as long as she has these, she still has her youth; her happy memories.'

'You're clearly very fond of her.'

'I am, yes. Maybe I see the person I'd like to have been in Mary. The explorer. The girl with no ties...'

'You still could be?'

'No, my travelling days are over. Besides, I'm happy now; working for Rudi.'

'So,' Bryant cast his eyes round the room. '*This* is Mary's life.' Everywhere he looked, there were huge chunks of rock. Of all shapes and sizes. Superficially, externally – dull, shadowy forms barely worth a second glance. But on closer inspection, *within* – where the outer casings had been expertly hewn away, there lay revealed the most beautiful and intricate of crystal formations. Every glance rewarded with shimmering, glistening facets. Some of the rock forms had been illuminated from various angles, the light picking out certain petrified anomalies. To a geologist the collection would undoubtedly have had an even greater meaning – but, limited though Bryant's understanding was, he still found it breathtaking. It didn't matter that he didn't know the rocks' names, nor that he was ignorant of their respective characteristics. He walked slowly round the exhibition, moving between rooms, reading the hand-written cardboard signs. The low-tech and, in places, unprofessional display somehow being a perfect accompaniment; complementing the naturalness of the Earth's innermost gifts. Here, a sign for heliotrope; and there, rhodonite; and elsewhere, sardonyx; and, just occasionally, something he did recognise. Opal... And *haematite* –

A sudden memory of Luisa...

Of the matching necklace and bracelet set he'd bought her in Venice; the cold, dark stones contrasting against the warmth of her delicate, Mediterranean tan. He dismissed her from his mind; but the thought of Paolo took longer to let go. Paolo – he *so* wished he could see him again...

'David? Over here,' Alice's words broke the internal concentration; distracted him from the sudden, unexpected feeling of despair. For even then, in that short time, it had begun to entwine itself – ivy-like in its constriction – around the few remaining branches of his already-fading memory-tree. 'Come and take a look at these.'

'What are they?'

'I think they're the most beautiful specimens in the whole exhibition. It's not like they're even the most valuable. But,' she waved him over, 'come and see for yourself.' Not that Alice intended to let on, but she *was* biased. For this was one of the cabinets she'd paid for. As well as the accompanying lighting effect –

Bryant came to stand beside Alice. He noticed straightaway that the rear and side panels had been painted black. He gazed in boyish wonder at the contents. There were seven items on show, each slightly smaller than the preceding one; like a line of Russian dolls. They had been recessed slightly into a Perspex ladder; one set above the other. Starting at the base, Bryant could see the largest of the seven exhibits radiating out a brilliant-red in all directions. Next in line was a slightly smaller mass, a vivid orange hue streaming out. Up another rung to an explosion of yellow. And then a vibrant aura of green – as if the gem itself had been charged with life's own spark. The green melted easily into a welcoming ethereal blue. And that, in turn, found itself absorbed into a night sky of indigo. And finally, king of colour, violet – though its source was the smallest of all the stones – shone out from its position of elevated elegance, cascading a superior luminescence over those of its inferior subjects beneath.

'Stunning,' Bryant said simply, observing Nature's rainbow-pallet. 'Tell me, what's causing the stones to glow so brightly? Are they special in some way? I've never seen anything like it.'

'Ah, the *glow*,' Alice sounded pleased with herself. 'It's because you're looking at them under *ultra-violet* light. That's why they appear so vivid. Different to how we usually see them.' She smiled. 'It was an idea of mine, actually. Add a bit of pizzazz to Mary's exhibition. Let people observe the rocks' true beauty. It's a bit like the rain forest. You know, the colours we see – birds, plants? That's just a fraction of what's there. Some in the animal kingdom are able to detect so many things we're unaware of. They just see it naturally for themselves.'

'I did not know that. Well, these gems, they're absolutely beautiful.'

'Right, then. Guess we ought to be going. If you'd like to find Mary, say thanks for letting us have a look round? I'll catch you up in a minute. I just need to make sure everything's turned off and locked up for her. Especially her summerhouse. You wouldn't believe how much some of these items are worth.'

'Just amazing.' Bryant added. He nodded his appreciation, turned and headed back along the corridor.

'It's certainly that,' Alice agreed. Then, when she could see Bryant had gone, she leaned round the side of the display case, fumbling for the switch.

She flicked it.

The special strip-light fired up and the cabinet seemingly came alive. The dull, hitherto lifeless contents instantly bathed themselves – *herself* – in a swirl of radiantly-energetic, arcing iridescence. For it was only now with the light switched on that she, too, could gaze on the wondrous colours revealed by the ultra-violet spectrum.

The colours that David Bryant had so *unnaturally* been able to see all by himself...

Alice had been impatient to get back.

She'd chatted happily enough to Bryant during their return drive. But it had all been superficial. She hadn't been able to help herself. Behind the scenes, her mind had been furiously at work.

Remembering. Theorising. Questioning. Extrapolating. Desperately trying to figure out what was going on. How could he be doing it? Was it conscious? Under his control? Did he even know? She'd have to tell Rudi. But think of the possibilities. Areas of research she'd long since dismissed as being futile, no more than anecdotal – founded on the quicksand of speculation – now clamoured for her attention. She'd have to decide which lines of investigation to prioritise –

But Alice the people-person intervened.

Must think of the patient. The patient comes first. Everything else is secondary. No place for egos. Must be careful not to frighten him, overburden him. He's been through a lot already. Mustn't scare him away. Time enough later to think about everything else...

She parked the car.

'David, I think we may be onto something.'

There was a pause, then Bryant asked, confused by the sudden change in conversation, 'Something... *meaning?*'

She realised they were talking crossed-purposes. He'd still been speaking about the community spirit he saw in evidence in the Highlands; and she'd – seemingly at least – been fully engaged in that conversation.

'Sorry. My fault. Listen, there's just so many things... and I think I'm beginning to put... oh, *stop!*' The rebuke was to herself, not to him. 'Right. Slow down, Alice. Think.' She took a deep breath. 'OK... Your experiences? What we discussed before?'

'Yes?'

'I said I thought I could explain some of them? The clinical synaesthesia, yes?' An affirmative nod from Bryant. 'Well, from what I've just seen back there...' He looked blank at that. 'Don't worry, I'll fill you in later. Well, I think now I can probably come up with a theory for *everything* that's been happening to you.'

'Right?' Excitement in Bryant's voice. 'Really?'

'Hopefully. Yes.'

Alice had invited Rudi to come over and join the two of them at her chalet to hear first-hand her emerging theories – radical concepts, perhaps, but ones she hoped they could explore relatively easily on site. While they waited for Rudi to arrive, Alice showed Bryant around.

'Nicely laid out,' Bryant observed, as they came back down to ground level from the living quarters upstairs. 'Compact – but room enough for a guest.'

'It does me just fine. Besides, I don't get that many visitors...' She let the thought trail off. 'But, I live in a wonderful setting, doing what I love; and with no bills. Can't ask for more than that, can I?'

'I take it Rudi does pay you something?'

'Oh, yes – but, obviously, it's not a patch on what I could have been earning if I'd stayed mainstream.'

'I guess not.'

'But it's a trade-off. Because I wouldn't have the freedom I've got now, would I? No, all things considered, I'm far better off here.' She shrugged her shoulders. 'It's funny though, the direction your life goes, isn't it?'

Bryant could empathise entirely. Just six months ago, he'd been *mainstream*, too. Conservative career. Affluent lifestyle. Comfortably placed among his corporate peers. Everything all neat and tidy. His life mapped out. Go back a year before that, and he'd still been happily married. *Funny though, the direction your life goes.* It was certainly that. He could never have predicted the point he'd now reached in his life.

'And back here,' Alice was walking him through to the next room, beyond the surgery area he'd sat in before, 'we've got my study.' It was all very ordered. There was a desk, swivel-chair, computer and printer. The walls were largely hidden by shelf after shelf of books, papers, lever-arch files; a lifetime's reference work.

'So where's the lab?' Bryant asked. 'I'd imagined, oh, I don't know...' memories of his schooldays came flooding back, '... Bunsen burners, retort stands, test tubes? At least a white coat hanging up somewhere? But not... *this* – one small room. Doesn't seem right somehow.'

'You don't miss much, do you?'

'Well...'

'The research centre's downstairs.'

'Downstairs?' It took Bryant a moment to figure it out. 'Ah, *subterranean.*' He remembered then. Some of the chalets had been built into the hill-sides, so why not down into the ground as well? All very eco-friendly. Helping reduce the visual impact, and no doubt saving on the heating and insulation costs. 'Can I see?'

'Of course.' Alice was in two minds whether to hang on for Rudi, but decided to press on with the tour. He'd soon realise they weren't there and make his own way down to the lab to find them. 'This way...'

They descended a narrow flight of stairs. Bryant half expected to feel colder the further down they went, but the temperature remained constant. He found it strangely welcoming; comforting almost, to be buried away out of sight. It reminded him of the familiar, inviting darkness to which he'd grown accustomed during his period of convalescence – when the blindness had been his constant companion, shielding him from the world outside. Maybe both sensations somehow tapped into a primordial, mental default-setting hard-wired into man's brain.

'Here we are.' Alice stopped and sized up a door. 'It sticks occasionally, so I'll just give it a helping hand.' She held the handle down, aimed carefully and delivered a forceful kick. The door creaked a half-hearted complaint, but opened to let them in to the room beyond. 'I'll just get the lights... There.'

Bryant had expected a bank of fluorescent strips to illuminate the room but, instead, natural daylight suddenly poured in. He looked up at the ceiling. There were strip-lights there, but none were switched on. The light was coming from diffusers at the end of several overhead pipes.

'Another of Rudi's ideas,' Alice explained. 'All the chalets have them. Light boxes. So we can use the natural daylight for as long as it's available.' Bryant had heard about the technology before. Tubes, mirrors and pipes that collected, then intensified the light that had been captured. 'The switch controls the shutters up at ground-level. And, as you can see, there's artificial lighting for when we do need it. But I reckon we've got another couple of hours' left yet.'

'You know, I'd have thought it would feel claustrophobic down here. But it doesn't. Not in the slightest.'

'Intelligent design. You've got to hand it to Rudi...'

Bryant looked round the room. Again, there was a distinct absence of anything clinical on show. Just the same calming pastels from the consulting room above. There was a light-blue massage couch in one corner and a chair beside it. A desk and another chair opposite. The room seemed unusually empty of gadgetry. He noticed Alice watching him.

'Shall I put you out of your misery?' She went over to one of the bare walls. She pressed against it and there was a *click* as a whole section swung down through 180 degrees. Revealed behind was a bank of computer monitors, just above a recessed keyboard. She gave the latter a gentle pull and it glided smoothly out on a concealed shelf. 'One control panel.' She moved across to another part of the wall. Again, a *click* – but this time, the chosen section popped out and slid to the side. Bryant let out a subdued whistle, impressed. He could see there was a room through there – or, at least, not a room but a *compartment*. 'This is where it all happens. My *brain-child*. Literally,' Alice explained. 'In there is a *very* expensive piece of kit. I don't think Rudi's quite recovered from the cost yet. But he's only himself to blame. He did ask what I needed – so I told him. I spent several months preparing the spec, right down to the last detail. And here it is. All paid for. It'll see us right for at least a decade. It may not look much but, with this, we can compete with the major research institutes. You know, there's a lot of hospitals would happily cut off several patients' right arms to get what we've got here.'

Bryant found the contrast amusing. The expensive medical resource hidden away in little more than a log-cabin. But he knew well enough that all ideas ultimately come from the mind – the writer setting pen to paper, the artist oil to canvas, the inventor hammer and blow-torch to metal. Irrespective of the tools at their disposal, first there had to be the spark of original thought – to light the kindling; to build up the fire of creation.

And he could see just such a spark in the eyes of the woman before him.

'So, what is it?' He asked.

'Well, put simply, it's a cross between an MRI and a PET scanner...'

'PET?' Bryant queried.

'*Positron emission tomography*,' Alice clarified teasingly, expecting she wouldn't be adding much to his understanding. 'Means we can watch the brain's activity. Pinpoint the areas that are being most used. Lots of colour, lots going on.'

'Right. Understood.'

'Ah, hello you two!' Fridriksson's voice swept into the room before the man himself. 'Thank you for your message, my dear, dear Alice.' He came over and gave her a great big hug. He patted Bryant warmly on the back. 'You think you have it cracked, yes? This is *so* exciting. It is good for you, I am thinking, David? We get now the answers. You and us.' Fridriksson went to sit on the edge of the desk, folded his arms and fixed Alice with an encouraging stare; like a school teacher – waiting for a contribution from his star pupil; something to wow the class.

Alice beckoned for Bryant to be seated also.

'OK. Here's what we know.' She quickly recapped what

Bryant had told her earlier. 'Also, I can now add to that what I witnessed at Mary's place – and, yes, I *promise* I will come to that soon. But, just let me run through this first while it's all still clear in my own mind. Right. Now, your blindness, David – *that*, I believe, can be attributed to some form of post-traumatic stress; similar to what the hospital told you. It also seems to be the case there never *was* any physical damage to your sight. So, we might legitimately infer that the blindness was self-induced. Think of it as self-preservation; a defence mechanism – the brain giving you a period of down-time. I mean, after what you'd gone through with the crash, it must have decided there was too much pressure on you – the guilt, anger, incomprehension; who knows what else – so it wanted to steer you away from mental overload...'

'In other words – that you were, Dr Alice thinks, going to be suffering with a nervous breakdown; yes?'

Alice nodded to Fridriksson. Then carried on with her theory.

'Now, your senses – they've all been jumbled up? But not permanently, and with no way of predicting when the next experience will occur. That, like I said before, I think is down to episodes of clinical synaesthesia. And those, again, could be attributed to your brain. Not yet fully recovered. Still a few ghosts in the machine, as it were. As for the voice you hear? That is, I admit, more tricky to pin down but I think it's a form of internalisation – you know, dual projection; a linkage you're creating between the conscious and unconscious minds. A way of letting you explore themes your conscience might otherwise find unacceptable. Again, I think it's linked to mental trauma. But, by arriving at decisions through a contrived medium – that is, the voice you hear; the voice you're creating – those aspects seem more acceptable to you...'

So far, so good. Bryant had been prepared to accept Alice's reasoning. But that last suggestion – about the voice – he wasn't at all sure about that. Hadn't it already revealed things to him that he couldn't possibly have known? Logically, then, it couldn't just be a case of his own mind arguing with itself. How could it be?

He tried to remember what the voice had told him; tried to isolate instances that might challenge Alice's explanation – not that he particularly wanted to disprove her theories – but nothing stood out. And as hard as he tried to remember examples, all he could focus on were conversations that fitted with Alice's explanation.

'This is interesting, all very interesting, is it not, David?'

Rudi was keen to hear more, and Alice obliged.

'Now, as for creating images – you'd said neither Sam nor Neve had been able to see the figure in the CCTV?' He nodded. 'Well, that again, I believe is some form of mental projection; seeing what you want to see. Personifying your emotions, perhaps?' Again Bryant wasn't convinced, but he kept that thought to himself as well. 'I am only speculating on that one,' Alice ventured candidly. 'I'd need to look into it more. I'll certainly need to view the footage. Decide what I can see...'

'So, do you think this is helping, David?' Fridriksson asked.

'Kind of,' Bryant replied, after a moment's hesitation. 'I'd like to hear what else Alice has to say.'

'Alice?' Fridriksson waited for her to speak again.

The doctor resumed where she'd left off, only this time she seemed less comfortable than before. It became clear why.

'As for the... forgive me... attempted suicide,' she could see Bryant was about to object, but put a finger to her lips, praying a few seconds' grace, 'no, I don't think it was any such attempt. More than likely you just passed out in the bath. It could even have been a case of sleep-walking...'

This time Bryant did interject. 'But I've never done that before.'

'No, OK; I accept that – but this *could* be another side effect of the post-crash trauma. Look at it this way. Brains are complex pieces of machinery. When they work, everything's fine. But no way do even the world's top neuro-scientists understand anything but the basics. You know what they say about us only ever using ten per cent of our true potential? So, let's just say for the time being it could have been some form of unconscious behaviour...'

'And David's multiple escapes? How has he avoided death on so many occasions?' Fridriksson asked.

'Well, Rudi, that one I think we'll just have to put down to a case of old-fashioned good fortune. Exceptional, though, I grant you.'

Fridriksson shot Bryant a knowing look. He, too, seemed unconvinced by some of Alice's theorising, but both men did sit up and take a keen interest in what she had to say next. For the doctor, fond as she was of empirical facts, was about to go out on a limb...

'Now, *this* I think you're going to find the most interesting of all. As you know, David, earlier today we went to see Mary's gemstone exhibition.'

'Yes?'

'And you commented on the beauty of the stones? How they shone under the ultra-violet light?'

'Yes. What about it?'

'Brace yourself. What you saw, you observed *without* the benefit of the ultra-violet.'

'*What?*' Fridriksson was stunned. 'That's impossible, isn't it?'

'*How* could I have done that?' Bryant demanded to know. 'You must be wrong.'

'No. And I've never been more certain of anything in my life,' Alice replied calmly. 'When you'd gone, it was only then that I turned on the ultra-violet. You *definitely* saw the effect before that.'

'But...' Bryant was confused.

'What do you think this can mean?' Fridriksson asked.

'Well, we know that certain animals have the ability to see outside the visible light spectrum. Take goldfish –'

'Yes, that is true,' Fridriksson confirmed.

'Now, what if...' Alice paused, thinking ahead – though not for effect, '... somehow, David, you're accessing parts of the brain that usually lie dormant?'

'Meaning, what? This other ninety per cent?'

'Yes, and no.' Alice wasn't meaning to confuse him. She tried to explain it better. 'It's not that simple. Look, as we've evolved as a species, we've set ourselves above the animal kingdom, but in doing so we've sacrificed a lot of what we'd call gut instinct. Think of indigenous tribes – the Aborigines, for example. We're always amazed how they can find water in the middle of nowhere. But isn't it just the case that they've not lost touch with nature? That they see – they *read* – the landscape as animals do? I think such tribes continue to rely on what we could label *primitive* cortices within the brain, whereas those of us who, as I say, have evolved have actually lost that ability. We may consider ourselves more technologically advanced, but there's been a price to pay.'

'So if I've got this right,' Bryant began, 'you're saying there are *old* parts of the brain? And these hold *old* skills we no longer need?'

'Correct.'

'And you think that's how I was able to see the colours coming from the rocks? All on my own, without the need for the ultra-violet light?' He couldn't help himself, and let out a snort of disbelief.

Alice folded her arms, annoyed he wasn't taking her seriously.

'Wait,' said Fridriksson, sensing the growing tension. 'I don't know if Alice is right or is not right. But, I have personally met people before who are experts in tracking. They can find their way anywhere. With no help – almost as if they are copying birds, yes? They are navigating in ways I for one do not understand. And, Alice, you are to tell me if I am mistaken, yes? But are there not magnetic materials in the nose?'

Bryant could already guess where this was headed. *Follow your nose.*

'There are, Rudi. But they're minute; trace materials, nothing more. If you're suggesting we can all follow some kind of electro-magnetic grid, well, the jury's out on that one...'

'But the sharks,' he went on, 'they do this also, yes?'

'I believe so.'

'Then why cannot man possibly have this gift?' He smiled as a thought occurred to him. 'Is this not something we could test – with David's help, of course? You would let us do that, David?'

Bryant didn't want to commit himself to anything. Not straight away. And certainly not without giving it serious thought. Alice's theorising was one thing, and he did want to get answers; but he wasn't about to agree to spending weeks – maybe months – as the pair's guinea pig; and it didn't matter how patient-friendly their testing regime might appear to be.

'Let me just finish on this note,' Alice offered. 'There's documented cases from the US, Russia and elsewhere of head-trauma victims being used by the military. You know, *remote-viewing*; that kind of thing?'

Bryant had a sudden flash-back; remembered Sam had mentioned remote-viewing the day they'd driven over – it was where he said he'd met Fridriksson; at a conference on the subject.

'Remote-viewing, but isn't that's all a –'

'Like you,' Alice pre-empted his objection, 'I also think most of it is just fabricated nonsense – disinformation to dupe the other side, if you like…' Bryant sensed a *But* coming, '*but* – I know, Rudi, you're a great believer in the potential for extra-sensory abilities. So, what if there *is* a deeper, more conventional capability hidden away? What if, after an accident, the patient has to rely on other parts of the brain? For example, they might need to learn to speak again. And if the usual part of the cortex has been damaged, make no mistake the brain *will* have to try and establish new neural pathways. So, what if, in the process of doing so it *also* accesses – uses – other areas that are in the historic, *primitive* cortices?'

'What, you think that's what's happening to me? That I'm going all caveman?' Bryant didn't mean to sound so dismissive, but he was finding Alice's suggestions increasingly outlandish.

Rudi, though, seemed more accepting of her theories; prepared to take them on nothing more than trust.

'You are thinking, perhaps, this is all related to David's crash?'

'Yes,' she replied, an edge now to her voice. She gazed directly at Bryant, anger in her eyes. 'I think we should at least be open to the possibility that in the period after the crash, when you thought your blindness was permanent, your brain was somehow recalibrating itself; trying to find ways of letting you see again. You didn't know – and it couldn't know – that the effect would only be temporary. So, just supposing it did succeed and in the process it opened – *created* – new neural pathways? Well, maybe these have *remained* open – even now, after the former ones have been reinstated...'

Bryant sighed, prepared now at least to consider the possibility of what she was saying.

'I'm sorry,' he began, 'Just now, I didn't mean to sound so...'

Alice nodded, satisfied she'd made her point. 'But you can see what I mean? Maybe that's what's behind all these strange experiences you've been having.' Her tone softened. 'And, come on, surely it's worth a day of your time to try and help me find out?' She fixed him with a look that he knew he wasn't going to be able to turn down. 'You did say you wanted answers? If I'm wrong, fine, I'll admit it. But think of what we could achieve, the areas of research we could open up, if we're able to show – *prove* – that you've somehow... *engineered* connections, created significant neural activity in those redundant cortices...'

'So, David? What do you say?' Fridriksson willing him to agree.

Bryant wondered where his little voice was. All quiet when he most needed him.

He sat still for a few moments, trying to weigh up the pros and cons. But, despite his initial misgivings, deep down he already knew what his answer would be.

'What would I have to do?' he finally asked.

'Nothing much,' said Alice. 'Just lie still in the scanner. I'll talk you through a number of scenarios and, while we're doing that, the computer will record the electrical activity it detects in different parts of your brain.'

'And that's all?'

'That's all.

'Simple as that?'

'As simple as that.'

'When?'

'Tomorrow,' Alice replied, pressing home her advantage.

CHAPTER NINETEEN

TOM CASEY WAS not his usually composed self.

He'd felt ill at ease all day. Not that it had anything to do with his playing the role of witchfinder general – that was something he enjoyed. It kept people on their toes. Ensured tacit subservience. Even gave those hankering after his own position pause for thought. They knew well enough – a word from him in Edward Graysbrook's ear and their promising careers would be over.

Or worse.

Far worse.

But the anxiety refused to disappear. And, unheard of for him, he'd even begun to question his own innate self-belief; had found himself wondering if his powers of persuasion had unexpectedly begun to wane. For he went back a long way with Edward. He'd been there pretty much from the start. There was history in their history. Through thick and thin, *always* his counsel had been accepted – even if only after a period of further, considered thought on Edward's part. Now, though, he was only too aware that Edward was clearly disturbed by David Bryant's continued survival. And the more so in the wake of their best efforts to see him dead...

But as he'd already been at pains to point out to Edward, he didn't share those concerns. To him, Bryant didn't constitute a threat. And, as he'd explained, the man Bryant couldn't know about them; couldn't challenge them; he, just one man against the power of their collective organisation. What were the chances of this David ever meeting – challenging, *overcoming* – their Goliath? Even so, despite his own protestations – and Edward's apparent, reluctant acceptance of them – still he knew the preoccupation would remain; for he knew Edward too well. All the signs were there – for one, the insistence that the traitor be unmasked; that whoever had been helping Bryant be summarily punished.

And therein lay the rub.

For two very good reasons.

First, as he'd already cautioned, they were sailing extremely close to the wind. Every change in tack, every gibe posed a further risk to the stability of their craft. There was so very little room left for manoeuvre – already they risked being driven by the squalls of secrecy towards a rapidly-approaching coastline of exposure. A single miscalculation now and they'd end up dashed against the rocks; or run-aground in the shallows – either way, their ship of anonymity would be there for all to see. And that they could not allow – afford – to happen.

But second – and of greater immediate concern to Casey – he simply *couldn't* offer up the traitor. Not yet. He needed more time. But he knew Edward wouldn't give it to him. True, he was well-accustomed to using the organisation's not inconsiderable resources and contacts to find people -- and, indeed, he *had* already set the wheels in motion – but if he failed to deliver the necessary head on the plate, he worried what Edward might do to *him*. The fear he was so used to instilling in others – and that he so selfishly exploited for his own gain – could only be relied upon up to a point. Fear, he knew, was completely useless when confronted with its opposing emotion –

Not bravery.

But *anger*.

For anger was intrinsically care-free; determined; typified by no thought for the consequences. Anger was a true force to be reckoned with. That would crush fear in its vice-like grip.

And Casey knew there were many in the organisation who had good reason to harbour anger and resentment towards him. Those he'd ensured had been overlooked for promotion. Those whose bonuses he'd suggested to Edward be withheld. And those whose ideas he'd stolen; ideas he'd then presented to Edward as being his own. For every one of his supporters, there were another ten saboteurs waiting quietly in the wings; biding their time until he slipped up. A suggestion of hesitation – just the slightest whisper of failure – and he'd find them suddenly emboldened; closing ranks to take him on. Out with the old guard, in with the new. That would be their battle cry. And if they did succeed in persuading Edward that he was a spent force, that would be it – status lost, irrecoverably; influence, zeroed; protection, gone. It would be open season for all-comers...

Casey pulled himself up.

Just what was he thinking? He shouldn't be entertaining such thoughts. The very fact that he was – that in itself amounted to a sign of weakness. He quickly marshalled his reserves, sent them into battle; watched as they took no prisoners; approved of the ensuing butchery. Seconds later, all doubt had been despatched. Dead – but purposely not buried. Instead, left on the mental battlefield of his mind to serve as a timely warning to any other insurgents – whether militias of insecurity; or guerrilla forces of neural impotence.

His confidence once more restored, Casey felt strong again. He allowed himself a few moments to reflect on his potential for ruthlessness. It was something he was proud of. And was it not, after all, why he and Edward worked so well together?

Then, quick as a flash, there was another attempted coup –

But, this time, his awareness focussed on something

insubstantial. A single seed. Struggling to germinate unnoticed in a soil of self-doubt. The battlefield now on the microcosmic scale. *Seed?* He recognised it contemptuously for what it was – a *weed*. He'd allow it no place to grow in his garden of eternal belief. But no matter how many times he turned the hoe, it still managed to escape being unearthed. It started to put down a solitary root... Casey found himself distracted. Realised he *did* risk being ham-strung. For he could only work with the information, the material available to him; and that didn't amount to much; not yet – and no matter how hard he wished it might otherwise be.

He was alone in the office, his secretary having long since left. He sat in his high-backed leather chair, turning from side to side; every so often, he'd propel himself with enough force to complete a full rotation. Back and forth he went. Round and round. All the while considering the options. Until, at last, a final spin –

He stopped the chair.

He *had* it.

Simple – as were all his best plans.

The seeded-weed had finally surfaced. He ripped it out.

Edward wanted his traitor – and that person he couldn't yet give him. So, he needed to buy himself more time; and the priority had to remain looking after his *own* interests. He could do that. Sure he could. He'd buy himself the time he needed and, as an added bonus, he'd also make certain he pointed the finger of suspicion at those close enough to threaten his position. *Win, win.* Edward would be happy. And he'd get much-needed breathing space.

Besides, by the time Edward discovered he'd been mistaken in his identification of the supposed traitors, matters would have moved on. He could have brought in his own people to fill the resulting gaps and, provided they soon showed themselves to be equally capable, Edward wouldn't give it a second thought. So long as the organisation was turning a healthy profit and its power was increasing, Edward would be happy.

He would, however, apologise profusely for his error. He'd plead that, with hindsight, he could see it might appear he'd acted in haste – but he'd also explain he'd only ever been acting in Edward's best interests; especially with the man Bryant still in the picture. For if the man was as great a threat as Edward believed, then that surely must have justified the action he'd taken?

Yes, that would all work out fine.

Casey got up from his chair and went over to sit at the conference table. Earlier security had wired up a TV and DVD player for him. He'd already watched several hours of collated CCTV footage.

He'd gone to them with a series of dates and times. His best estimate of when their traitor would have to have been at his most active – each opportunity to intervene coinciding with some notable event in the world of David Bryant. He'd been sure to include a few hours, as well as days in some cases, either side – in case the person had waited a while before returning to check progress; or to cover their tracks.

Ideally, Casey had wanted it to be clear-cut – just one person emerging as the key suspect. But it wasn't to be. Instead, security had given him a shortlist of five possibles. Five. But that hadn't necessarily been a bad thing, for there was no love lost between himself and three of the five.

He settled down to watch the recordings again. Twenty minutes later, he'd reached his decision. Two he'd let go, but he'd take decisive action against the remaining three; the three whose removal would – coincidentally – benefit him most. The duo would consider themselves lucky to have escaped. Word would soon get round. And any others who might yet have been tempted to cross him, to raise their heads above the parapet, they'd be given pause for thought.

As he'd thought – simple; but highly effective.

He took out his mobile, entered the memorised number and waited. Presently, a man's voice answered. It was one of his security contacts. Someone happy to take on a bit of freelance work.

Casey was succinct.

'The following three...' he spoke their names carefully, '... you're clear to proceed.'

He rang off and put the mobile away. He yawned, looked at his watch; decided he'd call it a night. He was just slipping his jacket on when the phone went on his desk; the ring indicating an internal call. He wondered who else would be working so late. He took it.

'Tom, Edward here. Glad I caught you.'

'Yes, Edward?'

'Listen, I've been giving it careful thought... this Bryant, I feel he's too much of a risk. Let's forget about the Pierfranco angle.' Casey had made the call as instructed, but had still been waiting to hear back from Pierfranco; to find out what job they might have been putting David Bryant's way. 'We're not going to offer him another position after all. I think it's time we ended it, don't you? I think I'm going to pay our Mr Bryant a visit personally. I'll take the jet. Do you want to come along for the ride?'

Casey had been wrong-footed. He hadn't expected Edward to strike out on his own. It was rare for him to do his own dirty work these days. And that spoke volumes about the way he perceived the threat. But there was something else that suddenly occurred to him. How had

Edward discovered the man's address? He'd still been working on it.

'You've traced him, then?' he asked, redundantly.

'Yes. Ways and means, Tom,' Graysbrook sounded pleased with himself. 'Easy, once I'd applied myself a little. So, are you coming?'

'Well, actually, Edward, I've got some news for you.'

'Oh?'

'As you know, I've been working on identifying our suspected traitor; whoever's been helping Bryant.'

'Ah, good. You've found him?'

Casey knew he'd have to be careful what he said next. How he handled this. A difficult balance to achieve.

'Well, I've narrowed it down to three suspects and I've...'

Graysbrook interrupted. 'Deal with it as you see fit, Tom. You can update me when I get back...'

'I hope you don't mind, Edward? I've already rather set the wheels in motion.'

Graysbrook understood exactly what Casey meant.

'I guess we can take a bit of friendly fire... as long as you're *sure* he's one of them?'

'As sure as I can be.'

'And you'll bring people in to back-fill?' Graysbrook didn't want any organisational down-time.

'Of course.'

'Very well, then.' An audible sigh of relief down the phone-line. 'Just think, Tom, 48 hours from now and we'll be free of David Bryant. And, thanks to your *precautions*, we'll have sent a firm message to anyone who might be thinking of stepping out of line. A good result all round.'

'So, should I wait to hear from you? Or would you prefer me to call when things have been taken care of this end?'

'I'll contact you. Good hunting...'

And with that, Graysbrook rang off.

By the time Alice turned up to collect Bryant, London was already missing three executives.

One had jumped in front of a rush-hour commuter train – at least, that's what a string of eye-witnesses would report. A second had overdosed on recreational drugs during the night. The third had fallen prey to a random street mugging.

The trio's office colleagues would, to varying degrees, feel obliged to sign the sympathy cards and contribute to the whip-round for flowers – but, three weeks on since last pay-day, bank accounts were running on empty and their show of respect would be noticeably less than if the deceased had had the good fortune to die later. The wheels of industry rolled on, and in six months' time the dead would be all but forgotten – their existence marked only by a string of numbers on a discontinued payroll-entry.

Sitting in the subterranean laboratory hundreds of miles north, Bryant was ignorant of the men; knew nothing about their deviously-orchestrated fate. But the significance of what had befallen the three would not be lost on him for much longer...

'David, are you ready?' Alice's voice was calmly authoritative; the professional in her element. Fridriksson was sitting quietly in the background, observing.

'Ready,' he replied, trying to sound as relaxed as he could.

He knew though he was anything but. His breathing was speeding up and his heart was pounding loudly in his ears. He concentrated, forced himself to slow the breaths; repeated over and over there was no need to be anxious. He was in safe hands, among friends. Alice's tests were quite safe. It wasn't like the hospital. And she was helping him find answers – *his* answers. A few hours, that was all and then it would be over. He'd be able to tell Sam and Neve about it over a drink that evening.

'Alright,' Alice continued, 'just like I explained before, this is what we're going to do. I'll lead you through a gentle visualisation. You just go with the flow. I'll introduce different elements as we go deeper and, if you fall asleep, that's fine. I'll still be talking to you – to your sub-conscious – and we'll see what parts of your brain we can get to light up. OK?'

'OK.'

'Right. Tell me, where would you rather spend time on holiday? Canadian Rockies, or Mediterranean beach?'

For Bryant, it had to be the beach. Associations so deeply instilled into the sands of his childhood; trickling now, grain by grain, through the hourglass of remembrance – the annual fortnight on the south Wales coast; donkey-rides; bucket and spade; the race to dig down to Australia before the tide came in; rock-pools with their miniature, stranded worlds; and keeping watch for pirates, forever threatening an attack from just over the horizon. And then there was candy-floss unwinding from the gooey stick; dodgems at the fun-fair – being told off by the angry man every time he drove into another car; and, best of all, fish and chips in the café by the old city wall. And the weather? Immaterial – a good time always had by all.

'Beach,' he answered, buoyed up by the happy memories.

'Beach it is.' He heard Alice herself draw a long breath. 'Now, just relax. Close your eyes and let your breathing settle into a steady rhythm...' She waited a few moments, watching both the physical Bryant as well as the virtual one displayed on her monitor. A click of the mouse and various graphics and readings appeared. His brain held centre-stage – three-dimensional blue hemispheres standing out from the two-dimensional background behind. When Alice was satisfied he was responding well, she continued, 'Now, imagine yourself lying on a sun-lounger, the wooden slats solid beneath your back.' She took her time, speaking slowly. 'Feel the warmth of the sun moving across your face, cooled by the lightest of breezes...'

As she continued, Bryant began relaxing more deeply. She could see his brain activity slowing, its rhythm moving from beta to alpha wave. He thought he heard Alice telling him to trail one hand over the side of the lounger, to draw his initials in the sand; but each time he did so the rippling waters swept in underneath, carried the writing away – just as the relaxing sensations seemed to be robbing him of his awareness. Bryant felt himself drifting off. Calm. No cares. Relaxed. At one with the scene he was mentally painting. And even as a thought occurred to him – as he slowly questioned whether this *was* all an imagination-induced dream world – he knew it didn't really matter anymore. Tangible reality, or neurally-generated fantasy, wasn't it all just the same?

Don't you just love doctors?

The voice reappeared. A stow-away come up on deck to have a look round, to share his sun-drenched idyll for free.

They think they're so clever. They tell you they have all the answers. What was it she said about me? Wait, I'll get it... yes, I'm a... dual projection; an internalisation. But that's not really true, is it? And you don't believe that for one minute?

Even the sudden return of the voice didn't unduly trouble Bryant. Not this time. In a strangely reassuring way, he found he even welcomed it – just another round-edged piece to slot into his jigsaw of mental recognition. But now he didn't care if he had all the pieces. He didn't feel the need to complete the puzzle. He could take it or leave it. And he was happy to leave it.

Are you listening to me?

No, Bryant replied by way of a single thought.

But you must be. How else can you reply? The voice as superior as ever. Bryant formed a mental picture of a cliff-edge. *What do you mean go throw myself off?* The voice didn't like his attitude. *What, you really think she's going to be able to find me? Is that it? A flare of electrical charge? Proof that I exist – that you are creating me? Such arrogance! You've been taken in!* The voice stayed quiet for a moment, before suggesting, *You really think you can get by without me? Is that it? Well just you look here...*

Alice was fascinated by the images she was observing on the screen. A neural firework display, exploding in scatter-gun fashion – and in areas where she'd definitely not expected to see them. She quickly checked Bryant's other vital signs – all perfectly normal; indicative of deep relaxation; mild hypnotic trance-state. So why then this sudden activity? It shouldn't be happening. She wondered where it was originating. She spoke to her subject gently, trying to bring him to a lighter level of awareness.

But Bryant didn't respond.

He was simply enjoying the moment. It didn't matter that the voice was there. He'd adjust the volume, fade it out. He couldn't be bothered being bothered any more. He pictured a great big dial, like on a stereo, and turned it from ten to eight. Then eight to five...

What are you doing?

His audio visitor clearly not happy with him. Then five to three. The complaining only now just discernible in his subdued consciousness.

Stop it! Stop it at once!

The protest almost mute, rather than his ears unhearing.

You don't know what you're doing...

And with that, Bryant turned the dial to zero.

Silence.

Bliss.

Alone now. Just himself.

And the sea.

And the sand.

And the warmth of the sun...

He felt like taking a dip to cool down. He shielded his eyes with a lazy hand and got up from the recliner. Crystal-clear waters lapped round his feet. He looked up and down the beach.

Deserted.

Except for himself, there was no-one there.

He stretched a little to wake himself up, then walked slowly into the inviting waters. On he went until the undulating sea reached his shoulders. Then he began to swim. Gentle, measured strokes. Gliding easily. Parallel now to the shore. He noticed the recliner had disappeared. But that wasn't a problem. It had probably been cleared away by an attentive member of the hotel staff. Paid to go unnoticed, but always there.

Always there...

Just like the *eyes* – not that they'd gone unnoticed.

But even the eyes could no longer induce any fear in him. No trace now of the customary anxiety. He was too relaxed for that. Besides, wasn't he on holiday? Enjoying himself? So everyone – *everything* – was surely there for one purpose? To make his stay as pleasurable as possible... He was the paying guest, after all. He called the shots, no-one else.

A sudden thought – no, more a *compulsion*.

He knew what he *wanted* to do – *had* to do.

He'd go find the cave.

Tell the eyes to stop watching him.

He was tired of their intrusion – just as he was of the little voice making its presence felt. Eyes, voice – they could all leave him alone. And he wouldn't be taking no for an answer. He'd be insistent.

He changed course and swam towards the beach.

He was rising up, coming out of the waves – but where he should have been dripping with water, he was *dry*. Face. Hair. Body. And *clothes* – wherever they'd come from – crisp, freshly-pressed cargo-pants and cotton shirt completing the look. A man casually in control, sure of himself; in charge; a force to be reckoned with.

A quick glance left; then right.

And there, in the distance – he saw it.

A finger of darkness, superimposed onto the vertical cliff-face.

The now-familiar entrance to the cave...

'That's helpful. Thanks, Paul.'

Tomlinson had had Riley check out any other addresses they had listed for Patrick Maltravers and the sergeant had come up with one. Tomlinson had chosen not to say anything about the warning he'd received, or that this message from *the other side* had seemingly come true. He knew what Riley would make of it – probably the same as he should too. But, then, *he'd* been there; Riley hadn't. And he *knew* he'd escaped death by inches...

How *could* Maltravers have known though? Or was it coincidence? He wondered if he was reading too much into it. Maybe it had just been another case of vagueness spoon-fed to the gullible? To him? But, then, he wouldn't fall into that category. He'd been alert to any cold-reading attempts; he knew he had. And he'd been careful not to give anything away.

But the more he analysed the accident, re-ran the scene in his mind, the more confusing it became. And yet...

'You still there, sir?' Riley's voice in his ear.

'Yes, sorry. What were you saying?'

'Just thought you might be interested to know that Anne and Geoff Wilson have decided to separate...'

Tomlinson wasn't that surprised. More often than not, the stresses involved in such tragedies served to widen the existing cracks in personal relationships; emotional chasms that no amount of support or counselling could bridge. Only the very closest of couples would reach the other side; each drawing strength from the other through a sorrow truly shared. Empathy – not sympathy – the true bonding agent.

'I feel for them. I really do…'

'And we've released Margaret Woods, sir.'

'You never did think she was involved, did you?'

'No, sir. But I think she'll still be in for a rough time of it. A lot of her friends have dropped her. Her house has been daubed with graffiti. And the press are following her every move.'

Tomlinson could just imagine the headlines. *Monster's Mother-in-Law Goes to Ground.* Or the pun-primed *Wood You Feel Safe with this Woman Living Next Door?*

'Sadly, I think you're right.' Tomlinson was in his car, flicking through the *A to Z*, looking up the grid for the street name Riley had given him. He found it. 'Right, got it. I'd best get over there. Thanks, again, for the new lead.'

'So, you really think this Maltravers can help, sir?'

'You'd be surprised…'

The over-riding feeling was one of dormancy.

As if the cave were slumbering; sleep rendering the eyes blind. So far there was no sign of the spotlight searching for him; seeking to announce his presence.

Bryant advanced slowly into the expanding cavern. Each silent footfall on the sand was leading him further away from the remaining shafts of daylight that penetrated the gloom from the entrance. He waited for his vision to adjust to the lower levels of light. And then the child in him – already waiting in the wings, recalled to consciousness by the fond holiday memories – prepared to do battle; wrapping itself in a cloak of invincibility, carrying a sword of self-belief by its side and a shield of faith on its arm.

A child that was supremely confident it could advance unnoticed, having long since mastered the game of statues – its movements timed to perfection, imperceptible; gaining ground, inch by stealthy inch; daring the eyes to open, but instantly ready to freeze. Forward once more, but only when it was sure the eyes really had closed again. On and on went the child, a knight creeping closer to his sleeping dragon until – within a sword's length of the prize – it lost interest in the game and returned to the toy-box of Bryant's mind, seeking out something else to amuse itself…

But leaving Bryant the grown-up perilously close to the scorching flames of detection –

He stood perfectly still, barely daring to breathe. Ready for the moment the first of the eyes would open – as he *knew* they must. Determined, though, to deny them further intrusion into his psyche.

And then, the first pair appeared –

Dark pools of apathy, centred in a white sea of oblivion...

He braced himself for the moment they saw him. When they'd try to coax him to join their number – coercion wedded to compulsion. But which of the happy couple would it be this time he wondered?

He had a sudden flash of insight – wondered why he'd not considered it before.

The eyes. Could they not be those of the dead? The pitiful souls lost on his flight? Envious of life – *his* life – urging him to let go and join them? Angry. Jealous. Refusing to accept that he alone had survived...

But just as quickly, another thought.

He was forgetting Graysbrook. The man had been there, too, and he had *also* survived. So why then were the eyes not pursuing him? He considered – maybe they had? But if so, how had Graysbrook managed to stay at large? He seemed somehow dominant there in the cave-world, able to come and go as he pleased.

Questions, but never answers...

A sudden nagging feeling, raising a flag of objection up the pole of comprehension.

The realisation he *was* on the wrong tack.

Not the dead...

Then *who*? *What*?

Bryant edged nearer to the eyes that had revealed themselves, but there was no recognition of his presence. The eyes just stared straight through him. As if he wasn't there. He backed away, carefully...

Without warning, a second pair of the ethereal orbs snapped open –

Then a third –

Now, he was certain they'd spotted him...

Nothing.

They took no notice of him.

But how could that be? What had changed? He just didn't know. He watched, confused, as pair upon pair multiplied – as far as *his* eyes could see. Domino-like, white dot chasing white dot materialised out of the endless gloom. And domino-like, too, he wondered if one flick could level the whole array. He closed in on the first pair again, let his own gaze penetrate their exterior. Still nothing.

It was only then – in such proximity – that he noticed something interesting.

The eyes were *not* single entities. For within each of the dark pupils, there lay other ebony spheres. And within each of those, yet more white globes existed. The pattern repeating endlessly, like a reflection in a mirror seen in another mirror.

Eyes within eyes. Within eyes.

And now it was he – *not* they – doing the observing; studying the structural complexity. More, sensing an *awareness* that seemed to have been fashioned from thought. Populated with memories. Each and every sphere possessed of a discrete intelligence. All part of some greater *being* –

No, that wasn't it. They were part of a... *Collective*. A *one*-ness. Thought form in joined, energetic existence.

He let himself be drawn inwards, curiosity his guide. Just how far could he penetrate the Collective before it knew he was there? He picked one of the white globes at random, intuitively commanded it to reveal its content. Instantly, a picture formed in his mind's eye. He saw a suited man on a platform – but there was someone behind, tripping him over in front of an approaching train... And there were others standing close by. Onlookers. Only not independent. Approving. All part of the same...

He recoiled in horror, realising he was witnessing a murder. He tried to distance himself from the secretive sphere – only to find himself colliding with dozens more. Images freed now to become absorbed into his very being. He was at once aware of another man – this time injecting himself; death slowly coursing into his veins.

And then a third – the alcohol he'd consumed numbing the knife blade...

Bryant began to panic; tried to get out of there; away from the Collective, before it overwhelmed him –

The cold-blooded killing-spree.

The pleasure derived by the many.

How could *they* enjoy it so? Orchestrate it? Encourage it? He scrambled backwards, immaterial hands clawing at shifting patterns of experience. He thought he'd made it, had got far enough away, but the Collective had other ideas.

The primary directive to serve the common good.

The eyes grew larger all around him, expanding in size – in *being* – until the clarity of their darkly-hidden mysteries enveloped him. Like a torrential rain hammering down, each liquid drop doused him in yet more of the revelations –

There was a woman. He couldn't see her clearly, but he knew

she was dressed like a nurse. She was in a car-park. There was a man adjacent to her. He was drawing a hand across his throat...

Bryant felt he ought to know the nurse; and there was something familiar about the man... a confused, muddled memory linked to the scene. But no time now to dwell on it –

For he saw *another* woman.

She had scalding to her face and arms. And there were two children, not moving though. Then, that same woman once more. He could hear an echo of voices that she herself had heard. He thought she was thanking them, grateful for their advice. And then there were bed-sheets being tied to fashion a noose...

Another image.

A young girl, surrounded by others in a classroom. They were older than her. They were laughing, taunting her and she was crying – her head bald; a wig lying where it had fallen to the floor...

A police-woman – being assaulted; beaten nearly to death...

And a man in a chair – a plastic bag over his head; being suffocated...

Everywhere, now... Sadness. Hurt. Pessimism. Grief. Hopelessness. Increasingly being revealed to him. Every image that quickly flashed by was full of negativity. Everything linked somehow to suffering, destruction or death...

Then, suddenly, a plane –

More than any of the other images, it resonated deeply in the core of his being. The lasting impression? The horror being experienced by those onboard during their final few seconds...

And then –

A startling incongruity.

For, amid all the tragedy, there was the faintest hint of hope.

A growing feeling of love. Compassion. Old-world concern for the wellbeing of others. Patience. Humility. A life's calling. And Bryant suddenly revelling in the feeling. Seeking out its source.

It was close now, but he still couldn't pinpoint the origin. He whirled round, blindly tried to locate it. He was aware of remembered smells – the oak dresser at his grandparents' house; the re-cycled tin of sugared jellies, home then to the weekly chocolate treats. And the lingering aroma of the spare room – the one he'd painted that summer holiday. Twenty miles on his bike every day for a week – but the effort all worth it for the heartfelt gratitude when he'd finished. Love and warmth. A perennial welcome. Memories of his grandfather. Something now seeking to extend a hand of love towards him...

He reached out his searching fingertips to make contact –

Get out of here! Now! Get out! Before they find you!

The voice there.

Next to him. Inside him. Shaking him to the core. Its tone panicked. Angry. Terrified.

Quick! Go! Now!

And then the voice itself was gone.

But the warmth – the feeling of love – persisted.

Bryant aware it was trying to become physical. There was a gentle brush against his mind – asking him where he was, who his friends were, how long he'd be staying there. It wanted to know. *Needed* to know. So it could help him…

It felt right to him to respond to something so inviting of trust. So he did.

Instantly he realised his mistake –

He felt the darkness returning, seeking to smother everything that stood against it; that tried to undermine its dominance. One by one the myriad eyes closed, lights winking out; allowing the gloom to hold sway once more.

All except for *one* pair of eyes.

Whiter, brighter than the others had been. Isolated, they shone defiantly – a brave last stand against the Collective.

Bryant peered through the darkness, trying to figure out how to get back to the light; to the beach beyond. But something – *someone* – held him there; begging him not to go; pleading for his help. He swung helplessly round, unsure how to find them. Then, all too briefly, he glimpsed the set of eyes. They were right there next to him. He knew they belonged to the source – *were* the source – of the happiness; of the love. But it was too late for him to do anything for them. They'd gone…

Only to be replaced by something –

Menacing. Inherently *evil.*

For even in that indistinct world of ebony half-light, Bryant could make out the shape of a man appearing beside him – replacing the eyes; substituting despair for hope, suffering for compassion, hate for love. But the body never fully materialised and, instead, a sharper darkness clung to the man's skeletal outline.

Bryant felt suddenly exposed, vulnerable – didn't know whether to run or hide. Should he stand firm, put up a fight? But how? He didn't even know what he was up against. With every second that passed, valuable time was running out.

Until it was too late.

A shadowy, ill-defined semblance of Edward Graysbrook walked forwards; turned to stand immediately before him.

'What *are* you?' The inquisitor demanded to know.

Bryant couldn't move. Panic welled up inside him. He knew he needed to stay silent, but he felt compelled to speak. But before he could form a single, terrified word, he heard – was *aware* – of an unspoken response coming from just *behind* him. The sense of friendship, love with him once more, protecting him. The realisation that a defiant pair of eyes were staring straight *through* him – forcing Graysbrook to keep his distance. There was a name, too, but Bryant couldn't quite grasp it. Then, an awareness of *something* – no, it was *someone* – possessed of holiness, from an age long since past. He shuddered contentedly as a wave of strength coursed through him that blanketed the panic.

'You have no place here!' The shadowy Graysbrook threatened. 'Leave now!' But the object of his anger stood firm. 'If you do not go, I *will* destroy you...'

It stayed put.

There *was* no second warning.

A focussed pulse of darkness, a blade of oblivion, sliced suddenly through Bryant's frame, impaling itself deep into the heart of its target. Momentarily, Bryant was transfixed as he experienced – *understood* – the destructive capability of the energetic lunge. Stunned motionless, he expected the worst, anticipated that pain would erupt throughout his body; that this would be the end for him...

But there *was* no pain. Not for him.

Unlike the intended target of Graysbrook's attack –

Bryant immediately sensed the desperation, the hurt, the cry; as existence was rendered non-existent. As life ebbed away...

'*Seth*? Ah, so that is your name?' came Graysbrook's triumphant cry. 'Well, Seth, whatever you are – or *were* – you are no more.'

Graysbrook inched closer to Bryant until he was almost nose to nose with him. He peered ahead, as if trying to locate a second target.

Bryant shut his eyes tightly. Held his breath. Anticipated the same fate as Seth.

But nothing happened –

He dared open his eyes.

In time to see Graysbrook dematerialising; disappearing back into the gloom...

CHAPTER TWENTY

EDWARD GRAYSBROOK WAS in two minds.

Although displeased at having had to interrupt a perfectly good lunch to attend to matters personally, even so he found himself savouring his achievement – one less adversary to worry about; or, rather, *two*.

For as well as despatching Seth to the realm of shade where he – more accurately, *it* – belonged, Graysbrook had also taken steps to ensure nothing more would be heard from the mortal mouthpiece.

Appetite for *foie gras* handsomely replaced by one for destruction.

He steered his heightened consciousness safely back to the harbour of immediacy – to the table, to the half-eaten meal, to the surroundings of the exclusive hunting lodge that was to be his home for the next week. And while there, he meant to indulge in one of his favourite pastimes – blood-sports. Enjoying the stalking. The test of stealth. The kill itself.

David Bryant, the target squarely in his sights –

But amid the anticipation, wine glass cradled in hand, Graysbrook still couldn't shake off a nagging doubt. He'd felt something had been wrong ever since the day of the crash. *His* survival, that had been a given. But for *another* – for the man, Bryant – to have walked away, that shouldn't have been possible. It was inexplicable. And Graysbrook didn't care for things he couldn't explain. For that meant ignorance. And ignorance, in the lexicon of influence, translated to vincibility; to weakness; to industrial impotence. And despite Tom Casey's continued assurances to the contrary, he was certain this hitherto inconsequential David Bryant was important in some way. He'd not experienced anything like this before, and he knew he couldn't afford to let the uncertainty run its course.

Draining the glass of its wine, Graysbrook reviewed what he already knew. Their early attempts – his people's repeat visits to the hospital, trying to induce apathy, feelings of insecurity, of self-doubt, and of suicidal tendencies in the vulnerable Bryant – had only met with partial successful. Sure, the man had cut himself, but those wounds had healed. Sectioning the man, that would have made matters easier, but even that had failed. Nor had the train been any more successful. And the plan to have Bryant end it all himself for the second time had similarly proved fruitless.

Graysbrook set the glass down and steepled his fingers in thought. While David Bryant appeared to be unaware of his potential, every day he seemed to be growing stronger; becoming a greater threat.

Just what was it about the man that troubled him so? He didn't think it could all be the doing of the mysterious protector either. Even he – or *she* – couldn't wield that much influence. No, Graysbrook concluded, there was an added dimension to all this; something he still needed to fathom out.

He cast the net wider, snaring more clues.

He'd sensed *another* presence there in the cave with Seth, and he had thought it was Bryant. But hard as he'd tried, he'd failed to pinpoint whoever, or whatever, it was. He'd not been able to penetrate the defences that had shielded that person – presence – from him. And that, too, he acknowledged was yet *another* reason to be concerned. Surely, though, it *had* been Bryant? Who else – *what* else – could it have been? He was suddenly angry with himself. Annoyed to find he was questioning his own judgement. It was simply not something he did.

He refocused.

There was the *cave*, for one thing. Always it was the cave with that man. Didn't that prove his suspicions? But why the cave? Why should the Collective manifest itself as a cave? What was the symbolism? What was the significance?

Again, ignorance. *His* ignorance. Yet another example of weakness. His weakness. The fear of his own power slipping away. But he wouldn't – *couldn't* – allow that to happen.

Tomorrow, he'd put an end to it.

Ensure David Bryant's hubris would feel the full force of his own Nemesis...

Tomlinson had a front row ticket.

He watched from his car as Maltravers walked along the pavement towards him, towards the second address that Riley had provided. The superintendent had decided to wait until Maltravers was right beside him. Then it was to be door open, quick interception, and a drive somewhere quiet to demand a full explanation; to establish just how Patrick Maltravers could possibly have predicted his near-miss with the van.

But even as Tomlinson's fingers were undoing the seat-belt, a strange paralysis began to seize the rest of his body. Insidious, it spread by quick degrees until even his fingers stiffened. His mind, though, remained alert – and foremost in his thoughts was the fear he was having a stroke. Part of his self was screaming at him. Telling him to move. *Anything. Anywhere.* Just as long as he did so right now, before his brain was equally affected by the seizure. But another part of him snapped instantly back, telling him he was fine. For the danger lay outside, not within...

But before Tomlinson had time to react, to coax movement back into his limbs, to get out of his car, he realised with a sense of foreboding what was about to happen. For there, right in front of him, the scene was already beginning to play out –

Maltravers had been about to step off the pavement to cross the final junction. Luckily for him, he'd glimpsed an approaching vehicle just in time. He'd slammed on his own mental brakes – the result, an abrupt halt and a comical sway as he'd teetered on the kerb edge. And there he'd stayed, waiting for car and driver to pass him by.

Spared to live another day.

Which he would have done, *but* for the kid on the bike –

Who'd come tearing round the corner from the other direction, his feet pedalling fast, not watching where he'd been going; who'd been looking back over his shoulder, goading the slower *Tour de France* wannabe trailing in his wake to catch him up. By the time he saw the car, it was too late to take avoiding action. The gift of life and death then lay squarely in the driver's hands – veer left, maim or kill the pedestrian; delay and the boy on the bike dies.

Roadcraft to test Solomon himself.

A quick toss of the coin of condemnation, and the driver arrived at his decision. Forty years without so much as a speeding ticket or parking fine now counted for nothing. The car swerved to the left. Wheel-rim sparked on stone kerb. A savage jolt bounced the vehicle up onto the pavement, and then the slow-motion cine-world of inevitability played out as, freeze-frame by freeze-frame, a tonne of metal collided with Maltravers.

He died instantly.

And in that moment he returned home to be with his mother, reunited in the eternal sleep of death. But for every such union, the scales of balance demanded there also be a separation – and Seth and Maltravers were forced to go their different ways. All that remained now was the man's lifeless body; contorted limbs, blood and exposed bone the would-be psychic's new calling card.

Not forgetting the boy, who'd also had to swerve, and who'd lost control. He'd tumbled to the road, but the price he'd paid had been incalculably less – winded, bruised, with grazed knees and elbows. But it would be his friend who would fare worse for, having witnessed the carnage first-hand, he'd find himself plagued by recurring nightmares for years to come.

The driver, the boys, Maltravers – every one of their lives had changed, and all because of a moment's carelessness. Or so it seemed.

And Tomlinson – thanks to his seat at this première, he'd not missed a single frame of Maltravers' final moments…

Only he *had* –

For what he couldn't have known was that Maltravers' close-up had already been filmed – more than once; and there *was* an alternate ending.

It was all about the letter.

The letter that Maltravers had posted. Just minutes earlier. The single most important communication he'd ever sent in his life. That would continue to have repercussions, long after his death...

Bryant had feared he'd be trapped there forever in the cave – imprisoned until Graysbrook returned to seek him out for a second time; to finish him off. But just as the despondency had threatened to hold him fast, he'd heard what he thought was Alice's voice. Barely audible, but there on the fringes of his sentience; so faint, it was little more than a decaying echo of reality. But it had given him a much-needed reference point – something on which to focus. He marshalled his neural reserves, re-wound the sonic string, let himself be guided out of the labyrinthine darkness and back to the welcoming light and safety of the laboratory.

Back to Alice. Back to Rudi. Back to sanity.

Bryant breathed a heavy, mental sigh of relief and wasted no time clambering out of the scanner compartment. His brow was covered in sweat, his pupils dilated – the fight or flight response automatically triggered. Free now of the cave, he chose flight.

Alice came forward to talk to him, keen to run through her observations, to cross-reference her thoughts with his experiences. But Bryant wasn't ready for that. No time to talk, not yet. Now, he just wanted to get away. To spend time on his own. To try to rationalise what he'd been through – if rationality *could* even be applied to the strange, other-worldly place into which he was increasingly being drawn.

Space.

The word suddenly uppermost in his consciousness. He knew that's what he really needed. Space. The antidote to the claustrophobia of the cave, to the scrutiny of the cavernous eyes. Space. The freedom to be himself – to *find* himself. Another echo...

A moment later and he was mentioning feeling nauseous. Feigning temporary discomfort. A complete lie. Just so he could be excused. Escape the intended questioning. And Alice, Rudi – he realised they were buying it. Ever-trusting. Ever-patient. Ever-accommodating. He started to feel guilty at the deceit. He felt even more so an hour later, after they'd driven him back. Good people – too good for him to be duping them so. But there was still more guilt to come. Guilt mixed with self-loathing, as he maintained the pretence. Sam and Neve – expecting to be all ears as he arrived home. But, instead, he'd identified them as the next willing marks, targets for the lies he was peddling. They, too, were trusting. Only too happy to let him be. Soup. Sandwiches. A light tea. All delivered to his room, so he could retire early for the night. And then there was the final promise he'd made them, that he'd be feeling better; be more approachable the next morning. All he needed was a good night's sleep.

But intuitively he judged the deceit to be necessary; accepting then there really was no time for the guilt-trip.

Because he'd *had* to put himself first. Selfishness the overriding necessity, to buy himself the down-time, the space – *that* word again – to breathe, to figure out in his own mind what he'd witnessed; where he'd actually been; the significance of it all. He needed to know why he'd been protected; and how *he'd* survived when the awareness known only to him as Seth had perished. Why would this Seth have sacrificed itself for him? No little voice was needed this time to tell him to keep quiet; not to share a word of this with anyone. That much he understood. *Knew*. If only, though, he could understand the rest of it…

It was no use. Sleep was proving elusive. The light meal hadn't helped, nor had turning in early. Bryant pushed the blanket down the bed, kicked off most of the sheet for good measure. It felt *so* hot in his room. He squinted in the darkness and looked at the clock; it showed 4:10 am.

It was a process he'd repeated throughout the night. And each time he'd checked, never more than half an hour had passed. He turned one of his pillows over, gained a temporary respite thanks to its cool, inviting surface. But the effect was short-lived.

He felt clammy – his body covered in sweat, the pyjamas clinging to his skin. He propped himself up on one arm. He was aware of a light breeze coming from somewhere, but it wasn't enough to cool him; only to increase the discomfort as the sweat became chilled. His body shivered. Warmth. And cold. Co-existing. Oxymoronic bed-fellows. Each keeping him awake.

He lay down again, trying to push the frustration and anger away. He could feel his eyes straining as they blindly sought a reference point in the dark. He sighed in exasperation and sat fully upright. He reached for the glass on his bedside-table and drank what little water was left. He considered going to the kitchen for a refill, but he didn't want to risk waking the others, so instead got up and went to open the window a little wider, hoping it would help cool the room.

He settled down again and challenged himself to get some rest…

The following hours were just as disjointed. Only when finally exhausted by tiredness itself, did Bryant get to sleep. The clock showed 8:43 am when he eventually came to. His neck ached, as did his back. He was aware of the beginnings of a groggy head, and his eyes felt gritty. He rose, then went over to the curtains and pulled them back, blinked a few times to let the now-familiar view come into focus. It was another sunny day. He threw on his dressing gown, tied it loosely round his waist and opened the door –

No-one batted an eye-lid as he walked from the washroom into the executive lounge.

As if it was the most natural thing in the world for him to parade about in his night-clothes. To his left, a businessman carried on reading his paper; to his right, fingers typed quickly on a laptop; and over at the bar, a loud voice was laughing into a mobile.

Bryant froze.

Did a double-take. Thought he must still be dreaming. Dream within a dream.

'This *can't* be...' he mumbled, trying to take in the absurdity of what he was seeing. He shook his head, turned round to go back into the bedroom to start again. But, instead, all he found was the highly-polished, white veneer door with its inlaid plaque – the universal, black-silhouetted figure indicating that the men's' room lay within.

Bryant's head was buzzing now, his brain addled with misunderstanding. He needed to rest. To figure out just what the hell was going on. He turned back towards the lounge and settled himself at an empty table. A newspaper rustled nearby. He glanced over, just in time to see a pair of blue eyes appear above the paper's headline. He thought he ought to recognise the face, but couldn't quite place it.

'You really should have tried the rainbow trout, you know,' said the familiar stranger, as recognition finally registered.

Graysbrook –

There, in the lounge with him for a second time. But none of this was real – it couldn't be. Bryant felt the confusion increase, swamping his already confused mental faculties. He so needed rest. Sleep. Sleep – that was it! He *was* still dreaming. He was sure of it. The somnambulist in him rose, wanting to get far away from this trick of the memory; back to the bed – no matter that it would be uncomfortably hot.

'Must you go so soon?' The man sounded disappointed. 'Are you sure you can't stay a while longer? There's so much we could talk about... Kindred spirits...'

Kindred spirits.

Half-remembered words. There, in the forefront of Bryant's consciousness. He remembered then. Graysbrook had said that the first time they'd met. Bryant ran back towards the washroom door, pressed firmly against it, forced himself through; determined to find the bedroom on the other side.

Only it wasn't to be –

For, with no warning, he suddenly found himself back in his old school yard. Once more looking for the ever-elusive bag. He was aware the afternoon bell had gone; double French and a free period before home-time. But first he *had* to find his bag. Where had he left it? Always the same. He looked left, then right – no sign of it. He turned round – only to see the double wooden doors, the right-hand one standing open; free admittance to the central teaching block; and, yet, so unusual that there was no prefect on duty. He walked up the three stone steps – each worn concave by hundreds of years of continuous schoolboy use – and eased himself through the opening. He misjudged the gap and caught his left shoulder on the still-bolted door.

Then, he was inside.

But the familiar was suddenly unfamiliar. No trace of the remembered line of glass-panelled doors that led to the French rooms. Nor the monolithic, marble staircase that climbed steeply to the upper classrooms – years of maths' lessons, and all but forgotten art classes. Everywhere, though, all he saw were long dark drapes that fell from ceiling to floor; as if he were at the foot of a stage gazing up, waiting for the performance to begin. And then the lights went down. Gloom encroaching all around. His awareness slowly fading. The obscurity becoming all too habitual. Comfortable. Incursive. Expansive. Ubiquitous. Shades simultaneously everywhere – and nowhere.

Without even thinking about it Bryant put his hands out, feeling for whatever was around him. Something soft – there, brushing against his finger-tips. Moving away from him. No, closer, now. But – further away. Ebbing and flowing… He made a grab for it. And an orange bar of light flooded around him, revealing the hotel room. A sudden click and *another* door opened.

A figure stood silhouetted in the intense light.

Serena, he wondered?

But the figure lost its form, turned rapidly to misty, dark smoke; insubstantial, dissipating before he could be certain. Spurred on by mounting curiosity he approached the doorway, shielded his eyes against the light with a splayed hand as he passed through…

Only to find himself standing outside the strange house at the end of his road; so near to his own home – so alike, but so totally different. He was turning fast on his heel to take in whatever was behind him. The mysterious door – barrier, as well as portal, to another world – stood firm; a memory of what might have been; where he might have journeyed – but for the timely appearance of the taxi.

He heard the familiar beep on the horn.

Car and remembered driver once more there, waiting for him. He climbed into the back. Observed the eyes in the mirror – eyes that observed him. He was getting out at the bus station, just as he had done before. Next, he was sitting at the table; settling himself comfortably into the window seat. Plenty of time yet to buy food and drink for later...

He closed his eyes –

Expecting to wake on the motorway slip-road...

Only to wake to the darkness. And, then, he felt a hand on his shoulder.

'David, would you like something to eat?' Nurse Jane was beside him.

Definitely Jane. But... he'd been through all this. This was his past. He'd got better. He didn't understand. How could this all be happening again? It had to be a nightmare. Graysbrook's doing.

'This isn't real, David.'

Not Jane this time.

But a *new* voice.

That belonged to a *man*.

One he didn't recognise.

But at least he was grateful it wasn't the oh-so-familiar chiding whine that assaulted his consciousness at will.

'Who?' But he didn't have time to finish the obvious question.

'Focus on me,' the newcomer continued. 'Follow my words.' But how *could* he focus on what he couldn't even see? As if he were blind again? 'Trust to your inner awareness, David; *not* your sight,' the voice offered. Try as he might though Bryant just couldn't manage it; neither visually, nor audibly. 'Here!' The man's voice now a shout. 'Pay attention! None of this is real! Follow my voice! *Only* my voice!' Bryant tried again. Nothing. But – then – a dim flash of insight; imperceptibly rewarding the further effort he'd made; and, then, there was an understanding growing within him; little by little; comprehension becoming ever more visible. 'Good! And again – keep up the focus,' the man's voice instructed him. Without understanding how he was doing it, Bryant allowed himself to be carried along on the stream of consciousness. 'Here, give me your hand!' He held out an arm, limp though it must have been, and felt a sudden grip tightening on his wrist.

And like a light switch being flicked on, the room came suddenly into view –

He could see an old man. Eastern in appearance. The man was standing before him, dressed in black. The man looked so thin and weak. And yet the pressure of his grip told Bryant there was a hidden, inner strength there.

'Who are you?'

'We don't have long.' The voice softly-spoken. 'He'll be coming for you...'

'Who's coming?'

'Always questions. Never prepared just to listen...'

'Wait!' Bryant interrupted. Noticing immediately the similarity. 'You're just like the *voice*, aren't you?' He didn't mean in the way the man sounded, but in the way he never got a straight answer. 'Are you *it*? I mean... You and the voice... are you the *same* thing? Or... are you me? Am I the voice? Well, tell me...'

It seemed the man *was* more prepared than the voice to give a straight answer; at least, of sorts.

'Yes – he and I; we are similar. Our paths cross – but there's no time to explain now. You must listen. Please, just listen. Your life depends on it...'

Another flicker of awareness from deep within Bryant's subconscious. It was not something he could have seen, but it was something he felt must be true.

'You... were at the hospital?'

'I was.'

'And...' It was as if Bryant was suddenly able to read the old man's mind. He could hear Jane shouting at the man; and he could see a doll, a pin sticking out of its chest. But he detected no malice there, just the man's intention to protect him from harm. 'You helped me, didn't you?'

'I did.'

'What's the doll I can see?' His first thought was *voodoo*, but it was immediately replaced by the word *poppet*; and an understanding of its true purpose – the traditional use for healing; never for inducing pain... 'And, wait, something to do with *Gravely*?'

A few more moments' probing and Bryant would have realised the man had impersonated Gravely; had assumed his appearance; had seen to it that they'd had to let him go. Had Bryant but been given the chance, he would then have questioned just *how* that could have been possible...

But the man from the Orient wasn't prepared to reveal any more of his secrets; and, even as Bryant was framing his next question – *who are you?* – the information stream was suddenly being dammed. No more trickling waters of lucidity.

'I'm sorry. It's too dangerous.' The old man had closed off his mind. 'You can't be allowed to know...'

'But...' Bryant wanted – *needed* – to know more; 'you... and the voice...'

'No more questions! There is *no* time left. He *is* coming. Understand this. *We* cannot oppose him – but *you* can.' The man stood hunched, turned to look round; an unspoken fear encircling him. 'I must go now. But remember – whatever he tells you, whatever you think you feel, it's all but a dream. A *dream*, I say again. Don't try. Don't think. Just allow yourself to see through it. Just be as you are. For the more you try to understand it, the more you'll find it confusing. And that confusion will bind you in chains that cannot be broken...'

Bryant was desperate for more answers. He felt the frustration rise in him as, once again, he was being left in the dark; alone, to face the unknown. But he wasn't going to give up this time. He'd question the old man further –

The man, though, had gone.

As had *Bryant* –

For he was no longer there, in the memory of the hospital; but instead he now found himself transported to the church pews. Observing that simple flagstone...

'It's amazing, isn't it?' The voice coming from right beside him. But not his father's. For in place of that figure of trust, there sat only arrogance personified. Edward Graysbrook. Once more encroaching into his world. 'You here? Me here? Who'd have thought it, David? Certainly not you, I'd wager.' Graysbrook laughed, mocking Bryant. 'Don't get me wrong,' he continued, 'but you can't possibly understand any of his, can you?' Bryant felt the long-forgotten – yet familiar – cloud of obscurity drifting airily closer towards him. Threatening to take away his sense of self. 'We've been here before, haven't we? And you nearly – *so* nearly – let it happen. So much easier just to have let it all go. Let yourself go. But, you know? You still can. And I can help you...'

A sudden feeling in the pit of Bryant's stomach.

Acidic contractions, warning him not to listen to the words he was being fed.

'No!' he countered immediately. 'Whatever you say, I'll not believe you!' He was on the offensive from the outset.

'Ah, did he tell you that?'

'He said –' Immediately, Bryant realised he'd been caught out. Knew he couldn't afford to give anything further away. He felt as if he were fighting with both hands tied behind his back. 'I don't know who you mean by *he*...'

'So, it *is* a he then?' Graysbrook collecting every piece of information he could. 'And is *he* working alone?' Before Bryant could prevent himself doing so, he'd already formed two mental pictures – Gravely, and the voice inside his head; *his* little voice. 'Then he's not working alone... Thank you for that. But, I think you must be mistaken... The man you see, *Gravely*; he can't be...' But this time, Bryant forced his own mental shutters down. Determined not to yield more secrets. 'Come now, David,' Graysbrook encouraged him, 'you can show me. Really, it's quite alright...' But he wasn't going to get anywhere; not now. 'Oh? I'm so disappointed in you. Still, that will have to do for the time being. You're really proving extremely helpful. Now, about us...'

'There is no us!' Bryant almost spat the words out.

'Ah, well there you're wrong, I'm afraid. You see there most certainly *is* an *us*... whether we like it or not. But, you're right in as much as there does just need to be... a *me*... So, we're going to have to straighten that out before we – or, rather, *I* – leave today. But rest assured, I'm extremely proficient. It's very simple. Now, if you'd just permit me to...'

'Get off!' Bryant's reaction was instant. Anger suddenly flaring deep within him at the realisation his mind was being violated; hijacked. As if someone were trying to remove a computer program. Interfere with his neural operating software. 'Leave me alone! You're not going to do this to me!'

Graysbrook sighed. 'I can see you're going to make this more difficult than it needs to be.' His eyes flashed a warning and his tone changed. 'Now, this is how it is going to be – you are going back to your hospital; back to your world of the dark, you pathetic little...'

'*No!*'

But even as Bryant uttered the objection, it felt as if he'd been mentally-floored. Raw energy – powerful, confusion-inducing, debilitating – assaulting his sense of being, his awareness of self. And next, there was physical pain in his neck. It quickly spread, flowing throughout his entire body. Graysbrook was quick to move in to press home his advantage. Bryant thought he understood what Seth must have gone through in the last moments of existence – as the destructive pulse had grown in potency...

Seth –

It was a memory. A thought. Just one word. Which slipped past his defences; broke free of his mental shield.

And the thought-form was not lost on his attacker.

'Ah, so you *were* there!' Graysbrook chuckled to himself, pleased at the eventual confirmation. 'I couldn't see you, but I knew you had to be there somewhere.' Bryant realised his mind was being read again, but this time he didn't try consciously to think what he was doing. Instead, he let the shield fall naturally back into place of its own accord; protecting him – his thoughts – from the continued, invasive scrutiny. 'How long do you really think you can keep this up, David?'

'As long as I need to...'

'But you don't even know *what* you're doing. Nor *how* you're doing it...'

'I know not to believe anything you say. I... have to see through it...'

'*See through it?* I take it he – *they* – told you that? Sound advice – *if* you know how to control it. But I don't think anyone's covered that, have they? No, there wouldn't have been time. The least you should have been told is that if you can't control it, it'll destroy you. But, look, David, I'm not vindictive. I don't want to see you hurt. None of this is, after all, any of your doing. You've just had the misfortune to be in the wrong place at the wrong time. So, what say we put it all right? Return you to where you should be? *Here!*'

Bryant had let himself be distracted again.

Had given Graysbrook the opportunity he'd been waiting for.

Instantly, everything disappeared.

Snatched away into the void.

And he was lying on a bed.

A hospital bed?

Jane's voice audible.

Away in the corner – talking to another patient.

'This *isn't* real!' Bryant cried defiantly.

'David, what's wrong?' Jane was there at once for him. Her calming touch applied to his shoulder.

'This *isn't* real!' he cried out again.

His determination to stand firm against the onslaught, to face down the close-massed ranks of oblivion, bought him time; time enough for cerebral reinforcements to bring up the rear; and time enough for them to carve a channel of enlightenment through the enemy's lines. By degrees, the wall of darkness began to grow lighter. The oppressive clouds started to be burned away by the force of the sun above. And, as the intensity of the shade decreased still further, Bryant became aware of a figure coming into view. There, before him, stood the figure in a nurse's uniform. Slender arms, gently holding him; imbuing him with an overwhelming feeling of –

Hatred.

Anger.

And destruction.

Graysbrook's fear-inducing face incongruously superimposed over that of the nurse. Jane's voice speaking quietly into Bryant's ear –

but the words so clearly those of his assailant.

'No,' the man taunted him, 'you never will get to see her.'

Bryant summoned yet more of his mental reserves. Pushed Graysbrook forcefully to one side. Swung his legs out of the bed. Stood. Then, certain he could support his own weight, ran out into the corridor. He could see a double swing-door ahead. He ran as fast as he could for the exit. His whole focus on escaping the madness all around him...

His momentum proved too much.

He almost careered off the end of the terrace –

Sam's arm shooting out; blocking his path; slowing him just enough.

'Hey, steady there, David!' Sam rose from his chair. 'Let me help you. Here...' he guided Bryant towards the seat he'd vacated, '... sit yourself down.'

Bryant felt grounded by the metal frame beneath him. The solidity under his arms helping anchor him back to normality once again. Yet *still* he couldn't quite be sure this truly was reality – what if it *was* just another level of make-believe; another rung to climb on the ladder of his mental reverie? He *so* wanted to believe he'd escaped...

This is real...

It wasn't the little voice speaking.

You are back...

Nor the old man.

This is reality. Stay with it...

Just an intuitive feeling; an inner assuredness that he had, finally, made it.

'I'm...' Bryant began, clearly still confused.

'... in need of some breakfast by the look of you,' Sam suggested, pulling out another of the chairs for himself. 'Followed by several more hours' sleep. You look half-dead...'

Bryant had only just noticed Neve. She must have been sat there with Sam all along. The two of them making time for their own breakfast – the guests presumably having left for the day.

'What time is it?' Bryant asked.

'Just after half-nine,' said Neve.

'But...' Bryant was trying to figure out where he'd been for the past forty-five minutes. He remembered – he'd got up just before quarter to. He'd put on his dressing gown and – It was all too much. None of it could have been real. A nightmare. Nothing more. But... Graysbrook... The flashbacks... *Were* they flashbacks?

'You sit there. I'll get you something.' Neve pushed her chair away from the table, a slight metallic scraping jarring his nerves as the legs argued with the paving slabs underneath. Neve went off to the kitchen.

'You don't look good at all, David,' said Sam. 'You coming down with something?'

'Sam?'

'Yes?'

'Sam?' Bryant had to be sure *this* wasn't another neural-induced fiction. Not least for his own sanity. That it wasn't more of Graysbrook's doing. He willed the shield to be there, to prevent his mind being read, as he asked, 'Where did we meet?'

'What do you mean, where did we meet?'

'Sam – just answer me. Please!'

'Here you go.' Neve was back with a cup of tea. 'I'll bring you some toast in a minute.'

Bryant was suddenly running through the scenarios. Neve's interruption. Deliberate? Planned? Yet another carefully-timed distraction, to prevent Sam answering his question – if it really *was* him. 'I'm waiting.' He wasn't going to be deflected from his purpose. 'Tell me. Now! Sam, *where* did we meet?'

'Well, at uni...'

'Where? *Exactly*, where?'

Bryant held his breath. Adrenalin kicking in. Preparing him to fight if he didn't get the answer he was looking for. He felt his whole body tense. Was aware of the uneasy silence. Saw the smile playing on the other man's face. Thought Graysbrook's laughing eyes would again superimpose themselves over another's features. And then –

'In the best traditions of Narnia,' Sam answered, 'we met in a wardrobe...'

'*Thank you!* You don't know how much that –'

But Bryant's relief was short-lived.

For there, over Sam's shoulder, he could see Edward Graysbrook coming towards him. The man had just rounded the side of the house; was striding out now, seeking to close the distance between them. Panicking, Bryant pushed himself away from the table, barely taking in Sam's startled expression. He absolutely had to get away. Now. But where to? Where could he go to be safe? Truly safe? There was no escape. For Graysbrook, he seemed to be able to be... *everywhere* –

Bryant lost his co-ordination. Feet moving before the body could follow suit.

He stumbled, but realised he had to force himself to stay calm. There *was* time. He *could* get away. Just so long as he kept his head. He exhaled. Counted to three. Then, turned tail and started running.

Up the incline, towards the stone circle –

A flash of approval in his awareness.

Again, not the voice; nor the man in black; but *something* spurring him on.

And a feeling that this was *his* secret. Nothing for Graysbrook to know about. As long as he made it to the circle, he'd be safe. He slipped again, palms instantly supporting his weight, pressing down into the cool grass. He cast a furtive glance back down the slope. Graysbrook there – gaining ground all the time. And Sam, still sat at the table as if nothing was going on; unaware of the intruder's presence. And Neve, walking out with the toast. But her movements, slower than usual. She, equally disinterested...

Graysbrook's voice was suddenly in Bryant's head – even though he could see the man's lips weren't moving.

'I know what you're thinking... but, no, they can't see me; nor can they see you. Look at them – blind fools; completely unaware of us.'

Bryant understood then – it was as if he and Graysbrook really were in some altered dimension. That had to explain his friends' behaviour, the speed of their actions. For them, time must have been passing slower. And he and Graysbrook, they were somehow out of synchronicity with the rest of the world around them. The world of reality. The world to which Bryant knew he had to return. If only he could break free of Graysbrook.

'You think that's going to save you?' Again, tendrils of inquisitiveness finding their way through the smallest of cracks in his consciousness; Graysbrook once more reading his mind, understanding where he was heading. 'Did they tell you to go to the circle? What? That it would protect you? That I couldn't enter?'

Bryant considered arguing, but knew intuitively he shouldn't allow himself to be side-tracked with such pointless engagement. For no matter what Graysbrook said to him, he'd still head for the circle. The old man had told him to see through it. He couldn't afford to believe anything Graysbrook told him. Getting to the safety of the circle was the only thing that mattered. And like a winger in the closing seconds of a rugby game, he allowed himself a final sprint; threw himself across the stones' threshold to secure that all-important try. Points that would safeguard his survival; see him return to play another home fixture...

A noise –

Sudden.

Arising out of nothing.

Not confined to his head – but all around.

And not Graysbrook…

But a familiar droning.

The same sound he'd heard before. The last time he'd been in the circle. The sense he'd had of an energy building within the stones; but he couldn't concentrate clearly enough to try to pinpoint the centre of the sonic anomaly.

And then – Graysbrook was there. He'd reached the circle. He was standing just outside the circumference. Deciding whether to enter, to pursue his quarry. Bryant edged backwards along the ground, as far as he could – but still within the protection of the circle.

'Look, David – why not come out? Can't we just talk about this? Forget what I said before. I was angry…'

Bryant noticed that Graysbrook was being careful not to enter. He watched the man walk left, then right; but never forward. He seemed to be looking for something; scanning the area. He couldn't tell if Graysbrook was also aware of the energetic pulsing.

'I'm just fine here.' Bryant answered at last. 'You can say what you need to from there.'

'Look, you're right. Fair enough, I can't come in. You're completely safe. I can only enter with your permission. So, will you come out to talk to me? Or may I come in?'

'We'll stay as we are. Now, what do you want?'

Graysbrook considered what to say for a moment, then replied, 'I want just one thing. *To kill you...*' Taking Bryant completely by surprise, he suddenly stepped inside the circle. 'Come now – don't look like that. You didn't really believe me, did you? That I couldn't enter? Or did you actually believe what *they* told you? Your ignorance is quite endearing. You can't honestly mean to say you thought – what – that I'd turn into to a pillar of salt if I stepped in here? Like I said, you shouldn't have trusted anything they told you…'

Bryant got to his feet again. Sidestepped Graysbrook. Ran as fast as he could back down the slope. Past Sam and Neve, both still moving as if in slow motion. He made for the door to the utility area that, in turn, led to the kitchen. Once inside, he halted, slammed the door shut behind him. He looked for the key. It *wasn't* there. But he realised he *could* still lock the door. There were two bolts; one each top and bottom; the top one above the door's frosted, double-glazed panel. He slid the bolts firmly home. Paused for a moment, collecting his thoughts. The windows. The front door. What if they were open? Graysbrook could get in that way…

He could see the man's shape already moving past the kitchen. Not running. Just walking slowly, confidently; arrogantly. Bryant tore through the house. Kitchen window – shut. On to the hallway. Front door – closed; but not bolted; no way of knowing if it was locked. He threw himself at it. Found the key in the barrel. Turned it. Then threw its bolts for good measure. On to his bedroom. He closed the window. Haring round the rest of the downstairs – all secure. He made his way back to the kitchen. Stepped through into the utility annexe. Slumped heavily down by the back door.

He jumped out of his skin –

Graysbrook suddenly banging a fist on the door, rattling the glass.

Now only inches away from him.

'David, I know you're there. Let me in...'

Bryant got to his feet. Dared to look through the frosted panel. He saw Graysbrook's outline, broken into a multiplicity of pieces. But, inexplicably, his features and colour appeared to be draining away. Only a spectral shadow remaining.

'Go away. You're not wanted.'

'David. Come on, let me in.'

'I've told you...' But he was aware his resolve was strangely wavering. Somewhere there in the back of his mind he was being asked to open the door. And even before he was consciously aware of his actions, his hand was already going for the top bolt. He slid it back.

'That's very good, David. Now the bottom one.'

His hand was there again. On the verge of repeating the movement...

See through it.

See through it.

See through it.

The repeated message flashing vividly into his awareness.

There was a faint droning starting up again, too.

He froze. Halted what he was doing.

'David?' Graysbrook aware something was up. Then, suddenly angry. 'David! Open this door now!'

Bryant slid the bolt...

The *top* one – firmly home again.

'No!' He countered with an air of finality. 'No, I won't allow you to come in!'

'Oh, David. That's where you're *so* wrong...'

Bryant saw Graysbrook's silhouette suddenly appear right there next to the glass. His own natural reaction was to pull away. He withdrew a couple of feet from the door.

And watched in stunned disbelief.

In horror...

As a shadowy arm appeared to melt *through* the door –

First the fingers.

Then the wrist.

Then the *entire* arm.

The disembodied limb fumbled for the top bolt. It found it; slid it open. Graysbrook knelt down, intent on freeing the second, lower bolt. Bryant used the few seconds he had left to step in close; to slide the top bolt home again.

'Oh, David, we'll be at this game all day,' Graysbrook laughed. 'Come now, stand back for me.'

And at that, Bryant did.

Driven back by the surprise...

As Graysbrook's *whole* body began to come forward towards him *through* the solid door –

The man halted.

Stood there before the terrified Bryant.

'I did warn you. You don't really consider yourself a match for me, do you? Far better just to let yourself go. As I've suggested all along...'

Graysbrook advanced.

Bryant retreated.

Another step forward.

A corresponding step back.

Forward and back.

Forward.

Back again.

Bryant tried to concentrate on where he was going – to ensure his route stayed clear – but he had to keep his attention focussed on Graysbrook as well. Not knowing what the man was capable of doing next. But he found himself fixating more and more on Graysbrook – watching the way the man's body grew ever less distinct; the physical, all but replaced by a wispy shadow of itself. The outline repeatedly morphing; becoming less substantial; devoid of all colour. Until it just resembled a smoky residue; an obscure essence of the man; trailing lightly behind; a little more being lost each time; like a ghostly comet's tail letting the fiery blackness burn off into the night-time sky.

'Are you ready to let it all go, David?'

Bryant retreated another step. Then another. Then one more. Found himself being edged into a point of no escape. He was in the sitting room now. His back to the fireplace. Was aware of a vibrating sensation. Frequency – volume – both low. The circle's droning penetrating the stonework; reverberating hypnotically in his ears; in his whole body; filling the room. But nowhere near loud enough to prevent him hearing Graysbrook's final offer. 'Shall we do it?'

Bryant felt possessed. Was aware his body was being manipulated. From without – and, yet, from within, too. Found himself kneeling. Bracing himself for the *coup de grâce*.

The end.

He closed his eyes.

Nothing.

He wondered if that's how it felt – being *dead*? Questioned whether his mother had been wrong? Maybe there *was* no after-life...

Still nothing.

Not even the faint droning any longer.

Nothing?

Just like... in the cave. After Graysbrook had destroyed Seth. Then, too, he'd been subjected to... *absolutely nothing.* It didn't make any sense.

As before, he dared open his eyes –

Just in time to see Graysbrook – his shadowy form once more rendered solid – unbolting the back door and leaving.

Bryant collapsed. Limbs shaking uncontrollably. Mind racing for the duration.

What the?

Why?

How?

Why didn't he?

Questions – but all pointless now.

Whatever the reason, Graysbrook had not seen fit to kill him. He'd survived.

And that was all that mattered. At least for now.

Only it wasn't –

For his ever-faithful friend, Sam, was almost immediately there in the room beside him. Lifting him to his feet.

'David. My God, are you alright?'

Bryant rose, still unsteady; the fear taking its time to subside. He didn't know how he was ever going to begin explaining this one. But there was no time. Sam suddenly trying to pull him towards the kitchen.

'Quick! We've got to get you out of here! Before he –'

He.

He.

The word came as a hammer blow.

'You... you mean...' Bryant stuttered in disbelief, '... you... *you* actually saw him? You saw Graysbrook?'

'*Graysbrook...*' Sam's suspicion confirmed. 'Yes, I saw him... Now come on, we've got to get you out!' Again, he was pulling at Bryant's arm.

Neve was suddenly there, too – the colour drained from her face. Her voice was little more than a terrified whisper as she said, 'We *both* saw him...' She was on the verge of tears. 'Oh, Sam, please, let's get out of here...'

'David, come on, you've got to help me.' Sam, still trying to support Bryant's weight; to manhandle him to safety.

It suddenly dawned on Bryant.

The urgency in his friends' action.

Their obvious concern for him – for themselves.

'No, wait... Look...' he interrupted, needing to reassure them quickly. 'We're safe. *We're safe...*' he repeated. 'Graysbrook's not here... *He's gone...*'

CHAPTER TWENTY-ONE

TOMLINSON HAD DECIDED to wait until early that morning, the day after the accident, before going into the local police station to give his witness statement.

His recollection of events would tally with that of the driver. Would help ensure the latter avoided prosecution for dangerous driving. And in some small way would help also, in the aftermath of the fatal crash, to lessen the unfortunate soul's guilt; the understandable feeling he could have done more, should have reacted more quickly.

Half an hour later and the superintendent was back in his car, considering his next step. With Maltravers dead, he knew he really did only have one line of enquiry open to him – David Bryant. He needed to find out if he *was* somehow connected to all of this. To Maltravers. The twins. The grandparents' murders. To Lucy Tanzer...

Again, Tomlinson just had that strangest of feelings.

Knew – or, perhaps more accurately, *felt* – something warranted his closer scrutiny. The familiar copper's nose urging him to find the link, no matter how improbable it might seem. Equally quickly, though, his thoughts returned to his suspension. Anger, disbelief, unease – all raised their emotive objections, wanting their voice to be heard first. He took a long, deep breath and purposely silenced the lot of them. He wasn't going to allow himself to be distracted. The accusation. The financial ramifications – they'd all have to wait for another day. For now, the priority had to be tracing David Bryant and getting answers.

Attic.

The word Tomlinson had jotted down earlier came suddenly to mind. He'd be sure to mention it to Riley. And speaking of Riley, he wondered why his sergeant hadn't called him back yet. Until he did, the superintendent was going nowhere. He checked his mobile. No missed calls. He turned the key in the ignition. He'd go get some breakfast, give it another hour and if Riley still hadn't phoned, he'd ring him.

Neve, Bryant and Sam had re-grouped in the kitchen.

Each now cautiously eyeing one another as they stood by the table, a shared sense of experience – of *knowing* – uniting them, drawing them closer than ever before. Bryant no longer the loner – the couple at last allowed a glimpse into the fringes of his alternate reality. There was no going back for them now, not after what they'd witnessed –

Graysbrook. A man who could walk *unseen*. Who'd appeared right there before their eyes from out of nowhere. And who'd passed *through* a solid door...

They'd panicked, confusion binding them to the spot, fearing for their safety; waiting for the man to emerge again from their house... But they'd not seen him.

And then Sam, spurred on by concern for his friend, mastered the fear; ran in to offer whatever help he could. There was no sign of Graysbrook; just an open door; Bryant collapsed on the floor...

Neve was holding Sam's hand tightly. She gave it a firm squeeze and, as he looked at her, arched her eyebrows, indicating he should say something. But before Sam had a chance to speak, it was Neve who broke the silence. Who, catching sight of the figure shooting past the window, raised the alarm –

'He's there! It's Graysbrook! Quick!' She realised they'd only have a few seconds before he'd reach them. 'Help me to –'

But it was too late. The man was already standing in the open doorway, his voice thundering into the room –

'Do you know? I'm lucky to be alive...'

Edward Graysbrook was angry to the core.

Not with Bryant. Nor the man who'd been coming towards him in the red van. But with *himself*. For having allowed his emotions too free a rein; emotions that had exposed him to such danger. *Danger*? He substituted another word, one more fitting. *Destruction*. That's what had been threatened. *His* destruction. A few more seconds would have meant death.

His death –

Death. Something he'd seldom had to worry about. For death only happened to others. But *life* – that was his birthright, as one of the privileged few. As one of those for whom time – and mortality itself – was governed by a different set of laws...

Ordinarily.

And so it still *should* have been. But after what had just happened, he now knew something *was* changing; *had* changed. For he'd been here before – the whole business with the plane...

Suddenly, a hint of recognition; his subconscious cornering the rogue emotion that had – twice now – threatened his existence.

Foolhardiness...

A liability. Expendable. Graysbrook signed its death warrant, let his mental firing squad do its work and foolhardiness was no longer a problem. Never again would he let his guard down...

'Damn fool nearly had me off the road! Not one of yours, was he?' The question was left hanging, waiting for confirmation either way. But Murdo, the postman, didn't really think the reckless driver would be one of the *Achavanandra* guesthouse's patrons. He knew well enough the sort of folk that Sam and Neve worked so hard to attract – courteous, pleasant types; middle-class tourists; away for ten days or so; time on their hands and no need to hurry; only too happy to pull over and give way. 'No, thought not,' he concluded, when there was no reply.

His arrival broke the spell.

Sam, Neve and Bryant had all been expecting to see Graysbrook; had been unsure of their next move. But now they realised the threat really had gone, for it had been Murdo passing the window.

'Can you excuse me a moment?' It was Neve. She felt she needed a few seconds to be alone, to compose herself. She withdrew from the kitchen.

'What's this, then?' Murdo joked, conscious there was an air in the room. 'Hope I'm not interrupting something?' He held Bryant and Sam's gaze, but they were giving nothing away. 'Best not to ask, eh?' He laughed, tapped his nose furtively. 'Aye, very good then.' He stepped forward to hand Sam the day's post, removing a red elastic band and fanning out the envelopes as he did so. He paused long enough to give them the once-over. 'Several bills for you, junk mail and... oh, a letter here for one of your guests, I reckon. It's addressed *Care Of*...' Sam took the items from him. 'Looks like we've a fine day ahead...' And with that, Murdo headed back towards his waiting van, hand waving a goodbye behind him.

Sam inspected the *guest's* letter. It was actually for Bryant.

'Here, this is for you.'

Bryant looked momentarily puzzled. 'But who'd be writing to me here?' He turned the envelope over, studied it to see if there was a return address. His first thought was that it might be something from the hospital. He could see the address had been hand-written. There were no sender's details and the post-mark had been smudged. He sat down. Sam remained standing. Neve came back into the room, circled an arm around her husband's waist. Bryant crossed his legs, then ripped the envelope slowly open, his finger sliding along the fold. He tried to remove the contents – several sheets of paper – but found the tear wasn't long enough. The letter caught inside one of the corners. He ran his finger down its length a second time.

As he unfolded and flicked the pages open, a small silvery object came free, falling first onto his leg then – as he was too slow to catch it – onto the floor. It *clinked*. The three of them could see it was a key. Sam retrieved it, placed it on the table. Bryant already seemed engrossed in the letter, his eyes darting quickly as he scanned the contents. No name or address on the first sheet. He quickly turned to the last. Saw two initials. And a name written underneath them.

'Who's it from?' Sam asked.

'Well...' Bryant paused, double-checking the sender's name. 'It's a... *Monty Maltravers*. And I've absolutely no idea who he is... Mean anything to you?'

'No,' Sam shook his head.

Bryant glanced at Neve, got the same reaction. He began skimming through the first page. And stopped dead. For there, only a few sentences in, he came across something familiar. A word. A name.

Seth –

He took a sharp intake of breath, eyes instantly drawn back to re-examine the beginning; the rest of the page. A quick turn of the paper and he was on to the second sheet. Then, the third. And, finally, the first again.

Where another word registered. Familiar, but for all the wrong reasons.

Graysbrook –

'What is it? Tell us!' Sam impatient to know.

But Bryant didn't answer straightaway. He was too immersed in what he was reading. Re-reading. And re-reading again. Over and over now, each time taking more care until he realised...

Graysbrook.

And... *himself.*

'Sam,' he began, an ominous gravity in his tone, 'Neve... please, you need to come and sit down.'

From what he'd read, he knew it wasn't over. Far from it.

The letter.

The key.

They signalled it was *just* the beginning...

'I *think* I've found him for you, sir.' A slight hesitancy in the sergeant's voice.

Riley had called the superintendent as Tomlinson had been tucking into a hearty meal of double egg, sausage and beans. He pushed the plate to one side and took a quick swig of his coffee.

'That's excellent, Paul; really good work. Hang on, let me get my pen...'

Riley had hoped the superintendent would have picked up on his tone. But, as it seemed he hadn't, he offered a more overt *caveat*. 'As I say, sir, it's *not* a hundred per cent...' He didn't want any flak if it turned out to be a wild goose chase.

'No, no; that's fine. I hear what you're saying.' Tomlinson took it in his stride. 'Run me through it...'

'OK. The home address? You already had that.'

'Yes.'

'Well, I called in a favour; got someone to go round. No sign of Mr Bryant. Neighbours said he'd not been home for several days; maybe a week...'

'Right?'

'So, next, I got his phone records – landline, no real help; but his mobile – bingo. Same number called over several days. I've traced it to an address in the Highlands of Scotland. It's a guesthouse...'

'Hm, guess I won't want to be driving all the way up there. I'll look into the plane times. Go on...'

'It's called *Acha*...' Riley stumbled over the pronunciation. 'Anyway, the electoral roll shows a Mr and Mrs Sam Girvan living there. Registered to vote a few years back. Before that, they were living down here.'

'What do you think? A previous work colleague of Bryant's?'

'Maybe. Or, perhaps, one of them went to school or college with him?'

'Do we know if he went to university?'

'Still waiting to hear back on that, sir. I'd guess he probably did, but I don't know where...'

'Well, don't worry for now. The calls show our man's been in touch with the Girvans. And, even if he's not there, at least it gives me another lead. I can still go talk to them. See what I can find out.'

'Oh, I've also checked with the DVLA and passport office and both have records for a David Bryant. I've asked for a copy of whatever photos they've got on their files. I'll send them on as soon as I get them.'

'Thanks.'

'Anyway, you'll be wanting the details for the guesthouse, sir?'

'Fire away.' Tomlinson jotted the address and phone number down, then read them back to his sergeant. 'Right, I'd better go pack something. See if I can get a flight out this afternoon. I'll give you a call in a few days. And, Paul?'

'Sir?'

'I owe you one. I know you're having to tread carefully.'

'You'd do the same for me, sir. Besides, you'll soon be back...'

Tomlinson hoped so. Then, Riley's last remark reminded him. 'Oh, hey... almost forgot. Look, while I'm away, can you do something else for me?'

It was the sergeant's turn to listen, to note something down his end.

'Good idea, sir. Consider it done.'

Graysbrook was back at the lodge, cradling a single malt – no ice, just a teaspoon of water added to release the flavour. He was dialling Tom Casey's number. He'd rehearsed what he was going to say. He knew Casey would want to know what had happened with Bryant. But he also knew there was only *so* much he was going to tell him...

'Hello?'

'Tom... Edward here.'

'Edward. Good to hear from you. How's the hunting?' The directness predictable – but polite.

Graysbrook was equally direct. 'I let him live.'

There was a distinct pause at the other end. 'Oh?' Casey sounded genuinely taken aback. 'But... I thought you said Bryant *definitely* was a threat to us? Why the change of mind?'

Graysbrook began his prepared speech. 'Tom, as you know... I'm not usually wrong, but... on this occasion, well... I do have to bow to your... seemingly-greater intuition. No...' Graysbrook feigning mock humility now; so out of character that he knew his second-in-command would have to take it at face value, '... let me finish... I *seriously* over-rated the man, and the risk he posed. You were right all along. I cornered him at his friends' house, and... well... I had *at least* expected some degree of opposition, but... do you know what? He was powerless. Totally. Just nothing there at all. Absolutely no awareness of his potential. Nothing to suggest he'll *ever* be able to use the abilities...'

'But... can we *know* that for sure? I mean, we don't even understand how he came to...'

'Tom,' Graysbrook gently interrupting, his tone avuncular; knowing best. 'This is truly ironic. Me now calming *your* fears...'

'I'm not afraid...' Casey interjected quickly.

Graysbrook liked that. He'd successfully put the man on the back foot. Psychological victory, reinforcing his own dominant position in their relationship. 'Forgive me. Poor choice of word. I know you're not *afraid*. Very well, then... not fears; but... *concerns*.' Casey stayed silent, Graysbrook interpreting that as compliance; recognition of his superiority. 'So... I judged it best to let him go. Besides, as you said yourself, we risked drawing attention to ourselves if we continued down that same road...'

'But what if he tells people about you?'

Graysbrook sighed for effect, before adding, 'So what if he does? He has no proof. His friends wouldn't have seen me. What's he going to say? People will just think he's crazy. You never know, he might end up being sectioned after all...'

Casey was still running through the worse case scenarios. 'And you're *sure* there's no way he might manage to..?'

Again, Graysbrook was straight in there, pressing home the advantage. 'Tom, I'm sure. Trust me. I was there. I saw him. But, if it'll make you feel less concerned, then, as we agreed before, go back to Pierfranco and get him to approach Bryant. See if he can't divert him a little. Tempt him back to the fold with an offer of promotion. After all, the man is still an employee of The Company. He needs a job. And, besides, that way we can keep an eye on him.'

'I guess you're right...' Casey still didn't sound entirely convinced. But he didn't want to argue the point.

'So, I can leave that to you? Arranging everything with Pierfranco?'

'Yes. I'll call him.' There was a silence as Casey thought something else through. 'It'll all need to be handled carefully, though. We can't have Bryant suspecting anything. Pierfranco will have to go through the hospital. And there's sure to be a delay while they make contact...'

'Yes, yes. Good. Now, I think I might as well stay on for a few more days.'

'Very well, Edward.'

Graysbrook ended the call. The conversation had gone far better than he'd expected. Reversal of roles achieved – Tom now the doubter; he, the reassurer. No more questions. And certainly, no suspicions over *his* abilities. Nor his resilience. Had Casey but known the truth – how weakened he'd actually been; *still was*; how the man, Bryant, had so *nearly* brought about his destruction – no matter he'd not consciously been aware what he'd been doing; then, Graysbrook knew, he would have reached the point of no return when, with his weakness exposed, his enemies would readily have seized the initiative; would have been quick to overthrow him once and for all. Maybe Casey would have been there, too; and would he have been leading them?

Graysbrook reflected again on just how close he'd come. How he'd so *nearly* not got out of there in time. He'd felt the warning signs – but, foolishly, had still pressed his luck. But – he had got away with it.

He circled the malt round his glass, drank the warming liquid down. A few more days to recuperate then, when his strength was fully restored, he'd head back to London. Have Casey undertake a spot of spring-cleaning for him. Remove a few more of those he suspected of being plotters.

And Casey? His loyal friend? Dear Tom?

Well, Graysbrook concluded, so long as Casey knew nothing of what had really happened, the *status quo* could remain. But, were he ever to find out, that would be another matter. One that he couldn't afford to ignore. At that point, their long-standing relationship would need to end. Permanently.

But he hoped not.

All things considered, he'd grown quite fond of Tom over the years...

Sam had finished reading Bryant's letter.

He wanted to know more about Seth. About Maltravers. About Graysbrook. What it all meant. He reached an arm out, intending to pass his wife the pages so she could read the content for herself. But Neve's interest lay elsewhere, her mind already focussed on a more immediate concern – the safety of her family; Katie's wellbeing in particular.

'What do we do now?' she asked.

'It's alright,' Sam tried to reassure her.

But she wasn't listening. 'What's going to happen to us? Are we safe? Is Katie going to be safe?' *Katie*. In all the confusion, Sam hadn't even stopped to consider her. Luck alone – certainly not design – had meant she'd been away at a sleep-over. But she'd be coming back later that morning. 'She mustn't know about *any* of this. Sam! Promise me!'

But it was Bryant's turn to speak now.

He felt so guilty. Responsible for involving his friends. If only he could have turned back time, he'd never have gone to stay with them. He braced himself for an expected wave of anger – fearing whatever he said would be wrong; that Neve would be quick to accuse him.

'Neve, listen... he's gone. I promise you, he's not coming back...'

Neve held her composure. 'How can you know that?' We didn't even see him go. We saw him... *there*,' she indicated beyond the back-door. 'He just *appeared* out of thin air... How the hell can someone do that? And then he was here in our house; and...'

'He's gone, Neve. Believe me, please... I saw him go...'

'But *we* didn't...' Sam interjected, voicing his own frustration. '*We* didn't see him go.'

Bryant spread his arms wide, apologetically; he simply didn't have the answers. 'Look, I *will* find out what's going on. I'd never – *never* – risk putting any of you in danger, and certainly not Katie. You must know that?'

The couple were hugging one another now, Neve in particular seeking reassurance through the physical bond.

'I know you wouldn't,' said Sam at last. 'And so does Neve; don't you?' She nodded slowly.

Bryant gave them a half smile; nervous, but grateful for their understanding. He was still holding the silver key, toying with it between fingers and thumb. He sighed, then said, 'You've read the letter, Sam. You *know* what I've got to do...'

Sam eased Neve gently free of him. Handed Bryant back the letter. Looking his wife in the eyes, he offered, 'David's going to have to go to London...'

'What? When?'

'Today,' Bryant answered softly.

Already, he was steeling himself; preparing to face his greatest fear...

Two hours later, Sam and Bryant were heading south along the A9 – destination, the airport; a little way east of Inverness. Bryant had gone online, checked availability and booked a return. Down that afternoon; back the following morning. In the interest of speed, he'd not looked into hotels. He'd just decided to find one that evening.

'Are you sure you're ready for this?'

Bryant didn't know whether he was ready or not. It was a grey area. Sure, his palms were sweating, his head was pounding and his heart was pumping like crazy – but what else did he expect? Despite all the other support he'd been given at the hospital, they'd never actually got round to his greatest fear –

Flying.

They'd just kept putting it off. Once or twice, early on, he'd heard them talking about it; as if he hadn't been there. Saying he shouldn't be unduly stressed. That there'd be plenty of time before they'd need to begin the... he couldn't remember the precise wording; but he knew they'd used some medical term...

Reciprocal inhibition.

But it wasn't the case that the phrase had suddenly popped into his mind of its own accord –

Instead, it marked the return of the all-knowing, irritating little voice; piping up, intent on making itself heard.

'Erm...' This, unintentionally directed at Sam *and* the voice. Its reappearance had caught him unawares.

Well, answer him... Are you ready? The voice teasing, now.

'Please be quiet. Just for once...'

'Sorry. It's only because I'm worried...' Sam apologised.

'No, Sam... I wasn't talking to *you*... It's just... oh, *it's* back – you know... *it*... the *voice* I've told you about...'

Sam started looking around him.

The Land Rover swerved slightly, and Bryant instantly reached out for the steering wheel, but Sam straightaway steadied their course.

'Sorry,' said Sam for the second time.

Bryant shook his head. '*You* can't see it. It's *here*,' he tapped a finger against his temple, 'in my head. It comes and goes...'

Yes, I do come and go, don't I? By the way, meant to say, well done, you... Who'd have thought it? I'd written you off, you know. You'll simply have to tell me how you did it. No-one – but no-one – gets the better of Graysbrook...

'Quiet!' Bryant was more forceful now. 'If you've nothing useful to say, just go...' He didn't even realise he'd stopped internalising; that he was now carrying on the crazy dialogue so openly.

Oh, bad time? Is that it? Ah... later's better for you?

Bryant gritted his teeth, trying to stifle his annoyance. Sarcastically, he suggested, 'Why don't you get me back the old guy; I think I liked him better...'

The old guy? Oh, him... Not too with it on the old dress front, is he? And you prefer him to me? Huh – now I am offended...

'Tough.'

Very well, I'll leave you to it. Consider me gone...

Bryant waited a few moments then, satisfied the voice really had left, sighed long then confirmed, 'Yes, Sam – I'm ready...' He paused, waited for his friend to say something; but he remained silent. So Bryant continued, 'I've got to go. You know that. You read the letter. You know I've no other choice. And I'm going to *have to* get on that plane...'

Sam knew as well as Bryant did it would still be weeks before the train line re-opened; and, with Bryant wanting to be down in London that very same afternoon, making the journey by coach or car was a non-starter. He'd have to fly. There was no other choice.

'Well, maybe we can ply you with a bit of Dutch courage before you get on.'

'Best not – you know, in case they think I'm some drunk tourist...'

'Fair point. But, hey... here, take this...' Sam fumbled a hand inside his jacket, then pulled clear a handful of notes.'

'I can't take those,' said Bryant, trying to refuse the money. But Sam's hand stayed put.

'Oh, go on. You'll want to buy a drink or something on the way down, won't you? And if it makes you feel any happier, consider it a loan until you get to a cash-point. You can pay me back when I pick you up tomorrow.'

'Sure?'

'Yes.'

'Alright, then. Thanks.' Bryant pocketed the cash.

The stewardess smiled as Bryant, reaching the top of the steps, ducked his head and entered the plane.

All things considered, he was bearing up far better than he'd expected. He'd had one slight wobble – walking out across the tarmac from the departure lounge, he'd taken several deep breaths to steady his resolve... only to catch the distinct waft of aviation fuel being carried on the breeze. But he'd acted quickly; had managed to hold fast the unpleasant memories before they'd had a chance to come flooding back – had forced himself to re-focus; to think only of the importance of what lay ahead.

He glanced at his boarding pass, checked the seat number again – not that there was any real need to do so; it was more a nervous reaction; finding something else to occupy his mind, however briefly. He counted mentally; eyed the layout. Two thirds of the way down, starboard side, he reckoned. He shuffled along slowly behind the line of other passengers and stopped when he reached the designated seat. A sizeable man was already there in the adjacent space, squashed up next to the window. The armrest was hidden under layers of his shirt. Bryant looked quickly round. Despite the short flight, he'd prefer a little more comfort. But the plane appeared to be nearly full. He cursed quietly to himself. Without his usual extra leg-room, it was going to be an extremely snug fit – but, at least, the seat was nearest the aisle so he'd be able to stretch out if it got too cramped. He swung his single item of hand-luggage up into the locker overhead.

'Sir?' A voice from further down in the plane. Another stewardess. Attentive, she'd picked up on his obvious disappointment and, noticing his height, had put two and two together. 'There *may* be a spare seat back here... if you'd prefer a little more room?'

Bryant scanned the rear, where she was indicating. The seating was different there – four solo seats; one in front of the other; arranged as pairs to either side of the central aisle. He nodded appreciatively, 'Oh, right. Thanks.' He was about to retrieve his bag – but she quickly continued,

'Sorry; if I could just ask you to stay put for the time being?' Bryant cocked his head. 'It's actually booked for one of our colleagues; but I think she might not make the flight.' The stewardess winced. 'Bit of a heavy night...'

'Ah, I see.'

'If you'd like to take that seat for now... and I'll come and get you when we're airborne, if she's a no-show.'

'OK, thanks.'

Bryant eased himself into the seat, jockeying for position with his fellow passenger's elbow. The man seemed to be dozing, so Bryant lined himself up next to him and used his own weight to push gently, until the slouching figure reached the vertical. It took all his effort to keep the man there. After only a few moments, though, he could feel the force of twenty plus stones beginning to press hard against his right shoulder. Bryant buckled himself in. Selfish though it was, he hoped the stewardess' friend had woken to the mother of all hangovers…

They were still climbing when he felt the gentle touch of a hand.

'Mr Bryant?'

'Yes?'

The stewardess was beside him, angling her body to counteract the incline of the plane. 'She didn't make it after all so, as soon as the seat-belt light goes out, you can move back there whenever you like.'

'Thanks, I'll do that.'

The stewardess left him to it.

Bryant's eyes were watering slightly. It was the air-con from overhead. He twisted the nozzle to reduce the flow; angled it away from his face. He looked at the man to his right. Out for the count. Unaware of – or, more likely, with *no* care for – those around him. Isolated selfishness, pure and simple. Still, Bryant thought, not long to go; just as soon as the light…

Ping –

He heard the sound, before actually seeing the backlight extinguish.

Grateful to be free, he undid his seat-belt, extricated his right elbow rather more forcefully than necessary. He didn't care whether it disturbed the other man. He shot him a quick glance. It hadn't.

He opened the overhead locker and took out his bag. He closed it again – conscious there was always a risk of turbulence. Not that he cared if something fell on the fat man… but it wouldn't do to endanger any of the other passengers. He walked slowly towards the back of the aircraft. His new seat was waiting for him – the very last one, port side; immediately in front of the rear bulkhead. He could hear people unbuckling their own belts behind him as he went.

As if on cue, one of the stewardesses came on the Tannoy: 'Ladies and gentlemen, we will shortly be commencing the in-flight refreshments' service. For your safety and convenience, please remain seated with your belts fastened. Thank you.'

Seeing there was ample room around the seat, Bryant decided not to stow his bag in the locker this time. Instead, he wedged it firmly between the seat's front leg and the curving wall of the plane. He settled back, enjoying the space; did his belt up.

'More comfortable?' It was the same stewardess; now pushing her trolley. Bryant nodded. 'Can I get you something?'

'Oh, yes... cup of tea, please and...' he eyed the available snacks, '...a muffin, I think.' He studied the stewardess' name-badge, too. *Heather*. He lowered the table in front of him. 'Thank you, Heather,' he said, taking first the cake, then the drink from her. 'And thanks again for the seat.'

'You're welcome.' She smiled. Then, turning to her right, she asked the adjacent passenger, 'Can I get you –'

But she never finished her sentence...

Bryant's hand shot out instinctively to catch the falling drink.

His stomach, like the tea, had suddenly plummeted. The sensation like drunkenness – falling rapidly into a bottomless pit.

The plane steadied itself.

The pilot was at once making an announcement. His voice just the right mix of casual professionalism and reassurance.

'Ladies and gentlemen, this is your Captain, Bob Anderson. I apologise for the slight rough patch back there. We seem to have encountered a spot of turbulence. All behind us now, but I'm going to engage the fasten seat-belt sign, just in case we run into any more. Thank you for listening – and I'll update you on our progress, a little further into the –'

Captain Anderson didn't finish his sentence either.

Again, the plane suddenly dropped. Only this time, the fall seemed to last considerably longer. People started screaming. Some tried to stand up.

Bryant watched as Heather returned to the rear bulkhead, her face panicked. A moment later, he could hear her on the internal phone. 'Come on, pick up!' He turned round. He could see her – the phone in one hand, the other waving frantically at the stewardess he'd passed when he'd first got on. But the other attendant was facing the other way – couldn't see her colleague trying to get her attention. Heather tried again. 'Pick up!' She demanded.

There was a quick burst of static, as Captain Anderson opened the intercom; but he never spoke –

The aircraft fell for a third time...

Oxygen masks automatically deployed into the cabin.

People were panicking. The carefully-rehearsed – but, as ever, largely-ignored – pre-flight safety drills all but forgotten. Those few who did apply the masks couldn't understand why there was no oxygen. Some grabbed the masks off those seated next to them. Fools, the lot of them – forgetting to *pull* the mask to release the oxygen stream.

Bryant made to stand up – but found himself restrained by his belt. Just as well – for the plane again dropped suddenly like a stone. Bryant was instantly nauseous; had to swallow down the rising bile. Felt his stomach race headlong towards his mouth.

The plane levelled-out and people were out of their seats now – trying to squeeze past one another. But it was hopeless – there was no room to manoeuvre. And futile – for where could they go?

Bryant swore.

Anger, though – and strangely *not* fear – was coursing through him as he shouted, 'This *cannot* be happening. You *cannot* do this to me again!' He released his own belt, indifferent to the likelihood the aircraft might plummet again any second. The anger blinding him to everything else. The seriousness. The fact they were all about to die. That he wouldn't escape. Not again –

Then, like a big-dipper, the plane suddenly lurched to one side. Bryant fell over; landed hard against the passenger in the seat to his right. The stupidity of it all; the complete absence of reality – he'd actually been about to apologise...

Time slowed.

The passenger's face turned. Bryant was staring at Graysbrook. He tried to lunge for the other man. To get in there first. But was thrown back into his seat. With a life of its own, the belt suddenly snaked round his middle; fastened itself securely around him. And then there was a woman's voice, there beside him. But not Heather's. He dared a look, knowing already that it could only be –

Serena.

'This is not real!' he bellowed.

He stared into Serena's eyes, seeing already in his mind's eye her excruciating fate... and, at once, she caught light like a living, Roman candle made human; screaming in agony, she whirled, a dervish of suffering, down the aisle...

And there, further down the plane, Bryant could see the pitiful blonde hostess – for the second time being suddenly lifted off her feet; the holed window – ironic – sealing her fate; air pressure dragging her, bones cracking and limbs twisting, to her death...

Barely a minute ahead of the rest of the passengers. Everything suddenly becoming nothing. Memory being transformed into forgetfulness. Existence hovering on the verge of oblivion...

The plane was in continuous free-fall; its course entirely vertical. Bryant sensed it was all about to end. Closed his eyes – helpless. Felt the thunderous, almighty impact. His mind was suddenly cart-wheeling – its movement choreographed to perfection – mimicking, Ixion-like, the motion of the seat to which he was still bound; round and round; and round it went; seemingly without end...

Until Graysbrook gave the command –

And then everything stopped. In an instant. *I'm alive!* Two words foremost in Bryant's consciousness. He opened his eyes. Began to take in the devastation around him. The crash site. The fires burning. The dead. The barely-alive. Flesh and blood. Bodies butchered...

And all to satisfy one man's desires –

But *still* Graysbrook was demanding more. Bryant, turning now to confront the doom-monger. But finding himself *as one* with the man...

The pair of them somehow *entwined*...

Lives. Awareness. Existence. All compressed into *a single being*. A united, *energetic* entity. Each – together; alone – safely encased within a ball of pulsating, strange blue light. Graysbrook *willing* the last few survivors to die. And then there'd followed the ultimate wave of searing, destructive flame as the air had grown thick with fuel vapour; a sudden spark, snuffing out all remaining life –

For Bryant, though, there was no little voice this time. No man in black to offer help. Nor even Graysbrook to taunt him. This time, it was different. *So* different. For this was no new crash. No fresh tragedy being visited upon him. This was *the now* – being fused with *the then*. Recalled elements; overlaying themselves; selectively chosen; time, reality – each being warped... as his subconscious *finally* showed him those last few, now-remembered seconds.

Revealing the *very* moment he'd survived the crash, all those months before –

'Sir?'

'What the –' Bryant sat bolt upright.

'Sorry, didn't mean to startle you.' The stewardess was beside him, angling her body to counteract the incline of the plane. 'She didn't make it after all so, as soon as the seat-belt light goes out, you can move back there whenever you like...'

CHAPTER TWENTY-TWO

'THIS CANNOT BE happening,' Bryant muttered under his breath.

It was *déjà vu*, alright. A repeat of the previous day.

He'd rushed off the plane, had only just caught a Gatwick Express and had flagged down a taxi the minute he'd arrived at Victoria Station. He'd managed to get over to the post office for 5:27 pm. Three minutes before closing time. It should all have been so straightforward – finding the PO Box referred to in Maltravers' letter; opening it with the key he'd been sent; retrieving the promised diary. But it had been anything but.

The cashier on duty had given him short shrift, telling him he'd have to come back the next day. So, back he was. Face to face with the same man. And no further forward.

'Look, I'm sorry,' the cashier was explaining. 'But without some form of matching identity, I can't give you access. It's the rules, see?'

'But, it's only through there... and I've got the key... Oh, this is madness!'

'I'm sorry. There's really nothing I can do.' The cashier pushed his button and the automated voice rang out, *Cashier Number Six, Please...*

But Bryant refused to budge. 'I want to see your supervisor.'

The cashier ignored him.

The next customer in line was already beside him. 'Hey, come on, mate. You've had your turn...'

'No, I have not,' Bryant intonated each word slowly. 'And I'm not leaving till you let me in there...'

'Then I'll call the police.' The cashier again.

'Be my guest.' Bryant folded his arms defensively, turning to the other customer. 'Look, *I'm* sorry – but I want to get in there to my box...'

'It's not *your* box, though, is it? That's the whole problem,' the cashier helpfully added to the debate.

'Now, look!' Bryant wasn't in the mood for taking prisoners. Not after the sleepless night he'd had. The crash; the memory of his escape; all of it had played in his mind over and over again into the small hours; and each time, he'd desperately tried to remember yet more of the detail...

But in vain. For it wasn't to be.

Wouldn't be. Not yet...

The cashier called over his shoulder, 'Clive, can you call the Old Bill?'

'Eh?' came a disinterested reply, from just round a corner.

'Can you call the Old Bill? To get rid of this guy...'

Clive came into view. Cup of tea in hand and a whole air of *I just want a quiet life* about him. 'What is it, Rich? We don't really want to be calling the police, do we? We'll have to write reports and all sorts...' He set his cup down on the counter, then pushed his glasses up, perching them on his thinning hair. Clive looked like he should have retired years back. He peered at Bryant. 'Now what's the problem, sir?'

'At last, someone with a brain!' Bryant began.

The cashier was about to come back at him, but Clive placed a steadying hand on the younger man's shoulder.

'No need for that, sir. You were saying...'

'OK,' Bryant sighed hard. 'I've come all the way down from Scotland. I rushed to get over here yesterday before you closed... *he* didn't even want to know, for starters... Now, I'm right up against it... I've a plane to catch... and I *just* want to get to that box in there. Is that too much to ask?' He pointed towards the post-boxes in the adjacent annexe that were shielded behind anti-vandal glass.

'Right. You've got your key?'

'Yes.'

'And a form of identity with you?'

'Well... yes, but as I was telling your colleague there,' Bryant managed to stay polite, 'I'm not actually the *lessee*; is that the right word?'

'So, *you* didn't actually rent the box yourself, then?'

'No, quite.'

'Hm...' Clive sucked meaningfully through his teeth. 'Like Rich says, it's the rules, I'm afraid. We're only supposed to give access to... Hang on...' Clive interrupted himself; the mental cogs whirring away. 'You a friend of his? Well, I suppose you must be, if he's given you the key. I mean, you don't look like a robber... Hm, I guess we *could* try calling him, to check. Rich, we got a number on file?'

Bryant seized the initiative. 'Wait, look... I've got a letter here; came with the key. That's good enough isn't it?' He opened a side zip in his bag; pulled out the letter. 'Here, see for yourself.' He handed the envelope over the small counter.

Clive studied the contents for a few seconds, laughed out loud to himself, then asked Rich whether a *Mr Maltravers* was the name shown on their records. The cashier nodded – grudgingly, Bryant thought.

'Very well. Rich, call it an executive decision, but I'm happy enough with this one. Let him through...'

'But Clive?'

'Rich, the letter looks kosher; it's addressed to him; and he's got the key.' The older man returned the paperwork to Bryant, then picked up his tea and went back to his quiet life.

The cashier pressed a release button under the desk and a door opened in the wall beside the glass panel.

'Thank you,' said Bryant, half-heartedly.

Once through, he set the bag down and put the letter safely away again in the pocket. He focussed then on the rows of boxes. He knew which number it was – twenty-seven. The key went in. A quarter turn anti-clockwise and the box opened. Inside, he found a brown-paper package; all the edges had been taped-up.

The diary –

It was about the size of a hardback book – but clearly not hard-backed, as it flopped slightly in his hand as he lifted it free of the box. There was nothing else in there. No other letter. No message left for him. He was in two minds whether to open the diary there and then. Impatience trying to get the better of him. The desire to know more. Urging him to tear the wrapping off. But he hesitated. It didn't feel like the right time. He decided he'd wait till he was in the airport. Then he'd find a quiet corner somewhere…

The package was too large to fit in the outer zip-pocket, so Bryant opened his bag. Pausing for a moment, he retrieved the letter from the pocket and placed it alongside the package inside the main compartment. He closed the bag, then the post-box and pocketed the key.

The time.

He glanced at his watch. He'd have to hurry to make the flight…

He reached the platform at Victoria with thirty seconds to spare. The guard was already blowing the final whistle. As on the way in, he'd booked First Class. He glanced at the carriage windows, but they all showed Standard.

'First Class?' he called.

'At the front!' the guard shouted back. 'Get on there and walk through, please!' A final blast of the whistle.

Bryant heard the automated doors begin to beep; they were about to close. He ran a further few steps ahead, drew up beside the now-closing opening; jammed his bag in to delay the mechanism. There was a burst of compressed air. The door opened wider. He leapt in. The door closed and the train pulled away.

Bryant was sweating as he started walking down through the train. It was absolutely packed. Standing room only. Bags, children's buggies and other paraphernalia were blocking the corridor. The train had reached East Croydon before Bryant managed to get through to

First. It was also busy, but there were a few spaces left. He chose the nearest two-seater, placed his bag in the overhead luggage-rack, then collapsed, exhausted; rested his head against the window pane.

'Tickets, please.' The guard had appeared at the far end of the carriage. Presently, he reached Bryant. 'Thank you, sir.' He was checking the man's ticket opposite, when Bryant asked,

'Excuse me, can I get a drink on board?'

'The trolley will be along in a minute, sir.'

'Thanks.'

'Tickets, please.' The guard was already on to the next table. He'd barely left the carriage when the refreshments' trolley arrived.

Bryant drummed his fingers on the table-top. He needed a cool drink. Everyone else seemed to want something too, so it was several minutes before the stewardess pulled up beside him. Early twenties, her accent pointed to somewhere from eastern Europe.

'You want a drink?'

'Please – something cold.'

'Beer?'

'No, a couple of soft drinks, if you've got any.' The girl produced two bottles of sparkling orange juice. 'Yes, that'll be fine.' Bryant handed over a ten pound note.

'What is this, please?'

'Ten pounds.'

The stewardess held the note up to the light. 'No, I'm not to accept this. You have other money?'

'But...' Bryant was about to protest. After the run-in at the post office, this was the last thing he needed. Then, he suddenly realised. He'd given her one of Sam's notes – it was Scottish. He pulled the others out of his pocket. All the same. Just his luck. She must have thought it was a fake. 'It's OK, you can accept it...'

But she wasn't going to. 'Please, you have other money?'

'Oh,' he shook his head. 'Let me look.' But, other than Sam's notes, all he had were a few coins – not enough to cover the cost of the drinks. 'Credit card?' he asked.

'No, not working.'

'But the guard, can't he...'

'He's busy.' She wasn't making it easy.

'Here, let me...'

The man seated opposite Bryant intervened. Taking out his wallet, he produced a crumpled English tenner.

'Thank you.' The girl gave the man his change, then set down the two bottles – together with a couple of plastic cups – on the table in front of Bryant. She moved on.